Praise for *Mothers & Other Monsters:*

Story Prize Finalist · Book Sense Nor   Reading

"All the gorgeously crafted storie   *Monsters* have
in common a profound understa   onships, to
which McHugh adds a touch of   what many
people might dismiss initially as   ın the right
hands.
      —Nancy Pearl (*Book Lust*), NPʀ, *Morning Edition*

"Wise and thoughtful; these stories left me deeply affected and unable to put many
of them out of my mind. A bookgroup looking for something a little different to
read would find in this collection plenty of fodder for discussion."
      —Lois Powers, Toadstool Bookshop, Milford, NH

"McHugh's stories are hauntingly beautiful, driven by the difficult circumstances of
their characters' lives—slices of life well worth reading and rereading."
      —*Booklist*

"The 13 stories in McHugh's debut collection offer poignant and sometimes heart-
wrenching explorations of personal relationships and their transformative power. . . .
McHugh (*Nekropolis*) relates her stories as slices of ordinary life whose simplicity
masks an emotional intensity more often found in poetry."
      —*Publishers Weekly*

"Wonderfully unpredictable stories, from the very funny to the very grim, by one of
our best and bravest imaginative writers."
      —Ursula K. Le Guin (*Changing Planes*)

"My favorite thing about her is the wry, uncanny tenderness of her stories. She has
the astonishing ability to put her finger on the sweet spot right between comedy and
tragedy, that pinpoint that makes you catch your breath. You're not sure whether to
laugh out loud or cry, and you end up doing both at once."
      —Dan Chaon (*Among the Missing*)

"When I first read *China Mountain Zhang* many years ago, Maureen McHugh instantly
became, as she has remained, one of my favorite writers. This collection is a welcome
reminder of her power—they are resonant, wise, generous, sharp, transporting, and
deeply, deeply moving. McHugh is enormously gifted; each of these stories is a gift."
      —Karen Joy Fowler (*The Jane Austen Book Club*)

""McHugh is enormously talented. . . . [She] has a light touch, a gentle sense of a
humor, and a keen wit."—*Strange Horizons*

"Passion and precision."—*Locus*

Praise for Maureen F. McHugh's novels:

Nekropolis
New York Times Notable Book
Book Sense 76 Pick
Amazon Best of the Year

★ "Exquisite."
　　—*Publishers Weekly* (starred review)

"This luminous tale of forbidden love in a near-future Morocco explores the evolution of human nature in a world where technology has redefined the meaning of the word human. . . . Speculative fiction at its best."
　　—*Library Journal*

China Mountain Zhang
Tiptree, Lambda, and Locus Award Winner

"McHugh's achievement recalls the best work of Delany and Robinson without being in the least derivative."
　　—*New York Times* Notable Book

Mission Child
★ "McHugh delivers another astonishing, compulsively readable novel."
　　—*Booklist* (starred review)

"Fans of Ursula Le Guin will find much to admire in McHugh's intelligent, carefully wrought novel of a world that is familiar yet very alien."
　　—*Publishers Weekly*

"Emotionally compelling . . . immensely satisfying . . . wonderfully structured and beautifully achieved . . . a splendid science fiction novel . . . McHugh makes an alien world and an imagined society feel compellingly real, and uses this setting to say something significant about being human."
　　—*Cleveland Plain Dealer*

"*Mission Child* is an epic map of voice meeting voice, world meeting world—tragic, heartfelt, and vibrant with life."
　　—Jonathan Lethem, author of *The Fortress of Solitude*

mothers
&
other
monsters

Maureen
F. McHugh

mothers
&
other
monsters

stories

Small Beer Press
Northampton, MA

Small Beer Press
176 Prospect Avenue
Northampton, MA 01060
www.smallbeerpress.com
info@smallbeerpress.com

Distributed to the trade by SCB Distributors.

The Library of Congress has cataloged the hardcover edition as follows:

McHugh, Maureen F.
  Mothers and other monsters : stories / Maureen F. McHugh.
     p. cm.
  ISBN 1-931520-13-5 (alk. paper)
  1. Parent and child--Fiction. 2. Science fiction, American. I. Title.
  PS3563.C3687M68 2005
  813'.54--dc22

                                                  2005005643

ISBN-13: 978-1-931520-19-5
ISBN-10: 1-931520-19-4

First edition 1 2 3 4 5 6 7 8 9 0

Printed in Canada on 55# Enviro Antique 100% Recycled Paper by Transcontinental.
Text set in Centaur 11.5
Cover image © Condé Nast Archive/Corbis. Photographer: Erwin Blumenfeld.

Contents

For Evelyn Lickliter McHugh, if she only knew.

Ancestor Money

I n the afterlife, Rachel lived alone. She had a clapboard cabin and a yard full of gray geese which she could feed or not and they would do fine. Purple morning glories grew by the kitchen door. It was always an early summer morning and had been since her death. At first, she had wondered if this were some sort of Catholic afterlife. She neither felt the presence of God nor missed his absence. But in the stasis of this summer morning, it was difficult to wonder or worry, year after year.

The honking geese told her someone was coming. Geese were better than dogs, and maybe meaner. It was Speed. "Rachel?" he called from the fence.

She had barely known Speed in life—he was her husband's uncle and not a person she had liked or approved of. But she had come to enjoy his company when she no longer had to fear sin or bad companions.

"Rachel," he said, "you've got mail. From China."

She came and stood in the doorway, shading her eyes from the day. "What?" she said.

"You've got mail from China," Speed said. He held up an envelope. It was big, made of some stiff red paper, and sealed with a darker red bit of wax.

She had never received mail before. "Where did you get it?" she asked.

"It was in the mailbox at the end of the hollow," Speed said. He said "holler" for "hollow." Speed had a thick brush of wiry black hair that never combed flat without hair grease.

"There's no mailbox there," she said.

"Is now."

"Heavens, Speed. Who put you up to this," she said.

"It's worse 'n that. No one did. Open it up."

She came down and took it from him. There were Chinese letters going up and down on the left side of the envelope. The stamp was as big as the palm of her hand. It was a white crane flying against a gilt background. Her name was right there in the middle in beautiful black ink.

> Rachel Ball
> b. 1892 d. 1927
> Swan Pond Hollow, Kentucky
> United States

Speed was about to have apoplexy, so Rachel put off opening it, turning the envelope over a couple of times. The red paper had a watermark in it of twisting Chinese dragons, barely visible. It was an altogether beautiful object.

She opened it with reluctance.

Inside it read:

> Honorable Ancestress of Amelia Shaugnessy: an offering of death money and goods has been made to you at Tin Hau Temple in Yau Ma Tei, in Hong Kong. If you would like to claim it, please contact us either by letter or phone. HK8-555-4444.

There were more Chinese letters, probably saying the same thing.

"What is it?" Speed asked.

She showed it to him.

"Ah," he said.

"You know about this?" she asked.

2

"No," he said, "except that the Chinese do that ancestor worship. Are you going to call?"

She went back inside and he followed her. His boots clumped on the floor. She was barefoot and so made no noise. "You want some coffee?" she asked.

"No," he said. "Are you going to write back?"

"I'm going to call," she said. Alexander Graham Bell had thought that the phone would eventually allow communication with the spirits of the dead and so the link between the dead and phones had been established. Rachel had a cell phone she had never used. She dialed it now, standing in the middle of her clean kitchen, the hem of her skirt damp from the yard and clinging cool around her calves.

The phone rang four times and then a voice said, "*Wei.*"

"Hello?" she said.

"*Wei,*" said the voice again. "*Wei?*"

"Hello, do you speak English?" she said.

There was the empty sound of ether in the airwaves. Rachel frowned at Speed.

Then a voice said, "Hello? Yes?"

Rachel thought it was the same voice, accented but clear. It did not sound human, but had a reedy, hollow quality.

"This is Rachel Ball. I got an envelope that said I should call this number about, um," she checked the letter, "death money." Rachel had not been able to read very well in life but it was one of those things that had solved itself in the afterlife.

"Ah. Rachel Ball. A moment . . ."

"Yes," she said.

"Yes. It is a substantial amount of goods and money. Would you like to claim it?"

"Yes," she said.

"Hold on," said the voice. She couldn't tell if it was male or female.

"What's going on?" Speed asked.

Rachel waved her hand to shush him.

"Honorable Ancestress, your claim has been recorded. You may

3

come at any time within the next ninety days to claim it," said the strange, reedy voice.

"Go there?" she asked.

"Yes," said the voice.

"Can you send it?"

"Alas," said the voice, "we cannot." And the connection was closed.

"Wait," she said. But when she pushed redial, she went directly to voicemail. It was in Chinese.

Speed was watching her, thoughtful. She looked at her bare feet and curled her toes.

"Are you going to go?" Speed asked her.

"I guess," she said. "Do you want to come?"

"I traveled too much in life," he said and that was all. Rachel had never gone more than twenty-five miles from Swan Pond in life and had done less in death. But Speed had been a hobo in the Depression, leaving his wife and kids without a word and traveling the south and the west. Rachel did not understand why Speed was in heaven, or why some people were here and some people weren't, or where the other people were. She had figured her absence of concern was part of being dead.

Rachel had died, probably of complications from meningitis, in 1927, in Swan Pond, Kentucky. She had expected that Robert, her husband, would eventually be reunited with her. But in life, Robert had remarried badly and had seven more children, two of whom died young. She saw Robert now and again and felt nothing but distant affection for him. He had moved on in life, and even in death he was not her Robert anymore.

But now something flickered in her that was a little like discontent. Amelia Shaugnessy was . . . her granddaughter. Child of her third child and second daughter, Evelyn. Amelia had sent her an offering. Rachel touched her fingers to her lips, thinking. She touched her hair.

What was it she had talked to on the phone? Some kind of Chinese spirit? Not an angel. "I'll tell you about it when I get back," she said.

She did not take anything. She did not even close the door.

"Rachel," Speed said from her door. She stopped with her hand on the gate. "Are you going to wear shoes?" he asked.

"Do you think I need them?" she asked.

He shrugged.

The geese were gathered in a soft gray cluster by the garden at the side of the little clapboard cabin where they had been picking among the tomato plants. All their heads were turned towards her.

She went out the gate. The road was full of pale dust like talcum powder, already warmed by the sun. It felt so good she was glad that she hadn't worn shoes.

As she walked, she seemed to walk forward in time. She came down and out the hollow, past a white farmhouse with a barn and silo and a radio in the windowsill playing a Reds baseball game against the Padres. A black Rambler was parked in the driveway and laundry hung drying in the breeze, white sheets belling out.

Where the road met the highway was a neat brick ranch house with a paved driveway and a patient German Shepherd lying in the shade under a tree. There was a television antenna like a lightning rod. The German Shepherd watched her but did not bark.

She waited at the highway and after a few minutes, saw a Greyhound bus coming through the valley, following the Laurel River. She watched it through the curves, listening to the grinding down and back up of its gears. The sign on the front of the bus said LEXINGTON, so that was where she supposed she would go next.

The bus stopped in front of her, sighing, and the door opened.

By the time she got to Lexington, the bus had modernized. It had a bathroom and the windows were tinted smoky colored. Highway 25 had become Interstate 75 and outside the window, they were passing horse farms with white board fence rising and falling across bluegreen fields. High-headed horses with manes like women's hair that shone in the sun.

"Airport, first," the driver called. "Then bus terminal with connections to Cincinnati, New York City and Sausalito, California." She thought he sounded northern.

Rachel stepped down from the bus in front of the terminal. The tarmac was pleasantly warm. As the bus pulled out, the breeze from its passing belled her skirt and tickled the back of her neck. She wondered if perhaps she should have worn a hat.

She wasn't afraid—what could happen to her here? She was dead. The bus had left her off in front of glass doors that opened to some invisible prompt. Across a cool and airy space was a counter for Hong Kong Air, and behind it, a diminutive Chinese woman in a green suit and a tiny green pillbox cap trimmed with gold. Her name tag said "Jade Girl" but her skin was as white as porcelain teeth.

Rachel hesitated for the first time since she had walked away from her own gate. This grandchild of hers who had sent her money, what obligation had she placed on Rachel? For more than seventy years, far longer than she had lived, Rachel had been at peace in her little clapboard house on the creek, up in the hollow. She missed the companionable sound of the geese and the longing was painful in a way she had forgotten. She was so startled by the emotion that she lifted her hand to her silent heart.

"May I help you?" the woman asked.

Wordlessly, Rachel showed her the envelope.

"Mrs. Ball?" the woman behind the counter said. "Your flight is not leaving for a couple of hours. But I have your ticket."

She held out the ticket, a gaudy red plastic thing with golden dragons and black. Rachel took it because it was held out to her. The Chinese woman had beautiful hands, but Rachel had the hands of a woman who gardened—clean but not manicured or soft.

The ticket made something lurch within her and she was afraid. Afraid. She had not been afraid for more than seventy years. And she was barefoot and hadn't brought a hat.

"If you would like to shop while you are waiting," the woman behind the counter said, and gestured with her hand. There were signs above them that said "Terminal A/Gates 1-24A" with an arrow, and "Terminal B/Gates 1-15B." "There are shops along the concourse," the Chinese woman said.

Rachel looked at her ticket. Amidst the Chinese letters it said "Gate 4A." She looked back up at the sign. "Thank you," she said.

The feeling of fear had drained from her like water in sand and she felt herself again. What had that been about, she wondered. She followed the arrows to a brightly lit area full of shops. There was a book shop and a flower shop, a shop with postcards and salt-and-pepper shakers and stuffed animals. It also had sandals, plastic things in bright colors. Rachel's skirt was pale blue so she picked a pair of blue ones. They weren't regular sandals. The sign said flip-flops and they had a strap sort of business that went between the big toe and second toe that felt odd. But she decided if they bothered her too much, she could always carry them.

She picked a postcard of a beautiful horse and found a pen on the counter. There was no shop girl. She wrote, "Dear Simon, The bus trip was pleasant." That was Speed's actual name. She paused, not sure what else to say. She thought about telling him about the odd sensations she had had at the ticket counter but didn't know how to explain it. So she just wrote, "I will leave for Hong Kong in a few hours. Sincerely, Rachel."

She addressed it to Simon Philpot, Swan Pond Hollow. At the door to the shop there was a mailbox on a post. She put the card in and raised the flag. She thought of him getting the card out of the new mailbox at the end of the hollow and a ghost of the heartsickness stirred in her chest. So she walked away, as she had from her own gate that morning, her new flip-flops snapping a little as she went. Partway down the concourse she thought of something she wanted to add and turned and went back to the mailbox. She was going to write, "I am not sure about this." But the flag was down and when she opened the mailbox, the card was already gone.

There were other people at Gate 4A. One of them was Chinese with a blue face and black around his eyes. His eyes were wide, the whites visible all the way around the very black pupils. He wore strange shoes with upturned toes, red leggings, elaborate red armor and a strange red hat. He was reading a Chinese newspaper.

Rachel sat a couple of rows away from the demon. She fanned herself with the beautiful red envelope, although she wasn't warm. There was a TV and on it a balding man was telling people what they should and should not do. He was some sort of doctor, Dr. Phil. He said oddly rude things and the people sat, hands folded like children, and nodded.

"Collecting ancestor money?" a man asked. He wore a dark suit, white shirt and tie and a Fedora. "My son married a Chinese girl and every year I have to make this trip." He smiled.

"You've done this before?" Rachel asked. "Is it safe?"

The man shrugged. "It's different," he said. "I get a new suit. They're great tailors. It's a different afterlife, though. Buddhist and all."

Buddhism. Detachment. And for a moment, it felt as if everything swirled around her, a moment of vertigo. Rachel found herself unwilling to think about Buddhism.

The man was still talking. "You know, I can still feel how strongly my son wants things. The pull of the living and their way of obliging us," he said, and chuckled.

Rachel had not felt much obligation to the living for years. Of her children, all but two were dead. There was almost no one still alive who remembered her. "What about," she pointed at the demon.

"Don't look at him," the man said, quietly.

Rachel looked down at her lap, at the envelope and the plastic ticket. "I'm not sure I should have come," she said.

"Most people don't," the man said. "What's your seat number?"

Rachel looked at her ticket. Now, in addition to saying "Gate 4A," it also said, "Seat 7A."

"I was hoping we were together," said the man. "But I'm afraid I'm 12D. Aisle seat. I prefer the aisle. 7A. That's a window seat. You'll be able to see the stars."

She could see the stars at home.

"There's the plane," he said.

She could hear the whine of it, shrill, like metal on metal. It was a big passenger 747, red on top and silver underneath, with a long, swirling gold dragon running the length of the plane. She didn't like it.

She stayed with the man with the Fedora through boarding. A young man in a golden suit, narrow and perfectly fitted, took their tickets. The young man's name tag said "Golden Boy." His face was as pale as platinum. At the door of the plane, there were two women in those beautiful green suits and little pillbox stewardess hats, both identical to the girl at the counter. Standing, Rachel could see that their skirts fell to their ankles but were slit up one side almost to the knee. Their nametags both said "Jade Girl." On the plane, the man with the Fedora pointed out to Rachel where her seat was.

She sat down and looked out the window. In the time they had been waiting for the plane, it had started to get dark, although she could not yet see the first star.

They landed in Hong Kong at dawn, coming in low across the harbor which was smooth and shined like pewter. They came closer and closer to the water until it seemed they were skimming it and then, suddenly there was land and runway and the chirp of their wheels touching down.

Rachel's heart gave a painful thump and she said, "Oh," quite involuntarily, and put her hand to her chest. Under her hand she felt her heart lurch again and she gasped, air filling her quiet lungs until they creaked a bit and found elasticity. Her heart beat and filled her with—she did not know at first with what and then she realized it was excitement. Rising excitement and pleasure and fear in an intoxicating mix. Colors were sharp and when one of the Jade Girls cracked the door to the plane, the air had an uncertain tang—sweet and underneath that, a many-people odor like old socks.

"Welcome to the Fragrant Harbor," the Jade Girls chorused, their voices so similar that they sounded like a single voice. The man with the Fedora passed her and looked back over his shoulder and smiled. She followed him down the aisle, realizing only after she stood that the demon was now behind her. The demon smelled like wet charcoal and she could feel the heat of his body as if he were a furnace. She did not look around. Outside, there were steps down to the tarmac and the heat took her breath away, but a fresh wind blew off the water. Rachel skimmed off her flip-flops so they wouldn't trip her up and went down the stairs to China.

A Golden Boy was waiting for her, as a Jade Girl had been waiting for the man with the Fedora. "Welcome to San-qing, the Heaven of Highest Purity," he said.

"I am supposed to be in Hong Kong," Rachel said. She dropped her flip-flops and stepped into them.

"This is the afterlife of Hong Kong," he said. "Are you here to stay?"

"No," she said. "I got a letter." She showed him the Chinese envelope.

"Ah," he said. "Tin Hau Temple. Excellent. And congratulations. Would you like a taxi or would you prefer to take a bus? The fares will be charged against the monies you collect."

"Which would you recommend?" she asked.

"On the bus, people may not speak English," he said. "So you won't know where to get off. And you would have to change to get to Yau Ma Tei. I recommend a taxi."

"All right," she said. People wouldn't speak English? Somehow it had never occurred to her. Maybe she should have seen if someone would come with her. This granddaughter, maybe she had burned ancestor money for Robert as well. Why not? Robert was her grandfather. She didn't know any of them, so why would she favor Rachel? That had been foolish, not checking to see if Robert had wanted to come. He hadn't been on the plane, but maybe he wouldn't come by himself. Maybe he'd gone to find Rachel and she'd already been gone.

She hadn't been lonely before she came here.

The Golden Boy led her through the airport. It was a cavernous space, full of people, all of whom seemed to be shouting. Small women with bowed legs carrying string bags full of oranges and men squatting along the wall, smoking cigarettes and grinning at her as she passed with the Golden Boy. There were monkeys everywhere, dressed in Chinese gowns and little caps, speaking the same language as the people. Monkeys were behind the counters and monkeys were pushing carts and monkeys were hawking Chinese newspapers. Some of the monkeys were tiny black things with wizened white faces and narrow hands and feet that were as shiny as black patent leather. Some were bigger and waddled, walking on their legs like men. They had stained yellow teeth and fingernails the same color as their hands. They were businesslike. One of the little ones shouted something in Chinese in a curiously human voice as she passed, and then shrieked like an animal, baring its teeth at another monkey. She started.

The Golden Boy smiled, unperturbed.

Out front, he flagged a taxi. The car that pulled up was yellow with a white top and said Toyota and Crown Comfort on the back—it had pulled past them and the Golden Boy grabbed her elbow and hustled her to it. Rachel expected the driver to be a monkey but he was a human. The Golden Boy leaned into the front seat and shouted at the driver in Chinese. The driver shouted back.

Rachel felt exhausted. She should never have come here. Her poor heart! She would go back home.

The Golden Boy opened the back door and bowed to her and walked away.

"Wait!" she called.

But he was already inside the airport.

The driver said something gruff to her and she jumped into the taxi. It had red velour seats and smelled strongly of cigarette smoke. The driver swung the car out into traffic so sharply that her door banged shut. A big gold plastic bangle with long red tassels swayed below his mirror. He pointed to it and said, "Hong Kong in-sur-ance pol-i-cy," and smiled at her, friendly and pleased at his joke, if it was a joke.

"I've changed my mind," she said. "I want to go back home."

But apparently, "Hong Kong insurance policy" was most, if not all, of his English. He smiled up into his rearview mirror. His teeth were brown and some were missing.

This was not what Rachel thought of as death.

The street was full of cars, bicycles, single-piston two-cycle tractors and palanquins. Her driver swung through and around them. They stopped at an intersection to wait for the light to change. Two men were putting down one of the palanquins. In it was a woman sitting in a chair. The woman put a hand on one of the men's shoulders and stood up carefully. Her gown was a swirl of greenish blues and silvers and golds. Her face was turned away but she was wearing a hat like a fox's head. There was something about her feet that was odd—they looked no bigger than the palm of a human hand. Rachel thought, "She's walking on her toes." The woman looked over towards the taxi and Rachel saw that it wasn't a hat, that the woman had marvelous golden fox eyes and that the tip of her tongue just protruded from her muzzle, dog-like. The light changed and the taxi accelerated up a hill, pushing Rachel back into her seat, queasy.

Narrow streets strung overhead with banners. The smells—dried fish and worse—made Rachel feel more and more sick. Nausea brought with it visceral memories of three years of illness before she died, of confusion and fear and pee in the bed. She had not forgotten before, but she hadn't felt it. Now she felt the memories.

The streets were so narrow that the driver's mirror clipped the shoulder of a pedestrian as they passed. The mirror folded in a bit and then snapped out and the angry startled cry dopplered behind them. Rachel kept expecting the face of the driver to change, maybe into a pig, or worse, the demon from the plane.

The taxi lurched to a stop. "Okay," the driver said and grinned into the mirror. His face was the same human face as when they had started. The red letters on the meter said $72.40. And then they blinked three times and said $00.00. When Rachel hadn't moved, the driver said, "Okay," again and said something in Chinese.

She didn't know how to open the car door.

He got out and came around and opened the door. She got out.

"Okay!" he said cheerfully and jumped back in and took off, leaving the smell of exhaust.

She was standing in an alley barely wider than the taxi. Both sides of the alley were long red walls, punctuated by wide doors, all closed. A man jogged past her with a long stick over his shoulders with baskets on both ends. The stick was bowed with the weight and flexed with each step. Directly in front of her was a red door set with studs. If she tilted her head back, above the wall she could see a building with curved eaves, rising tier upon tier like some exotic wedding cake.

The door opened easily when she pushed on it.

Inside was the temple, and in front of it, a slate-stone paved courtyard. A huge bronze cauldron filled with sand had incense sticks smoking in it, and she smelled sandalwood. After the relative quiet of the alley, the temple was loud with people. A Chinese band was playing a cacophony of drums and gongs, *chong, chong, chang-chong*, while a woman stood nodding and smiling. The band was clearly playing for her. Rachel didn't think the music sounded very musical.

There were red pillars holding up the eaves of the temple, and the whole front of the building was open, so that the courtyard simply became the temple. Inside was dim and smelled even more strongly of sandalwood. A huge curl of the incense hung down in a cone from the ceiling. The inside of the temple was full of birds; not the pleasant, comforting and domestic animals her geese were. They had long sweeping tails and sharply pointed wings and they flickered from ground to eaves and watched with bright, black, reptilian eyes. People ignored them.

A man in a narrow white suit came up to her, talking to the air in Chinese. He was wearing sunglasses. It took her a moment to realize that he was not talking to some unseen spirit, but was wearing a headset for a cell phone, most of which was invisible in his jet-black hair. He pushed the mic down away from his face a little and addressed her in Chinese.

"Do you speak English?" she asked. She had not gotten accustomed to this hammering heart of hers.

"No English," he said and said some more in Chinese.

The envelope and letter had Chinese letters on it. She handed it to him. After she had handed it to him, it occurred to her that she didn't know if he had anything to do with the temple or if he was, perhaps, some sort of confidence man.

He pulled the sunglasses down his nose and looked over them to read the letter. His lips moved slightly as he read. He pulled the mic back up and said something into it, then pulled a thin cell phone no bigger than a business card and tapped some numbers out with his thumb.

"Wei!" he shouted into the phone.

He handed her back the letter and beckoned for her to follow, then crossed the temple, walking fast and weaving between people without seeming to have had to adjust. Rachel had to trot to keep up with him, nearly stepping out of her foolish flip-flops.

In an alcove off to one side, the wall was painted with a mural of a Hong Kong street with cars and buses and red-and-white taxis, traffic lights and crosswalks. But no Jade Girls or fox-headed women, no palanquins or tractors. Everything in it looked very contemporary; the light reflecting off the plate-glass windows, the briefcases and fur coats. As contemporary as the white-suited man. The man held up his hand that she was to wait here. He disappeared back into the crowd.

She thought about going back out and getting in a taxi and going back to the airport. Would she need money? She hadn't needed money to get here, although they had told her that the amount of the taxi had been subtracted from her money. Did she have enough to get back? What if she had to stay here? What would she do?

An old woman in a gray tunic and black pants said, "Rachel Ball?"

"Yes?"

"I am Miss Lily. I speak English. I can help you," the woman said. "May I see your notification?"

Rachel did not know what a "notification" was. "All I have is this letter," she said. The letter had marks from handling, as if her hands had been moist. What place was this where the dead perspired?

"Ah," said Miss Lily. "That is it. Very good. Would you like your money in bills or in a debit card?"

"Is it enough to get me home?" Rachel asked.

"Oh, yes," Miss Lily said. "Much more than that."

"Bills," Rachel said. She did not care about debit cards.

"Very good," said Miss Lily. "And would you like to make arrangements to sell your goods, or will you be shipping them?"

"What do people do with money?" Rachel asked.

"They use it to buy things, to buy food and goods, just as they do in life. You are a Christian, aren't you?"

"Baptist," Rachel said. "But is this all there is for Chinese people after they die? The same as being alive? What happens to people who have no money?"

"People who have no money have nothing," said Miss Lily. "So they have to work. But this is the first of the seven heavens. People who are good here progress up through the heavens. And if they continue, they will eventually reach a state of what you would call transcendence, what we call the three realms, when they are beyond this illusion of matter."

"Can they die here?"

you *have* to be vapid," Michael says, oh so softly, softly enough that his voice might not even be there.

Michael is wearing a plaid shirt and a white T-shirt and boots. I realize that the shirt looks like one of Joe's. Which is probably on purpose, although, with Michael, I don't know if "purpose" is exactly the right description. (Does grass have "purpose" when it grows? Do cats have "purpose" when they hunt?)

Joe is still in Brooklyn and I'm here in Ohio, and I haven't seen Joe since he moved in with Keith five years ago, and I'm not a fag hag anymore, I'm a suburban matron. I don't even miss Joe or all that sexual tension—his for guys, mine for him.

I think about those abortive attempts at sex with Joe, and I'm embarrassed for both Joe and myself again.

"I'm middle-aged," I say.

Michael says nothing. He doesn't say that thirty-six is hardly middle-aged. He doesn't say that just because I've put on ten pounds and now weigh 140, that doesn't mean that I've become suddenly soft and frowsy and invisible.

I don't know why weighing 140 pounds means I'm middle-aged, but it does. It is a magic number. A matronly number. More important than wishing young people would get their hair out of their eyes and more important than thinking Green Day sounds banal and that MTV is too sexist. If I could lose ten pounds, then maybe I could put off middle age for a while. But the thought of dieting, of thinking of food *all the time,* seems like too much to contemplate.

"You need to get out of this place," Michael says. "You need to meet people."

So I join a dog club to stave off middle age.

The dog club meets at an armory. There are obedience classes and then a meeting. There are eleven people in the obedience class: eight women and three men. There are two golden retrievers, a Labrador retriever, a cocker spaniel, a Doberman, a boxer, two poodles, and three dogs that may be mutts for all I know. The cocker spaniel and one of the mutty-looking dogs are complete and total spazzes, which makes me feel better about

Miss Lily inclined her head. "Not die, but if they do not progress, they can go into the seven hells."

"But I have enough money to get back home," Rachel said. "And if I left you the rest of it, the money and the goods, could you give it to someone here who needs it?

"At home you will not progress," Miss Lily said gently.

That stopped Rachel. She would go back to her little clapboard cabin and her geese and everything would become as timeless as it had been before. Here she would progress.

Progress for what? She was dead. Death is eternity.

She had been dead for over seventy years, and she would be dead forever and forever. Dead longer than those buried in the tombs of Egypt, where the dead had been prepared for an afterlife as elaborate as this one. In her mind, forever spread back and forward through the epochs of dinosaurs, her time of seventy years getting smaller and smaller in proportion. Through the four billion years of the earth.

And still farther back and forward, through the time it took the pinwheel galaxy to turn, the huge span of a galactic day, and a galactic year, in which everything recognizable grew dwarfed.

And she would be dead.

Progress meant nothing.

It made no difference what she chose.

And she was back at her gate in Swan Pond standing in the talcum dust and it was no difference if this was 1927 or 2003 or 10,358. Hong Kong left behind in the blink of an eye. She wasn't surprised. In front of her was the empty clapboard cabin, no longer white-painted and tidy but satiny gray with age. The windows were empty of glass and curtains and under a lowering evening sky, a wind rhythmically slapped a shutter against the abandoned house. The tomatoes were gone to weeds, and there were no geese to greet her.

And it did not matter.

A great calm settled over her and her unruly heart quieted in her chest.

Everything was still.

In the Air

I join a dog club. I take along Smith, my seven-month-old go[lden] retriever, because, of course, if you are going to join a dog clu[b] should be because you want to train your dog. Smith can alr[eady] slap her butt on the floor when she hears the rattle of the biscuit [box.] Smith will even sometimes sit when told to, even if no puppy cook[ie is] in evidence. But Smith doesn't heel and doesn't stay.

This doesn't strike me as a major problem. Smith is housebro[ke] which is what really matters. And if she jumps on people when they c[ome] to the door, well, the only person who's come recently was UPS deli[ver]ing my videotape on "Decorating with Sheets," and if I've become [the] kind of person who lives in the suburbs and has a golden retriever [and] orders videotapes called "Decorating with Sheets," then life is already [too] surreal to worry about whether or not Smith can heel and stay.

"I'm thinking about sponge painting," I say, to the air, to Mich[ael,] who is practically air anyway.

Michael nods. Even though I'm not looking at him, I can tell t[hat] he nods; we're twins, and I know these things about Michael.

"Imagine it, *sponge* painting. Wallpaper." My back window op[ens] on trees and sometimes cows, and I'm looking out of it instead of [at] Michael. "Next will be fabric painting and decoupage."

"There's no rule that says that just because you live in the subur[bs]

17

Smith. Smith is a noodlehead, straining at the end of her leash until she strangles in her ecstasy of meeting other people and other dogs, but the cocker spaniel snaps at whoever comes near and the one mutty-looking dog is so oblivious to its owner that it might as well be deaf.

I get far away from both the cocker spaniel and the mutty-looking dog when they line up, and the Labrador retriever ends up behind us. A very large lady in stonewashed jeans is in front of us. The lady has a tiny pink poodle—it is really white, but it's so white that its skin shows through its fur and makes it look pink. It has a pink collar.

"It's probably named 'Angel' or 'Sweetie,'" the man with the Labrador says, *sotto voce*.

The pink poodle barely comes to the middle of the woman's calf. It doesn't have a clue what it is supposed to do, and the giant woman is quite uncomfortable.

"Jerk on the collar," the teacher says. The giant woman gives a tentative jerk that the pink poodle doesn't really notice. The pink poodle dances around on its tiny feet, looking up. Poodles have old faces, like midgets.

"No," the teacher says to the giant woman, "you have to be firm. He has to know what you want."

"Sit, Armand!" says the giant woman, and jerks, and the little poodle bounces up off its tiny poodle toes and flies up to about the woman's thigh. The giant woman goes to her knees, stricken, and comforts Armand, who doesn't seem particularly concerned. Armand's tongue is pink, too.

At least Smith weighs sixty pounds and is not likely to fly at the end of her lead like a tetherball.

The teacher finally gets the pink poodle to sit.

We are next. I reach into my pocket and say, "Sit." Smith, who knows what the hand in the pocket means, plops her butt obediently on the mat on the concrete armory floor.

"Is it okay if I give her a cookie?" I ask.

"No," the teacher says, "she'll learn to respond to you out of love."

"Good girl!" I say, full of enthusiasm, and Smith smiles with her eyes on my pocket. Smith does love me, but she'd really like a cookie and

I've implicitly promised one, so it is rotten not to give it to her, but at least Smith has sat on command. The teacher is pleased and moves on.

I could sneak the dog biscuit to Smith, but there is nothing subtle in the way Smith eats a dog biscuit. Ah well, sometimes even dogs have to have their expectations dashed. I kneel down and ruffle Smith's ears and whisper that the world is not fair, but Smith doesn't care about philosophy and wants into my pocket.

Behind us, the teacher is working with the man and the black Labrador. "Cruise," says the man, "sit!" The black Lab jumps excitedly at the teacher. Cruise is so black he shines like a wet seal under the fluorescent light.

"Cruise!" says the man, exasperated. Cruise's tongue appears to be about a foot long, and he wants desperately to lick the teacher.

"It's okay," the teacher says. He pets Cruise for a minute and then steps back.

"Sit!" says the man. Cruise wavers, looking up, intelligence perhaps creeping into that walnut-sized brain, as Michael would say. "Sit!" Cruise drops his butt to the ground.

"Good boy!" says the man, relieved. And Cruise lunges for the teacher, tail whipping, excited to death, all sloppy tongue and paws the size of dinner dishes. "Cruise!" says the man, bracing himself and grimacing; the shock of the Lab going to the end of the lead is almost enough to jerk him off his feet. The teacher goes on to the next student, and the man yanks at the leash. Cruise doesn't care. I know all about being yanked off my feet—Smith could happily strangle herself on her choke chain, apparently unconcerned that no oxygen is getting in. Michael always says it's because her brain is so small that it doesn't require a lot of oxygen.

The guy is obviously embarrassed. Cruise hadn't been that bad. "He's a happy fellow, isn't he?" I say. Cruise smiles at me with his long tongue and tries to leap on me.

"At least his toenails aren't pink," the man says, grimly hauling on the dog.

The man's name is Larry, and Cruise was named by his thirteen-year-old daughter, who is in love with Tom Cruise and the vampire movie, *Interview with a Vampire*. Larry isn't wearing a wedding ring. "I see her every other weekend," he says. "She lives with her mother." He smiles in a self-deprecating way. "Her mother lets her see R-rated movies. I live with Cruise here."

"Cruise is a good name for him," I say, not thinking about the vampire movie, which I haven't seen, but of the movies with the fighter jets and the race cars. Tom Cruise has a kind of boyishness that fits black Labradors.

Larry is okay. An ally in this class. One, because he is wicked in the right way, about things like poodles with pink toenails. Two, because Smith is better behaved than Cruise. I'm not sure I could have liked Larry if he'd had a perfect dog, which is petty, but there it is.

"Maybe we could get together this weekend to practice," Larry says.

"Okay," I say.

"I'm living in an apartment," Larry says. "Do you have a place where we could practice?"

"We could practice on my driveway," I say before I even think it through. "Edify the neighbors." Entertain Michael too.

Michael is there when I get home. "Were you waiting for us?" It's hard to tell if Michael waits for people or not.

"How was the first day of kindergarten?" he asks. He isn't dressed like Joe. This time he's dressed like Tony, khaki pants and loafers and cool, artsy black shirt. Married Tony.

"Why the costumed history of my romantic disasters?" I ask.

Michael doesn't answer.

Smith runs to him, tail waving in ecstasy. Smith appears to have just met someone she loves who she hasn't seen for months. Sometimes, I can get her to go nuts by going outside, ringing the doorbell, and coming back in. But Smith does love Michael, even when she can't touch him. She dances around him, leaping and jumping.

"You really should be dressed like Sharon," I say. Sharon was Tony's wife, and she haunted our affair much more than Michael ever did. I don't know what Sharon dressed like; I never met her. I only knew her through what Tony said. Tony said she went to a manicurist. "Class was okay," I say. I look in the fridge for a can of diet soda. "I met someone. A guy, named Larry, with a black Labrador named Cruise. We're going to practice together this weekend."

I look over the fridge door to see Michael's reaction, but Michael is gone.

Smith leaps onto the couch and sniffs. Did Michael leave a scent, an ectoplasmic remnant?

I suspect that Michael is pissed about Larry.

"He's divorced," I say to the still and empty air. "He has a thirteen-year-old daughter. I'm not interested in anybody with a kid."

The air stirs, which sometimes means Michael, and sometimes just means a draft.

"I'm not crazy," I say, meaning that I wouldn't be interested in someone with a thirteen-year-old girl.

There is no reaction.

Sometimes, at night, when I put the dog in her crate and go upstairs, Smith barks. Smith won't sleep with me; she's always slept in the crate, and if I bring her up to sleep in bed with me, she sits at the door and whines. But she's like a little kid, and sometimes she isn't ready to go to bed at bedtime.

Smith barks, and then there's the sound of something thumping against metal. The sound is Smith wagging her tail and hitting the crate. A muted ching, ching, ching. A greeting wag. A happy wag. Michael is with the dog. I don't ever hear anything else, not the crate opening, not Michael saying anything. Is he inside the crate with Smith?

Smith isn't the only one that Michael visits at night. Not every night, not even most nights, but enough. I never see anything. He just sits on the bed, or I feel his knees behind mine, my back is to his chest, warming me. I go to sleep with his arm around me. He used to steal my covers when I was little. He was all elbows when we were kids. He was gone for years and years, from about twelve to sometime in college. But came back then, sliding in with me while Laurie, my roommate the education major, slept unaware in the other bed. He is always my age. A ghost that grows older as I do. A ghost that was never legally alive.

My stillborn twin.

Larry drives an old Accord, and Cruise sits in the passenger seat next to him, pink tongue lolling. Cruise flings himself across the gearshift and across Larry's lap, and Larry can't open the door for a moment while he struggles with the dog, but finally they are both on the driveway.

Smith is wiggling, alternately crouching and leaping at the end of her lead. Cruise lunges against his lead. "Hi!" Larry calls, and he lets Cruise drag him up the walk to the house, and the two dogs meet nose to nose, then head to tail, and then start to tear madly around, tangling their leads.

I'm smiling, grinning, even though the two dogs are being such a pain and Larry is calling Cruise a "dumbshit." "Dumbshit" is said with such well-worn practice and deep affection that I know that Cruise thinks it's his name.

"Come in," I say.

"Are you sure you want me to?" Larry asks.

There's nothing two dogs are going to do to my house that one dog hasn't already done. So he comes into my empty house. There is no furniture in the living room or the dining room, just Smith's crate. There's a couch and two chairs in the family room, but I don't have any end tables, just a lettuce crate, a real one, taken from behind a grocery store. Real crates don't quite have the panache of the ones that people buy for furniture. There aren't any pictures on the walls.

"When I pulled up, I thought this neighborhood didn't look any-thing like I'd expect you to live in," Larry says.

"I haven't lived here long," I say. I practically apologize. "I just bought this place." I feel compelled to explain that my mother died and left her house that I sold so I could buy this place, but I don't want to tell him that because he will feel compelled to offer me sympathy, and my mother's death was awful and I don't want sympathy right now, I want to train dogs.

We train on the driveway, parading up and down and saying "SIT!" a lot. Larry is nervous, jerking Cruise roughly to get his attention. Not that this seems to bother Cruise, who sits on one hip, tongue lolling, looking around. Smith is in a flaky mood, more interested in chewing on the leash than listening.

"You can put bitter apple on that leash to stop her from chewing it," Larry says.

"I don't know, I mean, does it really *matter* if she chews it?" Is it bad? Are dogs not supposed to chew leashes? Smith always chews her leash.

"I guess not," Larry says. This seems to make him obscurely happy. "I read some dogs actually like bitter apple anyway."

"I spray it in the garbage can," I say.

"That's a good idea," Larry says—

Michael comes around the house, and Smith and Cruise both leap up and bound toward him.

It's hard not to look at Michael. But since no one else can see him, I try not to when anyone else is around.

"Shit," Larry is saying. "Cruise! You dumbshit! Cruise!"

Go away, I think. Michael, don't play games, go away.

Smith crouches, ears back, tail wagging, wheezing at the end of her leash. She is so sweet on Michael. Michael stops, watching the kids down the street. Cruise barks, but Michael doesn't seem to notice. I'm trying to watch him out of the corner of my eye.

"What is it?" Larry asks. "What are they after?"

"I don't know," I lie.

Larry lets Cruise drag him toward Michael, but Michael won't stay, of course. Cruise bounds around, barking, barking. Smith wants to look around the side of the house, but when she doesn't see Michael there, she decides instead to go to Larry. I realize too late, and Smith crosses leashes and Cruise comes back to see what's going on, and every time I try to get around Larry to untangle Smith, Smith and Cruise follow.

It should be funny, but it isn't because I'm upset about Michael. "Smith!" I keep yelling. "Smith, you damn dog!"

"Hold still," Larry is saying. "Wait, let me—no, go *that* way—"

He is too busy trying to get me to do it his way to see what I'm after, and I find myself thinking about how typical he is, while at the same time trying not to be angry. We're both entirely too polite when the dogs are finally untangled and Cruise is sitting on one hip, tongue lolling, watching the kids across the street, and Smith is belly to the driveway, trying to cool off.

I get the dogs some water and bring Larry a glass of iced tea, and we sit on the porch and contemplate the day.

"Caitlin's mother told me that her husband is probably going to be transferred to San Diego," Larry says.

It takes me a moment to remember that Caitlin is Larry's daughter. "Oh no," I say, "they can't do that, can they?"

"We'll have to renegotiate the visitation schedule. Maybe have her stay with me in the summer or something." Larry is looking at Cruise.

I don't know what to say.

"I think they've had enough of a break," Larry says. "Come on, you sluggard, let's whip you into shape."

Cruise levers himself up, and we go back to the driveway. Smith isn't at all interested in heeling.

Michael comes back around the house.

The dogs erupt.

"Damn it," Larry says. "Cruise!" and yanks the straining dog into a sitting position and smacks his back with the flat of his hand.

Startled, Cruise cringes.

For the first time this afternoon, Michael looks over at Cruise on his back, paws in the air, submissive, and then at me.

He's not cruel, I want to say. *You're* cruel, you're causing this!

I refuse to acknowledge Michael's presence. In the morning, Smith is rattling in her crate. I hear her before I get downstairs. Smith has her ball in her mouth and is growling delightedly. Dancing with her paws. Raugh-raugh-row-ru. Let me out. Let me out and play. Michael must be there, because Smith insists on believing that Michael can let her out. Maybe he does at night, how would I know? At the bottom of the stairs I can see only Smith and the crate. Smith looks over and sees me and happily switches her attention. Raugh-raugh-row-ru. No one else is there.

After I drink my coffee and go upstairs, he is reflected in my bathroom mirror as I brush my teeth, but I stoically brush without so much as flicking my eye in his direction. He leans against the doorframe, silent and apologetic. He shoves his hand in the pockets of his jeans. At least he's not dressed like some old boyfriend. Is his hairline receding? But I avoid the temptation to really look. Perhaps it's been receding all along and I just hadn't noticed, the way you don't notice the gradual change of something familiar. The way you don't notice things getting dusty until there they are, covered in dust.

I rap my brush against the sink, all efficiency and business. When I turn around, he's not there. I undress and take my shower. I'm used to showering with Michael around. I don't think he watches.

When I get out of the shower, the mirror is all steamed, and in the steam is written, "Without you I am not."

I turn on the fan and open the window, and the words dry up and leave no trace. If I had written it, after it was dry you could see the smear of my fingers, but when Michael does it, it just dries away.

I turn the fan off before I go to work.

Larry calls me at work. He's called me twice before, once to get directions to my house and another time just to chat. He *is* interested in me, which I sort of like and sort of don't. I'm not really attracted to him, so in the end this will probably end up being more trouble than it's worth. He misrepresented himself. He said he wasn't interested in dating, that he just wanted to spend a little time getting himself back on his feet, concentrating on his job. "I don't want to rebound," he said. I had the image of him leaping up after a basketball, which, since Larry is tall, is not so strange.

Larry wants to know if we could meet for dinner. "I'd ask you for lunch," he said, "but I'm all the way downtown. I don't want to ask you on a date," he says and then stops. "I mean, it's not that I think you're not attractive or anything, but I really have the feeling that we're going to be friends, you know? And I don't have very many friends. I mean, it's not that I don't have *friends*, I'm not saying that. I really *do* have friends. I don't know why I said that. But I don't want to jeopardize our friendship, you know?"

"Why don't we go Dutch," I say. "I like the idea of friendship and I'm not looking for a relationship either."

He sighs on the other end of the phone, relieved. He is having trouble with his daughter, Caitlin, the thirteen-year-old, he says. "I don't know anything about thirteen-year-old girls," he says.

"It's a pretty horrible age," I say, sympathetic.

He laughs. "So there's hope she'll grow out of it?"

"Well," I say, "if her only problem is that she's thirteen, then she's in pretty good shape."

After work, I drive home to let Smith out of the crate. Out into the backyard, let the dog pee, throw a stick a couple of times, and then back into the crate. Smith isn't happy after having been in the crate all day.

I don't want to go back and meet Larry. I have this feeling, this antipathy, before parties, before most social events. If I just go, it will be fine. Most of the time, once I get there I have a much better time than I expected. It seems like so much trouble to sit and listen to a man I hardly know sit and talk about his daughter.

The air stirs, warms. Smith looks up, ears forward, nose working. The tip of Smith's tail twitches. I could stay home. I could stay home with Michael and Smith. It would be easy.

I grab my jacket and run.

Applebee's is crowded, and we have to stand and wait for a table. "We should have gotten here earlier," Larry says.

"The price of dependents," I say, and then realize that since Larry is worried about his daughter, calling our dogs dependents may suggest that I think they're as important as Caitlin. But Larry grins.

Larry is wearing a suit, which makes him look very different. His dog clothes change him, make him accessible and a little silly, the way men's casual clothes do. He isn't silly at all in a gray suit. He makes me uncomfortable, but interested somehow.

I expect him to start talking about Caitlin, his daughter. I am braced for him to do so, but instead he starts talking about his job. He runs the graphics and design department for a stationery company. He used to be an artist, but, he says, he sold out for the promise of a mortgage and a family. "Not really such a bad idea," he explains. "I really don't have the right temperament for a fine artist. I hate to be by myself. You know, working in my studio, nothing but me and my muse. My muse doesn't carry on much of a conversation, I guess."

He likes his job, something that comes through even his talk of too-short deadlines. He likes working with the young designers, he likes their music and their strange haircuts.

He is really much more interesting than I expected. We never actually do get around to talking about Caitlin.

I'm a little sorry when he doesn't kiss me before I get into my car. I hope he is, too.

Michael is in the air, but that is all. I don't know if that is good or not. I'll have to pick. Michael has never made me pick before. It isn't fair that he is going to make me pick, because I've only gone out with this man for dinner and that was only just as friends. Why is he doing this? What if I pick Larry and it doesn't work out?

"Puppy," I whisper to Smith, looking for comfort. Smith holds my fingers in her mouth, not biting, not really. Smith is happy, lying there on the couch, holding on to my fingers.

In the kitchen, something hits the floor and shatters. Smith starts. The plate I ate dinner on is broken on the floor. My glass slides off the counter, shatters on the hardwood.

"Michael," I say.

The refrigerator door opens and a jar of mustard slides out and hits the floor, but does not break. It rolls toward the cabinet.

He has never done anything like this.

"Michael," I whisper. "Stop it."

Nothing else happens.

Smith cowers behind my legs. "It's okay, baby," I say. I sit on the floor and she runs to me and stands on my lap, sixty pounds of dog.

"You scared the *dog*," I say accusingly to the air. Michael likes Smith. At least, I think Michael likes Smith.

If Michael starts doing things like this, what will I do? I can't leave Michael; it isn't some building he haunts, it's *me*. Anywhere I go to live, Michael will come *with* me.

Imagine life without Michael.

I cannot, I cannot.

"You use me." That's what it says in the steam on the mirror the next morning.

I don't know what it means, so I pretend not to see it.

I open my closet and look at my clothes. I can't wear my city clothes anymore, I'm too fat. My gypsy skirts and silk shirts. All I can wear are the things I have bought since then. My wardrobe of suburbia, my fat-assed jeans and sweatshirts.

"Are you warning me?" I ask the air. "What's so different about Larry?"

The indifferent air doesn't answer.

Choose. Choose the living or the dead. Put like that, it should be easy.

I have to do something. I call Larry, half expecting that when I pick up the phone, the contents of my desk will go flying across the room, or the file cabinets will open and spill tongues of manila. But nothing happens.

Larry sounds as if I woke him up. Eight-thirty on a Saturday morning, maybe *he* was asleep, but Smith won't let me sleep that late.

"I was just wondering if you wanted to bring Cruise over and do some practice," I say.

"Sure," he says. "Yeah. What time is it?"

"Maybe you can come over in a while and leave Cruise here and we'll go get breakfast. Unless you've eaten." Although I know he hasn't eaten.

"Okay," he says.

"He's coming," I tell the room after I hang up the phone.

There's no response. I don't expect one.

I let Smith out in the backyard. I turn on the television and flip through the channels, turn off the television. I start to put dishes in the dishwasher and decide to make tea first, and then while the tea is brewing, I go upstairs and make my bed and forget about tea. The house is empty.

Where does Michael *go* when he isn't here?

It is forever before Larry calls back and says he's awake now, that he's on his way, should we eat at Bob Evans?

Does the room air stir as his car pulls up, or am I only anticipating?

"You want a cup of coffee before we go?" I ask, standing on my front step.

"Sure," says Larry. He's wearing khaki shorts, and briefly I think of Tony, but Tony always wanted to look like he was on his way to a Soho gallery opening and Larry looks like a department manager. What is different about Larry? Why does Michael suddenly want me to choose?

Cruise leaps exuberantly into the foyer. Larry looks tired. From work? From getting up in the morning? What do I know about this man?

The air stirs. Smith barks, and Cruise whirls in ecstasy. I look for Michael, but I don't see anything.

"Cruise!" Larry says. "Jesus, why does he always do this?"

"No," I say, "it's okay."

I can't see Michael. Has there ever been a time when Smith could see Michael and *I* couldn't? There've been times Michael left just as I got there, but never a time Smith could see him and I couldn't.

I feel sick.

Cruise bounds and rears to put his paws on Michael's chest or shoulders or something—and falls through. The dog's astonishment would be comic if I weren't so frightened. Smith barks, tail happy and delighted.

Larry watches without comprehension.

Cruise tries again, then tries to shove his nose in Michael's hand.

Larry goes over to see what's going on, walks into the space where Cruise is trying to get to Michael. Are Michael and Larry occupying the same space? The idea makes me feel ill, Michael within Larry, Larry within Michael.

I cover my mouth with my hand, but I can't think of anything to say. For a moment, I feel so angry at Larry. Bumbling, unwitting man in my house! Outsider! But Larry is on one knee, trying to calm Cruise.

"Hey, hey, hey," Larry is saying, letting Cruise lick his face and dance and just be the big, black animal that he is. Larry likes Cruise. Of course Larry likes Cruise, but somehow every time I see Larry, he's worried about whether or not Cruise is behaving.

Smith flops down, tongue out. Is Michael gone?

And if he's gone, is he ever coming back?

Michael. Michael. Don't leave me!

Something thuds upstairs, and for a second I think it's a body. Something big and heavy. Suicide! But Michael doesn't really *have* a body. I run upstairs and find my bookcase pushed over.

So he's not gone.

I don't mind that he's angry, as long as he's not *gone*.

Larry comes upstairs slowly. "What happened?"

"The bookcase fell over," I say.

There's no earthly reason for the bookcase to have fallen over, and yet, there it is. As we stand there, looking at it, my tall, four-drawer filing cabinet tips slowly and majestically forward, drawers sliding open, papers just beginning to spill when it completely overbalances and falls.

"Oh, my God," says Larry.

"It's a ghost," I say. "It's the ghost of my brother. We're having an argument about you."

Larry looks at me, frowning.

"I'm really sorry," I say lamely. "Michael, stop it, you'll scare the dogs." And then to Larry again, "He likes dogs. At least, I think he does."

"Is this a *joke*?" Larry asks. He looks at the wall and then at the four-drawer. Probably wondering if this is some sort of bizarre humor. Like I'm David Copperfield or Penn and Teller or something, and this is what I do to all my prospective boyfriends.

Michael is standing in the middle of the room, chest heaving from exertion. "Don't ignore me," he says to me.

Larry is standing gape-mouthed.

"Do you *see* him?" I ask.

"What," Larry says, "what's going on?" He *does* see him! No one has *ever* seen Michael before!

"Larry," I say, "this is my brother, Michael. Michael, this is Larry."

I feel light-headed. Looking at Larry, I don't know if he'll leave or if he'll stay. I don't know what *either* of them is going to do. But I don't care. I am oddly, in fact, deliriously, happy.

The Cost to Be Wise

The sun was up on the snow and everything was bright to look at when the skimmer landed. It landed on the long patch of land behind the schoolhouse, dropping down into the snow like some big bug. I was supposed to be down at the distillery helping my mam but we needed water and I had to get an ice axe so I was outside when the offworlders came.

The skimmer was from Barok. Barok was a city. It was so far away that no one I knew in Sckarline had ever been there (except for the teachers, of course) but for the offworlders the trip was only a few hours. The skimmer came a couple of times a year to bring packages for the teachers.

The skimmer sat there for a moment—long time waiting while nothing happened except people started coming to watch—and then the hatch opened out and an offworlder stepped gingerly out on the snow. The offworlder wasn't a skimmer pilot though, it was a tall, thin boy. I shaded my eyes and watched. My hands were cold but I wanted to see.

The offworlder wore strange colors for the snow. Offworlders always wore unnatural colors. This boy wore purples and oranges and black, all shining as if they were wet and none of them thick enough to keep anyone warm. He stood with his knees stiff and his body rigid because the snow was packed to flat, slick ice by the skimmer and he wasn't sure of his balance. But he was tall and I figured he was as old as I am so it looked odd that he still didn't know how to walk on snow. He was beardless, like a boy. Darker than any of us.

Someone inside the skimmer handed him a bag. It was deep red, and shined as if it were hard, and wrinkled as if it were felt. My father crossed to the skimmer and took the bag from the boy because it was clear that the boy might fall with it and it made a person uncomfortable to watch him try to balance and carry something.

The dogs were barking, and more Sckarline people were coming because they'd heard the skimmer.

I wanted to see what the bags were made of, so I went to the hatch of the skimmer to take something. We didn't get many things from the offworlders because they weren't appropriate, but I liked offworlder things. I couldn't see much inside the skimmer because it was dark and I had been out in the sun, but standing beside the seat where the pilot was sitting there was an old white-haired man, all straight-legged and tall. As tall as Ayudesh the teacher, which is to say taller than anyone else I knew. He handed the boy a box, though, not a bag, a bright blue box with a thick white lid. A plastic box. An offworlder box. The boy handed it to me.

"Thanks," the boy said in English. Up close I could see that the boy was really a girl. Offworlders dress the same both ways, and they are so tall it's hard to tell sometimes, but this was a girl with short black hair and skin as dark as wood.

My father put the bag in the big visitors' house and I put the box there, too. It was midday at winterdark, so the sun was a red glow on the horizon. The bag looked black except where it fell into the red square of sunlight from the doorway. It shone like metal. So very fine. Like nothing we had. I touched the bag. It was plastic, too. I liked the feeling of plastic. I liked the sound of the word in lingua. If someday I had a daughter, maybe I'd name her Plastic. It would be a rich name, an exotic name. The teachers wouldn't like it, but it was a name I wished I had.

Ayudesh was walking across the snow to the skimmer when I went back outside. The girl (I hadn't shaken free from thinking of her as a boy) stuck out her hand to him. Should I have shaken her hand? No, she'd had the box, I couldn't have shaken her hand. So I had done it right. Wanji, the other teacher, was coming, too.

I got wood from the pile for the boxstove in the guest house, digging it from under the top wood because the top wood would be damp. It would take a long time to heat up the guest house, so the sooner I got started the sooner the offworlders would be comfortable.

There was a window in the visitor's house, fat-yellow above the purple-white snow.

Inside, everyone was sitting around on the floor, talking. None of the teachers were there, were they with the old man? I smelled whisak but I didn't see any, which meant that the men were drinking it outside. I sat down at the edge of the group, where it was dark, next to Dirtha. Dirtha was watching the offworld girl who was shaking her head at Harup to try to tell him she didn't understand what he was asking. Harup pointed at her blue box again. "Can I see it?" he asked. Harup was my father's age so he didn't speak any English.

It was warming up in here, although when the offworlder girl leaned forward and breathed out, her mouth in an O, her breath smoked the air for an instant.

It was too frustrating to watch Harup try to talk to the girl. "What's your kinship?" he asked. "I'm Harup Sckarline." He thumped his chest with his finger. "What's your kinship?" When she shook her head, not understanding all these words, he looked around and grinned. Harup wouldn't stop until he was bored, and that would take a long time.

"I'm sorry," the girl said, "I don't speak your language." She looked unhappy.

Ayudesh would be furious with us if he found out that none of us would try and use our English.

I had to think about how to ask. Then I cleared my throat, so people would know I was going to talk from the back of the group. "He asks what is your name," I said.

The girl's chin came up like a startled animal. "What?" she said.

Maybe I said it wrong? Or my accent was so bad she couldn't understand? I looked at my boots; the stitches around the toes were fraying.

They had been my mother's. "Your name," I said to the boots.

The toes twitched a little, sympathetic. Maybe I should have kept quiet.

"My name is Veronique," she said.

"What is she saying?" asked Harup.

"She says her kinship is Veronique," I said.

"That's not a kinship," said Little Shemus. Little Shemus wasn't old enough to have a beard, but he was old enough to be critical of everything.

"Offworlders don't have kinship like we do," I said. "She gave her front name."

"Ask her kinship name," Little Shemus said.

"She just told you," Ardha said, taking the end of her braid out of her mouth. Ardha was a year younger than me. "They don't have kinship names. Ayudesh doesn't have a kinship name. Wanji doesn't."

"Sure they do," Shemus said. "Their kinship name is Sckarlineclan."

"We give them that name," said Ardha and pursed her round lips. Ardha was always bossy.

"What are they saying?" asked the girl.

"They say, err, they ask, what is your—" your what? How would I even ask what her kinship name was in English? There was a word for it, but I couldn't think of it. "Your other name."

She frowned. Her eyebrows were quite black. "You mean my last name? It's Veronique Twombly."

What was so hard about "last name"? I remembered it as soon as she said it. "Tawomby," I said. "Her kinship is Veronique Tawomby."

"Tawomby," Harup said. "Amazing. It doesn't sound like a word. It sounds made-up, like children do. What's in her box?"

"I know what's in her box," said Erip. Everybody laughed except for Ardha and me. Even Little Sherep laughed and he didn't really understand.

The girl was looking at me to explain.

"He asks inside, the box is." I had gotten tangled up. Questions were hard.

"Is the box inside?" she asked.

I nodded.

"It's inside," she said.

I didn't understand her answer so I waited for her to explain.

"I don't know what you mean," she said. "Did someone bring the box inside?"

I nodded, because I wasn't sure exactly what she'd said, but she didn't reach for the box or open it or anything. I tried to think of how to say it.

"Inside," Ardha said, tentative. "What is?"

"The box," she said. "Oh wait, you want to know what's in the box?"

Ardha looked at the door so she wouldn't have to look at the off-worlder. I wasn't sure so I nodded.

She pulled the box over and opened it up. Something glimmered hard and green and there were red and yellow boxes covered in lingua and she said, "Presents for Ayudesh and Wanji." Everybody stood up to see inside, so I couldn't see, but I heard her say things. The words didn't mean anything. Tea, that I knew. Wanji talked about tea. "These are sweets," I heard her say. "You know, candy." I know the word "sweet," but I didn't know what else she meant. It was so much harder to speak English to her than it was to do it in class with Ayudesh.

Nobody was paying any attention to what she said, but me. They didn't care as long as they could see. I wished I could see.

Nobody was even thinking about me, or that if I hadn't been there she never would have opened the box. But that was the way it always was. If I only lived somewhere else, my life would be different. But Sckarline was neither earth nor sky, and I was living my life in-between. People looked and fingered, but she wouldn't let them take things out, not even Harup, who was as tall as she was and a lot stronger. The younger people got bored and sat down and finally I could see Harup poking something with his finger, and the outland girl watching. She looked at me.

"What's your name?" she asked.

"Me?" I said. "Umm, Janna."

She said my name. "What's your last name, Janna?"

"Sckarline," I said.

"Oh," she said, "like the settlement."

I just nodded.

"What is his name?" She pointed.

"Harup," I said. He looked up and grinned.

"What's your name?" she asked him and I told him what she had said.

"Harup," he said. Then she went around the room, saying everybody's names. It made everyone pleased to be noticed. She was smart that way. And it was easy. Then she tried to remember all their names, which had everyone laughing and correcting her so I didn't have to talk at all.

Ayudesh came in, taller than anyone, and I noticed, for the first time in my life, that he was really an offworlder. Ayudesh had been there all my life, and I knew he was an offworlder, but to me he had always been just Ayudesh.

Then they were talking about me and Ayudesh was just Ayudesh again. "Janna?" he said. "Very good. I'll tell you what, you take care of Veronique, here. You're her translator, all right?"

I was scared, because I really couldn't understand when she talked, but I guessed I was better than anybody else.

Veronique unpacked, which was interesting, but then she just started putting things here and there and everybody else drifted off until it was just her and me.

Veronique did a lot of odd things. She used a lot of water. The first thing I did for her was get water. She followed me out and watched me chip the ice for water and fill the bucket. She fingered the wooden bucket and the rope handle.

She said something I didn't understand because it had "do" in it and a lot of pronouns and I have trouble following sentences like that. I smiled at her, but I think she realized I didn't understand. Her boots were purple. I had never seen purple boots before.

"They look strange," she said. I didn't know what looked strange. "I like your boots," she said, slowly and clearly. I did understand, but then I didn't know what to do, did she want me to give her my boots? They were my mother's old boots and I wouldn't have minded giving them to her except I didn't have anything to take their place.

"It is really cold," she said.

Which seemed very odd to say, except I remembered that off-worlders talk about the weather, Ayudesh had made us practice talking about the weather. He said it was something strangers talked about. "It is," I said. "But it will not snow tonight." That was good, it made her happy.

"And it gets dark so early," she said. "It isn't even afternoon and it's like night."

"Where you live, it is cold as this, ummm," I hadn't made a question right.

But she understood. "Oh no," she said, "where I live is warm. It is hot, I mean. There is snow only on the mountains."

She wanted to heat the water so I put it on the stove, and then she showed me pictures of her mother and father and her brother at her house. It was summer and they were wearing only little bits of clothes.

Then she showed me a picture of herself and a man with a beard. "That's my boyfriend," she said. "We're getting married."

He looked old. Grown up. In the picture, Veronique looked older, too. I looked at her again, not sure how old she was. Maybe older than me? Wanji said offworlders got married when they were older, not like the clans.

"I have boyfriend," I said.

"You do?" She smiled at me. "What's his name?"

"Tuuvin," I said.

"Was he here before?"

I shook my head.

Then she let me see her bag. The dark red one. I loved the color. I stroked it, as slick as leather and shining. "Plastic?" I said.

She nodded.

"I like plastic," I said.

She smiled a little, like I'd said something wrong. But it was so perfect, so even in color.

"Do you want it?" she asked. Which made me think of my boots and whether she had wanted them. I shook my head.

"You can have it," she said. "I can get another one."

"No," I said. "It isn't appropriate."

She laughed, a startled laugh. I didn't understand what I'd done and the feeling that I was foolish sat in my stomach, but I didn't know what was so foolish.

She said something I didn't understand, which made me feel worse. "What did you say?" she said. "'Appropriate?'"

I nodded. "It's not appropriate," I said.

"I don't understand," she said.

Our lessons in appropriate development used lots of English words because it was hard to say these things any other way, so I found the words to tell her came easily. "Plastic," I said, "it's not appropriate. Appropriate technologies are based on the needs and capacities of people, they must be sustainable without outside support. Like the distillery is. Plastic isn't appropriate to Sckarline's economy because we can't create it and it replaces things we can produce, like skin bags." I stroked the bag again. "But I like plastic. It's beautiful."

"Wow," Veronique said. She was looking at me sharp, all alert like a stabros smelling a dog for the first time. Not afraid, but not sure what to think. "To me," she said slowly, "your skin bags are beautiful. The wooden houses," she touched the black slick wood wall, "they are beautiful."

Ayudesh and Wanji were always telling us that offworlders thought our goods were wonderful, but how could anyone look at a skin bag and then look at plastic and not see how brilliant the colors were in plastic? Dye a skin bag red and it still looked like a skin bag, like it came from dirt.

"How long you, um, you do stay?" I asked.

"Fourteen days," she said. "I'm a student, I came with my teacher."

I nodded. "Ayudesh, he is a teacher."

"My teacher, he's a friend of Ayudesh. From years ago," she said. "Have you always lived here? Were you born here?"

"Yes," I said. "I am born here. My mother and father are born in Tentas clan, but they come here."

"Tentas clan is another settlement?" she asked.

I shook my head. "No," I said. "No. Sckarline only is a settlement."

"Then, what is Tentas clan?"

"It is people." I didn't know how to explain clans to her at all. "They have kinship, and they have stabros, and they are together—"

"Stabros, those are animals," she said.

I nodded. "Sckarline, uh . . . is an appropriate technology mission."

"Right, that Ayudesh and Wanji started. Tentas clan is a clan, right?"

I nodded. I was worn out from talking to her.

After that, she drank tea and then I took her around to show her Sckarline. It was already almost dark. I showed her the generator where we cooked stabros manure to make electricity. I got a lantern there.

I showed her the stabros pens and the dogs, even though it wasn't really very interesting. Tuuvin was there, and Gerdor, my little uncle, leaning and watching the stabros who were doing nothing but rooting at the mud in the pen and hoping someone would throw them something to eat. The stabros shook their heads and dug with their long front toes.

"This is Tuuvin?" Veronique said.

I was embarrassed. One of the stabros, a gelding with long feathery ears, craned his head toward me. I reached out and pulled on the long guard hairs at the tips of his ears and he lipped at my hand. He had a long purple tongue. He breathed out steam. Their breath always reminded me of the smell of whisak mash.

"Do you ride them?" Veronique asked.

"What?" I asked.

"Do you, um, get on their backs?" She made a person with her fingers walking through the air, then the fingers jumped on the other hand.

"A stabros?" I asked. Tuuvin and Gerdor laughed. "No," I said. "They have no like that. Stabros angry, very much." I pretended to kick. "They have milk, sometimes. And sleds," I said triumphantly, remembering the word.

She leaned on the fence. "They are pretty," she said. "They have pretty eyes. They look so sad with their long drooping ears."

"What?" Tuuvin asked. "What's pretty?"

"She says they have pretty eyes," I said.

Gerdor laughed, but Tuuvin and I gave him a sharp look.

The dogs were leaping and barking and clawing at the gate. She stopped and reached a hand out to touch them. "Dogs are from Earth," she said.

"Dogs are *aufworld*," I said. "Like us. Stabros are *util*."

"What's that mean?" she asked.

"Stabros can eat food that is *aunworld*," I said. "We can't, dogs can't. But we can eat stabros, so they are between."

"Are stabros from Earth?" Veronique asked.

I didn't know, but Tuuvin did, which surprised me. "Stabros are from here," he said. "Ayudesh explained where it all came from, remember? *Util* animals and plants were here, but we could use them. *Aunworld* animals and plants make us sick."

"I know they make us sick," I snapped. But I translated as best I could.

Veronique was looking at the dogs. "Do they bite?" she asked.

Bite? "You mean," I clicked my teeth, "like eat? Sometimes. Mostly if they're fighting."

She took her hand back.

"I'll get a puppy," Tuuvin said, and swung a leg over the side of the pen and waded through the dogs. Tuuvin took care of the dogs a lot so he wasn't afraid of them. I didn't like them much. I liked stabros better.

"There's a winter litter?" I said.

"Yeah," he said. "But it hasn't been too cold, they might be okay. If it gets cold we can always eat 'em."

The puppy looked like a little sausage with short arms and legs and a pink nose. Veronique cooed and took it from Tuuvin and cradled it in her arms. She talked to it, but she talked in a funny way, like baby talk, and I couldn't understand anything she said. "What's its name?" she asked.

"Its name?" I said.

"Do you name them?" she asked.

I looked at Tuuvin. Even Tuuvin should have been able to understand that; the first thing anybody learned in lingua was "What's your name?" But he wasn't paying any attention. I asked him if any of the dogs had names.

He nodded. "Some of them do. The dark male, he's a lead dog, he's called Bigman. And that one is Yellow Dog. The puppies don't have names, though."

"I think this one should have a name," Veronique said, when I told her. "I think he'll be a mighty hunter, so call him Hunter."

I didn't understand what hunting had to do with dogs, and I thought it was a bitch puppy anyway, but I didn't want to embarrass her, so I told Tuuvin. I was afraid he would laugh, but he didn't.

"How do you say that in English?" he asked. "Hunter? Okay, I'll remember." He smiled at Veronique and touched the puppy's nose. "Hunter," he said. The puppy licked him with a tiny pink tongue.

Veronique smiled back. And I didn't like it.

Veronique went to find her teacher. I went down to the distillery to tell Mam why I wasn't there helping. Tuuvin followed me down the hill. The distillery stank so it was down below Sckarline in the trees, just above the fields.

He caught me by the waist and I hung there so he could brush his lips across my hair.

"It's too cold out here," I said and broke out of his arms.

"Let's go in the back," he said.

"I've got to tell Mam," I said.

"Once you tell your mam, there'll be all these things to do and we won't get any time together," he said.

"I can't," I said, but I let him make up my mind for me.

We went around the side, tracking through the dry snow where no one much walked, through the lacey wintertrees to the door to the storage in the back. It was as cold in the back as it was outside, and it was dark. It smelled like mash and whisak and the faint charcoal smell of the charred insides of the kegs. Brass whisak, Sckarline whisak.

He boosted me on a stack of kegs and kissed me.

It wasn't that I really cared so much about kissing. It was nice, but

43

Tuuvin would have kissed and kissed for hours if I would let him and if we could ever find a place where we could be alone for hours. Tuuvin would kiss long after my face felt overused and bruised from kissing. But I just wanted to be with Tuuvin so much. I wanted to talk with him, and have him walk with me. I would let him kiss me if I could whisper to him. I liked the way he pressed against me now; he was warm and I was cold.

He kissed me with little kisses; kiss, kiss, kiss. I liked the little kisses. It was almost like he was talking to me in kisses. Then he kissed me hard and searched around with his tongue. I never knew what to do with my tongue when he put his in my mouth, so I just kept mine still. I could feel the rough edge of the keg beneath my legs, and if I shifted my weight it rocked on the one below it. I turned my face sideways to get my nose out of the way and opened my eyes to look past Tuuvin. In the dark I could barely make out Uukraith's eye burned on all the kegs, to keep them from going bad. Uukraith was the door witch. Uukraith's sister Ina took souls from their mother and put them in seeds, put the seed in women to make babies. The kegs were all turned different directions, eyes looking everywhere. I closed mine again. Uukraith was also a virgin.

"Ohhhh, Heth! Eeeuuuu!"

I jumped, but Tuuvin didn't, he just let go of my waist and stepped back and crossed his arms the way he did when he was uncomfortable. The air felt cold where he had just been warm.

My little sister, Bet, shook her butt at us. "Kissy, kissy, kissy," she said. "MAM, JANNA'S BACK IN THE KEGS WITH TUUVIN!"

"Shut up, Bet," I said. Not that she would stop.

"Slobber, slobber," she said, like we were stabros trading cud. She danced around, still shaking her butt. She puckered up her lips and made wet, smacking noises.

"Fucking little bitch," I said.

Tuuvin frowned at me. He liked Bet. She wasn't his little sister.

"MAM," Bet hollered, "JANNA SAID 'FUCKING'!"

"Janna," my mother called, "come here."

I tried to think of what to do to Bet. I'd have liked to slap her silly.

44

But she'd just go crying to Mam and I'd really be in trouble. It was just that she thought she was so smart and she was really being so stupid.

Mam was on her high stool, tallying. My mam wore trousers most often, and she was tall and man-faced. Still and all, men liked her. I took after her, so I was secretly glad that men watched her walk by, even if she never much noticed.

"Leave your little sister alone," she said.

"Leave her alone!" I said. "She came and found me."

"Don't swear at her. You talk like an old man." Mam was acting like a headman, her voice even and cool.

"If she hadn't come looking—"

"If you had been working as you're supposed to, she'd have had no one to look for, would she."

"I went to see the visitors," I said. "There are two. An old man and a girl. I helped Da carry their things to the visitors' house."

"So that means it is okay to swear at your sister."

It was the same words we always traded. The same arguments, all worn smooth and shining like the wood of a yoke. The brand for the kegs was heating in the fire and I could smell the tang of hot iron in the dung.

"You treat me like a child," I said.

She didn't even answer, but I knew what she would say, that I acted like a child. As if what Tuuvin and I were doing had anything to do with being a child.

I was so tired of it I thought I would burst.

"Go back to work," Mam said, turning on her stool. Saying "this talk is done" with her shoulders and her eyes.

"It's wrong to live this way," I said.

She looked back at me.

"If we lived with the clans, Tuuvin and I could be together."

That made her angry. "This is a better life than the clans," she said. "You don't know what you're talking about. Go back to work."

I didn't say anything. I just hated her. She didn't understand anything. She and my Da hadn't waited until they were old. They hadn't waited for anything, and they'd left their clan to come to Sckarline when it was new. I stood in front of her, making her feel me standing there, all hot and silent.

"Janna," she said. "I'll not put up with your sullenness—" It made her furious when I didn't talk.

So she slapped me, and then I ran out, crying, past Bet who was delighted, and past Tuuvin, who had his mouth open and a stupid look on his face. And I wished they would all disappear.

Veronique sat with Tuuvin and me at dinner in the guesthouse. The guesthouse was full of smoke. We all sat down on the floor with felt and blankets. I looked to see what Veronique would be sitting on and it was wonderful. It was dark, dark blue and clean on the outside, and inside it was red and black squares. I touched it. It had a long metal fastener, a cunning thing that locked teeth together, that Veronique had unfastened so she could sit on the soft red and black inside. Dark on the outside, red on the inside; it was as if it represented some strange offworld beast. My felt blanket was red, but it was old and the edges were gray with dirt. Offworlders were so clean, as if they were always new.

Ayudesh was with the old man who had come with Veronique. Wanji was there, but she was being quiet and by herself, the way Wanji did.

Tuuvin had brought the puppy into the guesthouse. "She asked me to," he said when I asked him what he was doing.

"She did not," I said. "People are watching a dog in this house. Besides, you don't understand her when she talks."

"I do, too," he said. "I was in school, too."

I rolled my eyes. He was when he was little, but he left as soon as he was old enough to hunt. Men always left as soon as they were old enough to hunt. And he hated it anyway.

Veronique squealed when she saw the puppy and took it from Tuuvin as if it were a baby. Everyone watched out of the corner of their eyes. Ayudesh thought it was funny. We were all supposed to be equal in Sckarline, but Ayudesh was really like a headman.

She put the puppy on her offworld blanket and it rolled over on its back, showing her its tan belly. It would probably pee on her blanket.

My da leaned over. "I hope it isn't dinner." My da hated dog.

"No," I said. "She just likes it."

My da said to her, "Hie." Then to me he said, "What is she called?"

"Veronique," I said.

"Veronique," he said. Then he pointed to himself. "Guwk."

"Hello, Guwk," Veronique said.

"Hello, Veronique," said my da, which surprised me because I had never heard him say anything in English before. "Ask her for her cup," he said to me.

She had one; bright yellow and smooth. But my da handled it matter-of-factly, as if he handled beautiful things every day. He had a skin and he poured whisak into her cup. "My wife," he waved at Mam, "she makes whisak for Sckarline."

I tried to translate, but I didn't know what 'whisak' was in English.

Veronique took the cup. My da held his hand up for her to wait and poured himself a cup. He tossed it back. Then he nodded at her for her to try.

She took a big swallow. She hadn't expected the burn, you could see that. She choked and her face got red. Tuuvin patted her on the back while she coughed. "Oh my God," she said. "That's strong!" I didn't think I needed to translate that.

II.

The sound of the guns is like the cracking of whips. Like the snapping of bones. The outrunners for the Scathalos High-on came into Sckarline with a great deal of racket; brass clattering, the men singing and firing their guns into the air. It started the dogs barking and scared out stabros and brought everyone outside.

Scathalos dyed the toes and ridgeline manes of their stabros kracken yellow. They hung brass clappers in the harnesses of their caravan animals and bits of milky blue glass from the harnesses of their dogs. On this sunny day everything winked. Only their milking does were plain, and that's only because even the will of a hunter can't make a doe stabros tractable.

Veronique came out with me. "Who are they?" she asked.

47

Even after just three days I could understand Veronique a lot better. "They are from a great clan, Scathalos," I said. "They come to buy whisak." We hoped they would buy it. Sometimes, when Scathalos outrunners came, they just took it.

"They're another clan?" she asked. "Where are the women?"

"They're outrunners," I said. "They go out and hunt and trade. Outrunners are not-married men."

"They have a lot of guns," she said.

They had more guns than I had ever seen. Usually when outrunners came they had one or two guns. Guns are hard to get. But it looked as if almost every outrunner had a gun.

"Does Sckarline have guns?" Veronique asked.

"No," I said.

'They're not appropriate, right?"

A lot of people said we should have guns, whether Ayudesh and Wanji thought they were appropriate or not. They had to buy the clips that go with them. Ayudesh said that the offworlders used the need of the clips to control the clans. He said that it wasn't appropriate because we couldn't maintain it ourselves.

My da said that maybe some things we should buy. We bought things from other clans, that was trade. Maybe guns were trade, too.

The dogs nipped at the doe stabros, turning them, making them stop until outrunners could slip hobbles on them. The stabros looked pretty good. They were mostly dun, and the males were heavy in the shoulders, with heads set low and forward on their necks. Better than most of our animals. The long hairs on their ears were braided with red and yellow threads. Handlers unhooked the sleds from the pack stabros.

Two of them found the skimmer tracks beyond the schoolhouse. They stopped and looked around. They saw Veronique. Then another stared at her, measuring her.

"Come with me," I said.

Our dogs barked and their dogs barked. The outrunner men talked loudly. Sckarline people stood at the doors of their houses and didn't talk at all.

"What's wrong?" Veronique asked.

"Come help my mam and me." She would be under the gaze of them in the distillery, too, but I suspected she would be under their gaze anywhere. And this way Mam would be there.

"Scathalos come here for whisak," I said to my mam, even though she could see for herself. Mam was at the door, shading her eyes and watching them settle in. Someone should have been telling them we had people in the guesthouse and offering to put their animals up, but no one was moving.

"Tuuvin is in the back," Mam said, pointing with her chin. "Go back and help him."

Tuuvin was hiding the oldest whisak, what was left of the three-year-old brass whisak. Scathalos had come for whisak two years ago and taken what they wanted and left us almost nothing but lame stabros. They said it was because we had favored Toolie Clan in trade. The only reason we had any three-year-old whisak left was because they couldn't tell what was what.

So my da and some of the men had dug a cellar in the distillery. Tuuvin was standing in the cellar, taking kegs he had stacked at the edge and pulling them down. It wasn't very deep, not much over his chest, but the kegs were heavy. I started stacking more for him to hide.

I wondered what the outrunners would do if they caught us at our work. I wondered if Tuuvin was thinking the same thing. We'd hidden some down there in the spring before the stabros went up to summer grazing but then we'd taken some of the oldest kegs to drink when the stabros came back down in the fall.

"Hurry," Tuuvin said softly.

My hands were slick. Veronique started taking kegs, too. She couldn't lift them, so she rolled them on their edge. Her hands were soft and pretty, not used to rough kegs. It seemed like it took a long time. Tuuvin's hands were rough and red. I'd never thought about how hard his hands were. Mine were like his, all red. My hands were ugly compared to Veronique's. Surely he was noticing that, too, since every time Veronique rolled a keg over, her hands were right there.

And then the last keg was on the edge. Uukraith's eye looked at me, strangely unaffected. Or maybe amused. Or maybe angry. Da said that spirits do not feel the way we feel. The teachers never said anything at all about spirits, which was how we knew that they didn't listen to them. There was not much space in the cellar, just enough for Tuuvin to stand and maybe a little more.

Tuuvin put his hands on the edge and boosted himself out of the cellar. In front of the store we heard the crack of the door on its hinges and we all three jumped.

Tuuvin slid the wooden cover over the hole in the floor. "Move those," he said, pointing at empty kegs.

I didn't hear voices.

"Are you done yet?" Mam said, startling us again.

"Are they here?" I asked.

"No," she said. "Not yet." She didn't seem afraid. I had seen my mam afraid, but not very often. "What is she doing here?" Mam asked, pointing at Veronique.

"I thought she should be here, I mean, I was afraid to leave her by herself."

"She's not a child," Mam said. But she said it mildly, so I knew she didn't really mind. Then Mam helped us stack kegs. We all tried to be quiet, but they thumped like hollow drums. They filled the space around us with noise. It seemed to me that the outrunners could hear us thumping away from outside. I kept looking at Mam, who was stacking kegs as if we hid whisak all the time. Tuuvin was nervous, too. His shoulders were tense. I almost said to him, "you're up around the ears, boy," the way the hunters did, but right now I didn't think it would make him smile.

Mam scuffed the dirt around the kegs.

"Will they find them?" I asked.

Mam shrugged. "We'll see."

There was a lot to do to get ready for the outrunners besides hiding the best whisak. Mam had us count the kegs, even Veronique. Then when we all three agreed on a number she wrote it in her tally book. "So we know how much we sell," she said.

We were just finishing counting when outrunners came with Ayudesh.

They came into the front. First the wind like a wild dog sliding around the door and making the fires all sway. Then Ayudesh and then the out-runners. The outrunners looked short compared to Ayudesh. And they looked even harder than we did. Their cheeks were winter red. Their felts were all dark with dirt, like they'd been out for a long time.

"Hie," said one of the men, seeing my mother. They all grinned. People always seemed surprised that they were going to trade with my mam. The outrunners already smelled of whisak so people had finally made them welcome. Or maybe someone had the sense to realize that if they gave them drink we'd have time to get things ready. Maybe my da.

My mam stood as she always did, with her arms crossed, tall as any of them. Waiting them out.

"What's this," said the man, looking around. "Eh? What's this? It stinks in here." The distillery always stank.

They walked around, looked at the kegs, poked at the copper tub-ing and the still. One stuck his finger under the drip and tasted the raw stuff and grimaced. Ayudesh looked uncomfortable, but the teachers always said that the distillery was ours and they didn't interfere with how we ran it. Mam was in charge here.

Mam just stood and let them walk around her. She didn't turn her head to watch them.

They picked up the brand. "What's this?" the man said again.

"We mark all our kegs with the eye of Uukraith," Mam said.

"Woman's work," he said.

He stopped and looked at Veronique. He studied her for a moment, then frowned. "You're no boy," he said.

Veronique looked at me, the whites of her eyes bright even in the dimness, but she didn't say anything.

He grinned and laughed. The other two outrunners crowded close to her and fingered the slick fabric of her sleeve, touched her hair. Veronique pulled away.

The first outrunner got bored and walked around the room some more.

He tapped a keg. Not like Mam thumped them, listening, but just as if everything here were his. He had dirty brown hair on the backs of his hands. Everywhere I looked I was seeing people's hands. I didn't like the way he put his hands on things.

Then he pointed to a keg, not the one he was tapping on, but a different one, and one of the other men picked it up. "Is it good?" he asked.

My mam shrugged.

He didn't like that. He took two steps forward and hit her across the face. I looked at the black, packed dirt-floor.

Ayudesh made a noise.

"It's good," my mam said. I looked up and she had a red mark on the side of her face. Ayudesh looked as if he would speak, but he didn't.

The outrunner grabbed her braid—she flinched as he reached past her face—and yanked her head. "It's good, woman?" he asked.

"Yes," she said, her voice coming almost airless, like she could not breathe.

He yanked her down to her knees. Then he let go and they all went out with the keg.

Ayudesh said, "Are you all right?" Mam stood back up again and touched her braid, then flipped it back over her neck. She didn't look at any of us.

People were in the schoolhouse. Ayudesh sat on the table at the front and people were sitting on the floor talking as if it were a meeting. Veronique's teacher was sitting next to Ayudesh and Veronique started as if she was going to go sit with him. Then she looked around and sat down with Mam and Tuuvin and me.

"So we should just let them take whatever they want?" Harup said. He wasn't clowning now, but talking as a senior hunter. He sat on his heels, the way hunters do when they're waiting.

Ayudesh said, "Even if we could get guns, they're used to fighting and we aren't. What do you think would happen?"

Veronique was very quiet.

"If we don't stand up for ourselves, what will happen?" Harup said.

"If you provoke them they'll destroy us," Ayudesh said.

"Teacher," Harup said, spreading his hands as if he was telling a story. "Stabros are not hunting animals, eh. They are not sharp-toothed like haunds or dogs. Haunds are hunters, packs of hunters, who do nothing but hunt stabros. There are more stabros than all the haunds could eat, eh. So how do they choose? They don't kill the buck stabros with their hard toes and heads, they take the young, the old, the sick, the helpless. We do not want to be haunds, teacher. We just want the haunds to go elsewhere for easy prey."

Wanji came in behind us, and the fire in the boxstove ducked and jumped in the draft. Wanji didn't sit down on the table, but, as was her custom, lowered herself to the floor. "Old hips," she muttered as if everyone in the room wasn't watching her. "Old women have old hips."

When I thought of Kalky, the old woman who makes the souls of everything, I thought of her as looking like Wanji. Wanji had a little face and a big nose and deep lines down from her nose to her chin. "What happened to you, daughter?" she asked my mam.

"The outrunners came to the distillery to take a keg," Mam said.

I noticed that now the meeting had turned around, away from Ayudesh on the table towards us in the back. Wanji always said that Ayudesh was vain and liked to sit high. Sometimes she called him "High-on." "And so," Wanji said.

My mother's face was still red from the blow, but it hadn't yet purpled. "I don't think the outrunners like to do business with me," Mam said.

"One of them hit her," I said, because Mam wasn't going to. Mam never talked about it when my da hit her, either. Although he didn't do it as much as he used to when I was Bet's age.

Mam looked at me, but I couldn't tell if she was angry with me or not.

Harup spread his hands to say, "See?"

Wanji clucked.

"We got the three-year-old whisak in the cellar," Mam said.

I was looking, but I didn't see my da.

"What are they saying," Veronique asked.

"They are talking," I said, and had to think how to say it, "about what we do, but they, eh, not, do not know? Do not know what is right.

Harup want guns. Wants guns. Ayudesh says guns are bad."

"Wanji," Tuuvin whispered, "Wanji she ask—eh," and then in our own tongue, "tell her she was asking your mam what happened."

"Wanji ask my mother what is the matter," I said.

Veronique looked at Tuuvin and then at me.

"Guns are bad," Veronique said.

Tuuvin scowled. "She doesn't understand," he said.

"What?" Veronique said, but I just shook my head rather than tell her what Tuuvin had said.

Some of the men were talking about guns. Wanji was listening without saying anything, resting her chin on her hand. Sometimes it seemed like Wanji didn't even blink, that she just turned into stone and you didn't know what she was thinking.

Some of the other men were talking to Ayudesh about whisak. Yet, Harup's wife, got up and put water on the boxstove for the men to drink and Big Sherep went out the men's door in the back of the schoolhouse, which meant that he was going to get whisak or beer.

"Nothing will get done now," Tuuvin said, disgusted. "Let's go."

He stood up and Veronique looked up at him, then scrambled to her feet.

"Now they talk, talk, talk," I said in English. "Nothing to say, just talk, you know?"

Outside there were outrunners. It seemed as if they were everywhere, even though there were really not that many of them. They watched Veronique.

Tuuvin scowled at them and I looked at their guns. Long black guns slung over their backs. I had never seen a gun close. And there was my da, standing with three outrunners, holding a gun in his hands as if it were a fishing spear, admiring it. He was nodding and grinning, the way he did when someone told a good hunting story. Of course, he didn't know that one of these people had hit Mam.

Still, it made me mad that he was being friendly.

"We should go somewhere," Tuuvin said.

"The distillery?" I asked.

"No," he said, "they'll go back there." And he looked at Veronique.

54

Having Veronique around was like having Bet, you always had to be thinking about her. "Take her to your house."

"And do what?" I asked. A little angry at him because now he had decided he wasn't going back with us.

"I don't know, teach her to sew or something," he said. He turned and walked across to where my da was standing.

The outrunners took two more kegs of whisak and got loud. They stuck torches in the snow, so the dog's harnesses were all glittering and winking, and we gave them a stabros to slaughter and they roasted that. Some of the Sckarline men like my da—and even Harup—sat with them and talked and sang. I didn't understand why Harup was there, but there he was, laughing and telling stories about the time my da got dumped out of the boat fishing.

Ayudesh was there, just listening. Veronique's grandfather was out there, too, even though he couldn't understand what they were saying.

"When will they go?" Veronique asked.

I shrugged.

She asked something I didn't understand.

"When you trade," she said, "trade?"

"Trade," I said, "trade whisak, yes?"

"Yes," she said. "When you trade whisak, men come? Are you afraid when you trade whisak?"

"Afraid?" I asked. "When Scathalos come, yes."

"When other people come, are you afraid?" she asked.

"No," I said. "Just Scathalos."

She sat on my furs.

My mam was on the bed and Bet had gone to sleep. Mam watched us talk, sitting cross-legged and mending Bet's boots. She didn't understand any English. It felt wrong to talk when Mam didn't understand, but Veronique couldn't understand when I talked to Mam, either.

"I have to go back to my hut," Veronique said. "Ian will come back and he'll worry about me."

Outside the air was so cold and dry that the insides of our noses felt it.

"Don't you get tired of being cold?" Veronique asked.

The cold made people tired, I thought, yes. That was why people slept so much during winterdark. I didn't always know what to say when Veronique talked about the weather.

"We tell your teacher, you sleep in our house, yes?" I offered.

"Who?" she said. "You mean Ian? He isn't really my teacher like you mean it. He's my professor."

I tried to think of what a professor might be, maybe the person who took you when your father died? It always seemed English didn't have enough words for different relatives, but now here was one I didn't know.

The outrunners and the Sckarline hunters were singing about Fhidrhin the hunter and I looked up to see if I could make out the stars that formed him, but the sky had drifting clouds and I couldn't find the stars.

I couldn't see well enough, the light from the bonfire made everyone else just shadows. I took Veronique's hand and started around the outside of the circle of singers, looking for Ayudesh and Veronique's teacher or whatever he was. Faces glanced up, spirit faces in the firelight. The smoke blew our way and then shifted, and I smelled the sweat smell that came from the men's clothes as they warmed by the fire. And whisak, of course. The stabros was mostly bones.

"Janna," said my da. His face was strange, too, not human, like a mask. His eyes looked unnaturally light. "Go on back to your mother."

"Veronique needs to tell the offworlder that she's staying with us."

"Go on back to the house," he said again. I could smell whisak on him, too. Whisak sometimes made him mean. My da used to drink a lot of whisak when I was young, but since Bet was born he didn't drink it very often at all. He said the mornings were too hard when you got old.

I didn't know what to do. If I kept looking for Veronique's grandfather and he got angry he would probably hit me. I nodded and backed away, pulling Veronique with me, then when he stopped watching me, I started around the fire the other way.

One of the outrunners stumbled up and into us before we could get out of the way. "Eh——?"

I pulled Veronique away but he gripped her arm. "Boy?"

His breath in her face made her close her eyes and turn her head.

"No boy," he said. He was drunk, probably going to relieve himself. "No boy, outsider girl, pretty as a boy," he said. "Outsider, they like that? Eh?"

Veronique gripped my hand. "Let's go," she said in English.

He didn't have to speak English to see she was afraid of him.

"I'm not pretty enough for you?" he said. "Eh? Not pretty enough?" He wasn't pretty, he was wiry and had teeth missing on one side of his mouth. "Not Sckarline? With their pretty houses like offworlders? Not pretty, eh?"

Veronique drew a breath like a sob.

"Let go of her, please," I said, "we have to go find her teacher."

"Look at the color of her," he said, "does that wash off? Eh?"

"Do you know where her teacher is?" I asked.

"Shut up, girl," he said to me. He licked his thumb and reached towards her face. Veronique raised her hand and drew back, and he twisted her arm. "Stand still." He rubbed her cheek with his thumb and peered closely at her.

"Damn," he said, pleased. "How come the old man isn't dark?"

"Maybe they are different clans," I said.

He stared at her as if weighing what I'd said. As if thinking. Although he actually looked too drunk to do much thinking. Then he leaned forward and tried to kiss her.

Veronique pushed him away with her free arm. He staggered and fell, pulling her down, too.

"Let go!" she shrieked.

Shut up, I thought, shut up, shut up! Give in, he's too drunk to do much. I tried to pull his arm off, but his grip was too strong.

"What's this?" another outrunner was saying.

"Fohlder's found some girl."

"It would be fucking Fohlder!"

Veronique slapped at him and struggled, trying to get away.

"Hey now," Ayudesh was saying, "hey now, she's a guest, an offworlder." But nobody was paying attention. Everybody was watching the outrunner wrestle with her. He pinned her with her arms over her head and kissed her.

Veronique was crying and slapping. Stop it, I kept thinking, just stop it, or he won't let you alone.

Her grandfather tried to pull the outrunner off. I hadn't even seen him come up. "No no no no no," he was saying as if scolding someone. "No no no no no—"

"Get off him," another outrunner hauled him away.

Ayudesh said, "Stop! She is our guest!"

"She's yours, eh?" someone said.

"No," Ayudesh said, "she should be left alone. She's a guest."

"Your guest, right. Not interested in the likes of us."

Someone else grunted and laughed.

"She likes Sckarline better, eh?"

"That's because she doesn't know better."

"Fohlder'll show her."

You all stink like drunks, I wanted to scream at them, because they did.

"Think she's dark inside like she is outside?"

"Have to wait until morning to see."

Oh, my da would be so mad at me, the stupid bitch, why didn't she stop, he was drunk, he was drunk, why had she slapped at him, stupider than Bet, she was as stupid as Bet my little sister, I was supposed to be taking care of her, I was supposed to be watching out for her, my da would be so mad—

There was the bone crack of gunfire and everybody stopped.

Harup was standing next to the fire with an outrunner gun pointed up, as if he were shooting at Fhidrhin up there in the stars. His expression was mild and he was studying the gun as if he hadn't even noticed what was going on.

"Hey," an outrunner said, "put that down!"

Harup looked around at the outrunners, at us. He looked slowly. He didn't look like he usually did, he didn't look funny or angry, he looked as if he were out on a boat in the ice. Calm, far away. Cold as the stars. He could kill someone.

The outrunners felt it too. They didn't move. If he shot one of them, the others would kill him, but the one he shot would still be dead. No one wanted to be the one that might be dead.

"It's a nice piece," Harup said, "but if you used it for hunting you'd soon be so deaf you couldn't hear anything moving." Then he grinned.

Someone laughed.

Everyone laughed.

"Janna," Harup said, "take your friend and get us more whisak."

"Fohlder, you old walking dick, get up from that girl." One of them reached down and pulled him off. He looked mad.

"What," he said, "what."

"Go take a piss," the outrunner said.

Everyone laughed.

III.

Veronique stayed with me that night, lying next to me in my blankets and furs. She didn't sleep, I don't think. I was listening to her breath. I felt as if I should help her sleep. I lay there and tried to think if I should put my arm around her, but I didn't know. Maybe she didn't want to be touched.

And she had been a stupid girl, anyway.

She lay tense in the dark. "Are you going to be a teacher?" I asked.

She laughed. "If I get out of here."

I waited for her to say more, but she didn't. "Get out of here" meant to make someone leave. Maybe she meant if she made herself.

"You come here from Earth?" I asked. To get her to talk, although I was tired of lingua and I didn't really want to think about anything.

"My family came here from Earth," she said.

"Why?"

"My father, he's an anthropologist," she said. "Do you know anthropologist?"

"No," I said.

"He is a person who studies the way people live. And he is a teacher."

59

All the offworlders I had ever met were teachers. I wondered who did all the work on Earth.

"Because Earth had lost touch with your world, the people here are very interesting to my father," she said. Her voice was listless in the dark and she was even harder to understand when I couldn't see her properly. I didn't understand so I didn't say anything. I was sorry I'd started her talking.

"History, do you know the word 'history'?" she asked.

Of course I knew the word "history." "I study history in school," I said. Anneal and Kumar taught it.

"Do you know the history of this world?"

It took my tired head a long time to sort that out. "Yes," I said. "We are a colony. People from Earth come here to live. Then there is a big problem on Earth, and the people of Earth forget we are here. We forget we are from Earth. Then Earth finds us again."

"Some people have stories about coming from the Earth," Veronique said. "My father is collecting those stories from different peoples. I'm a graduate student."

The clans didn't have any stories about coming from Earth. We said the first people came out of the sun. This somehow seemed embarrassing. I didn't understand what kind of student she was.

"Are you here for stories?" I asked.

"No," she said. "Ian is old friends with your teacher, from back when they were both with the survey. We just came to visit."

I didn't understand what she'd said except that they were visiting.

We were quiet after that. I pretended to sleep. Sometimes there was gunfire outside and we jumped, even Mam on the bed. Everyone but Bet. Once Bet was asleep it was impossible to wake her up.

I fell asleep thinking about how I wished that the Scathalos outrunners were gone. I dreamed that I was at the offworlder's home, where it was summer but no one was taking care of the stabros, and they were all glad, and so I was a hero—and I was startled awake by gunfire.

Just more drinking and shooting.

I wished my da would come home. It didn't seem fair that we should lie here and be afraid while the men were getting drunk and singing.

❄

The outrunners stayed the next day, taking three more kegs of whisak but not talking about trade. The following day they sent out hunters, but didn't find their own meat and so took another stabros, the gelding I'd shown to Veronique. And more whisak.

I went down to the distillery after they took some more whisak. It was already getting dark. The dark comes so early at this time of year. The door was left open and the fire was out. Mam wasn't coming anymore. There was no work being done. Kegs had been taken down and some had been opened and left open. Some had been spilled. They had started on the green stuff, not knowing what was what and had thrown most of it in the snow, probably thinking it was bad. Branded eyes on the kegs looked everywhere.

I thought maybe they wouldn't leave until all the whisak was gone. For one wild moment I thought about taking an axe to the kegs. Give them no reason to stay.

Instead I listened to them singing, their voices far away. I didn't want to walk back towards the voices, but I didn't want to be outside in the dark, either. I walked until I could see the big fire they had going, and smell the stabros roasting. Then I stood for a while, because I didn't want to cross the light more than I wanted to go home. Maybe someone was holding me back, maybe my spirit knew something.

I looked for my father. I saw Harup on the other side of the fire. His face was in the light. He wasn't singing, he was just watching. I saw Gerdor, my little uncle, my father's half brother. I did not see my father anywhere.

Then I saw him. His back was to me. He was just a black outline against the fire. He had his hands open wide, as if he was explaining. He had his empty hands open. Harup was watching my father explaining something to some of the outrunners and something was wrong.

One of the outrunners turned his head and spat.

My father, I couldn't hear his voice, but I could see his body, his shoulders moving as he explained. His shoulders working, working hard as if he were swimming. Such hard work, this talking with his hands open, talking, talking.

The outrunner took two steps, bent down and pulled his rifle into the light. It was a dark thing there, a long thing against the light of the fire. My father took a step back and his hands came up, pushing something back.

And then the outrunner shot my father.

All the singing stopped. The fire cracked and the sparks rose like stars while my father struggled in the snow. He struggled hard, fighting and scraping back through the snow. Elbow-walking backwards. The outrunner was looking down the long barrel of the rifle.

Get up, I thought. Get up. For a long time it seemed I thought, Get up, get up. Da, get up! But no sound came out of my mouth and there was black on the snow in the trampled trail my father left.

The outrunner shot again.

My father flopped into the snow and I could see the light on his face as he looked up. Then he stopped.

Harup watched. No one moved except the outrunner who put his rifle away.

I could feel the red meat, the hammering muscle in my chest. I could feel it squeezing, squeezing. Heat flowed in my face. In my hands.

Outrunners shouted at outrunners. "You shit," one shouted at the one who shot my father. "You drunken, stupid shit!" The one who shot my father shrugged at first, as if he didn't care, and then he became angry, too, shouting.

My breath was in my chest, so full. If I breathed out loud the outrunners would hear me out here. I tried to take small breaths, could not get enough air. I did not remember when I had been holding my breath.

Harup and the hunters of Sckarline sat, like prey, hiding in their stillness. The arguing went on and on, until it wasn't about my father at all and his body was forgotten in the dirty snow. They argued about who was stupid and who had the High-on's favor. The whisak was talking.

I could think of nothing but air.

I went back through the dark, out of Sckarline, and crept around behind the houses, in the dark and cold until I could come to our house without going past the fire. I took great shuddering breaths of cold air, breathed out great gouts of fog.

My mother was trying to get Bet to be quiet when I came in. "No," she was saying, "stop it now, or I'll give you something to cry about."

"Mam," I said, and I started to cry.

"What," she said. "Janna, your face is all red." She was my mam, with her face turned towards me, and I had never seen her face so clearly.

"They're going to kill all of us," I said. "They killed Da with a rifle."

She never said a word but just ran out and left me there. Bet started to cry although she didn't really know what I was crying about. Just that she should be scared. Veronique was still. As still as Harup and the hunters.

Wanji came and got me and brought me to Ayudesh's house because our house is small and Ayudesh's house had enough room for some people. Snow was caked in the creases of my father's pants. It was in his hands, too, unmelted. I had seen dead people before, and my father looked like all of them. Not like himself at all.

My mother had followed him as far as the living can go—or at least as far as someone untrained in spirit journeys—and she was not herself. She was sitting on the floor next to his body, rocking back and forth with her arms crossed in her lap. I had seen women like that before, but not my mother. I didn't want to look. It seemed indecent. Worse than the body of my father, since my father wasn't there at all.

Bet was screaming. Her face was red from the effort. I held her even though she was heavy and she kept arching away from me like a toddler in a tantrum. "MAM! MAM!" she kept screaming.

People came in and squatted down next to the body for a while. People talked about guns. It was important that I take care of Bet, so I did, until finally she wore herself out from crying and fell asleep. I held her on my lap until the blood was out of my legs and I couldn't feel the floor and then Wanji brought me a blanket and I wrapped Bet in it and let her sleep.

Wanji beckoned me to follow. I could barely stand, my legs had so little feeling. I held the wall and looked around, at my mother sitting next to the vacant body, at my sister, who though asleep was still alive. Then

I tottered after Wanji as if I was the old woman.

"Where is the girl?" Wanji said.

"Asleep," I said. "On the floor."

"No, the girl," Wanji said, irritated. "Ian's girl. From the university."

"I don't know," I said.

"You're supposed to be watching her. Didn't Ayudesh tell you to watch her?"

"You mean Veronique? She's back at my house. In my bed."

Wanji nodded and sucked on her teeth. "Okay," she said. And then again to herself. "Okay."

Wanji took me to her house, which was little and dark. She had a lamp shaped like a bird. It had been in her house as long as I could remember. It didn't give very much light, but I had always liked it. We sat on the floor. Wanji's floor was always piled high with rugs from her home and furs and blankets. It made it hard to walk but nice to sit. Wanji got cold and her bones hurt, so she always made a little nest when she sat down. She pulled a red and blue rug across her lap. "Sit, sit, sit," she said.

I was cold, but there was a blanket to wrap around my shoulders. I couldn't remember being alone with Wanji before. But everything was so strange it didn't seem to make any difference and it was nice to have Wanji deciding what to do and me not having to do anything.

Wanji made tea over her little bird lamp. She handed me a cup and I sipped it. Tea was a strange drink. Wanji and Ayudesh liked it and hoarded it. It was too bitter to be very good, but it was warm and the smell of it was always special. I drank it and held it against me. I started to get warm. The blanket got warm from me and smelled faintly of Wanji, an old dry smell.

I was sleepy. It would have been nice to go to sleep right there in my little nest on Wanji's floor.

"Girl," Wanji said. "I must give you something. You must take care of Veronique."

I didn't want to take care of anybody. I wanted someone to take care of me. My eyes started to fill up and in a moment I was crying salt tears into my tea.

"No time for that, Janna," Wanji said. Always sharp with us. Some people were afraid of Wanji. I was. But it felt good to cry, and I didn't know how to stop it, so I didn't.

Wanji didn't pay any attention. She was hunting through her house, checking in a chest, pulling up layers of rugs to peer in a corner. Was she going to give me a gun? I couldn't think of anything else that would help very much right now, but I couldn't imagine that Wanji owned a gun.

She came back with a dark blue plastic box not much bigger than the span of my spread hand. That was almost as astonishing as a gun. I wiped my nose on my sleeve. I was warm and tired. Would Wanji let me sleep right here on her floor?

Wanji opened the plastic box, but away from me so I couldn't see inside it. She picked at it as if she were picking at a sewing kit, looking for something. I wanted to look in it but I was afraid that if I tried she'd snap at me.

She looked at me. "This is mine," she said. "We both got one and we decided that if the people who settled Sckarline couldn't have it, we wouldn't either."

I didn't care about that. That was old talk. I wanted to know what it was.

Wanji wasn't ready to tell me what it was. I had the feeling that Ayudesh didn't know about this, and I was afraid she would talk herself out of it. She looked at it and thought. If I thought, I thought about my father being dead. I sipped tea and tried to think about being warm, about sleeping, but that feeling had passed. I wondered where Tuuvin was.

I thought about my da and I started to cry again.

I thought that would really get Wanji angry so I tried to hide it, but she didn't pay any attention at all. The shawl she wore over her head slipped halfway down so when I glanced up I could see where her hair parted, and the line of pale skin. It looked so bare that I wanted it covered up again. It made me think of the snow in my father's hands.

"It was a mistake," Wanji said.

I thought she meant the box, and I felt a terrible disappointment that I wouldn't get to see what was inside it.

"You understand what we were trying to do?" she asked me.

With the box? Not at all.

65

"What are the six precepts of development philosophy?" she asked.

I had to think. "One," I said, "that economic development should be gradual. Two, that analyzing economic growth by the production of goods rather than the needs and capacities of people leads to displacement and increased poverty. Three, that economic development should come from the integrated development of rural areas with the traditional sector—"

"It's just words," she snapped at me.

I didn't know what I had done wrong so I ducked my head and sniffed and waited for her to get angry because I couldn't stop crying.

Instead she stroked my hair. "Oh, little girl. Oh, Janna. You are one of the bright ones. If you aren't understanding it, then we really haven't gotten it across, have we?" Her hand was nice on my hair, and it seemed so unlike Wanji that it scared me into stillness. "We were trying to help, you know," she said. "We were trying to do good. We gave up our lives to come here. Do you realize?"

Did she mean that they were going to die? Ayudesh and Wanji?

"This," she said, suddenly brisk. "This is for, what would you call them, runners. Foreign runners. It is to help them survive. I am going to give it to you so that you will help Veronique, understood?"

I nodded.

But she didn't give it to me. She just sat holding the box, looking in it. She didn't want to give it up. She didn't feel it was appropriate.

She sighed again, a terrible sound. Out of the box she pulled shiny foil packets, dark blue, red, and yellow. They were the size of the palm of her hand. Her glasses were around her neck. She put them on like she did in the schoolroom, absent from the gesture. She studied the printing on the foil packets.

I loved foil. Plastic was beautiful, but foil, foil was something unimaginable. Tea came in foil packets. The strange foods that the teachers got off the skimmer came in foil.

My tea was cold.

"This one," she said, "it is a kind of signal." She looked over her glasses at me. "Listen to me, Janna. Your life will depend on this. When you have this, you can send a signal that the outsiders can hear. They can hear it all the way in Bashtoy. And after you send it, if you can wait in the same place, they will send someone out to get you and Veronique."

"They can hear it in Bashtoy?" I said. I had never even met anyone other than Wanji and the teachers who had ever been to Bashtoy.

"They can pick it up on their instruments. You send it every day until someone comes."

"How do I send it?"

She read the packet. "We have to set the signal, you and I. First we have to put it in you."

I didn't understand, but she was reading, so I waited.

"I'm going to put it in your ear," she said. "From there it will migrate to your brain."

"Will it hurt?" I asked.

"A little," she said. 'But it has its own way of taking pain away. Now, what should be the code?" She studied the packet. She pursed her lips.

A thing in my ear. I was afraid and I wanted to say no, but I was more afraid of Wanji so I didn't.

"You can whistle, can't you?" she asked.

I knew how to whistle, yes.

"Okay," she said, "here it is. I'll put this in your ear, and then we'll wait for a while. Then when everything is ready, we'll set the code."

She opened up the packet and inside was another packet and a little metal fork. She opened the inside packet and took out a tiny little disk, a soft thing almost like egg white or like a fish egg. She leaned forward and put it in my left ear. Then she pushed it in hard and I jerked.

"Hold still," she said.

Something was moving and making noise in my ear and I couldn't be still. I pulled away and shook my head. The noise in my ear was loud, a sort of rubbing, oozing sound. I couldn't hear normal things out of my left ear. It was stopped up with whatever was making the oozing noise. Then it started to hurt. A little at first, then more and more.

I put my hand over my ear, pressing against the pain. Maybe it would eat through my ear? What would stop it from eating a hole in my head?

"Stop it," I said to Wanji. "Make it stop!"

But she didn't, she just sat there, watching.

The pain grew sharp, and then suddenly it stopped. The sound, the pain, everything.

I took my hand away. I was still deaf on the left side but it didn't hurt.

"Did it stop?" Wanji asked.

I nodded.

"Do you feel dizzy? Sick?"

I didn't.

Wanji picked up the next packet. It was blue. "While that one is working, we'll do this one. Then the third one, which is easy. This one will make you faster when you are angry or scared. It will make time feel slower. There isn't any code for it. Something in your body starts it."

I didn't have any idea what she was talking about.

"After it has happened, you'll be tired. It uses up your energy." She studied the back of the packet, then she scooted closer to me, so we were both sitting cross-legged with our knees touching. Wanji had hard, bony knees, even through the felt of her dress.

"Open your eyes, very wide," she said.

"Wait," I said. "Is this going to hurt?"

"No," she said.

I opened my eyes as wide as I could.

"Look down, but keep your eyes wide open," she said.

I tried.

"No," she said, irritated, "keep your eyes open."

"They are open," I said. I didn't think she should treat me this way. My da had just died. She should be nice to me. I could hear her open the packet. I wanted to blink but I was afraid to. I did, because I couldn't help it.

She leaned forward and spread my eye open with thumb and forefinger. Then she swiftly touched my eye.

I jerked back. There was something in my eye. I could feel it, up under my eyelid. It was very uncomfortable. I blinked and blinked and blinked. My eye filled up with tears, just the one eye, which was very, very strange.

My eye socket started to ache. "It hurts," I said.

"It won't last long," she said.

"You said it wouldn't hurt!" I said, startled.

"I lied," Wanji said, matter-of-fact.

It hurt more and more. I moaned. "You're hateful," I said.

"That's true," she said, unperturbed.

She picked up the third packet, the red one.

"No," I said, "I won't! I won't! You can't do it!"

"Hush," she said, "this one won't hurt. I saved it until last on purpose."

"You're lying!" I scrambled away from her. The air was cold where the nest of rugs and blankets had been wrapped around me. My head ached. It just ached. And I still couldn't hear anything out of my left ear.

"Look," she said, "I will read you the lingua. It is a patch, nothing more. It says it will feel cold, but that is all. See, it is just a square of cloth that will rest on your neck. If it hurts, you can take it off."

I scrambled backwards away from her.

"Janna," she said. "Enough!" She was angry.

I was afraid of it, but I was still more afraid of Wanji. So I hunched down in front of her. I was so afraid that I sobbed while she peeled the back off the square and put it on me.

"See," she said, still sharp with me, "it doesn't hurt at all. Stop crying. Stop it. Enough is enough." She waved her hands over her head in disgust. "You are hysterical."

I held my hand over the patch. It didn't hurt but it did feel cold. I scrunched up and wrapped myself in a rug and gave myself over to my misery. My head hurt and my ear still ached faintly and I was starting to feel dizzy.

"Lie down," Wanji said. "Go on, lie down. I'll wake you when we can set the signal."

I made myself a nest in the mess of Wanji's floor and piled a blanket and a rug on top of me. Maybe the dark made my head feel better, I didn't know. But I fell asleep.

Wanji shook me awake. I hadn't been asleep long, and my head still ached. She had the little metal fork from the ear packet, the yellow packet. It occurred to me that she might stick it in my ear.

I covered my ear with my hand. My head hurt enough. I wasn't going to let Wanji stick a fork in my ear.

"Don't scowl," she said.

"My head hurts," I said.

"Are you dizzy?" she asked.

I felt out of sorts, unbalanced, but not dizzy, not really.

"Shake your head," Wanji said.

I shook my head. Still the same, but no worse. "Don't stick that in my ear," I said.

"What? I'm not going to stick this in your ear. It's a musical fork. I'm going to make a sound with it and hold it to your ear. When I tell you to, I want you to whistle something, okay?"

"Whistle what?" I said.

"Anything," she said, "I don't care. Whistle something for me now."

I couldn't think of anything to whistle. I couldn't think of anything at all except that I wished Wanji would leave me alone and let me go back to sleep.

Wanji squatted there. Implacable old bitch.

I finally thought of something to whistle, a crazy dog song for children. I started whistling—

"That's enough," she said. "Now don't say anything else, but when I nod my head you whistle that. Don't say anything to me. If you do, it will ruin everything. Nod your head if you understand."

I nodded.

She slapped the fork against her hand and I could see the long tines vibrating. She held it up to my ear, the one I couldn't hear anything out of. She held it there, concentrating fiercely. Then she nodded.

I whistled.

"Okay," she said. "Good. That is how you start it. Now whistle it again."

I whistled.

Everything went dark and then suddenly my head got very hot. Then I could see again.

"Good," Wanji said. "You just sent a signal."

"Why did everything get dark?" I asked.

"All the light got used in the signal," Wanji said. "It used all the light in your head so you couldn't see."

My head hurt even worse. Now, besides my eyes aching, my temples were pounding. I had a fever. I raised my hand and felt my hot cheek.

Wanji picked up the blue packet. "Now we have to figure out about the third one, the one that will let you hibernate."

I didn't want to learn about hibernating. "I feel sick," I said.

"It's probably too soon, anyway," Wanji said. "Sleep for a while."

I felt so awful I didn't know if I could sleep. But Wanji brought me more tea and I drank all that and lay down in my nest and presently I was dreaming.

IV.

There was a sound of gunfire, far away, just a pop. And then more pop-pop-pop.

It startled me, although I had been hearing the outrunners' guns at night since they got here. I woke with a fever and everything felt as if I were still dreaming. I was alone in Wanji's house. The lamp was still lit, but I didn't know if it had been refilled or how long I had slept. During the long night of winterdark it is hard to know when you are. I got up, put out the lamp, and went outside.

Morning cold is worst when you are warm from sleep. The dry snow crunched in the dark. Nothing was moving except the dogs were barking, their voices coming at me from every way.

The outrunners were gone from the center of town, nothing there but the remains of their fire and the trampled slick places where they had walked. I slid a bit as I walked there. My head felt light and I concentrated on my walking because if I did not think about it I didn't know what my feet would do. I had to pee.

Again I heard the pop-pop-pop. I could not tell where it was coming from because it echoed off the buildings around me. I could smell smoke and see the dull glow of fire above the trees. It was down from Sckarline, the fire. At first I thought they had gotten a really big fire going, and then

I thought they had set fire to the distillery. I headed for home.

Veronique was asleep in a nest of blankets, including some of my parents' blankets from their bed.

"They set fire to the distillery," I said. I didn't say it in English, but she sat up and rubbed her face.

"It's cold," she said.

I could not think of anything to respond.

She sat there, holding her head.

"Come," I said, working into English. "We go see your teacher." I pulled on her arm.

"Where is everybody?" she said.

"My father die, my mother is, um, waiting with the die."

She frowned at me. I knew I hadn't made any sense. I pulled on her again and she got up and stumbled around, putting on boots and jacket.

Outside I heard the pop-pop-pop again. This time I thought maybe it was closer.

"They're shooting again?" she asked.

"They shoot my father," I said.

"Oh God," she said. She sat down on the blankets. "Oh God."

I pulled on her arm.

"Are you all right?" she asked.

"Hurry," I said. I made a pack of blankets. I found my axe and a few things and put them in the bundle, then slung it all over my shoulders. I didn't know what we would do, but if they were shooting people we should run away. I had to pee really bad.

She did hurry, finally awake. When we went outside and the cold hit her she shuddered and shook off the last of the sleep. I saw the movement of her shoulders against the glow of the fire on the horizon, against the false dawn.

People were moving, clinging close to houses where they were invisible against the black wood, avoiding the open spaces. We stayed close to my house, waiting to see whose people were moving. Veronique held my arm. A dog came past the schoolhouse into the open area where the outrunners' fire had been and stopped and sniffed—maybe the place where my father had died.

I drew Veronique back, along to the back of the house. The spirit door was closed and my father was dead. I crouched low and ran, holding her arm, until we were in the trees and then she slipped and fell and pulled me down, too. We slid feet first in the snow, down the hill between the tree trunks, hidden in the pools of shadow under the trees. Then we were still, waiting.

I still felt feverish and nothing was real.

The snow under the trees was all powder. It dusted our leggings and clung in clumps in the wrinkles behind my knees.

Nothing came after us that we could see. We got up and walked deeper into the trees and then uphill, away from the distillery, but still skirting the village. I left her for a moment to pee, but she followed me and we squatted together. We should run, but I didn't know where to run to and the settlement pulled at me. I circled around it as if on a tether, pulling in closer and closer as we got to the uphill part of the town. Coming back around, we hung in the trees beyond the field behind the schoolhouse. I could see the stabros pens and see light. The outrunners were in the stabros pens and the stabros were down. A couple of men were dressing the carcasses.

We stumbled over Harup in the darkness. Literally fell over him in the bushes.

He was dead. His stomach was ripped by rifle fire and his eyes were open. I couldn't tell in the darkness if he had dragged himself out here to die or if someone had thrown the body here. We were too close.

I started backing away. Veronique was stiff as a spooked stabros. She lifted her feet high out of the snow, coming down hard and loud. One of the dogs at the stabros pen heard us and started to bark. I could see it in the light, its ears up and its tail curled over its back. The others barked, too, ears towards us in the dark. I stopped and Veronique stopped, too. Men in the pen looked out in the dark. A couple of them picked up rifles, and cradling them in their arms walked out towards us from the light.

I backed up, slowly. Maybe they would find Harup's body and think that the dogs were barking at that. But they were hunters and they would see the marks of our boots in the snow and follow us. If we ran they would hear us. I was not a hunter. I did not know what to do.

We backed up, one slow step and then another, while the outrunners walked out away from the light. They were not coming straight at us, but they were walking side by side and they would spread out and find us. I had my knife. There was cover around, mostly trees, but I didn't know what I could do against a hunter with a rifle, and even if I could stop one the others would hear us.

There were shouts over by the houses.

The outrunners kept walking, but the shouts didn't stop, and then there was the pop of guns. That stopped one and then the other and they half-turned.

The dogs turned barking towards the shouts.

The outrunners started to jog towards the schoolhouse.

We walked backward in the dark.

There were flames over there, at the houses. I couldn't tell whose house was on fire. It was downhill from the schoolhouse, which meant it might be our house. People were running in between the schoolhouse and Wanji's house and the outrunners lifted their guns and fired. People, three of them, kept on running.

The outrunners fired again and again. One of the people stumbled, but they all kept running. They were black shapes skimming on the field. The snow on the field was not deep because the wind blew it into the trees. Then one was in the trees. The outrunners fired again, but the other two made the trees as well.

There was a summer camp out this way, down by the river, for drying fish.

I pulled on Veronique's arm and we picked our way through the trees.

There were people at the summer camp and we waited in the trees to make sure they were Sckarline people. It was gray, false dawn by the time we got there. I didn't remember ever having seen the summer camp in the winter before. The drying racks were bare poles with a top covering of snow, and the lean-to was almost covered in drifted snow. There was no shelter here.

There were signs of three or four people in the trampled snow. I didn't think it would be the outrunners down there because how would they even know where the summer camp was, but I was not sure of anything. I didn't know if I was thinking right or not.

Veronique leaned close to my ear and whispered so softly I could barely hear. "We have to go back."

I shook my head.

"Ian is there."

Ian. Ian. She meant her teacher.

She had a hood on her purple clothing and I pulled it back to whisper, "Not now. We wait here." So close to the brown shell of her ear. Like soft, dark leather. Not like a real people's ear. She was shivering.

I didn't feel too cold. I still had a fever—I felt as if everything were far from me, as if I walked half in this world. I sat and looked at the snow cupped in a brown leaf and my mind was empty and things did not seem too bad. I don't know how long we sat.

Someone walked in the summer camp. I thought it was Sored, one of the boys.

I took Veronique's arm and tugged her up. I was stiff from sitting and colder than I had noticed, but moving helped. We slid down the hill into the summer camp.

The summer camp sat in a V that looked at the river frozen below. Sored was already out of the camp when we got there, but he waved at us from the trees and we scrambled back up there. Veronique slipped and used her hands.

There were two people crouched around a fire so tiny it was invisible and one of them was Tuuvin.

"Where is everyone else?" Sored asked.

"I don't know," I said. Tuuvin stood up.

"Where's your mother and sister?" he asked.

"I was at Wanji's house all night," I said. "Where's your family?"

"My da and I were at the stabros pen this morning with Harup," he said.

"We found Harup," I said.

"Did you find my da?" he asked.

75

"No. Was he shot?"

"I don't know. I don't think so."

"We saw some people running across the field behind the school-house. Maybe one of them was shot."

He looked down at Gerda, crouched by the fire. "None of us were shot."

"Did you come together?"

"No," Sored said. "I found Gerda here and Tuuvin here."

He had gone down to see the fire at the distillery. The outrunners had taken some of the casks. He didn't know how the fire started, if it was an accident or if they'd done it on purpose. It would be easy to start if someone spilled something too close to the fire.

Veronique was crouched next to the tiny fire. "Janna," she said, "has anyone seen Ian?"

"Did you see the offworlder teacher?" I asked.

No one had.

"We have to find him," she said.

"Okay," I said.

"What are you going to do with her?" Sored asked, pointing at Veronique with his chin. "Is she ill?"

She crouched over the fire like someone who was sick.

"She's not sick," I said. "We need to see what is happening at Sckarline."

"I'm not going back," Gerda said, looking at no one. I did not know Gerda very well. She was old enough to have children but she had no one. She lived by herself. She'd had her nose slit by her clan for adultery, but I never knew if she had a husband with her old clan or not. Some people came to Sckarline because they didn't want to be part of their clan anymore. Most of them went back, but Gerda had stayed.

Tuuvin said, "I'll go."

Sored said he would stay in case anyone else came to the summer camp. In a day or two they were going to head towards the west and see if they could come across the winter pastures of Haufsdaag Clan. Sored had kin there.

"That's pretty far," Tuuvin said. "Toolie clan would be closer."

"You have kin with Toolie Clan," Sored said.

Tuuvin nodded.

"We go to Sckarline," I said to Veronique.

She stood up. "It's so damn cold," she said. Then she said something about wanting coffee. I didn't understand a lot of what she said. Then she laughed and said she wished she could have breakfast.

Sored looked at me. I didn't translate what she had said. He turned his back on her, but she didn't notice.

It took us through the sunrise and beyond the short midwinter morning and into afternoon to get to Sckarline. The only good thing about winterdark is that it would be dark for the outrunners, too.

Only hours of daylight.

Nothing was moving when we got back to Sckarline. From the back the schoolhouse looked all right, but the houses were all burned. I could see where my house had been. Charred logs standing in the red afternoon sun. The ground around them was wet and muddy from the heat of the fires.

Tuuvin's house. Ayudesh's house. Wanji's house. In front of the schoolhouse there were bodies. My da's body, thrown back in the snow. My mam and my sister. My sister's head was broken in. My mam didn't have her pants on. The front of the schoolhouse had burned, but the fire must have burned out before the whole building was gone. The dogs were moving among the bodies, sniffing, stopping to tug on the freezing flesh.

Tuuvin shouted at them to drive them off.

My mam's hip bones were sharp under the bloody skin and her sex was there for everyone to see, but I kept noticing her bare feet. The soles were dark. Her toenails were thick and her feet looked old, an old, old woman's feet. As if she were as old as Wanji.

I looked at people to see who else was there. I saw Wanji, although she had no face, but I knew her from her skin. Veronique's teacher was there, his face red and peeled from fire and his eyes baked white like a smoked fish. Ayudesh had no ears and no sex. His clothes had been taken.

The dogs were circling back, watching Tuuvin.

77

He screamed at them. Then he crouched down on his heels and covered his eyes with his arm and cried.

I did not feel anything. Not yet.

I whistled the tune that Wanji had taught me to send out the message, and the world went dark. It was something to do, and for a moment, I didn't have to look at my mother's bare feet.

The place for the Sckarline dead was up the hill beyond the town, away from the river, but without stabros I couldn't think of how we could get all these bodies there. We didn't have anything for the bodies, either. Nothing for the spirit journey, not even blankets to wrap them in.

I could not bear to think of my mother without pants. There were lots of dead women in the snow and many of them did have pants. It may not have been fair that my mother should have someone else's, but I could not think of anything else to do so I took the leggings off of Maitra and tried to put them on my mother. I could not really get them right—my mother was tall and her body was stiff from the cold and from death. I hated handling her.

Veronique asked me what I was doing, but even if I knew enough English to answer, I was too embarrassed to really try to explain.

My mother's flesh was white and odd to touch. Not like flesh at all. Like plastic. Soft looking but not to touch.

Tuuvin watched me without saying anything. I thought he might tell me not to, but he didn't. Finally he said, "We can't get them to the place for the dead."

I didn't know what to say to that.

"We don't have anyone to talk to the spirits," he said. "Only me."

He was the man here. I didn't know if Tuuvin had talked with spirits or not, people didn't talk about that with women.

"I say that this place is a place of the dead, too," he said. His voice was strange. "Sckarline is a place of the dead now."

"We leave them here?" I asked.

He nodded.

He was beardless, but he was a boy and he was old enough that he had walked through the spirit door. I was glad that he had made the decision.

78

I looked in houses for things for the dead to have with them, but most things were burned. I found things half-burned and sometimes not burned at all. I found a fur, and used that to wrap the woman whose leggings I had stolen. I tried to make sure that everybody got something—a bit of stitching or a cup or something, so they would not be completely without possessions. I managed to find something for almost everybody, and I found enough blankets to wrap Tuuvin's family and Veronique's teacher. I wrapped Bet with my mother. I kept blankets separate for Veronique, Tuuvin, and me and anything I found that we could use I didn't give to the dead, but everything else I gave to them.

Tuuvin sat in the burned-out schoolhouse and I didn't know if what he did was a spirit thing or if it was just grief, but I didn't bother him. He kept the dogs away. Veronique followed me and picked through the blackened sticks of the houses. Both of us had black all over our gloves and our clothes, and black marks on our faces.

We stopped when it got too dark, and then we made camp in the schoolhouse next to the dead. Normally I would not have been able to stay so close to the dead, but now I felt part of them.

Tuuvin had killed and skinned a dog and cooked that. Veronique cried while she ate. Not like Tuuvin had cried. Not sobs. Just helpless tears that ran down her face. As if she didn't notice.

"What are we going to do?" she asked.

Tuuvin said, "We will try for Toolie Clan."

I didn't have any idea where their winter pastures were, much less how to find them, and I almost asked Tuuvin if he did, but I didn't want to shame his new manhood, so I didn't.

"The skimmer will come back here," Veronique said. "I have to wait here."

"We can't wait here," Tuuvin said. "It is going to get darker, winter is coming and we'll have no sun. We don't have any animals. We can't live here."

I told her what Tuuvin said. "I have, in here," I pointed to my head, "I call your people. Wanji give to me."

Veronique didn't understand and didn't even really try.

I tried not to think about the dogs wandering among the dead. I tried not to think about bad weather. I tried not to think about my house or my mam. It did not leave much to think about.

Tuuvin had kin with Toolie Clan but I didn't. Tuuvin was my clankin, though, even if he wasn't a cousin or anything. I wondered if he would still want me after we got to Toolie Clan. Maybe there would be other girls. New girls, that he had never talked to before. They would be pretty, some of them.

My kin were Lagskold. I didn't know where their pastures were, but someone would know. I could go to them if I didn't like Toolie Clan. I had met a couple of my cousins when they came and brought my father's half brother, my little uncle.

"Listen," Tuuvin said, touching my arm.

I didn't hear it at first, then I did.

"What?" Veronique said. "Are they coming back?"

"Hush," Tuuvin snapped at her, and even though she didn't understand the word, she did.

It was a skimmer.

It was far away. Skimmers didn't land at night. They didn't even come at night. It had come to my message, I guessed.

Tuuvin got up, and Veronique scrambled to her feet and we all went out to the edge of the field behind the schoolhouse.

"You can hear it?" I asked Veronique.

She shook her head.

"Listen," I said. I could hear it. Just a rumble. "The skimmer."

"The skimmer?" she said. "The skimmer is coming? Oh God. Oh God. I wish we had lights for them. We need light, to signal them that someone is here."

"Tell her to hush," Tuuvin said.

"I send message," I said. "They know someone is here."

"We should move the fire."

I could send them another message, but Wanji had said to do it one time a day until they came and they were here.

Dogs started barking.

Finally we saw lights from the skimmer, strange green and red stars. They moved against the sky as if they had been shaken loose.

Veronique stopped talking and stood still.

The lights came towards us for a long time. They got bigger and brighter, more than any star. It seemed as if they stopped, but the lights kept getting brighter and I finally decided that they were coming straight towards us and it didn't look as if they were moving, but they were.

Then we could see the skimmer in its own lights.

It flew low over us and Veronique shouted, "I'm here! I'm here!"

I shouted, and Tuuvin shouted, too, but the skimmer didn't seem to hear us. But then it turned and slowly curved around, the sound of it going farther away and then just hanging in the air. It got to where it had been before and came back. This time it came even lower and it dropped red lights. One. Two. Three.

Then a third time it came around and I wondered what it would do now. But this time it landed, the sound of it so loud that I could feel it as well as hear it. It was a different skimmer from the one we always saw. It was bigger, with a belly like it was pregnant. It was white and red. It settled easily on the snow. Its engines, pointed down, melted snow beneath them.

And then it sat. Lights blinked. The red lights on the ground flickered. The dogs barked.

Veronique ran towards it.

The door opened and a man called out to watch something, but I didn't understand. Veronique stopped and from where I was, she was a black shape against the lights of the skimmer.

Finally a man jumped down, and then two more men and two women and they ran to Veronique.

She gestured and the lights flickered in the movements of her arms until my eyes hurt and I looked away. I couldn't see anything around us. The offworlders' lights made me quite nightblind.

"Janna," Veronique called. "Tuuvin!" She waved at us to come over. So we walked out of the dark into the relentless lights of the skimmer.

I couldn't understand what anyone was saying in English. They asked me questions, but I just kept shaking my head. I was tired and now, finally, I wanted to cry.

"Janna," Veronique said. "You called them. Did you call them?"

81

I nodded.

"How?"

"Wanji give me . . . In my head . . ." I had no idea how to explain. I pointed to my ear.

One of the women came over, and handling my head as if I were a stabros, turned it so she could push my hair out of the way and look in my ear. I still couldn't hear very well out of that ear. Her handling wasn't rough, but it was not something people do to each other.

She was talking and nodding, but I didn't try to understand. The English washed over us and around us.

One of the men brought us something hot and bitter and sweet to drink. The drink was in blue plastic cups, the same color as the jackets that they all wore except for one man whose jacket was red with blue writing. Pretty things. Veronique drank hers gratefully. I made myself drink mine. Anything this black and bitter must have been medicine. Tuuvin just held his.

Then they got hand lights and we all walked over and looked at the bodies. Dogs ran from the lights, staying at the edges and slinking as if guilty of something.

"Janna," Veronique said. "Which one is Ian? Which is my teacher?"

I had to walk between the bodies. We had laid them out so their heads all faced the schoolhouse and their feet all faced the center of the village. They were more bundles than people. I could have told her in the light, but in the dark, with the hand lights making it hard to see anything but where they were pointed, it took me a while. I found Harup. Then I found the teacher.

Veronique cried and the woman who had looked in my ear held her like she was her child. But that woman didn't look dark like Veronique at all and I thought she was just kin because she was an offworlder, not by blood. All the offworlders were like Sckarline; kin because of where they were, not because of family.

The two men in blue jackets picked up the body of the teacher. With the body they were clumsy on the packed snow. The man holding the teacher's head slipped and fell. Tuuvin took the teacher's head and I took his feet. His boots were gone. His feet were as naked as my mother's.

I had wrapped him in a skin, but it wasn't very big, and so his feet hung out. But they were so cold, they felt like meat, not like a person.

We walked right up to the door of the skimmer and I could look in. It was big inside. Hollow. It was dark in the back. I had thought it would be all lights inside and I was disappointed. There were things hanging on the walls but mostly it was empty. One of the offworld men jumped up into the skimmer and then he was not clumsy at all. He pulled the body to the back of the skimmer.

They were talking again. Tuuvin and I stood there. Tuuvin's breath was an enormous white plume in the lights of the skimmer. I stamped my feet. The lights were bright but they were a cheat. They didn't make you any warmer.

The offworlders wanted to go back to the bodies, so we did. "Your teachers," Veronique said. "Where are your teachers?"

I remembered Wanji's body. It had no face but it was easy to tell it was her. Ayudesh's body was still naked under the blanket I had found. The blanket was burned along one side and didn't cover him. Where his sex had been, the frozen blood shone in the hand lights. I thought the dogs might have been at him, but I couldn't tell.

They wanted to take Wanji's and Ayudesh's bodies back to the skimmer. They motioned for us to take Ayudesh.

"Wait," Tuuvin said. "They shouldn't do that."

I squatted down.

"They are Sckarline people," Tuuvin said.

"Their spirit is already gone," I said.

"They won't have anything," he said.

"If the offworlders take them, won't they give them offworlder things?"

"They didn't want offworld things," Tuuvin said. "That's why they were here."

"But we don't have anything to give them. At least if the offworlders give them things, they'll have something."

Tuuvin shook his head. "Harup—," he started to say, but stopped. Harup talked to spirits more than anyone. He would have known. But I didn't know how to ask him and I didn't think Tuuvin did either. Although

83

I wasn't sure. There wasn't any drum or anything for spirit talk anyway.

The offworlders stood looking at us.

"Okay," Tuuvin said. So I stood up and we picked up Ayudesh's body and the two offworld men picked up Wanji's body and we took them to the skimmer.

A dog followed us in the dark.

The man in the red jacket climbed up and went to the front of the skimmer. There were chairs there and he sat in one and talked to someone on a radio. I could remember the world for *radio* in English. Ayudesh used to have one until it stopped working and then he didn't get another.

My thoughts rattled through my empty head.

They put the bodies of the teachers next to the body of Veronique's teacher. Tuuvin and I stood outside the door, leaning in to watch them. The floor of the skimmer was metal.

One of the blue-jacket men brought us two blankets. The blankets were the same blue as his jacket and had a red symbol on them. A circle with words. I didn't pay much attention to them. He brought us foil packets. Five. Ten of them.

"Food," he said, pointing to the packets.

I nodded. "Food," I repeated.

"Do they have guns?" Tuuvin asked harshly.

"Guns?" I asked. "You have guns?"

"No guns," the blue jacket said. "No guns."

I didn't know if we were supposed to get in the skimmer or if the gifts meant to go. Veronique came over and sat in the doorway. She hugged me. "Thank you, Janna," she whispered. "Thank you."

Then she got up.

"Move back," said the red jacket, shooing us.

We trotted back away from the skimmer. Its engines fired and the ground underneath them steamed. The skimmer rose, and then the engines turned from pointing down to pointing back and it moved off. Heavy and slow at first, but then faster and faster. Higher and higher.

We blinked in the darkness, holding our gifts.

84

The Lincoln Train

S oldiers of the G.A.R. stand alongside the tracks. They are General Dodge's soldiers, keeping the tracks maintained for the Lincoln Train. If I stand right, the edges of my bonnet are like blinders and I can't see the soldiers at all. It is a spring evening. At the house, the lilacs are blooming. My mother wears a sprig pinned to her dress under her cameo. I can smell it, even in the crush of these people all waiting for the train. I can smell the lilac, and the smell of too many people crowded together, and a faint taste of cinders on the air. I want to go home, but that house is not ours anymore. I smooth my black dress. On the train platform we are all in mourning.

The train will take us to St. Louis, from whence we will leave for the Oklahoma territories. They say we will walk, but I don't know how my mother will do that. She has been poorly since the winter of '62. I check my bag with our water and provisions.

"Julia Adelaide," my mother says, "I think we should go home."

"We've come to catch the train," I say, very sharp.

I'm Clara, my sister Julia is eleven years older than me. Julia is married and living in Tennessee. My mother blinks and touches her sprig of lilac uncertainly. If I am not sharp with her, she will keep on it.

I wait. When I was younger I used to try to school my unruly self in Christian charity. God sends us nothing we cannot bear. Now I only try to keep it from my face, try to keep my outer self disciplined. There is a feeling inside me, an anger, that I can't even speak. Something is being bent, like a bow, bending and bending and bending—

"When are we going home?" my mother says.

"Soon," I say because it is easy.

But she won't remember and in a moment she'll ask again. And again and again, through this long, long train ride to St. Louis. I am trying to be a Christian daughter, and I remind myself that it is not her fault that the war turned her into an old woman, or that her mind is full of holes and everything new drains out. But it's not my fault either. I don't even try to curb my feelings and I know that they rise up to my face. The only way to be true is to be true from the inside and I am not. I am full of unchristian feelings. My mother's infirmity is her trial, and it is also mine.

I wish I were someone else.

The train comes down the track, chuffing, coming slow. It is an old, badly used thing, but I can see that once it was a model of chaste and beautiful workmanship. Under the dust it is a dark claret in color. It is said that the engine was built to be used by President Lincoln, but since the assassination attempt he is too infirm to travel. People begin to push to the edge of the platform, hauling their bags and worldly goods. I don't know how I will get our valise on. If Zeke could have come I could have at least insured that it was loaded on, but the Negroes are free now and they are not to help. The notice said no family Negroes could come to the station, although I see their faces here and there through the crowd.

The train stops outside the station to take on water.

"Is it your father?" my mother says diffidently. "Do you see him on the train?"

"No, Mother," I say. "We are taking the train."

"Are we going to see your father?" she asks.

It doesn't matter what I say to her, she'll forget it in a few minutes, but I cannot say yes to her. I cannot say that we will see my father even to give her a few moments of joy.

"Are we going to see your father?" she asks again.

"No," I say.

"Where are we going?"

I have carefully explained it all to her and she cried every time I did. People are pushing down the platform toward the train, and I am trying to decide if I should move my valise toward the front of the platform. Why are they in such a hurry to get on the train? It is taking us all away.

"Where are we going? Julia Adelaide, you will answer me this moment," my mother says, her voice too full of quaver to quite sound like her own.

"I'm Clara," I say. "We're going to St. Louis."

"St. Louis," she says. "We don't need to go to St. Louis. We can't get through the lines, Julia, and I . . . I am quite indisposed. Let's go back home now, this is foolish."

We cannot go back home. General Dodge has made it clear that if we did not show up at the train platform this morning and get our names checked off the list, he would arrest every man in town, and then he would shoot every tenth man. The town knows to believe him, General Dodge was put in charge of the trains into Washington, and he did the same thing then. He arrested men and held them and every time the train was fired upon he hanged a man.

There is a shout and I can only see the crowd moving like a wave, pouring off the edge of the platform. Everyone is afraid there will not be room. I grab the valise and I grab my mother's arm and pull them both. The valise is so heavy that my fingers hurt, and the weight of our water and food is heavy on my arm. My mother is small and when I put her in bed at night she is all tiny like a child, but now she refuses to move, pulling against me and opening her mouth wide, her mouth pink inside and wet and open in a wail I can just barely hear over the shouting crowd. I don't know if I should let go of the valise to pull her, and for a moment I think of letting go of her, letting someone else get her on the train and finding her later.

A man in the crowd shoves her hard from behind. His face is twisted in wrath. What is he so angry at? My mother falls into me, and the crowd pushes us. I am trying to hold on to the valise, but my gloves are slippery, and I can only hold with my right hand, with my left I am trying to hold up my mother. The crowd is pushing all around us, trying to push us toward the edge of the platform.

The train toots as if it were moving. There is shouting all around us. My mother is fallen against me, her face pressed against my bosom, turned up toward me. She is so frightened. Her face is pressed against me in improper intimacy, as if she were my child. My mother as my child. I am filled with revulsion and horror. The pressure against us begins to lessen. I still have a hold of the valise. We'll be all right. Let the others push around, I'll wait and get the valise on somehow. They won't have us travel without anything.

My mother's eyes close. Her wrinkled face looks up, the skin under her eyes making little pouches, as if it were a second, blind eyelid. Everything is so grotesque. I am having a spell. I wish I could be somewhere where I could get away and close the windows. I have had these spells since they told us that my father was dead, where everything is full of horror and strangeness.

The person behind me is crowding into my back and I want to tell them to give way, but I cannot. People around us are crying out. I cannot see anything but the people pushed against me. People are still pushing, but now they are not pushing toward the side of the platform but toward the front, where the train will be when we are allowed to board.

Wait, I call out, but there's no way for me to tell if I've really called out or not. I can't hear anything until the train whistles. The train has moved? They brought the train into the station? I can't tell, not without letting go of my mother and the valise. My mother is being pulled down into this mass. I feel her sliding against me. Her eyes are closed. She is a huge doll, limp in my arms. She is not even trying to hold herself up. She has given up to this moment.

I can't hold on to my mother and the valise. So I let go of the valise.

Oh merciful God.

I do not know how I will get through this moment.

The crowd around me is a thing that presses me and pushes me up, pulls me down. I cannot breathe for the pressure. I see specks in front of my eyes, white sparks, too bright, like metal and like light. My feet aren't under me. I am buoyed by the crowd and my feet are behind me. I am unable to stand, unable to fall. I think my mother is against me, but I can't tell, and in this mass I don't know how she can breathe.

I think I am going to die.

All the noise around me does not seem like noise anymore. It is something else, some element, like water or something surrounding me and overpowering me.

It is like that for a long time, until finally I have my feet under me, and I'm leaning against people. I feel myself sink, but I can't stop myself. The platform is solid. My whole body feels bruised and roughly used.

My mother is not with me. My mother is a bundle of black on the ground, and I crawl to her. I wish I could say that as I crawl to her I feel concern for her condition, but at this moment I am no more than base animal nature and I crawl to her because she is mine and there is nothing else in the world I can identify as mine. Her skirt is rucked up so that her ankles and calves are showing. Her face is black. At first I think it something about her clothes, but it is her face, so full of blood that it is black.

People are still getting on the train, but there are people on the platform around us, left behind. And other things. A surprising number of shoes, all badly used. Wraps, too. Bags. Bundles and people.

I try raising her arms above her head, to force breath into her lungs. Her arms are thin, but they don't go the way I want them to. I read in the newspaper that when President Lincoln was shot, he stopped breathing, and his personal physician started him breathing again. But maybe the newspaper was wrong, or maybe it is more complicated than I understand, or maybe it doesn't always work. She doesn't breathe.

I sit on the platform and try to think of what to do next. My head is empty of useful thoughts. Empty of prayers.

"Ma'am?"

It's a soldier of the G.A.R.

"Yes sir?" I say. It is difficult to look up at him, to look up into the sun.

He hunkers down but does not touch her. At least he doesn't touch her. "Do you have anyone staying behind?"

Like cousins or something? Someone who is not "recalcitrant" in their handling of their Negroes? "Not in town," I say.

"Did she worship?" he asks, in his northern way.

"Yes sir," I say, "she did. She was a Methodist, and you should contact the preacher. The Reverend Robert Ewald, sir."

"I'll see to it, ma'am. Now you'll have to get on the train."

"And leave her?" I say.

"Yes ma'am, the train will be leaving. I'm sorry ma'am."

"But I can't," I say.

He takes my elbow and helps me stand. And I let him.

"We are not really recalcitrant," I say. "Where were Zeke and Rachel supposed to go? Were we supposed to throw them out?"

He helps me climb onto the train. People stare at me as I get on, and I realize I must be all in disarray. I stand under all their gazes, trying to get my bonnet on straight and smoothing my dress. I do not know what to do with my eyes or hands.

There are no seats. Will I have to stand until St. Louis? I grab a seat back to hold myself up. It is suddenly warm and everything is distant and I think I am about to faint. My stomach turns. I breathe through my mouth, not even sure that I am holding on to the seat back.

But I don't fall, thank Jesus.

"It's not Lincoln," someone is saying, a man's voice, rich and baritone, and I fasten on the words as a lifeline, drawing myself back to the train car, to the world. "It's Seward. Lincoln no longer has the capacity to govern."

The train smells of bodies and warm sweaty wool. It is a smell that threatens to undo me, so I must concentrate on breathing through my mouth. I breathe in little pants, like a dog. The heat lies against my skin. It is airless.

"Of course Lincoln can no longer govern, but that damned actor made him a saint when he shot him," says a second voice, "And now no one dare oppose him. It doesn't matter if his policies make sense or not."

"You're wrong," says the first. "Seward is governing through him. Lincoln is an imbecile. He can't govern, look at the way he handled the war."

The second snorts. "He won."

"No," says the first, "we *lost*, there is a difference, sir. We lost even though the north never could find a competent general." I know the type of the first one. He's the one who thinks he is brilliant, who always knew what President Davis should have done. If they are looking for a recalcitrant southerner, they have found one.

"Grant was competent. Just not brilliant. Any military man who is not Alexander the Great is going to look inadequate in comparison with General Lee."

"Grant was a drinker," the first one says. "It was his subordinates. They'd been through years of war. They knew what to do."

It is so hot on the train. I wonder how long until the train leaves.

I wonder if the Reverend will write my sister in Tennessee and tell her about our mother. I wish the train were going east toward Tennessee instead of north and west toward St. Louis.

My valise. All I have. It is on the platform. I turn and go to the door. It is closed and I try the handle, but it is too stiff for me. I look around for help.

"It's locked," says a woman in gray. She doesn't look unkind.

"My things, I left them on the platform," I say.

"Oh, honey," she says, "they aren't going to let you back out there. They don't let anyone off the train."

I look out the window, but I can't see the valise. I can see some of the soldiers, so I beat on the window. One of them glances up at me, frowning, but then he ignores me.

The train blows that it is going to leave, and I beat harder on the glass. If I could shatter that glass. They don't understand, they would help me if they understood. The train lurches and I stagger. It is out there, somewhere, on that platform. Clothes for my mother and me, blankets, things we will need. Things I will need.

The train pulls out of the station and I feel so terrible I sit down on the floor in all the dirt from people's feet, and sob.

The train creeps slowly at first, but then picks up speed. The clack-clack clack-clack rocks me. It is improper, but I allow it to rock me. I am in others' hands now and there is nothing to do but be patient. I am good at that. So it has been all my life. I have tried to be dutiful, but something in me has not bent right, and I have never been able to maintain a Christian frame of mind, but like a chicken in a yard, I have always kept my eyes on the small things. I have tended to what was in front of me, first the house, then my mother. When we could not get sugar, I learned to cook with molasses and honey. Now I sit and let my mind go empty and let the train rock me.

"Child," someone says. "Child."

The woman in gray has been trying to get my attention for awhile, but I have been sitting and letting myself be rocked.

"Child," she says again, "would you like some water?"

Yes, I realize, I would. She has a jar and she gives it to me to sip out of. "Thank you," I say. "We brought water, but we lost it in the crush on the platform."

"You have someone with you?" she asks.

"My mother," I say, and start crying again. "She is old, and there was such a press on the platform, and she fell and was trampled."

"What's your name," the woman says.

"Clara Corbett," I say.

"I'm Elizabeth Loudon," the woman says. "And you are welcome to travel with me." There is something about her, a simple pleasantness, that makes me trust her. She is a small woman, with a small nose and eyes as gray as her dress. She is younger than I first thought, maybe only in her thirties? "How old are you? Do you have family?" she asks.

"I am seventeen. I have a sister, Julia. But she doesn't live in Mississippi anymore."

"Where does she live?" the woman asks.

"In Beech Bluff, near Jackson, Tennessee."

She shakes her head. "I don't know it. Is it good country?"

"I think so," I say. "In her letters it sounds like good country. But I haven't seen her for seven years." Of course no one could travel during the war. She has three children in Tennessee. My sister is twenty-eight, almost as old as this woman. It is hard to imagine.

"Were you close?" she asks.

I don't know that we were close. But she is my sister. She is all I have, now. I hope that the Reverend will write her about my mother, but

I don't know that he knows where she is. I will have to write her. She will think I should have taken better care.

"Are you traveling alone?"

"My companion is a few seats farther in front. He and I could not find seats together."

Her companion is a man? Not her husband, maybe her brother? But she would say her brother if that's who she meant. A woman traveling with a man. An adventuress, I think. There are stories of women traveling, hoping to find unattached girls like myself. They befriend the young girls and then deliver them to the brothels of New Orleans.

For a moment Elizabeth takes on a sinister cast. But this is a train full of recalcitrant southerners, there is no opportunity to kidnap anyone. Elizabeth is like me, a woman who has lost her home.

It takes the rest of the day and a night to get to St. Louis, and Elizabeth and I talk. It's as if we talk in ciphers; instead of talking about home, we talk about gardening, and I can see the garden at home, lazy with bees. She is a quilter. I don't quilt, but I used to do petit pointe, so we can talk sewing and about how hard it has been to get colors. And we talk about mending and making do, we have all been making do for so long.

When it gets dark, since I have no seat, I stay where I am sitting by the door of the train. I am so tired, but in the darkness all I can think of is my mother's face in the crowd and her hopeless open mouth. I don't want to think of my mother, but I am in a delirium of fatigue, surrounded by the dark and the rumble of the train and the distant murmur of voices. I sleep sitting by the door of the train, fitful and rocked. I have dreams like fever dreams. In my dream I am in a strange house, but it is supposed to be my own house, but nothing is where it should be, and I begin to believe that I have actually entered a stranger's house, and that they'll return and find me here. When I wake up and go back to sleep, I am back in this strange house, looking through things.

I wake before dawn, only a little rested. My shoulders and hips and back all ache from the way I am leaning, but I have no energy to get up. I have no energy to do anything but endure. Elizabeth nods, sometimes awake, sometimes asleep, but neither of us speak.

Finally the train slows. We come in through a town, but the town seems to go on and on. It must be St. Louis. We stop and sit. The sun comes up and heats the car like an oven. There is no movement of the air. There are so many buildings in St. Louis, and so many of them are tall, two stories, that I wonder if they cut off the wind and that is why it's so still. But finally the train lurches and we crawl into the station.

I am one of the first off the train by virtue of my position near the door. A soldier unlocks it and shouts for all of us to disembark, but he need not have bothered for there is a rush. I am borne ahead at its beginning, but I can stop at the back of the platform. I am afraid that I have lost Elizabeth, but I see her in the crowd. She is on the arm of a younger man in a bowler. There is something about his air that marks him as different—he is sprightly and apparently fresh even after the long ride.

I almost let them pass, but the prospect of being alone makes me reach out and touch her shoulder.

"There you are," she says.

We join a queue of people waiting to use a trench. The smell is appalling, ammonia acrid and eye-watering. There is a wall to separate the men from the women, but the women are all together. I crouch, trying not to notice anyone and trying to keep my skirts out of the filth. It is so awful. It's worse than anything. I feel so awful.

What if my mother were here? What would I do? I think maybe it was better, maybe it was God's hand. But that is an awful thought, too.

"Child," Elizabeth says when I come out, "what's the matter?"

"It's so awful," I say. I shouldn't cry, but I just want to be home and clean. I want to go to bed and sleep.

She offers me a biscuit.

"You should save your food," I say.

"Don't worry," Elizabeth says, "We have enough."

I shouldn't accept it, but I am so hungry. And when I have a little to eat, I feel a little better.

I try to imagine what the fort will be like where we will be going. Will we have a place to sleep, or will it be barracks? Or worse yet, tents? Although after the night I spent on the train I can't imagine anything

94

that could be worse. I imagine if I have to stay awhile in a tent then I'll make the best of it.

"I think this being in limbo is perhaps worse than anything we can expect at the end," I say to Elizabeth. She smiles.

She introduces her companion, Michael. He is enough like her to be her brother, but I don't think that they are. I am resolved not to ask; if they want to tell me they can.

We are standing together, not saying anything, when there is some commotion farther up the platform. It is a woman. Her black dress is like smoke. She is running down the platform, coming toward us. There are all of these people and yet it is as if there is no obstacle for her. "NO NO NO NO, DON'T TOUCH ME! FILTHY HANDS! DON'T LET THEM TOUCH YOU! DON'T GET ON THE TRAINS!"

People are getting out of her way. Where are the soldiers? The fabric of her dress is so threadbare it is rotten and torn at the seams. Her skirt is greasy black and matted and stained. Her face is so thin. "ANIMALS! THERE IS NOTHING OUT THERE! PEOPLE DON'T HAVE FOOD! THERE IS NOTHING THERE BUT INDIANS! THEY SENT US OUT TO SETTLE BUT THERE WAS NOTHING THERE!" I expect she will run past me, but she grabs my arm and stops and looks into my face. She has light eyes, pale eyes in her dark face. She is mad.

"WE WERE ALL STARVING, SO WE WENT TO THE FORT BUT THE FORT HAD NOTHING. YOU WILL ALL STARVE, THE WAY THEY ARE STARVING THE INDIANS! THEY WILL LET US ALL DIE! THEY DON'T CARE!" She is screaming in my face, and her spittle sprays me, warm as her breath. Her hand is all tendons and twigs, but she's so strong I can't escape.

The soldiers grab her and yank her away from me. My arm aches where she was holding it. I can't stand up.

Elizabeth pulls me upright. "Stay close to me," she says and starts to walk the other way down the platform. People are looking up, following the screaming woman.

She pulls me along with her. I keep thinking of the woman's hand and wrist turned black with grime. I remember my mother's face was black when she lay on the platform. Black like something rotted.

"Here," Elizabeth says at an old door, painted green but now weathered. The door opens and we pass inside.

"What?" I say. My eyes are accustomed to the morning brightness and I can't see.

"Her name is Clara," Elizabeth says. "She has people in Tennessee."

"Come with me," says another woman. She sounds older. "Step this way. Where are her things?"

I am being kidnapped. Oh merciful God, I'll die. I let out a moan.

"Her things were lost, her mother was killed in a crush on the platform."

The woman in the dark clucks sympathetically. "Poor dear. Does Michael have his passenger yet?"

"In a moment," Elizabeth says. "We were lucky for the commotion."

I am beginning to be able to see. It is a storage room, full of abandoned things. The woman holding my arm is older. There are some broken chairs and a stool. She sits me in the chair. Is Elizabeth some kind of adventuress?

"Who are you?" I ask.

"We are friends," Elizabeth says. "We will help you get to your sister."

I don't believe them. I will end up in New Orleans. Elizabeth is some kind of adventuress.

After a moment the door opens and this time it is Michael with a young man. "This is Andrew," he says.

A man? What do they want with a man? That is what stops me from saying, "Run!" Andrew is blinded by the change in light, and I can see the astonishment working on his face, the way it must be working on mine. "What is this?" he asks.

"You are with Friends," Michael says, and maybe he has said it differently than Elizabeth, or maybe it is just that this time I have had the wit to hear it.

"Quakers?" Andrew says. "Abolitionists?"

Michael smiles. I can see his teeth white in the darkness. "Just Friends," he says.

Abolitionists. Crazy people who steal slaves to set them free. Have they come to kidnap us? We are recalcitrant southerners, I have never heard of Quakers seeking revenge, but everyone knows the Abolitionists are crazy and they are liable to do anything.

"We'll have to wait here until they begin to move people out, it will be evening before we can leave," says the older woman.

I am so frightened; I just want to be home. Maybe I should try to break free and run out to the platform. There are northern soldiers out there. Would they protect me? And then what, go to a fort in Oklahoma?

The older woman asks Michael how they could get past the guards so early and he tells her about the madwoman. A "refugee," he calls her.

"They'll just take her back," Elizabeth says, sighing.

Take her back—do they mean that she really came from Oklahoma? They talk about how bad it will be this winter. Michael says there are Wisconsin Indians resettled down there, but they've got no food, and they've been starving on government handouts for a couple years. Now there will be more people. They're not prepared for winter.

There can't have been much handout during the war. It was hard enough to feed the armies.

They explain to Andrew and to me that we will sneak out of the train station this evening, after dark. We will spend a day with a Quaker family in St. Louis, and then they will send us on to the next family. And so we will be passed hand to hand, like a bucket in a brigade, until we get to our families.

They call it the underground railroad.

But we are slave owners.

"Wrong is wrong," says Elizabeth. "Some of us can't stand and watch people starve."

"But only two out of the whole train," Andrew says.

Michael sighs.

The old woman nods. "It isn't right."

Elizabeth picked me because my mother died. If my mother had not died, I would be out there, on my way to starve with the rest of them.

I can't help it, but I start to cry. I should not profit from my mother's death. I should have kept her safe.

"Hush, now," says Elizabeth. "Hush, you'll be okay."

"It's not right," I whisper. I'm trying not to be loud, we mustn't be discovered.

"What, child?"

"You shouldn't have picked me," I say. But I am crying so hard I don't think they can understand me. Elizabeth strokes my hair and wipes my face. It may be the last time someone will do these things for me. My sister has three children of her own, and she won't need another child. I'll have to work hard to make up my keep.

There are blankets there and we lie down on the hard floor, all except Michael, who sits in a chair and sleeps. I sleep this time with fewer dreams. But when I wake up, although I can't remember what they were, I have the feeling that I have been dreaming restless dreams.

The stars are bright when we finally creep out of the station. A night full of stars. The stars will be the same in Tennessee. The platform is empty, the train and the people are gone. The Lincoln Train has gone back south while we slept, to take more people out of Mississippi.

"Will you come back and save more people?" I ask Elizabeth.

The stars are a banner behind her quiet head. "We will save what we can," she says.

It isn't fair that I was picked. "I want to help," I tell her.

She is silent for a moment. "We only work with our own," she says. There is something in her voice that has not been there before. A sharpness.

"What do you mean?" I ask.

"There are no slavers in our ranks," she says and her voice is cold.

I feel as if I have had a fever; tired, but clear of mind. I have never walked so far and not walked beyond a town. The streets of St. Louis are empty. There are few lights. Far off a woman is singing, and her voice is clear and carries easily in the night. A beautiful voice.

"Elizabeth," Michael says, "she is just a girl."

"She needs to know," Elizabeth says.

"Why did you save me then?" I ask.

"One does not fight evil with evil," Elizabeth says.

"I'm not evil!" I say.

But no one answers.

Interview: *On Any Given Day*

(Pullout quote at top of site.)

Emma: I had this virus, and it was inside me, and it could have been causing all these weird kinds of cancers—

Interviewer: What kind of cancers?

Emma: All sorts of weird stuff I'd never heard of like hairy cell leukemia, and cancerous lesions in parts of your bones and cancer in your pancreas. But I wasn't sick. I mean I didn't feel sick. And now, even after all the antivirals, now I worry about it all the time. Now I'm always thinking I'm sick. It's like something was stolen from me that I never knew I had.

(The following is a transcript from an interview for the *On Any Given Day* presentation of 4.12.2021. This transcript does not represent the full presentation, and more interviews and information are present on the site. *On Any Given Day* is made possible by the National Public Internet, by NPIBoston.org affiliate, and by a grant from the Carrol-Johnson Charitable Family Trust. For information on how to purchase this or any other full site presentation on CDM, please check NPIBoston.org.)

> Pop-up quotes and site notes in the interview are included with this transcript.

The following interview was conducted with Emma Chicheck. In the summer of 2018, a fifteen-year-old student came into a health clinic in the suburban town of Charlotte, outside Cleveland, Ohio with a sexually transmitted version of a proto-virus called pv414, which had recently been identified as a result of contaminated batches of genetic material associated with the telemerase therapy used in rejuvenation. The virus had only been seen previously in rejuvenated elders, and the presence of the virus in teenagers was at first seen as possible evidence that the virus had changed vectors. The medical detective work done to trace the virus, and the picture of teenaged behavior that emerged was the basis of the site documentary, called "The Abandoned Children." Emma was one of the students identified with the virus.

> The <u>Site map</u> provides links to <u>a description of the proto-virus</u>, a <u>map of the transmission</u> of the virus from Terry Sydnowski through three girls to a total of eleven other people, and <u>interviews with state health officials</u>.

Emma: I was fourteen when I lost my virginity. I was drunk, and there was this guy named Luis, he was giving me these drinks that taste like melon, this green stuff that everybody was drinking when they could get it. He said he really liked all my Egyptian stuff and he kept playing with my slave bracelet. The bracelet has chains that go to rings you wear on your thumb, your middle finger, and your ring finger. "Can you be my slave?" he kept asking and at first I thought that was funny because he was the one bringing *me* drinks, you know? But we kept kissing and then we went into the bedroom and he felt my breasts and then he wanted to have sex. I felt as if I'd led him on, you know? So I didn't say no.

I saw him again a couple of times after that, but he didn't pay much attention to me. He was older and he didn't go to my school. I regret it. I wish it had been a little more special and I was really too young.

Sometimes I thought that if I were a boy I'd be one of those boys who goes into school one day and starts shooting people.
(Music—"Poor Little Rich Girl" by Tony Bennett.)

❄

Interviewer: What's a culture freak?

Emma: You're kidding, right? This is for the interview? Okay, in my own words.

A culture freak is a person who really likes other cultures, and listens to culture freak bands and doesn't conform to the usual sort of jumpsuit or Louis Vuitton wardrobe thing. So I'm into Egyptian a lot, in a spiritual way, too. I tell Tarot Cards. They're really Egyptian, people think they're Gypsy but I read about how they're actually way older than that and I have an Egyptian deck. My friend Lindsey is like me, but my other friend, Denise, is more into Indian stuff. Lindsey and I like Indian, too, and sometimes we'll all henna our hands.

Interviewer: Do you listen to culture freak music?

Emma: I like a lot of music, not just culture music. I like Black Helicopters, I really like their *New World Order* CDM, because it's really retro and paranoid. I like some of the stuff my mom and dad like, too; Tupac and Lauryn Hill. I like the band Shondonay Shaka Zulu. It's got a lot of drone. I like that.

(Music—"My Favorite Things" by John Coltrane.)

I'm seventeen. I'll be eighteen in April. I went to kindergarten when I was only four. I've already been accepted at Northeastern. I wanted to go to Barnard but my parents said they didn't want me going to school in New York City.

My dad's in telecommunications. He's in Hong Kong for six weeks. He's trying to get funding for a sweep satellite. They're really cool. The satellites are really small, but they have this huge, like, net in front of them, like miles in front and miles across. The net, like, spins itself. See, if space debris hits something hard it will drill right through it, but when it hits this big net, the net gives and just lets the chunk of metal or whatever slide away so it doesn't hit the satellite. That way it won't be like that satellite in '07 that caused the chain reaction so half the United States couldn't use their phones.

My mom is a teacher. She's taking a night class two nights

a week to recertify. She's always having to take classes, and she's always gone one night a week for that. Then there's after school stuff. She never gets home before six. When I was little, she took summers off, but now she does bookkeeping and office work in the summer for a landscaper, because my older brother and sister are in college already.

The landscaper is one of those babyboomers on rejuvenation. He's a pain in the ass. Like my dad says, they're all so selfish. Why won't they let anyone else have a life? I mean, the sixties are over, and they're trying to have them all over again. I hate when we're out and we see a bunch of babyboomers all hopped up on hormones acting like teenagers. But then they go back and go to work and won't let people like my dad get promoted because they won't retire.

They want to have it both ways. My mom says when we're all through school, she's going to retire and start a whole different life. A less materialistic life. She says she's going to get out of the way and let us have our lives. People have to learn how to go on to the next part of their lives. Like the Chinese. They had five stages of life, and after you were successful you were supposed to retire and write poetry and be an artist. Of course, how successful can you consider a high school teacher?

(Music—"When I'm Sixty-Four" by the Beatles.)

Okay, we were out this one Saturday, hanging outside the bowling alley because the cops had thrown us out. The cops here are the worst. They discriminate against teenagers. Everybody discriminates against teenagers. Like, the pizza place has this sign that says only six people under eighteen are allowed in at a time—which means teenagers. If they had a sign that only six people *over* eighteen or six *black* people were allowed in at a time everybody would be screaming their heads off, right? We rented shoes and everything, but we weren't bowling yet, we were just hanging out, because we hadn't decided if we were going to bowl and they threw us out.

We went over to the grocery store and the CVS to hang out on the steps and there was this boomer there. He was trying to dress like a regular kid. See most boomers dress in flared jeans and black and stuff and they all have long hair, especially the men, I guess because so many of them were, like, bald before the treatments. This guy had long hair, too, pulled back in a dorky pony tail, but he was wearing a camo jumpsuit. He'd have looked stupid in county orange, like he was trying too hard, but the camo jumpsuit was okay.

> In 2018, Terry Sydnowski was seventy-one years old. Click here for information on <u>telemerase repair</u>, <u>endocrinological therapy</u> and <u>cosmetic surgery techniques</u> of rejuvenation.

We were ignoring him. It was me and Denise and Lindsey, and this older black guy named Kamar and these two guys from school, DC and Matt. Kamar had bought a bunch of forty-fives. You know, malt liquor. I was kind of nervous around Kamar. Kamar seemed so grown up, in a lot of ways. He'd been arrested twice as a juvenile. Once for shoplifting and once, I think, for possession. He always called me "little girl." Like when he saw me he said, "What you doing, little girl?" and smiled at me.

> Interview with <u>Kamar Wilson</u>, conducted in the Summit County jail where Wilson is serving eighteen months for possession of narcotics.

I was feeling pretty drunk and I started feeling sorry for this dorky boomer who was just standing over by the wall watching us. I told Denise he looked really sad.

Denise didn't really care. I remember she had a blue caste mark right in the middle of her forehead and it was the kind that glowed under streetlights. When she moved her head it kind of bobbed around. She thought boomers were creeps.

I said he probably had money and ID. But she didn't really care because DC always had money and this other guy, Kamar, he had ID.

I know that boomers already had childhoods and all that, but this guy looked really sad. And maybe he didn't have a childhood. Maybe his mom was an alcoholic and he had to watch his brothers and sisters. Just looking at him I felt like there was this real sadness to him. I don't know why. Maybe because he wasn't being pushy. He sure wasn't like the guy my mom worked for, who was kind of a jerk. He wasn't getting in our faces or anything. boomers usually hang out with each other, you know?

Then DC sort of noticed him. DC is really kind of crazy, and I was afraid he and Kamar would decide to mess him up or something.

I said something about how I felt sorry for him.

And DC said something like, you want him to be really sorry? Kamar laughed.

I told them to leave him alone. DC is crazy. He'll do anything. Anything anybody does, DC has to be badder.

Interviewer: Tell me about DC.

Emma: DC always had a lot of money, he lived with this guy who was his godfather because his parents were divorced and his mom was really depressed or something and just lay around all the time. His godfather was always giving him anything. Kamar was nineteen and he had a fake phone ID, so he'd order stuff and they'd do a check against his phone ID and then he'd just pick it up and pay for it.

DC did all kind of crazy things. DC and Matt decided they were going to kill a bunch of kids. Just because they were mad. They were going to do a Columbine. So they drank like one of those fifths of Popov vodka, you know the kind I mean? They were going to get guns from some guy Kamar knew, but instead DC just took a baseball bat and started beating on this kid, Kevin, who he really hated.

Interviewer: Why did he hate Kevin?

Emma: I don't know, Kevin was just annoying, you know? He was this dweeby kid who was always bad-mouthing people. He used to get in a fight with this black kid, Stan, at the beginning of every school year. Stan wasn't even that good at fighting, but he'd punch Kevin a couple of times and that would be it until Kevin started bad-mouthing him the next year. It's like everything Kevin said got on

DC's nerves. So DC is totally wasted, driving around with a bunch of kids, and he sees Kevin hanging out in front of Wendy's and he screams, "Stop the car!" and he jumps out with this baseball bat and goes running up to Kevin and swings at him and Kevin raises his arm and gets his arm broken and then some other people haul DC off.

No, I wasn't there. I heard all about it the next day, though. And Kevin's arm was in a cast. Kevin was real proud of it, actually. He's that kind of a dork.

No, Kevin's parents were going to go to court, but they never did. I don't know why.

> No charges were ever filed. Kevin and his parents declined to be interviewed.

Anyway, that's why I was really worried about DC and this boomer. Luckily, Lindsey had a real thing about DC that night and they went off to walk back down to the bowling alley to look for this other girl whose parents were gone for the weekend. We were all going to that girl's house for a party.

Interviewer: Where were your parents?

Emma: My parents? They were home. I had to be in by midnight, but if it was a really good party I'd just go home at midnight and my parents would already be in bed, so I'd tell them I was home and then sneak back out through the side door in the basement and go back to the party.

Interviewer: Do you think your parents should have kept closer watch on you?

Emma: No. I mean, they couldn't. I mean, like, Denise has a PDA with a minder. They caught her this one time she went to Rick's in the Flats using Lindsey's sister's ID—

> An industry has developed around the arsenal of monitoring devices used to track teenagers, <u>pagers, minders, snitch packs and chips</u>, as well as the <u>variety of tricks</u> teenagers use to subvert them.

Interviewer: Can you describe a minder?

Emma: It's like a chip or something, and it's supposed to tell your parents where you are. Denise walked into the club and now all the clubs have these things, like, in the door or something that sets off the minder, and then this company calls your home and tells your parents where you are. But Kamar downloaded this program for Denise and put it on her PDA, and when she runs it, it tells her minder that she's somewhere else. Like, she puts my phone number in, and then it tells her minder that she's at my house.

So it was me and Denise and Kamar and this guy, Matt, and Kamar went somewhere . . . I don't remember where. Denise starts kidding me about talking to the boomer.

I was kind of drunk by then, and when I got drunk I used to think everything was funny. Oh, yeah, Kamar had gone to look for some other kids we knew, but anyway. We were kind of goofin'. You know? And Denise kept saying that she didn't think I would talk to the guy. So finally I did. I just went up to him and said hi.

And he said hi.

Up close he had that kind of funny look that geezers—I mean, boomers do. You know, like their noses and their chins and their ears are too big for their faces or something. I was pretty drunk and I didn't know what to say, so I just started laughing, because I was kind of nervous and when I'm nervous, sometimes I laugh.

He asked me what I was doing, but nice. Smiling. And I told him, "Talking to you." I thought it was funny.

He said I seemed a little drunk. He said "tipsy" which was funny because it sounded so old-fashioned.

For a minute I thought he might be a cop or something. But then I decided he wasn't because he could have busted us a long time ago, and besides, we weren't doing anything but drinking. So I introduced him to Denise and Matt. He said his name was Terry, which seemed like a real geezer name, you know? He was really nice, though. Quiet.

Interviewer: Do you know any rejuvenated people?

Emma: No, I didn't know any boomers, I mean, not any rejuvenated ones, except the guy my mom works for, and I don't really know him. My grandmother is going to do it next year but she has to wait until some kind of stock retirement thing happens.

I think I asked him if he was a cop, but I didn't really mean it. I was laughing because I knew he really wasn't.

He said he was just looking for someone to hang out with.

I asked him why he didn't hang out with other people like him? I mean now it sounds kind of rude, but really, it was weird, you know?

He said that they were all old, and he wanted to be young. He didn't want to hang around with a bunch of old people who thought they were young. He said that he hadn't really enjoyed being a kid so he was going to try it again.

That made me think I was right about what I'd thought before about his not having a childhood or something. I liked the idea of his having one now, so I asked if he wanted to go to the party.

Denise thought it was stupid, I could see from her face, but I knew once I explained about the childhood thing she'd feel bad for him, too.

He asked where the party was and we told him it was at this girl's house but we needed to wait for DC and Lindsey and Kamar to come back. Then I started worrying about DC.

Then he said he'd go get beer, which was the coolest thing, because that would convince a lot of people he was okay. He asked us what kind of beer we wanted.

Denise really liked that lemon beer, what's it called, squash, so we told him to get that. He got in this all-gasoline car—really nice. No batteries, a real muscle car like a Mercury or something. I told Denise my theory about him not having a childhood.

She was worried DC might be crazy but I thought that if Terry had beer, DC wouldn't care. Denise kept saying that DC was going to be really cranked.

Matt kept saying DC wouldn't care if Terry had beer, but I was getting really nervous about DC, because if he decided he wanted to be a pain in the ass—I'm sorry, I shouldn't swear, but that's the way we talk when it's just us. Is that okay?

Well, I was afraid DC would be a pain in the ass, just because you never know with DC. I was kind of hoping maybe Kamar and DC and Lindsey would get back before the geezer did so we could just go on to the party and forget about it. Kamar got back. But then Terry got back before DC and Lindsey.

But when DC and Lindsey got back, DC didn't even pay any attention to Terry. They told us that Brenda had already gone to her house so we all went to the party.

(Music—"Downtown" by Petula Clark.)

So the next time I saw Terry was with Kamar at another party. I was really surprised. Just because of the way Kamar was. But he and Terry were like good friends, which I figured really pissed DC off. Kamar liked DC, but part of the reason was because DC always had money, and Terry always had money. Terry was always buying beer and stuff. I thought Terry would ignore me because that's what guys do, they're nice to you one night and ignore you the next. But Terry was really nice and brought me a squash because he thought it was what I liked.

It's Denise that really likes it but I thought it was neat that he remembered.

He hung around with me for a while. He was cute, for a geezer. I bet when he was a kid he was really cute. I just forgot that he was different. He just seemed like a regular kid, only really nice. Then all the sudden I'd look at him and I'd think about how odd he looked, you know, just the way his face was different, and his knuckles were thick. I mean his hands and face were smooth. He told me once that he was self-conscious about it, and that some people, people in movies and stuff, have the cartilage on their nose and chin shaved. After a while though, I got so used to it I didn't even notice it anymore.

So I hung out with him and after a while we started kissing and stuff. He got really turned on, really fast. It was already maybe 10:30 and I was drunk, so we went upstairs and Matt and Lindsey were in the bedroom, so we kind of snuck in. They were on the bed, but we

spread out some coats. It's really embarrassing to talk about.
(Music—"Days of Wine and Roses" by Frank Sinatra.)

Emma: Oh my God! I just thought of something. I shouldn't say it.
Interviewer: You don't have to unless you want to.
Emma: You won't put it on tape if I don't want you to, will you?
(Laughing.) Oh my God, my face is so red. He was a mushroom.
Interviewer: What?
Emma: You know, a mushroom. I can't believe I'm saying this. He was
cut. I don't remember the word for it.
Interviewer: Circumcised?

> More than ninety percent of all men born between 1945
> and 1963 were circumcised.

Emma: Yeah. I'd never seen a boy like that before. Denise had sex with
a guy who was, but I never had before. It was weird. I know my face
is so red. I guess you can leave it in. A lot of boomers are circumcised, right?
Oh my God. (Covers face with hands, laughing.) It's such a
stupid thing to remember.
(Music—More of "Days of Wine and Roses" by Frank Sinatra, which
has been playing underneath this portion of the interview.)

Interviewer: How many people have you had sex with?
Emma: Four. I've had sex with four guys. Yeah, including Terry and
Luis.
Interviewer: Do you have any regrets?
Emma: Sure I wish I hadn't. The antivirals made me sick. I missed
almost a month of school that year because every time I had a treatment I'd be sick for three days. And everybody knew why I was
missing school, which was so embarrassing. There were seventeen
of us who had it.
They think that the antivirals took care of it, and we won't
get cancer, but they don't know because it's so new. So I've got to
have blood tests and check-ups every year. I hate it because I never

thought about being sick before, not really, and now, every time I feel weird, I'm thinking, is it a tumor? Every headache, I'm thinking, is this a brain tumor?

Sometimes I'm so mad, because Terry got to be rejuvenated, he gets like forty extra years, and I may not even get to be old because of him. Most of the time I think the antivirals took care of it, and like my mom says, all the check-ups mean if I ever do get sick, it will get caught a lot faster than it would in another person, so in a way, I might be lucky.

I usually believe that the antivirals did it, but sometimes, like when I'm getting blood drawn, I'm really aware of how I feel and I'm afraid I've got cancer, and right then I don't believe it. I was unlucky enough to have this happen, so why would I be lucky about it working? I know that doesn't make any sense.

Terry and DC were arguing one time. DC was saying that when he was old he wouldn't get rejuvenated. He'd let someone else have a chance. But Terry said he'd change his mind once he got old. And Terry was right. I always thought I wouldn't want to be rejuvenated, but every time I think I'm sick, I really want to live and I don't think I'll feel different when I'm old.

Terry didn't know he had the virus. It wasn't really his fault or anything. But sometimes I still get really mad at him.

That's kind of why I'm doing this. So that maybe someone else won't have to go through what I did.

Interviewer: Have you kept in touch with Terry?

Emma: No. I haven't seen him for three years.

Interviewer: Your parents wanted to file statutory rape charges, didn't they?

Emma: Yeah, but I thought it would be stupid. It wasn't like that.

Interviewer: Why not?

Emma: Statutory rape is stupid. He didn't rape me. He was nice, nicer than a lot of other guys.

Interviewer: But Terry is an adult. Terry is in his seventies.

Emma: I know. But it's not like a guy who looks seventy years old . . . It's different. I mean, in a way it's not, I know, but it is, because

Terry was sort of being one of us, you know? I mean, he wasn't all that different from Kamar. It would have been statutory rape with Kamar, too, but nobody says anything about that. I didn't sleep with Kamar, but I know a lot of girls who did, and nobody is trying to pin that on Kamar.

They're trying to pin everything else on Kamar. They said he was dealing drugs to us and he was the ringleader, but you can get drugs anywhere. You can get them at school. And he wasn't the ringleader. There wasn't any ringleader. We didn't need to be led to do all those things.

Interviewer: Was Terry one of you?

Emma: Yeah . . . no. No. Not really. He wanted to be. I mean, I wish I had known stuff before, I wish I had known not to get involved with Terry and all this stuff—but I wish I could have been a kid longer.

(Music—"The Kids Are All Right" by The Who.)

The last time I saw Terry? It was before I got tested, before anyone knew about the virus. Before all these people said to me, "You're lucky it's not AIDS, then you'd have to take medicine your whole life."

We went together for four months, I think. From November to March because we broke up right after Denise's birthday. We didn't break up really, so much as decide that maybe we should see other people, that we shouldn't get serious. Terry was weird to talk to. I never knew what he was thinking. I knew a little bit about him. He was retired and he'd had some kind of office job. I found out that he hadn't had a rotten childhood, he just hadn't liked it. He said he didn't have many friends and he was too serious before.

Interviewer: Why did you break it off?

Emma: We weren't in sync. He liked all that boomer music, rock and roll and Frank Sinatra and stuff. And we couldn't exactly fall in love, because he was so different.

He was always nice to me afterwards. He wasn't one of those guys who just ignores you.

We were all hanging out at the park next to the library after school. It was the end of the year, school was almost over. Kamar was hanging out with Brenda. He wasn't exactly her boyfriend because she was also hanging out with this other guy named Anthony and one weekend she'd be with Kamar and the next weekend she'd be with Anthony.

Everybody was talking and something Terry said made DC really mad. I don't know what it was. It really surprised me because DC always acted like Terry didn't even exist. When Terry was around, he'd ignore him. When he wasn't around, DC would hang with Kamar. But DC started screaming, stuff like, why don't you have any friends! You loser! You fucking loser! You have to hang around with us because you don't have any friends! Well, we don't want you, either! So why don't you just go die!

Terry had this funny look on his face.

A couple of guys pulled DC away and calmed him down. But everyone was looking at Terry, like it was his fault. I don't know why, I mean, he didn't do anything.

That evening I was supposed to stay at Denise's house, for real, not like when I told my mom I would be at Denise's and then went out. So I took my stuff over to her house, and then my brother, who was home from Duke, took us and dropped us off at Pizza Hut so we could get something to eat and then we wandered over to the steps outside the CVS because we saw people hanging out there.

Lindsey was there and she told me that DC was looking for Terry. That DC said he was going to kill Terry. Kamar got arrested, she said. Which meant that there was nobody to calm down DC.

Kamar had gotten arrested before, for shoplifting, but he got probation. But this time he got arrested for possession. Partly it was because Kamar is black.

Everybody was talking about Kamar getting busted and DC going off the deep end.

Lindsey kept saying, "Oh my God." It really got on my nerves. I mean, I knew DC hated Terry. DC just hated Terry. He said Terry was a poser and was just using people.

Interviewer: Were you friends with DC?

Emma: I knew DC, but we never really talked, but Lindsey had been seeing him for a couple of months so she knew him better than Denise and me.

Lindsey thought DC and Kamar were really friends. I thought Kamar just hung around with DC because he had money. Kamar was something like three years older than DC. But Lindsey said Kamar was just using Terry, but he and DC were really close.

I don't know what was true.

After a while Terry showed up. I didn't know what we should do, if we should tell him or not, but finally I thought I should. Terry was sitting with his car door open, talking to some people.

I told him Kamar got arrested for possession.

He wanted to know what happened, and I didn't know anything but what Lindsey had told me.

Terry wanted to know if he had a lawyer?

I never thought about a lawyer. Like I said before, mostly it was easy to forget that Terry wasn't just a kid like everyone else.

Terry called the police station on his cellphone. Just punched up the information and called. He said he was a friend of Kamar Wilson's. They wouldn't tell him anything on the phone, so he hung up and said he was going to go down.

I felt really weird suddenly talking to him, because he sounded so much like an adult. But I told him DC was looking for him.

"Fuck DC," Terry said.

I thought Terry would take off right then and there to go to the police station. But he kept talking to people about Kamar and about what might have happened, so I gave up and I went back to sit on the steps with Denise and Lindsey. We were working on our tans because it would make us look more Egyptian and Indian. Not that I would even think of doing that now, even though skin cancer isn't one of the types of cancer.

So finally DC came walking from over towards the hardware store and Denise saw him and said, "Oh shit."

I just sat there because Terry was an adult and he could just deal with it, I figured. I'd tried to tell him. And I was kind of pissed at him, too, I don't know why.

DC started shouting that Terry was a loser.

I don't remember if anybody said anything, but Terry didn't get out of the car. So DC came up and kicked the car, really hard. That didn't do anything so he jumped up on the hood.

Terry told him to get off the car, but DC wanted him to get out of the car and talk to him. After awhile Terry got out of the car and DC said something like, "I'm going to kill you, man."

DC had a knife.

Denise wanted us to go inside the CVS. But we were pretty far away. And the people inside the CVS are creeps anyway. They were calling the police, right then. Terry stood right by the door of his car, kind of half in and half out.

Lindsey was going, "Oh my God. Oh my God." She was really getting on my nerves. I didn't think anything was really going to happen. Terry kept saying stuff like, "Calm down man."

DC was ranting and raving that Terry thought that just because he was older he could do anything he wanted.

Terry finally got in his car and closed the door. But DC didn't get off the hood. He jumped up and down on it and the hood made this funny kind of splintery noise. Terry must have gotten mad, he drove the car forward, like, gunned it, and DC fell off, really hard.

Terry stopped to see if DC was okay. He got out of his car and DC was lying there on his side, kind of curled up. Terry bent over DC and DC said something . . . I couldn't see because Terry was between me and DC, Matt was one of the kids up there and he said that Terry pulled open his jacket and he had a gun. He took the gun out in his hand, and showed it to DC and said to fuck off. A bunch of kids saw it. Matt said that Terry called DC a fucking rich kid.

Interviewer: Have you ever seen a gun?

Emma: I saw one at a party once. This kid I didn't know had it. He was showing it to everyone. I thought he was a creep.

Interviewer: When did you see Terry next?

Emma: I never saw Terry after that, although I told the clinic about him, so I'm sure they contacted him. He was where the disease came from.

I wasn't the only one to have sex with him. Brenda had sex with him, and this girl I don't know very well, JaneAnne. JaneAnne had sex with some other people, and I had sex with my boyfriend after that. I don't know about Brenda.

> JaneAnne and Brenda's interviews. JaneAnne was interviewed from her home in Georgetown, MD, where her family moved six months ago. Brenda is still living in Charlotte, with her mother.

It taught me something. Adults are different. I don't know if I want to be one.

Interviewer: Why not?

Emma: Because DC was acting stupid, you know? But DC was a kid. And Terry really wasn't, no matter how bad he wanted to be. So why would he do that to a kid?

Interviewer: So it was Terry's fault?

Emma: Not his fault, not exactly. But he was putting himself in the wrong place at the wrong time.

Interviewer: Should he have known better?

Emma: Yeah. No, I mean, he couldn't know better. It was my fault in a way. Because most of the time if, like, we're at the bowling alley and a couple of geezers come in trying to be young, we just ignore them and they just ignore us. It's just instinct or something. If I hadn't talked to Terry, none of this would have happened.

Terry has different rules than us. I'm not saying kids don't hurt each other. But Terry was always thinking, you know?

Interviewer: What do you mean?

Emma: I don't know. Just that he was always thinking. Even when he wasn't supposed to be, even when he was mad, he was always thinking.

(Music—"Solitude" by Duke Ellington.)

Emma: When my parents found out they were really shocked. It's like they were in complete denial. My dad cried. It was scary.

We're closer now. We still don't talk about a lot of things, though. We're just not that kind of family.

Interviewer: Do you still go to parties? Still drink?

Emma: No, I don't party like I used to. When I was getting the antivirals, I was so sick I just stopped hanging out. My parents got me a PDA with a minder, like Denise's. But I wasn't doing anything anymore. Lindsey still sees everyone. She tells me what's going on. But it feels different now. I don't want to be an adult. That must have been what Terry felt like. Funny, to think I'm like him.

(Music—"My Old School" by Steely Dan.)

Oversite

It doesn't hurt, Gram," Renata says. My sixteen-year-old daughter pulls up her T-shirt sleeve to show her bare arm, the skin summer brown and the muscle swelling slightly into smooth biceps, flawless. "I had it done when I was little and see, you can't even tell."

My mother is sitting in the little examining room at the assisted living. Everything is white and hospital-like but there's no examining couch. There's just a desk, a little white table with two chairs and a scale. The doctor, a woman I don't know, is sitting in the other chair. My mother is bewildered, her face turned up towards me. She's got Alzheimer's.

"It's okay, Mom," I say.

She wants to understand, I can see that. So I explain again. "It's an implant that will let them know where you are, and how you are. It won't hurt."

Her eyes water constantly, now. In the time it takes me to explain she grasps and loses the words, grasps and loses phrases as they go past.

She looks at me and then at Renata, who is smiling, and finally submits uncomprehendingly. We have worn her down. The doctor bares my mother's arm, where the crepey flesh hangs loosely on the bones. The doctor swabs her upper arm with antiseptic and says, "I'm going to give you something to numb it, okay?" To me the doctor says in her normal voice, "It's just a little lidocaine." I don't like the doctor, but I don't know why. She is no-nonsense. She has professional hair, lightly streaked. This is no reason to dislike her.

My mother winces at the injection and is surprised again. She looks up at me, at Renata. We are smiling, both of us.

"Okay," my mother says. What is okay? I have no idea.

We wait for a few minutes.

My mother says, "Is it time to go?"

"Not yet," I say. "They're going to give you an injection."

"What?" my mother says.

"They're going to implant a chip. It will help them take care of you."

I try to say it every time as if it was the first time I said it. I don't want to embarrass her. Her head swings around, from Renata to me to the doctor and then back to Renata.

"It's okay, Gram," Renata says.

"Renata," my mother says.

The doctor has an injection gun and while my mother is focused on my daughter, she puts it firmly against my mother's arm and puts the chip in.

"Oh!" says my mother.

It's another low-grade moment of horror, but I think about that particular time with my mother because Renata was there and we were united, she and I. So that's a good memory. I come back to it a lot. In the background, shining, is Renata, who is young and healthy and good, raising her arm to show her grandmother that the chip is nothing, nothing at all.

The last two nights I have dreamed of dogs in trouble. I don't dream about Renata, although when the dreams wake me up, it's thinking about Renata that keeps me awake. The first night I dreamed of seeing a stray dog and not stopping to pick it up although it was wandering in an empty parking lot near a busy road. That was the first night Renata didn't come home and it doesn't take Freud to figure out what that meant. Seventeen-year-olds sleep on friends' couches, I know. Or Renata might be sleeping in her car.

The second night I dreamed that I was on a desert island and Sonia, our golden retriever, was with me. There was some horrible fate impending for Sonia and I had to kill her before something worse happened. I laid her down on some sticks. She trusts me, she's more my dog than anyone's, and she didn't like it but for me she lay there. In my dream I told her, "Stay, Sonia. Stay."

She stayed because I held her there by looking at her, the way you can sometimes will a dog into submission. She stayed while I lit the fire. And then the horror of it all hit me and I said, "Sonia, up!"

And I woke up.

That was last night, the second night Renata didn't come home.

Today is Tuesday and on Tuesdays I drive from work to the nursing home where my mother is. I go to see her Tuesday and Thursday and Saturday and even though she doesn't know what day it is or what days I visit, I think maintaining the pattern is important.

It's a nice place. The hallways are carpeted, and there is none of the clatter and echo, the institutionalization I associate with nursing homes. It's more like a hotel near the freeway, the kind that includes breakfast in the lobby. My mom's room has her own furniture from her condo—her gold couch, her bed, her little dinette table, the white ceramic angel that sat on an end table. She got the angel in a Christmas gift swap with her bridge club, but she thinks it's something inherited, antique.

"Clara," she says when she sees me. "What are you doing here?"

For a moment, everything seems normal.

"Hi, Mom," I say. "I came to see you."

She leans forward and whispers, "Take me home."

"Okay," I say. My mother wanders. She tries to get away. That's why they implanted the chip. It's called a Digital Angel and it monitors her blood pressure and temperature and has a GPS so that at the reception desk they can track her. When she was living at her condo, the police found her in her nightgown and a pair of black high-heeled shoes, carrying an empty pocketbook, walking down Ashleigh Drive. It was five in the morning. When I picked her up at the police station, her bare ankles almost broke my heart.

"Where's Renata?" she asks. She thinks Renata is still eight.

"She's at home," I say.

My mother frowns. She has an inkling she's missing something. She doesn't really know anymore that she has Alzheimer's, but sometimes she knows something is wrong. That she is disappearing. Plaque filling up the interstitial spaces between her neurons, her brain like Swiss cheese filled with fibrous mold. "She's with the babysitter," she says.

"Renata is seventeen now," I say brightly, as if it were utterly normal that nine years had been absorbed into the fungus. And of course, Renata isn't home. I don't know where Renata is.

My mother purses her lips. She senses I'm lying. Sometimes she makes the connections, and sometimes she is fiercely there, fully firing. She looks at me, her pale eyes bright, her Einstein hair flaring around her head. She leans forward. My smile is fixed on my face.

"Take me home," she whispers.

We got a Digital Angel for Renata when she was nine. There had been a rash of abductions, another summer of disappearing girls. Matt and I knew that statistically she was in more danger in our car. But while I was getting ready for work in the morning, I got into the habit of switching on Court TV and there was a trial going on of a man who had abducted a girl. He lived in a camper. He was fiftyish, balding and had a handlebar moustache like some character actor in a realistic Western. I would get into the shower and when I got out, I would dry off and come back into the bedroom, and absently pat Sonia the golden retriever, lying on the foot of the bed hoping not to be thrown off. On the television, they would be talking about there being no body. About how hard that would make it to convict him. About the girl's palm print found on the wall above his bed. I would picture her, leaning her weight for a moment to steady herself.

So I told Matt I was going to do it, and he agreed. Matt is such a softy. I told him on the phone, and I heard him sigh softly, relieved. Relieved that I had made the decision that we both wanted, but both knew was a little foolish. We agreed it was foolish, but it wasn't expensive, only about a hundred dollars, so why not?

I could track her on the computer on DigitalAngelMap.com. It's a street map, zoom in, zoom out, like the ones for driving directions, only

Renata shows up on it as a yellow triangle. While I was at work, I could plug in her number and my password and see the yellow triangle that was Renata at 2216 Gary—the house of Kerry, her best friend. I left it up on my computer, running in the background, while I talked on the phone or did columns in spreadsheets. I'm a planner. I order parts for manufacture. Planning is an inexact science, a kind of art. If I have too many parts ordered, then money is sitting around as inventory—costing us space. If I order the parts too slow, and we run out, then the assembly line shuts down, and that's even worse.

When I took Renata to the doctors to get the chip implanted, she sat on the examining table, frightened, while the doctor swabbed her arm to give her the lidocaine. I held her there with my eyes, the way I could sometimes hold Sonia, the golden retriever.

Renata did not cry out. She only flinched.

There is no trace of Renata on DigitalAngelMap.com. We were arguing. I told her to be in by eleven and she said she'd try and I said trying wasn't good enough. It escalated from there. She told me, "You watch! You watch your computer! One minute I'll be there and the next I won't! You won't know where I am and that will kill you!"

The kids wrap metal tape around their arms to cut off the signal. I knew that. I didn't know she did it.

Matt says, "Should we call the police? Report her as missing? As a runaway?"

I say, "She'll be eighteen in five months. What would we do then?"

"Don't we want to send a message?" he asks. "Let her know we take this seriously?"

"I think she has to come back herself," I say.

"I think we should get the police," he says.

"But won't they arrest her? She could end up in some sort of juvenile detention place. Or have a record. What if Keith has something in the car?" We think they smoke pot. We've discussed it.

"I'm going to make some calls," he says. "I'm going to call Kerry, and then Keith's aunt."

"Okay," I say, although I don't expect anything. Kerry and Renata have been drifting apart—Kerry on track for college, Renata going . . . wherever it is that Renata is going.

Matt gets in the car and drives around. He calls me from the park to tell me she's not there.

Renata has a boyfriend, Keith. Keith is short and skinny and has three lines branded beneath his lower lip, radiating like the rays of a sun. We won't let Renata get branded, tattooed, or pierced. Keith shaved his head for a while, but now he's letting his hair grow. Matt remarked one time, "Have you ever noticed how Keith always needs something?"

That was the evening Keith needed a jump for his car. Matt stood out on the driveway, dressed in his business casual (Matt is an engineer) and hooked up the jumper cables, talking amiably with Keith, while Renata sat on the front steps with her bare arms crossed over her knees and her chin on her forearms, staring at nothing. Renata had dyed her hair black a week before. She was wearing a pair of men's pants, suit pants, charcoal gray. As far as I could tell she had stopped wearing underwear.

I don't think there's a day in my life when I haven't worn under-wear.

When she dyed her hair black, she challenged me, "Are you going to tell me I can't dye my hair?"

"No," I said. "You can dye your hair any color you want. You can shave it off if you want." I hoped that by telling her she could shave it off, she wouldn't. But Matt and I had decided she could do anything temporary—just nothing permanent—no tattoos, piercings or brands.

It is a phase, adolescent rebellion, the process of separation. I want to blame Keith, of course. Renata got all A's and B's all the way through middle school. Now she's getting an A in art and C's and D's in every-thing else.

Renata is getting an A in art, despite the fact that she doesn't even bother to do some of the projects. Mr.. Vennemeyer, her young art teacher, just shrugs his shoulders and says, "Of all the people I've taught, Renata is a real artist." When she was fifteen, he started an Art

Club where he taught her to stretch canvas, prime it, and choose colors for the ground. Other kids do sculpture and collage and work with the kiln. Renata paints. Every so often she gets interested in something he assigns, and does a 3-D maze or a collage, but mostly she paints.

She paints in our basement. I buy her oils and canvas and stretchers. Matt doesn't know how much I've spent on tubes of Windsor and Newton oils. "How can you paint in the basement?" I ask. "Don't you need more light?"

She shrugs. "I need space," she says. She and Keith are down there for hours, music playing quietly on her dad's old boom box. I've gone down often enough to make sure and I never have the sense that they are doing anything. No hurry, no dishevelment. Just Renata painting and Keith sitting in a ratty old armchair they found set out for the garbage.

Matt doesn't go down in the basement. His workbench and tools are in the garage. I go down for something now and then—boxes for Christmas gifts, or glasses stored down there. I shouldn't look at Renata's paintings. They're hers. There is something private about them. But I do.

"Come downstairs," I say to Matt on the second night Renata is gone.

He comes down with me and we stand with our arms around each other's waists while he looks at Renata's paintings.

Renata paints pictures of girls hit by cars. There are always four paintings: the moment when the girl is struck, the girl sliding across the hood or against the windshield, the girl in the air, and the girl crumpled on the ground. Renata has all sorts of photos stuck up on her easel and on the table she uses for her paints. She has pictures of her best friend, Kerry. Keith has Kerry around the waist and yanks her backwards forcefully—all you can see of Keith are his arms. Renata used Matt's digital camera. In her first series of girl hit by car, you can see it is based on Kerry.

There are also pictures of cars and car hoods; Matt's, mine, Keith's, cars I don't recognize.

In the first series, the Kerry series, the girl looks awkward, not quite right, except in the painting where she is flying through the air. I think Renata really caught something there.

125

In the second series, the girl is a black girl who looks around ten. There's a magazine photo of a black woman falling off a fire escape, and you can see that in the girl in the air. In that series, the best painting is the girl crumpled on the pavement. In the third series, the girl is an enormously fat white girl with red hair. She bobs in the flying in the air painting like a huge pink Macy's Parade balloon. She has on a red jumper and white anklets and Mary Janes. She doesn't look frightened. And when she is lying crumpled on the pavement, her haunch is exposed so her white panties show. Her huge thigh is painted pink and smooth as strawberry yogurt.

The one Renata is working on right now is an Amish girl series. She works on them all at once, so they are sitting around in stages. On her easel is the Amish girl being hit by the car. The Amish girl is in gray, with a white bonnet sketched over her hair. She is wearing sneakers. The car is Keith's car.

"Well," Matt says slowly. "She'll have to come back for all this, won't she. She wouldn't leave all this."

I don't know.

There is a folder, open, full of pictures of girls cut out from magazines, and just visible, the scalloped corner of an old photograph. I reach for it, and Matt says, "Don't touch that," but I do anyway. It's from one of my photo albums. It's an old black and white picture of a young woman, maybe Renata's age, wearing a forties-style one-piece bathing suit. She's soft and by today's standards, a little heavy in the hips and her bangs make her look something like Betty Page. The bathing suit is a jazzy number with polka dots. She's sexy and solid as a pin-up. It's my mother. I show it to Matt and then take it upstairs with me. He doesn't say anything.

Brenda, one of the aides where my mother lives, left me a voicemail at work that my mother was out of some things—lipstick (Cool Watermelon by Revlon, a strange, overly vivid shade that my mother prefers) and lotion and menstrual pads because sometimes my mother has a little urinary leakage. It's Wednesday and I'll see her Thursday, but I stop on my way home from work and pick things up at the grocery store and drop them off.

I always want to leave right away, so I always make myself sit down and say something to Mom. I touch her a lot, on the arm, on the shoulder. I kiss her cheek sometimes. We were not a huggy family. We're not as remote as the classic Presbyterian family (my husband says that in moments of great emotion, the men in his family would shake hands) but we don't touch each other much. My mother seems to like to be touched now, though.

Her phone rings. I can't think who would call. I call her and tell her I'm coming over, although I have no sign that she remembers. I used to see notes written to herself, CLARA COMING. But not anymore. I pick it up, expecting it to be a telemarketer. It's Matt.

"Renata called," he says. "She's on her way home."

"Is she all right?" I ask.

"She didn't say," he says.

"I'll be right there."

My mother is watching me, birdlike. "Where's Renata?" she asks.

Lost, I want to say. "I don't know where she is, Mom. She's run away. She's seventeen and she's run away. But she's on her way home now."

My mother looks at me and reaches out and covers my hand with hers. Her hand is cool. She searches my face. I think she is together in this moment and I know what she is going to say. It's what she said to me when Renata was two and I told her that sometimes I was so afraid I would get up in the middle of the night to see if Renata was breathing. She said, "Our children are hostages to the world."

She pets my hand and then she says, "Take me home."

Our driveway is a bit of an incline. Keith parks at the bottom, the way he always does, and Matt and I stand at the door, watching. The car sits for a long moment, while Renata and Keith are apparently talking. Then the doors open and Renata gets out and comes up the driveway, head down, leaning forward against the slope. She's wearing plumber's tape around her upper arm. Keith gets out and leans up against the door of his car, arms crossed across his chest.

I gasp and Matt says, "Oh shit." Keith's lip is split and his face is bruised all down one side, swelling now so that one eye is half closed.

Renata doesn't look back at him, doesn't say anything to us, just goes in the house.

Matt goes down driveway and I know what he is asking. Are you all right? he is asking. Do you want me to go with you to the emergency room? But Keith is shaking his head.

I follow Renata inside. "Have you had anything to eat?" I ask. I hear the door behind me, Matt coming in.

"We stopped at McDonald's," Renata says. She tried to be vegetarian for a week or two, but she's a carnivore. Even as a baby, Renata would choose steak over ice cream.

"So where did you go?" Matt asks her.

"Some guy Keith knows has a friend who has a trailer. He uses it for fishing or something. Out near Sandusky." I can imagine the trailer, low and mean and narrow. The story comes out in little bits, and before much of it has come out, Renata is crying. The guy who owns the trailer is named Don, and he showed up there today. He was high on something, Renata thinks maybe crack.

"He's missing a bunch of teeth," she says, "and I can't understand him when he talks." She is crying in the way that is almost like hiccoughing. "So I kept smiling and nodding my head like I knew what he was talking about but I was afraid I was nodding my head at the wrong times or something.

"And then he got mad at Keith, I don't know why. And he got all ugly and he, like, winged this ashtray at Keith and it hit him in the head and they started fighting and then Keith and I got out of the house and he said he was going to get his gun and we were out in the middle of nowhere and I was so scared and we ran to Keith's car. While we were trying to back out his crappy driveway he shot at us and he hit the back of Keith's car. There's a hole in the trunk. We kept backing up really fast, and his driveway is really long. It's just these two ruts, not even gravel or anything."

We are sitting on the couch and at seventeen, she almost crawls into my lap. I stroke her hair, coarse with black dye.

We ground her, of course.

"Here's the deal," I say. "I'll take you to the doctor and get the chip taken out. But you've got to do your part. You've got to tell us where you're going and what you're doing."

She is subdued and listens without agreeing or disagreeing.

Matt and I lecture, even if we know it is the worst thing to do. How can we not? All our feelings spill out in warnings. She's got to straighten up. She'll be eighteen in five months, and she's got to make some decisions. If we're going to help her go to art school, she's got to get her grades up. And on, and on.

Her dad goes to the bathroom and I take the photo of my mother out of my purse. I slide it towards her on the coffee table.

She frowns at it, and looks up at me, puzzled.

"You can have it," I say. "But please don't paint her being hit by a car. I couldn't stand it."

She covers her mouth with her hand, thinking. What words are trapped behind that hand?

Then she nods and says softly, "Okay, Mom."

At two that morning, I wake up, frightened from some dream. I lie in bed and catalogue my sins; obsessive, insufficiently understanding, self-absorbed. Then I get up and call up DigitalAngelMap.com. First I put in Renata's code, which I know by heart. The yellow triangle is steady on our street. I watch it a long time. Sonia climbs the steps. I can hear her. She's an old dog now and she has arthritis. She comes into the extra bedroom where we keep the computer and lies down and sighs.

I put in my mother's code. As soon as I start typing it, I am gripped by the deep conviction, the premonition that my mother is out wandering around.

But the triangle is right where it should be, unmoving. I turn off the computer and then step over the dog and turn out the light, step blindly back over the dog and sit in the chair. The dark and stillness spread around me, blanketing the house and the street. The cars are silent and still and the girls are all safe in their beds.

Wicked

The first thing that burst into flame was a bag of groceries in the back of the Explorer. Taking groceries in the house was a moment she joked about with the cashier at the grocery store. The grocery store nearest her house was a little upscale, a little chichi and when she shopped there instead of the less expensive Kroger's, she knew it was another moral lapse. But she liked to get shopping over with as fast as possible so she mostly shopped at the expensive place.

The bag boys loaded the groceries in the car for the customers and as Joe was bagging, she said, "Could you come home and put them away for me?"

Joe, who was still in high school, just laughed.

But she really hated putting groceries away. Picking them was ripe with possibility. Putting them away was like cleaning up after the party. Joyless. She opened the back of the SUV and saw the pile of bags and felt the creeping edge of despair. She just stood there, looking, and then a curl of smoke drifted up past the box of Life cereal, and suddenly, instead of a bag of cereal and macaroni and cheese, it was a bag of flame.

It was gorgeous. And her heart warmed to it. She felt nothing but pleasure for a moment and then she thought distantly that she should pull the bag out. But she didn't. Instead she just watched the next bag of groceries—onions, red bell peppers and portabella mushrooms—catch. Upscale groceries, double-bag, and outer plastic sack melted, then blackened. The back of the seat caught, too, heavy black smoke, stinking and acrid with chemicals.

She backed out of the garage. Would the car explode? But it didn't. It burned flamboyantly, the flames flattening against the ceiling of the garage.

The next-door neighbor shouted, "I'll call 911!"

She hadn't even noticed that the neighbor had come out.

Let it burn, she thought.

She looked at the mailbox down by the street and in a moment, smoke leaked around the opening, and then the top of the post flared, fire almost invisible in the daylight.

The garage was engulfed and she could see smoke behind the windows in the front of the house. Her husband was at work. Her kids were at school. Wouldn't they be surprised?

Who was going to clean this up?

Not me, she thought.

Laika Comes Back Safe

There was a special program when I was in fourth grade where this photographer came and taught us. It was called the Appalachian Art Project and it was supposed to expose us to art. We all got these little plastic cameras called Dianas that didn't have a flash or anything, and black-and-white film. The first week we took pictures of our family and then we developed them and picked one for our autobiography. Then the next week we took pictures of each other. Then the third week we took pictures of important things in our lives. The fourth week we took pictures of dreams.

Not hopes and dreams—we were supposed to take a picture of something that was like something we would dream about. I had a book from the school library about exploration in space. It was old, from the seventies, and it talked about the history of space exploration. It was really more of a boy's book. My favorite books were horse books. All I remember from it was the part about Laika the dog. They trained this dog and they sent her up in space and they used her to see if people could survive in space and then because they couldn't bring her back down they left her to die up there.

That really bothered me because I had a German shepherd named Lacey and I kept thinking about Laika up there all by herself and then just her bones going around and around. I had a bad dream about Lacey being taken to go to space. So when it was time to do the photograph of a dream, I took string and tape and I taped Lacey up with spots of tape on her chest and her head and I took her picture sitting there in the backyard. I had a parachute from one of those plastic soldiers you get that you wrap up in the parachute and throw in the air and hope the parachute opens and I taped that on Lacey, too, and had my mom hold the parachute—you can see her hand and a little of her arm in the picture—and then, while mom kept Lacey from pawing all the tape and the string off, I took her picture. It's a good picture—she's looking at me and she has her ears up. I titled it *Laika Comes Back Safe*.

We put all the pictures on the chalk rail. I remember somebody took a picture of their steps down to their cellar. Nobody seemed to think anything of *Laika Comes Back Safe* maybe because you could see my mom's hand and the parachute was really too little.

Tye Petrie stood behind me in the lunch line. "Brittany, is that your dog?" he asked.

"Yeah," I said.

"She looks like a neat dog."

That was more than Tye Petrie had ever said to me in my life. Even though he was my second cousin, we didn't have picnics and family reunions or anything with the Petries. "Her name is Lacey," I said, and then I said, "I love her more than anyone else on Earth."

I thought it sounded like a stupid thing to say, but Tye Petrie just said, "Really?" in this way that made it sound like he thought that was good thing.

"Do you have a dog?" I asked.

"No," he said. "I'm not allowed."

"You can come and pet Lacey," I said.

We had a little white house on cinder block—my dad had built most of it himself. I was doing my homework and my dad was getting ready to leave for second swing, the shift he was working at the plant before he got messed up, and my dad looked out the window and said, "What's that briar doing hanging on the fence?"

My dad didn't mean anything by it, he called everybody a briar, but Tye Petrie had a real light head of hair and real pale eyes in a dark face and he did look a bit like white trash. He was waiting around by our gate. "He's come to see Lacey," I said, and went out.

By that time Lacey was barking her fool head off. I untied her—Dad said she had to stay tied up even though we had a chain link fence because she crapped all over the front yard—and she went bounding over towards Tye. She stopped when she got close to him, looking back at me with one paw raised like she wasn't sure of something. Then she lowered her head the way she did when she was being introduced to another dog, tail sort of neither up or down and wagging just a little.

She was acting that way because Tye was a werewolf, although he wasn't really, not yet. I didn't know Tye was a werewolf, because he didn't tell me for years and years. In movies, dogs are afraid of werewolves, but that's not true. They just think they're other dogs and if your dog hates other dogs, then they'll hate a werewolf, too. I'm like an expert on werewolves, after knowing Tye all these years, but it's not something that will ever do me any good. I thought about calling the *X-Files* people and seeing if they could use all that stuff for a movie, but I really can't tell, and besides, I wouldn't know how to get the phone number for a television show.

Tye and Lacey liked each other fine and we took her for a walk down the street. We hung out and he took me to the place where he'd made a fort in the woods. He came over pretty often after that and I think he went roller skating with my mom and me once. We never talked at school, because I was always hanging out with Rachel and Melissa and Lindsey and he was always hanging out with Mike and Justin or somebody.

When my dad was in the motorcycle accident and messed up his back and his leg and lost his job, we had to go on the county until he got his social security pension settled. We moved into town and I transferred from the Knox County school system to Barbourville City Schools and went to Landry middle school. We had to give up Lacey. The people down the street from our old house took her. I only saw Tye Petrie at church and we never said anything to each other.

I was in 4-H then, doing sewing stuff, and I ran into Tye at the Knox County Fair. He wasn't in 4-H, he was just at the fair. He wasn't hanging around with anybody and I was in the barn looking at the big draft horses. He walked up beside me like it was the school cafeteria lunch line and looked at the horse.

"Hi, Tye," I said.

"I checked on Lacey last week," he said. "She's doing fine."

When we gave up Lacey I didn't get mad and scream and cry like they do on TV. I didn't say, "You can't have her!" and she didn't run away and find me, but it really hurt me deep inside and I never ever got over it. It was the worst thing that ever happened to me, even worse than when my dad got hurt. I couldn't say anything, because I was afraid I was going to cry.

"I meant to tell you at church, but I never got a chance," he said. "I go check on her about once a week. They take good care of her. They don't tie her up, they let her run around their yard."

I took a deep breath and it was like a sob. "Thanks," I said. It came out a little shaky.

"So how's it going?"

I shrugged. "It sucks," I said.

"Yeah," he said. "It does."

"You want to go on the Octopus?" I said. I don't know why, the Octopus always makes me sick. But it was the only ride I could think of.

We hung around the whole day. My mom had to take my dad home because his back hurt so bad, it gave him a migraine and Tye's mom and dad said they'd take me home. Tye's mom had the same coloring that Tye did, pale hair, a dark face, real pale eyes and she wore her hair up on the back of her head, kind of old-fashioned. She had an accent, Tye said, because she came from a Parish in Louisiana. She wasn't pretty or anything, she looked real plain and kind of country. She didn't say nearly anything when I was around.

Mostly, though, we were on our own and in the evening it got cool and the lights came on in the midway and the rides would take you up and back into the dark and then down and into the light.

"Brittany's got a beau," my mom said when I got home and I thought it was true.

On the Tuesday of the last week before school started I walked all the way out to Swan Pond to see him and Lacey. I got there before him. Lacey went nuts, jumping and barking, and Mrs. West came out to see what was wrong, but when she saw me she just waved and said I could come in the fence. I went inside and hugged Lacey and she licked my face. Mrs. West had a pretty garden and it had marigolds and red and white petunias.

Tye came and I said he could come in the fence. Lacey jumped all over him. Then he lay down on his back and I petted Lacey. "Do you ever wish you were a dog?" he asked.

"Yeah," I said. "A lot."

"It's not all it's cracked up to be," he said.

I thought about that. It probably wasn't. Lacey hadn't asked to have new owners, but then I hadn't asked to move into town and have to live on food stamps, either.

We talked about the life of a dog, and he told me about how his parents never talked to each other. They never fought, they just never talked to each other, and his father had told him once that he'd made a mistake to marry his mother. His mother took Lithium for her nerves. I told him that my mom was a bitch sometimes, which she was, and she probably should be on Lithium or something, and that since he got messed up, my dad had just given up on everything.

By the time I started home I was late for dinner, but since my dad didn't go to work anymore we just all sort of ate whenever anyway and it really didn't matter.

I told my mom that I'd gone to see Lacey. I didn't tell her about Tye, because I didn't want her to tease me.

Tye and I met pretty often after that. We'd play with Lacey and then we'd walk out the gravel road to the Pope-Ball cemetery. It's just a little farm family cemetery, just a place fenced in with a wire fence and a bunch of tombstones halfway up Pope-Ball mountain. It's not any bigger than Mrs. West's yard but there are some trees all along the back fence. Some of the tombstones are pretty old, from 1890 and stuff, but most of them are my grandparents and great-aunts and -uncles.

Tye told me he would never have a girlfriend, never get married. There was a genetic problem in his family and he wasn't going to pass it on. He wouldn't say what it was but the way he talked I always thought it had to do with his penis or something and that's why he wouldn't say.

I still liked talking though, and I thought maybe he would change his mind about me. I thought about never having children and I didn't know if I could marry someone like that.

We met at least once a week until it got too cold, and then when it got warm I called him and told him I was going to see Lacey, slogged up through the mud and there he was and everything was pretty much the same. We started high school, and still kept it up, even when I started dating Rick. I told Tye all about Rick although I never told Rick about Tye. Tye thought Rick was a poser. Rick wore skateboarder stuff like the big pants and he really did skateboard although he didn't do stunts.

My mom was having trouble with diabetes and a lot of it was her own fault. She found out she had diabetes when she went on that liquid diet where you drink a can of stuff in the morning and a can of stuff at noon and she blacked out. Then the doctor told her to lose weight and it got worse. I never knew what we were going to eat at home—for a while she was on this Susan Powter kick. Susan Powter is the chick with the white buzz cut, and basically she says you can't eat anything good. Mom tried vegetarian for a little while until Dad said we had to have meat at dinner. Then she did the cabbage soup diet and lost some weight but then she gained it all back. Most of the time, Rick picked me up and we went down to Taco Bell or Dairy Queen and ate. A lot of times we brought stuff back for Dad.

Tye's parents filed for divorce. He said it was a relief. His mom got a job in town at Kmart and his dad moved out. Since his mom was at work in the afternoon, he'd bring a six-pack of beer and stash it in the cemetery and after we saw Lacey we'd go sit and I'd drink two and he'd drink four and we'd talk about stuff.

Rick started hanging out with his friends and not coming over. He got a paintball gun and played paintball all the time and he never had any money to do anything, never wanted to come over much. He was a pain anyway because all he ever talked about was how he was going to join the Air Force and be a pilot, or the music he liked which was all Jimi Hendrix and Led Zeppelin and singing "Sweet Home Alabama," or it was Garth Brooks and Clint Black. I got sick and tired of him never having time to come over and we had a big argument and broke up and then I cried for a week.

I'd go out to see Tye almost every evening and we'd sit in the cemetery, bundled up in our winter coats, long after it got dark. I didn't think of Tye as a possible boyfriend anymore, he was more like a brother or something. He had this old plaid cloth coat and he'd sit there with his back up against my great-aunt Ethel's red granite tombstone—it was the biggest in the cemetery even though both her and my great-uncle Jake drank all the time and never had any money, because John, her son, and my cousin once removed, had a good job with the nuclear plant down in Knoxville, Tennessee, and he paid for the funeral—and we'd listen to Pearl Jam or U2 or Sublime until the batteries ran out on his CD player. I was talking about being a vet. That's what I wanted to do, be a vet.

"I can't come over the next few nights," he said.

"Is your mom working days?"

"Yeah," he said. He stared at his beer. "And, um, I go kinda crazy sometimes and I'm going to do it for the next couple of days."

"You mean you like schedule it?" I said. I didn't know if I was supposed to laugh or what.

"No," he said, "I just know when it's going to happen." He was dead serious.

"Tye," I said, "what do you mean?"

He shrugged. "It's a hereditary condition. I told you I had a hereditary condition."

"It makes you crazy sometimes?"

"Sort of," he said.

"What do you mean, 'sort of'?"

He wouldn't say any more than that.

It was too cold and it was late. He promised me he'd be back out here on Tuesday unless it was raining. We had an unspoken agreement that if it was raining we just came the next time it was dry.

I rolled up our blanket and stuck it in the plastic bag we kept it in, then stashed it half under this fallen-down tree and sprayed it with this Pet Off stuff we used to keep the animals out. I took the beer cans and Tye took the CD player. I threw out the beer cans in the Dumpster in the back of the Chinese place I passed on the way home.

We lived in an apartment complex then, and I cut across the back parking lot. I could see the light through the curtains of the sliding glass door. We had a first-floor apartment because of my dad's leg.

My mom was loaded for bear when I got in. "Where have you been?"

"Shelly's," I said.

"I called Shelly's and you weren't there."

"I went for a walk."

"For four hours?"

"Yeah. I went out to see Lacey, my dog, and then I walked around."

She didn't buy it. I don't know why I didn't tell her I was with Tye except that I didn't want her coming up to the cemetery and catching me drinking beer. She was screaming at me about never being home and I just said, "Yeah, whatever," and she slapped me.

My dad said, "For God's sake, Betty, hitting her isn't going to do any good!"

"Jesus!" my mom shouted, "you want your daughter running around all night?"

Oh God, they'd been arguing. I stood there, holding my face, feeling these little sobs like hiccoughs.

"She's been out for hours without telling anyone where's she's been! Don't I have a right to know where my daughter's been?"

"You don't have any goddamn right to hit her!"

"Maybe if you acted like a father—"

"Maybe if you got off your fat ass and got a job!"

"You don't have the sense God gave a cockroach! You know something, Joseph Gaines Ball! You know something? I grew up! You never grew up! You just kept drinking and running around on a goddamn motorcycle!"

I ran to my bedroom and locked the door.

"Goddamn it!" my mother roared. "You get out here, you little bitch!"

My mom started hammering on my door. My dad must have tried to grab her because I heard her slap him. Then she must have punched him because he fell out in the hall. He had trouble getting up because of his back and his leg, so she could punch him when he was down, too.

"Goddamn it!" he was yelling. "Goddamn it!"

Then I could hear my mother run down the hall sobbing.

My dad was lying out there on the floor on the mauve carpeting that didn't go with any of our furniture. "I'm going to get my gun," my dad said in a monotone. "I'm going to get it and blow my fucking head off." I could hear it clearly through the thin walls.

"Sure," my mother called from the kitchen. "Lie there and pity yourself! If you think I'm going to beg you to save your sorry-ass excuse for a life, you're wrong!"

"I'm going to blow my fucking head off," my dad said again.

I lay on my bed in the dark and pulled my big stuffed dog up against my chest and pretended it was Lacey.

My mom and dad were still asleep when I got up. I was late for school the next day and missed first period General Math, which was no great loss.

When I got home, my mom was waiting for me and she started in on me again, so I said, "I'm going."

She grabbed me by the arm but I just twisted out of her grip and ran out the door. I went to see Lacey but she was in the house so I went up to the cemetery and found our blanket and wrapped up in it. I couldn't face going home yet, and I didn't know what to do. It was chilly, but not really cold. I sat leaning up against my great-aunt's tombstone in the sun. My parents had argued until two or three in the morning and I was tired and I fell asleep there.

I woke a couple of times and then suddenly it was dark and I'd gotten cold. It wasn't completely dark, because the moon was up but it was strange and creepy to be walking home in the dark. My mom was waiting for me, still mad. We had another fight, and I told her I was afraid to come home to a psycho mom. She said the school had called and said I was tardy and I said that maybe if she got up and sent me off to school like a normal mom, I wouldn't be tardy.

My dad came out and said I wasn't being fair and they told me I was grounded for a week.

I didn't get to go out to the cemetery until my punishment was up. I called Tye Petrie and told him I'd been grounded. We didn't talk about it on the phone. Tye didn't like to talk on the phone. He just told me he'd see me in a week.

He was waiting in Mrs. West's yard, and Lacey was happy to see me. I did all the things she liked, rubbing my knuckles in her ears and scratching her chest to apologize for not having seen her.

"What happened?" he asked.

"My mom and dad were having an argument so I came out to the cemetery and I fell asleep and I didn't get home until about nine."

"Yeah?" Tye said. He looked tired. He'd been suddenly getting taller and he'd gone from looking like a little middle school kid to looking like one of the juniors. He even had a little bit of a mustache.

"Did you go crazy?" I asked.

"Yeah," he said.

I wanted to know what it was like to go crazy. "What did you do?"

"Just, sorta went crazy."

That's all he would say and then neither one of us knew what to talk about. "When I woke up at the cemetery," I said, "it was already dark. Scared the living shit out of me," I said.

"Brittany," he said, "you shouldn't be out alone after dark."

"I didn't expect to be out after dark," I said, irritated.

"No, really. I mean, I . . . um, what if something attacked you?"

"The only people that ever go to the cemetery are you and me," I said.

"What if I attacked you?" he said.

"Don't be weird, Tye," I said.

"I am weird," he said, and I grinned, but he started to cry.

I'd never seen Tye cry. "Jesus," I said, "what's wrong?"

That's when he told me he was a werewolf.

I thought that maybe he really was crazy, you know? Here he was crying and telling me that he was a werewolf, for Christ' sake. I patted him and said it was okay, he was okay. I wondered a lot of things about Tye, like was he gay, or was his father like, molesting him, but I never expected that he was crazy. He told me a bunch of crazy things like how he hadn't started changing into a wolf until this year, because the change didn't happen until you started going through puberty. He told me about how he'd been dreading it for years, and how he couldn't really remember what had happened afterward, because it was like he had experiences in a whole different way, like through smell. "So, see," he said, "I could have hurt you really bad, Brittany. Really bad!"

"You didn't hurt me," I said, because I didn't know what else to say. It was really crazy. Some ways, Tye was really crazy. Sometimes he was so excited, it was like he was on something and he'd be talking a mile a minute. Sometimes he would sleep all Saturday and Sunday and be real depressed.

We sat there a long time while he told me about how his mom's family in Louisiana was like this and how his mom had run away to try to get away from all that. It was crazy stuff and it was creepy listening to Tye because he really believed it but it was so strange, it was really interesting. I knew if I acted like I wanted to go, Tye would think I didn't believe him. He kept saying, "I know it sounds crazy, you probably don't believe me, but it's true," and he kept watching me in this desperate way like I was the last person in his life.

Finally I had to go home or I'd get grounded again.

The next day I half thought he wouldn't be at the Wests', but he was there, just hanging by the fence and Lacey was sitting, looking up at him as if she were trying to talk to him. I thought about how much he had changed lately and I realized for the first time how, well, sexy he seemed suddenly.

Lacey and I said hello.

I asked Mrs. West if we could take Lacey for a walk—sometimes we did that and Tye had me so weirded out that I wanted her with me. I took her on the leash and we walked up to the cemetery. Tye got the beers and I poured some into my hand for Lacey. She liked beer.

Lacey licked my face and then stood with her front paws on my legs. She usually only did that when I was crying or something. "Lacey," I said, "what's up with you today!"

"She knows you're scared," Tye said. "She can smell your fear. She's trying to make you feel better."

I almost said, "Scared of what, you?" but it was true, I was scared. Not that Tye was going to hurt me, but that he was crazy and I didn't know what to do.

"I can smell it, too," he said.

I petted Lacey, trying to think of something to say.

"You don't believe me," he said. "I can smell that, too. It's okay, it's all pretty crazy. But I can smell your feelings. I can smell what you had for lunch—you had a cheeseburger."

I had a cheeseburger almost every day at lunch because it was about the only thing I could stand in the school cafeteria. I mean, probably Tye could have guessed that. I mean, we'd talked about it because we'd talked about how school lunches sucked. But the way he said it scared me even more.

"I can smell that you're worried," he said. "I can smell feelings that I don't even have names for. I can smell you better than I can see you, Brittany."

It was then that I either had to believe him or I had to quit seeing him.

Things changed after that; like we were falling, out, away. I'd walk out to the cemetery and it was as if I wasn't in Barbourville anymore. Tye was taller than I remembered and the pale hair on his forearms looked so soft, I wanted to touch it. I knew he had to smell that change on me, too, but he didn't say anything about it. So I studied the way his shirtsleeve was cuffed back against his skin.

He told me how when he went out at night during what we called his "crazy times" the whole world was different because his brain was different. "I can't remember it afterwards," he said.

It started to rain. I had a jacket with a hood and the rain was hard enough that it pattered on it like a roof. All around me I heard the rain on the dead leaves and the cemetery was deep in maple and oak leaves.

"I watched a place last night," Tye said. His eyes were dark looking underneath like he hadn't had much sleep. "When I got there the light was on and I could see it through the curtains, so I lay there next to the door with my nose pressed up against the crack. I smelled macaroni and cheese."

I felt the hair lift on the back of my neck because I knew whose place he had watched.

"I wasn't thinking 'macaroni and cheese,'" he said. "But today I can remember the smell, and the smell of people inside, a man and two women."

He told me all the things we'd done, watched TV and stuff. I thought about how when I was doing my Spanish homework there he was, not five foot away, smelling me. I had a funny image of Tye lying there in the dark on the patio: a person, not a wolf. It was creepy.

He told me how the lights had gone out and how he had heard the television still on. My dad sat in the dark and watched TV.

Tye coughed. He had a cold.

I wanted to touch his arm, but I sat on the tombstone and felt the rain on my chilly hands. "I went to the next window," he said, "and I smelled that smell almost as familiar as my own."

I started to cry. I lifted my face to the November rain. Everything was spinning so fast, we were on the spinning earth whirling along. The cold rain was wet on my upturned face and Tye leaned over and kissed me and we fell out into the sky, like Laika, whirling away.

His lips were cold from the rain and so very soft.

"I'll hurt you, Brittany," he said. "I won't mean to. I'll follow your smell."

"No you won't," I said. I was crying so hard that the words came out all muddled. "You'd never hurt me!"

But he got up and walked out of the cemetery and down the mountain.

The next afternoon I went out to see Lacey and Tye never showed up. I went every day for a week and he still didn't show up. So I called his house—something we almost never did—and he came to the phone.

"Hey, Tye," I said, "it's Brittany."

"Hi," he said. The silence hung there. "I'm going to get a part-time job."

"You can't get a job," I said, "you're only fifteen."

"I can get a work permit for hardship because my mom's divorced, and there's this guy that's going to hire me to work in his bait shop. I won't be able to come up to see Lacey anymore."

"You can't," I whispered.

"Brit, I gotta go." And then he hung up.

I didn't see him for over a year after that but then he got a job at the Pick-n-Pay as a stockboy and I'd see him when I went in sometimes. He'd say hello to me and act friendly, but not really personal. More like polite. And by that time I was dating Kevin and I had a job at Dairy Queen so I didn't have a lot of time. I was saving money to move out, but the radiator and the water pump went out on the old Accord and we had to have a car so I had to fix it because my mom didn't have the money. Things just kept coming up.

It was Jack Pope who first told us the news. I was sitting at the kitchen table after school watching my tape of *General Hospital* and my mom was eating some of those fat-free cookies, even though I'd told her they didn't do her sugar any good, they had more sugar in them than the regular kind.

Jack doesn't drive and he and his wife live out on the mountain near the Pope-Ball cemetery, so he walks miles and miles, and when he comes by our house sometimes he stops in for a glass of water. I didn't think anything about it when he poked his head in. He said to my mom, "Betty, did you hear about Tye Petrie? He done killed himself."

Normally I wouldn't believe him. Jack doesn't lie but his two kids are in special education and they come by it honestly, so I'd have figured that he got something mixed up, but when he said it I just knew it.

My mom said, "Tye Petrie? Roger Petrie's oldest boy? You knew him, didn't you, Brit." And then she called to my dad, "Joe? Joe? Jack Pope's here and he says Roger Petrie's oldest boy killed himself!"

My dad was in the bedroom like usual, but he limped out into the kitchen even though he probably didn't know or care about Roger Petrie or Tye Petrie. He didn't say nothing, just stood there looking at Mom and Jack.

Mom asked Jack Pope what happened, but I didn't want to listen. There was a ring of water on the kitchen table where my glass of diet coke had been sitting and I drew lines across the ring with my finger, drawing out the water.

My dad was standing there in the kitchen, and my mom was talking to Jack Pope. I just sat there and died and no one noticed.

My mom's been having more and more trouble with her sugar, and now she has trouble seeing. The way she keeps eating I figure she's going to go blind and I don't know how my dad is going to take care of everything. Lacey died the year Tye did. Her hips got bad with hip dysplasia and she had to be put to sleep. I hadn't seen her since Tye stopped going to the cemetery. Sometimes, when I was remembering Tye and everything that had happened, I thought she was me.

Kevin, my boyfriend, has a job at a machine shop and he's talking about getting married. He wants a little land so we can raise a couple of beef cows, like his dad does. I don't know any reason not to get married and Kevin says a dog would be great. I'm going to have a bunch of dogs, German shepherds and huskies and stuff. I'm going to be a veterinarian assistant, but I can't yet because we need more money than that so I've got a cashier job at the Pick-n-Pay.

Sometimes we go down to Corbin to a bar down there that plays country and teaches line dancing, and we go out the interstate. Jack Pope told us they found his car parked on the interstate on one of the bridges. As we cross the bridges I find myself thinking. Could I do it? Is it hard? Did he have to work up the nerve?

They say when you jump there's no feeling of falling. Maybe he just leaned forward and fell into the smoky blue-green air.

Presence

Mila sits at her desk in Ohio and picks up the handle of the new disposable razor in . . . Shen Zhen, China? Juarez, Mexico? She can't remember where they're assembling the parts. She pans left and right and decides it must be Shen Zhen, because when she looks around there's no one else in camera range. There's a twelve-hour time-zone difference. It's eleven at night in China, so the only other activity is another production engineer doing telepresence work—waldos sorting through a bin of hinge joints two tables over in a pool of light. Factories are dim and dirty places, but cameras need light, so telepresence stations are islands in the darkness.

She lifts the dark blue plastic part in front of the CMM and waits for it to measure the cavity. She figures they're running about 20 percent out of spec, but they are so far behind on the razor product launch, they can't afford to have the vendor resupply, so tomorrow, underpaid Chinese employees in Shen Zhen raw materials will have to hand-inspect the parts, discard the bad ones, and send the rest to packaging.

Her phone rings.

She disengages the waldos and the visor. The display is her home number and she winces.

"Hello?" says her husband, Gus. "Hello, who is this?"

"It's Mila," she says. "It's Mila, honey."

"Mila?" he says. "That's what the Speed Dial said. Where are you?"

"I'm at work," she says.

"At P&G?" he says.

"No, honey, now I work for Gillette. You worked for Gillette, too."

"I did not," he says, suspicious. Gus has Alzheimer's. He is fifty-seven.

"Where's Cathy?" Mila asks.

"Cathy?" his voice lowers. "Is that her name? I was calling because she was here. What is she doing in our house?"

"She's there to help you," Mila says helplessly. Cathy is the new home health. She's been watching Gus during the day for almost three weeks now, but Gus still calls to ask who she is.

"She's black," Gus says. "Not that it matters. Is she from the neighborhood? Is she Dan's friend?" Dan is their son. He's twenty-five and living in Boulder.

"Are you hungry?" Mila asks. "Cathy can make you a sandwich. Do you want a sandwich?"

"I don't need help," Gus says. "Where's my car? Is it in the shop?"

"Yes," Mila says, seizing on the excuse.

"No it's not," he says. "You're lying to me. There's a woman here, some strange woman, and she's taken my car."

"No, baby," Mila says. "You want me to come home for lunch?" It's eleven, she could take an early lunch. Not that she really wants to go home if Gus is agitated.

Gus hangs up the phone.

Motherfucker. She grabs her purse.

Cathy is standing at the door, holding her elbows. Cathy is twenty-five and Gus is her first assignment from the home healthcare agency. Mila likes her, likes even her beautifully elaborate long, polished fingernails. "Mrs. Schuster? Mr. Schuster is gone. I was going to follow his minder but he took my locator. I'm sorry, it was in my purse and I never thought he'd take it out—"

"Oh, Jesus," Mila says. She runs upstairs and gets her minder from her bedside table. She flicks it on and it says that Gus is within three hundred meters. The indicator arrow says he's headed away from Glenwood, where all the traffic is, and down toward the dead end or even the pond.

"I'm so sorry, Mrs. Schuster," Cathy says.

"He's not far," Mila says. "It's not your fault. He's cunning."

They go down the front steps. Cathy is so young. So unhappy right now, still nervously hugging her elbows as if her ribs hurt. Her fingernails are pink with long sprays like rays from a sunrise on each nail. She trails along behind Mila, scuffing in her cute flats. She's an easy girl, usually unflustered. Mila had so hoped that Gus would like her.

Gus is around the corner toward the dead end. He's in the side yard of someone's house Mila doesn't know—thank God that nobody is ever home in the daytime except kids. He's squatting in a flower garden and he has his pants down; she can see his hairy thighs. She hopes he isn't shitting on his pants. Behind him, pale pink hollyhocks rise in spikes.

"Gus!" she calls.

He waves at her to go away.

"Gus," she says. Cathy is still trailing her. "Gus, what are you doing?"

"Can't a man go to the bathroom in peace?" he says, and he sounds so much like himself that if she weren't used to all the craziness, she might have burst into tears.

She doesn't cry. She doesn't care. That's when she decides it all has to stop. Because she just doesn't care.

"It is sometimes possible to cure Alzheimer's, it's just not possible to cure the person who has Alzheimer's," the treatment info explains. "We can fix the brain and replace the damaged neurons with new brain but we can't replace the memories that are gone." It's the way Alzheimer's has been all along, Mila thinks, a creeping insidious disease that takes away the person you knew and leaves this angry, disoriented stranger. The video goes on to explain how the treatment—which is nearly completely effective in only about 30 percent of cases, but which arrests the progress of the disease in 90 percent of the cases and provides some functional improvement in almost all cases—cannot fix the parts of the brain that have been destroyed.

Mila is a quality engineer. This is a place she is accustomed to, a place of percentages and estimations, of statements of certainty about large groups, and only guesses about particular individuals. She can translate it, "We can promise you everything, we just can't promise it will happen to Gus."

Gus is gone anyway, except in odd moments of habit.

When Gus was diagnosed they had talked about whether or not they should try this treatment. They had sat at the kitchen table, a couple of engineers, and looked at this carefully. Gus had said no. "In five years," he'd said, "there's a good chance the Alzheimer's will come back. So then we'll have spent all this money on a treatment that didn't do any good and where will you be then?"

In some people it reverses in five years. But they've only been doing it for seven years, so who knows?

Gus had diagrammed the benefits. At very best he would be cured. Most likely they would only have spent a lot of money to slow the disease down. "And even if I'm cured, the disease could come roaring back," he'd said. "I don't think I want to have this disease for a long time. I know I don't want to have it twice."

His hands are small for a man, which sounds dainty but isn't. His hands are perfect, the nails neat and smooth, but he hadn't been fussy. He'd been deft with a pencil, had been good at engineering drawings before they did them on computer, and his diagram of benefits and liabilities on a piece of computer paper had been neat. "Don't cry," he'd said.

Gus couldn't handle it when she cried. For the thirty years of their marriage, when she'd had to cry—which was always at night, at least in her memory—she'd gone downstairs after he'd gone to sleep and sat on the couch and cried. She would have liked him to comfort her, but in marriage you learn what other people's limits are. And you learn your own.

For the cost of her house, she can have them put an enzyme in Gus's brain that will scrub out the Alzheimic plaque that has replaced so much of his neural structure. And then they will put in undifferentiated cells and a medium called Transglycyn and that medium will contain a virus that tells the DNA within the cells to create neurons and grow him a new brain.

She calls Dan in Boulder.

"I thought you and Dad didn't want to do this," Dan says.

"I thought so, too," she says. "But I didn't know what it would be like."

Dan is silent. Digital silence. You can hear a pin drop silence. "Do you want me to come home?" he asks.

"No," she says. "No, you stay out there. You just started your job." Dan is a chef. He studied at the Culinary Institute of America, and spent a couple of years as a line chef in the Four Seasons in New York. Now Étienne Corot is opening a new restaurant in Boulder called, of course, Corot, and Dan has gotten a job as sous-chef. It's a promotion. The next step in making a name for himself, so that someday he can open his own restaurant.

"You need to keep your eye on Schuster's," she says. It's an old joke between them, that he's going to open a four-star restaurant called Schuster's. They both agree that Schuster's sounds like a Big Boy franchise.

"Artesia," he says.

"Is that it?" she asks.

"That's the latest name," he says. They have been trading names for the restaurant he will someday open since he started at the Culinary Institute. "You like it?"

"As long as I don't think about the cattle town in New Mexico."

"No shit," he says, and she can imagine him at the other end of the phone, ducking his head the way his dad does. Dan is an inch taller than Gus, with the same long legs and arms. Unfortunately, he got her father's hairline and already, at twenty-five, his bare temples make her tender and protective.

"I can fly out," he says.

"It's not like surgery," she says, suddenly irritated. She wants him to fly out, but there isn't any point in it. "And I'd get tired of us sitting there holding hands for the next three months while they eradicate the plaque, because as far as you and I will be able to tell, nothing will be happening."

"Okay," he says.

"Dan," she says. "I feel as if I'm spending your money."

"I don't care about the money. I don't like to talk about it that way, anyway," he says. "I just feel weird because Dad said not to do it."

"I know," she says. "But I don't feel as if this person is your dad anymore."

"It won't be Dad when it's done, will it?" Dan says.

"No," Mila says. "No, but at least maybe it will be a person who can take care of himself."

"Look, Mom," he says, his voice serious and grown-up. "You're there. You're dealing with it every day. You do what you have to do. Don't worry about me."

She feels tears well up in her eyes. "Okay, honey," she says. "Well, you've got stuff you need to do."

"Call me if you want me to come out," he says.

She wants him off the phone before she cries. "I will," she says.

"Love you, Mom," he says.

She knows he can tell she was crying.

"I'm not sick," Gus says.

"It's a checkup," Mila says.

Gus sits on the examining room table in his shorts and T-shirt. It used to be that she said the litany of what she loved when she saw him like this—his nose, his blue eyes made to look the distance, the hollow of his collar bone, his long legs. Show me your butt, she'd say, and he'd turn and shake it at her and they'd cackle like children.

"We've waited long enough," Gus says.

"It's not that long," Mila says, and at that moment the doctor knocks and opens the door. With him is a technician, a black woman, with a cart.

"Who are you?" Gus says.

"I'm Dr. Feingold." He is patient, is Dr. Feingold. He met with them for an hour yesterday and he talked with them for a few minutes this morning before Gus had his blood work. But Gus doesn't remember. Gus was worse than usual. They are in Atlanta for the procedure. Lexington, Kentucky, and Windsor, Ontario, both have clinics that do the procedures, but Dr. Feingold had worked with Raymond Miller, the Ph.D. who originated the treatment. So she picked Atlanta.

Gus is agitated. "You're not my doctor," he says.

Dr. Feingold says, "I'm a specialist, Mr. Schuster. I'm going to help you with your memory problems."

Gus looks at Mila.

"It's true," she says.

"You're trying to hurt me," Gus says. "In fact, you're going to kill me, aren't you?"

"No, honey," she says. "You're sick. You have Alzheimer's. I'm trying to help you."

"You've been poisoning me," Gus says. Is it because he's scared? Because everything is so strange?

"Do you want to get dressed?" Dr. Feingold says. "We can try this in an hour."

"I don't want to try anything," Gus says. He stands up. He's wearing white athletic socks and he has the skinny calves of an old man. The disease has made him much older than fifty-seven. In a way she is killing him. Gus will never come back and now she's going to replace him with a stranger.

"Take some time," Dr. Feingold says. Mila has never been to a doctor's office where the doctor wasn't scheduled to death. But then again, she's never paid $74,000 for a doctor's visit, which is what today's injection of brain-scrubbing Transglycyn will cost. Not really just the visit and the Transglycyn. They'll stay here two more days and Gus will be monitored.

"God damn," Gus says, sitting back down. "God damn you all."

"All right, Mr. Schuster," Dr. Feingold says.

The technician pushes the cart over and Dr. Feingold says, "I'm going to give you an injection, Mr. Schuster."

"God damn," Gus says again. Gus never much said *God damn* before.

The Transglycyn with the enzyme is supposed to be injected in the spine but Dr. Feingold takes a hypodermic and gives Gus a shot in the crook of his arm.

"You just lie there a moment," Dr. Feingold says.

Gus doesn't say anything.

"Isn't it supposed to be in his back?" Mila says.

"It is," Dr. Feingold says, "but right now I want to reduce his agitation. So I've given him something to calm him."

"You didn't say anything about that," she says.

"I don't want him to change his mind while we're giving him the enzyme. This will relax him and make him compliant."

"Compliant," she says. She's supposed to complain, they're drugging him and they didn't tell her they would. But she's pretty used to him not being compliant. Compliant sounds good. It sounds excellent. "Is it a tranquilizer?" she asks.

"It's a new drug," Dr. Feingold says. He is writing it down on Gus's chart. "Most tranquilizers can further agitate patients with Alzheimer's."

"I have Alzheimer's," Gus says. "It makes me agitated. But sometimes I know it."

"Yes, Mr. Schuster," Dr. Feingold says. "You do. This is Vicki. Vicki is someone who helps me with this all the time, and we're very good at doing it, but when we roll you on your side, I need you to lie very still, all right?"

Gus, who hated when doctors patronized him, says dopily, "All right." Gus, who during a colonoscopy, higher than a kite on Demerol, asked his doctor if they had gotten to the ileum, because even with his brain cradled in opiates, Gus just liked to know.

Vicki and Dr. Feingold roll Gus onto his side.

"Are you comfortable, Mr. Schuster?" Vicki asks. She has a down-home Atlanta accent.

Dr. Feingold goes out the door. He comes back in with two more people, both men, and they put a cushion behind Gus's knees so it's hard for him to roll over, and then another cushion at the back of his neck.

"Are you all right, Mr. Schuster?" Dr. Feingold asks. "Are you comfortable?"

"Okay," Gus says, fuzzy.

Vicki pulls his undershirt up and exposes his knobby backbone. Dr. Feingold marks a place with a black pen. He feels Gus's back like a blind woman, his face absent with concentration, and then he takes a needle and says, "There will be a prick, Mr. Schuster. This will make the skin on your back numb, okay?" He gives Gus another shot.

Gus says "Ow" solemnly.

And then Dr. Feingold and Vicki make some marks with the pen. Then there is another needle, and Dr. Feingold makes a careful injection in Gus's back. He leaves the needle in a moment, pulls the part of the hypodermic out that had medication in it, and Vicki takes it and gives him another one and he puts that in the hypodermic and injects it.

Mila isn't sure if that's more painkiller or the Transglycyn.

"Okay, Mr. Schuster," Dr. Feingold says. "We're done with the medicine. But you lie still for a few minutes."

"Is it like a spinal tap?" Mila asks. "Will he get a headache?"

Dr. Feingold shakes his head. "No, Mrs. Schuster, that's it. When he feels like sitting up, he can."

So now it is inside him. Soon it will start eating the plaque in his brain.

The places it will eat clean were not Gus anymore, anyway. It's not as if Gus is losing anything more. It bothers her, though, the Transglycyn goo moving along the silver-gray pathways of his neurons, dissolving the Swiss cheese damage of the disease. And then, what, there are gaps in his head? Fluid-filled gaps in his brain, the tissue porous as a sponge and poor Gus, shambling along, angry and desperate.

She wants to stroke his poor head. But he is quiet now, sedated, and maybe it's best to let him be.

The clinic is more like a hotel than a hospital, the bed has a floral bedspread and over it is a painting of cream and peach roses in a vase. After being sedated during the day, Gus is restless. He will not go to bed. If she goes to bed, he'll try to go out into the hall, but the door is locked from the inside so he can't get out. There's a touchpad next to the door and she's used 0815, Dan's birthday, as the code. She doesn't think Gus knows Dan's birthday anymore. A sign on the door says, IN CASE OF FIRE,

ALL DOORS WILL OPEN AUTOMATICALLY. Gus runs his fingers along the crack between the door and the wall. "I want to go out," he says, and she says that he can't. "I want to go out," he says, and she says, "We're not home, we have to stay here."

"I want to go out," he says, again and again, long after she stops answering him. He finally sits and watches five minutes of television but then he gets up and goes back to the door. "Let's go home," he says this time, and when she doesn't answer, he runs his long fingers like spiders up and down the edge of the door. He sits, he gets up and stands at the door for minutes, twenty, thirty minutes at a time, until she is blind with fatigue and her eyes burn with tears and she finally shrieks, "There's no way out!"

For a moment he looks at her, befuddled. The he turns back to the door and says querulously, "I want to go out."

At one point she goes to him and folds both his hands in hers and says, "We're both trapped." She is dizzy with fatigue but if she cries, he will just get worse. He looks at her and then goes back to searching the door, moth fingers fluttering. She turns out the light and he howls, "Oww-ow-oww-ow——" until she snaps the light back on.

Finally, she shoves past him and locks him in the room. She goes down to the lounge and sits on a couch, pulling her bare feet up and tucking them under her nightgown. The lounge is deserted. She thinks about sleeping here for a few hours. She feels vacant and exposed. She leans her head back and closes her eyes and there is the distant white noise of the ventilation system and the strange audible emptiness of a big room and she can feel her brain swooping instantly into a kind of nightmare where she is sliding into sleep thinking someone is sick and she needs to do something and when she jerks awake her whole body feels a flush of exhaustion.

She can't stay here. Is Gus howling in the room?

When she opens the door he is standing there, but she has the odd feeling he may not have noticed she was gone.

He finally lets her talk him into lying down around 3:15 in the morning but he is up again a little after six.

She asks the next day if it is the stuff they've injected, but of course, it's not. It's the strangeness. The strange room, the strange place, the Alzheimer's, the ruin of his brain.

The social worker suggests that until they are ready to insert the cellular material and stimulate neural growth, Gus should go to a nursing facility for elderly with dementia.

Even if she could afford it, Mila thinks she would have to say no. When they resculpt his brain, he will be a different person, but she will still be married to him, and she wants to stay with him and to be part of the whole process, so that maybe her new husband, the new Gus, will still be someone she loves. Or at least someone she can be married to.

Mila is lucky they can afford this. It is an experimental treatment, so insurance doesn't cover the cost. She and Gus have money put away for retirement from his parents and hers, but she can't touch that or capital gains taxes will go off, as her accountant says, like a time bomb. But they can sell their house.

The old house sells for $217,000. The first half of the treatment is about $74,000. The second half of the treatment is a little over $38,000. Physical therapy is expected to cost a little over $2,100 a month. Home health is $32,000 through an agency (insurance will no longer pay because this is an experimental treatment). That doesn't include airfare and a thousand incidentals. At least the house is paid off, and the tax man does some finagling and manages to save her $30,000 for a down payment on a little town house.

It has two floors, a postage stamp–sized backyard, and monthly maintenance fees of $223 a month. Her mortgage is $739 a month.

It has a living room and kitchen downstairs and two bedrooms upstairs. The carpet is a pale gray, and her living room furniture, which is all rich medieval reds and ochre and ivory, doesn't go well, but it doesn't look bad, either.

"Why is our couch here?" Gus asks plaintively. "When can we go home?"

One evening when he says he wants to go home she puts him in the car and starts driving. When Dan was a baby, when he wouldn't go to sleep, the sound of a car engine would soothe him, and this evening it seems to have the same effect on Gus. He settles happily into the passenger seat of their seven-year-old Honda sedan, and as she drives he strokes the armrest and croons. She's not sure at first if the crooning means he's agitated, but after a while she decides it's a happy sound.

"You like going for a ride?" she says to him.

He doesn't answer but he keeps on crooning, "ooo-ooo-ooo-ooo."

Another night she wakes up alone in the bed. Alzheimer's victims don't sleep much. Used to be that if Gus or Dan got up in the night she heard them, but she's pretty tired these days.

She finds him downstairs in the kitchen, taking the bowl of macaroni and cheese out of the refrigerator. It's covered in foil because she's out of plastic wrap. "Are you hungry?" she asks.

Gus says, "I can take care of it." His tone is ordinary and reassuring. He puts the bowl in the microwave.

"You can't put it in the microwave, honey," Mila says. "You have to take the foil off the top first." She hates that she only calls him *honey* when she is exasperated with him, and when she doesn't want to make him angry. It feels passive aggressive. Or something.

Gus closes the microwave door and pushes the time button.

"Gus," she says, "don't do that." She reaches past him and opens the microwave door, and he pushes her away.

"Gus," she says, "don't." She reaches for the door and he pushes her away again.

"Leave it alone," he says.

"You can't," she says. "It's got foil on it." Gus is an engineer, for God's sake. Or was.

She tries to stop him, puts her hand on his forearm, and he turns to face her, his face a grimace of anger, and he pulls his arm back and punches her in the face.

He is still a strong, tall man and the punch knocks her down.

She doesn't even know how to feel it. No one has punched her since she was maybe twelve, and that was a pretty ineffective punch, even if her nose did bleed. It stops her from thinking. She is lying on the kitchen floor. Gus pushes the START button on the microwave.

Mila touches her face. Her lip is cut; she can taste the blood. Her face hurts.

There is a flicker as the microwave arcs. She doesn't have it in her to get up and do anything about it. Gus frowns. Not at her, at the micro-wave.

Mila sits up and explores her face. One of her teeth feels wobbly to her tongue. Gus doesn't pay any attention. He's watching the microwave. He's intent. It's a parody of the engineer solving a problem.

The microwave starts arcing in earnest and Gus steps back.

Mila sits on the floor until the microwave starts smoking and only then does she get up. She doesn't even feel like crying, although her mouth and cheek hurt. She pushes CANCEL on the microwave and then pulls it out of the alcove and unplugs it. She leaves it half pulled out and goes over to the sink and spits bloody saliva. She rinses her mouth and then washes the sink out.

"Go on up to bed," she says.

Gus looks at her. Is he angry? She steps back, out of range. Now she is scared. He's not a child; he's a big man. Is he going to be upset with her because he's still hungry?

"I'll heat you up some soup," she says. "Okay?"

Gus looks away, his mouth a little open.

She grabs an oven mitt, opens the smoking microwave carefully, and takes out the macaroni and cheese. The ceramic bowl has cracked in half and the foil is blackened, but she holds it together until she can throw it out. Gus sits down. She takes the microwave outside on the grass. She doesn't think it's burning inside, but she isn't sure. She can't sit and watch it, not with Gus unsupervised. So if it starts to smolder, it starts to smolder. The grass is damp.

Back inside she finds Gus in the living room eating ice cream out of the carton with a serving spoon. There is ice cream on him and on the couch.

She's afraid to go near him, so she sits on a chair and watches him eat.

She cannot shake the feeling that the man in front of her should not be Gus, because the Gus she has been married to would not, would never, hit her. The Gus she was married to had certain characteristics that were inalienable to him—his neatness—almost fussiness. His meticulousness. His desperate need to be good, to be oh so good. But this is still Gus, too. Even as the ice cream drips on his legs and on the couch. What exactly is Gus? What defines Gusness? What is it she married? It is not just this familiar body. There is some of Gus inside, too. Something present that she can't put her finger on, maybe only habits of Gusness.

Later, when he goes up to bed, sticky with ice cream, she throws out the carton even though it is still half-full. Outside, the microwave sits inert and smelling faintly of hot appliance. She goes upstairs and goes to bed in the other bedroom.

She tries to think of what to do. The Transglycyn is eating out the plaque, but he won't start to get better until they replace the neurons and the neurons grow and they don't even go to Atlanta until next month. It will be three months after that before she begins to see any improvement.

The old bastard. Alzheimer's is the bastard.

She doesn't know what to do. She can't even afford a leave of absence at work. Saturday, she thinks, she'll hire a sitter and then she'll rent a hotel room and sleep for a few hours. That will help. She'll think better when she's not so tired.

At work, Mila's closest friend is Phyllis. Phyllis is also a quality engineer. More and more engineers in QA are women and Phyllis says that's why QA engineers make ten thousand a year less than design and production engineers. "It's like Human Resources," she says. "It's a girl-ghetto of engineering now." *Girl-ghetto* is a little ironic, coming from Phyllis who is five ft two inches, weighs close to two hundred pounds, and who has close-cut iron gray hair.

Phyllis comes by Mila's cubicle at midmorning and says, "So how's the old bastard." Phyllis knew Gus when he was still Gus.

"A real bastard," Mila says, and looks up away from the computer monitor, up at Phyllis, the side of her face all morning-glory purple.

"Oh my God!" Phyllis says, "What happened?"

"Gus decked me."

"Oh God," Phyllis says. In the cafeteria, sitting with a cup of coffee in front of her, she says dryly, "You really look quite amazing," which is a relief, because Phyllis's initial shock, her initial speechlessness was almost more than Mila could bear. If Phyllis can't joke about it . . .

She does not say, "You've got to put him in a home." The other thing Phyllis does say is, "Gus would be appalled."

"He would," Mila says, utterly grateful. "He would, wouldn't he."

They go to the Cleveland Clinic and Gus is anesthetized and some of his bone marrow is extracted. The frozen bone marrow is shipped to Atlanta so they can extract undifferentiated stem cells to inject in him to replace his own missing neurons.

After the anesthetic he is agitated for two days. His balance is off and his hip hurts where they extracted the bone marrow and he calls her a bitch.

Two weeks later they go to Atlanta and the procedure to inject the undifferentiated cells and virus trigger are almost identical to the first procedure. Gus swings at her twice more; once at the clinic in Atlanta and once back in the town house, but she's watching because she's afraid of him now, and she gets out of the way both times. She warns Iris, the new home health. (Cathy left because her boyfriend has a cousin in Tampa who can get him some sort of job.) Iris is in her thirties, heavy and not friendly. Not unfriendly. Iris says Gus never gets that way around her. Is she lying? Mila wonders. And then, why would she?

Is Iris saying that Gus likes Iris better than Mila? Mila always has the feeling that Iris thinks Mila should be home more. That Mila should be taking care of Gus herself.

Gus likes car rides, sometimes. They climb into her car.

"Where are we going?" he asks.

"To therapy," she says. He'll start to get agitated now, she thinks.

But he puts the window down and the trees go past, and he leans his head back and croons.

"Are you happy, Saxophone Man?" Mila says.

Everything is in stasis now—he grows no better but no worse until something happens with the cells they put in his brain. Three months until they see any difference, at the earliest. But now, one month after they injected new cells into his gap-ridden brain, they will do some tests to benchmark.

It all makes perfect sense. Too bad we never benchmark when we're healthy, she thinks. Maybe she should have herself benchmarked. Mila Schuster, cognitive function raw scores at age fifty-one. Then if dementia got her in its jaws, they could chart the whole cycle. Hell, benchmark the whole population, like they benchmark women with mammograms between the ages of forty-five and fifty.

Unless it has already started. She forgets things at work. She knows it is just because she is so worried about Alzheimer's. Senior moments, Allen, one of the home health used to call those times when you stand in the kitchen and can't remember what you came for.

If she got Alzheimer's, who would take care of her? She and Gus would end up in an institution, both in diapers and unaware of each other.

Gus croons.

"Saxophone Man," she says. There is something dear to her about the ruined Gus, even through all the fear and the anger and the dismay. This great ruin of a fine brain. This engineer who could so often put his finger on a problem and say, "There. That's it. The higher the strength of the plastic in the handle, the more brittle it is. You want to back off on the strength a bit and let the thing flex or it's going to shatter. Particularly if it sits in sunlight and the UV starts breaking down the plastic."

What a marvelous brain you had, she thinks. You'd say it and I'd see it, everybody would see it, obvious then. But everything is obvious once you see it.

The therapy is done at a place called Baobab Tree Rehab in a strip shopping mall. The anchor store in the mall is a Sears Hardware, which is Sears with just tools. Inside, Baobab Tree Rehab is like insurance companies and mortgage companies—there are ficus trees in pots in front of the windows, and rat's maze cubicles like there are in older office buildings. Once, years before, Gus was walking with Mila at work when suddenly he

crouched a bit so he was her height—she is five three—and said, it really
is a maze for you. That was the first time she realized he could see over the
tops of the cubicles, and so they didn't really work like walls for him.

Gus is looking over the cubicles now, too.

Their therapist is young. She comes out to meet them. "Mr.
Schuster, Mrs. Schuster, I'm Eileen."

Mila likes that she talks to Gus. Gus may or may not care, but Mila
figures it means that they think about things.

Eileen takes them back past the cubicles to a real room with a table
in it. There are shelves on the wall.

"Mrs. Schuster," she says, "I'd like you to sit in with us this first
time." Mila has not even thought about not sitting in, but now, suddenly
she longs to be allowed to leave. She could go for a walk. Go take a nap.
But Gus will probably get upset if she leaves him with a stranger.

And nearly everyone is a stranger.

Gus sits down at the table, bemused.

Eileen takes a puzzle with big wooden pieces off a shelf and says,
"Mr. Schuster? Do you like to do puzzles?"

Gus says, "No."

Did Gus like to do puzzles? Isn't engineering a kind of puzzle? Mila
can't remember Gus ever doing regular puzzles—but they were so busy.
Their life wasn't exactly conducive to sitting down and doing puzzles.
Gus built telescopes for a while. And then he built model rockets. He
made such beautiful rockets. He would sit in front of the television and
sand the rocket fins to get the perfect airfoil shape, sawdust falling into a
towel on his lap, and then he would glue them to the rocket body using
a slow-setting epoxy, and finally, when they were about set, he'd dip his
finger in rubbing alcohol and run it down the seam to make the fillet
smooth and perfect. He made beautiful rockets and then shot them off,
risking everything.

"Let's try a puzzle," Eileen says.

"Mila?" It is Gus on the phone.

"I'll get back to you," Mila tells Roger. Roger is the manufacturing
engineer on the project she's working on.

"Look," Roger says, "I just need a signature and I'll get out of your hair—"

"It's Gus," Mila says.

"Mila, honey," Roger says, "I'm sorry, but I've got four thousand parts in IQA." He wants her to sign off on allowing the parts to be used, even though they're not quite to spec, and she's pretty sure he's right that they can use them. But her job is to be sure.

"Mila," Gus says in her ear, "I think I've got bees in my head."

Roger knew Gus. And Roger is a short-sighted bastard who doesn't care about anything but four thousand pieces of ABS plastic pieces. Actually Roger is just doing his job. Roger is thorough.

"I promise it's okay," Roger says. "I assembled twenty of them, they worked fine."

Mila signs.

"Mila?" Gus says. "Can you hear me? I think I've got bees in my head."

"What do you mean, honey," she says.

"It itches in my head."

Gus isn't supposed to feel anything from the procedures. There aren't nerve endings in the brain, he can't be feeling anything. It's been four months since the second procedure.

"It itches in your head," Mila says.

"That's right," Gus says. "Can you come pick me up? I'm ready to go home now."

Gus is at home, of course, with Iris, the home health. But if Mila says that he's at home, Gus will get upset. "I'll be there in a while to pick you up. Let me talk to Iris."

"My head itches," Gus says. "Inside."

"Okay, honey," Mila says. "Let me talk to Iris."

Gus doesn't want to give the phone to Iris. He wants . . . something. He wants Mila to take care of this head-itching thing, or whatever it is that's going on. Mila doesn't know what Gus knows about the procedure. Maybe he's sort of pieced this together to get her to come and take him home. Maybe something strange is going on. It is an experimental procedure. Maybe this is just more weird Alzheimer's behavior. Maybe he has a headache and this is what he can say.

"It's bees," he says.

Finally he lets her talk to Iris.

"Does he have a temperature? Does anything seem wrong?" she asks Iris.

"No," says Iris. "He's real good today, Mrs. Schuster. I think that brain cells are growing back because he's really good these last couple of days."

"Do I need to come home?" Mila asks.

"No, ma'am. He just insisted on calling you. I don't know where the bees thing comes from, he didn't say that to me."

Maybe the tissue in his head is being rejected. It shouldn't be. The cells are naïve stem cells. They're from his own body. Maybe there was a mistake.

When she gets home he doesn't mention it.

Sitting across from him at the dinner table, she can't decide if he's better or not. Is he handling a fork better?

"Gus?" she says. "Do you want to look at some photographs after dinner?"

"Okay," he says.

She sits him down on the couch and pulls out a photo album. She just grabs one, but it turns out to be from when Dan was in first grade. "There's Dan," she says. "There's our son."

"Uh-huh," Gus says. His eyes wander across the page. He flips to the next page, not really looking.

So much is gone. If he does get smarter, she'll have to teach him his past again.

There is a picture of Dan sitting on a big pumpkin. There is someone, a stranger, off to one side, and there are rows of pumpkins, clearly for sale. Dan is sitting with his face upturned, smiling the over-big smile he used to make every time his picture was being taken. He looks as if he is about six.

Mila can't remember where they took the picture.

What was Dan that year for Halloween? She used to make his costumes. Was that the year he was the knight? And she made him a shield and it was too heavy to carry, so Gus ended up carrying it? No, because she made the shield in the garage in the house on Talladega Trail, and they didn't move there until Dan was eight. Dan had been disappointed in the shield, although she couldn't remember why. Something about the emblem. She couldn't even remember the emblem, just that the shield was red and white. She had spent hours making it. It had been a disaster, although he had used it for a couple of years afterwards, playing sword fight in the front yard.

How much memory did anybody have? And how much of it was even worth keeping?

"Who is that?" Gus asks, pointing.

"That's my mother," Mila says. "Do you remember my mother?"

"Sure," Gus says, which doesn't mean anything. Then he says, "Cards."

"Yeah," Mila says. "My mother played bridge."

"And poker," Gus says. "With Dan."

The magpie mind, she thinks. He can't remember where he lives but he can remember that my mother taught Dan to play poker.

"Who is that?" he asks.

"That's our neighbor on South Bend," Mila says. Thankfully, his name is written next to the photo. "Mike. That's Mike. He was a volunteer fireman, remember?"

Gus isn't even looking at the photos. He's looking at the room. "I think I'm ready to go home now," he says.

"Okay," she says. "We'll go home in a few minutes."

That satisfies him until he forgets and asks again.

Dan comes in the door with his suitcase. "It's nice, Mom," he says. "It's really nice. The way you talked I thought you were living in a project."

Mila laughs, so delighted to see him, so grateful. "I didn't say it was that bad."

"It's plain," he says, his voice high to mimic her, "it's just a box, but it's all right."

"Who's there?" Gus calls.

"It's me, Dad. It's Dan." His face tightens with . . . worry?

Nervousness, she decides.

"Dan?" his dad says.

"Hi, Dad," he says. "It's me, Dan. Your son." He is searching his father's face for recognition.

It is one of Gus's good days, and Mila has only a moment of fear before Gus says, "Dan. Visiting. Hello." And then in that astonishingly normal way he sometimes does, "How was your flight?"

Dan grins. "Great, Dad, it was great."

Is it the treatment that makes Gus remember? Or is it just one of those odd moments?

Dan is home for Christmas. It's his Christmas gift for her, he says, to give her a break. It's no break, because she's been cleaning and trying to buy presents off the net. Thank God for the net. She's bought Dan cookbooks and CDs, a beautiful set of German knives that he's always wanted but would never get because he never cooks at home. She's spent way too much money, but what would she buy Gus? She's bought Gus chocolates for a palate gone childlike. A couple of warm bright shirts. A puzzle.

"I can't believe you're here," she says, and she can feel her face stretched too wide.

"I'm here," he says. "Of course I'm here. Where else would I be? Lisa says hello."

Lisa is the new girlfriend. "You could have brought her," Mila says. Gus stands there, vacant and uninterested.

Dan says, "Dad, I've met a really nice girl." She's told Gus about Lisa, but mostly it's to hear her own chatter and because Gus seems soothed by chatter. Whether what the magpie left of his mind has noticed the name, she doesn't know.

"I didn't bring her," Dan says. "I thought I would be enough disruption."

Gus doesn't even appear to try to follow the conversation.

"I'll show you your room," Mila says. She's putting Dan in the guest room, which means she'll have to sleep with Gus. This week he has been going to sleep at ten or even earlier. And sleeping until early morning, say, five or six. That, she thinks, has to be the treatment.

❄

On Christmas Eve, Dan makes a fabulous feast. On Christmas Eve they used to eat roast beef, and then on Christmas Day they'd eat roast beef sandwiches all day, but in the last few years she's made just a normal meal for the two of them. Dan makes a Christmas roast and Yorkshire pudding. There are puréed chestnuts and roasted potatoes and a salad with pomegranate and champagne dressing. "For dessert," he says, "crème brûlée. I borrowed a torch from Corot's." He brandishes a little handheld torch like the ones in the Williams-Sonoma catalog. "This is going to be the best Christmas ever!" he cackles, which has been his joke for years, an ironic reference to all those Christmas television specials.

Gus does a puzzle. He has been doing them in therapy and the therapist (a different one from the first one, who is now on maternity leave) says that there are definite signs that the cells are grafting, filling in. Gus likes puzzles. She buys the ones for children eight to twelve. Cannonball Adderly is on the CD player. The tightness in her eases a bit. Christmas has never been a time for good things to happen, not in her experience. Too much at stake, she always supposed. All those expectations of the best Christmas ever.

But at this moment she is profoundly grateful.

"Do you need help?" she calls into the kitchen. Dan has told her she isn't allowed in on pain of death.

"No," Dan calls out.

The smell of beef drippings is overwhelming. She has been living on microwavable dinners and food picked up at the grocery where they have already cooked stuff to take home and eat and Chinese takeout.

"Why'd you get rid of the microwave?" Dan asks from the kitchen.

"It shorted out," Mila says.

Gus doesn't look up from his puzzle. Does he remember that evening at all? That was after his brain was scrubbed out, so it isn't something he would have lost. But did he ever have it? Does he know what he is living through, moment to moment, or is it like sand?

"Are you in there?" she whispers.

At six o'clock, there is more food than three people could ever eat in a month. Dan has sliced the beef and put beautifully finished slices on their plates. (Gus's is cut up, she notices, and her eyes fill with gratitude.) The beef is cooked beautifully, and sits in a brown sauce with a swirl of horseradish. There is a flower cut out of carrot sitting on bay leaves on her plate and on Dan's—Gus's has the flower, but no bay leaf to mistake for food. The salad glistens and the pomegranate berries are like garnets. There is wine in her glass and in Dan's—Gus's glass has juice.

"Oh, my," she breathes. It's a dinner for grown-ups in a place that has never seen anything but frozen lasagna and Chinese takeout. "Oh, Dan," she says. "It's so beautiful."

"It had better be," Dan says. "It's what I do for a living."

"Gus," she says. "Come eat Dan's dinner."

"I'm not hungry," Gus says.

"Come and sit with me while I eat, then."

Sometimes he comes and sometimes he doesn't. Tonight he comes and she guides him to his seat.

"It's Christmas Eve, Dad," Dan says. "It's roast beef for Christmas Eve dinner." She wants to tell him not to try so hard, to just let Gus make his own way, but he has worked so hard. Please, no trouble, she thinks.

"Roast beef?" Gus says. He takes his fork and takes a bite. "It's good," he says. She and Dan smile at each other.

Mila takes a bite. "Where did you get this meat?" she asks.

"Reider's Stop and Shop," Dan says.

"No you didn't," she says.

"Sure I did," Dan says. "You've just cooked so many years, you don't remember how it tastes when you've just been smelling. I got all my cooking talents from you, Mom."

Not true. He is his father over again, with the same deep thoughtfulness, the same meticulousness. It is always a puzzle, cooking. She cooked as a hobby. Dan cooks with the same deep obsessiveness that Gus brought to model rockets.

"I don't like that," Gus says.

"What?" Dan says.

"That." Gus points to the swirl of horseradish. "It's nasty."

"Horseradish?" Dan says. "You always liked horseradish."

Gus had made a fetish of horseradish. And wasabi and chilies and ginger. He liked licorice and kimchee and stilton cheese and everything else that tasted strongly.

"It's nasty," Gus says.

"I'll get you some without," Mila says, before Dan fights. Never contradict, she thinks at Dan. It's not important. "He's not used to strong tastes anymore," she says quickly to Dan, hoping Gus won't pay attention, that she won't have to explain.

"I'll get it," Dan says. "You sit."

Dan brings a plate. "What have you been eating, Dad?" he asks. "Cottage cheese? Mom, shouldn't he be getting tastes to, I don't know, stimulate him?"

Gus frowns.

"Don't," she says. It's hard enough without Dan making accusations.

Gus has retreated from all but the bland. He eats like a three-year-old might. Macaroni and cheese. Grilled cheese sandwiches. Tomato soup. Ice cream. And she's let him because it was easy. She thinks about telling him that Gus has hit her. That they have been getting through the days.

Maybe inviting Dan was a mistake. Gus needs routine, not disruption.

"How's that, Dad?" Dan says.

"Good," Gus says. Gus eats the roast beef without horseradish, the potatoes, the chestnut purée. He cleans out the ramekin of crème brûlée with his index finger while Dan sits, smiling and bemused.

And then, full, he goes upstairs and goes to bed in his clothes. After an hour she goes up and takes off his shoes and covers him up. He sleeps, childlike and serene, until almost seven on Christmas morning.

"I'm getting better," Gus announces after therapy one day in February.

"Yes," Mila says, "you are." He goes to therapy three times a week now, and does the kind of things they do with children who have sensory integration problems. Lots of touching and moving. Evenings after therapy he goes to bed early, worn out.

"I remember better," he says.

He does, too. He remembers, for instance, that the town house is where they live. He doesn't ask to go home, although he will say that he wishes they still lived in the other house. She thinks there is some small bit of recrimination in this announcement.

"Do you want to go out to eat?" she asks one evening. They haven't gone out to eat in, oh, years. She is out of the habit.

She decides on Applebee's, where the food is reassuringly bland. These days, Gus might be someone who had a stroke. He no longer looks vacant. There is someone there, although sometimes she feels as if the person there is a stranger.

After dinner at Applebee's she takes him to rent a DVD. He wanders among the racks of DVDs and stops in the area of the store where they still have videotapes. "We used to watch these," he says.

"We did," she says. "With Dan."

"Dan is my son," he says. Testing. Although as far as she can tell he's never forgotten who Dan is.

"Dan is your son," she agrees.

"But he's grown," Gus says.

"Yes," she says.

"Pick a movie for me," he says.

"How about a movie you used to like?" She picks out *Forbidden Planet.* They had the tape until she moved them to the town house. She got rid of all of Gus's old tapes when they moved because there wasn't enough room. He had all the *Star Wars* tapes including the lousy ones. He had all the *Star Trek* movies, and *2001, Blade Runner, Back to the Future* i and iii.

"This is one of your favorites," she says. "You made a model of the rocket."

When Dan was a kid he loved to hear about when he was a baby, and Gus is that way now about what he was like "before." He turns the DVD over and over in his hands.

At home he puts it in the player and sits in front of the screen. After a few minutes he frowns. "It's old," he says.

"It's in black-and-white," she says.

"It's dumb," he says. "I didn't like this."

She almost says, It was your favorite. They watched it when they were dating, sitting on the couch together. He had shown her all his science fiction movies. They'd watched them on television. But she doesn't, doesn't start a fight. When he gets angry he retreats back into Alzheimer's behavior, restless and pacing and then opaque.

She turns on the TV and runs the channels.

"Wait," he says, "go back."

She goes back until he tells her to stop. It's a police show, one of the kind everyone is watching now. It's shot three-camera live and to her it looks like a cross between *Cops* and the old sitcom *Barney Miller*. Part of the time it's sort of funny, like a sitcom, and part of the time it's full of swearing and idiots with too many tattoos and too few teeth.

"I don't like this," she says.

"I do," Gus says. And watches the whole show.

She lets the home health go.

Iris quit to go to another agency, Mila doesn't know why, and then they got William. Luckily by the time they got William it was okay if Gus was alone sometimes because William never got there before eight thirty and Mila had to leave for work before eight. William was an affable and inept twenty-something, but Gus seemed to like him. Because William was a man instead of a woman?

Gus says, "Thank you for putting up with me," and William smiles.

"I'm so glad you got better, Mr. Schuster," he says. "I never left before because a patient got better."

"You helped a lot," he says.

Gus can stay by himself. There's so much he doesn't know these days, among the strange things that he does. But he can follow directions. The latest therapist—they have had four in the ten months Gus has been going, and the latest is a patient young man named Chris—the latest therapist says that Gus has the capacity to be pretty much normal. It's just a matter of relearning. And he is relearning as if he were actually much younger than he is, because of those new neurons forming connections.

There is some concern about those new neurons. Children form more and more connections until they hit puberty, and then the brain seems to sort through the connections and weed out some and reinforce others, to make the brain efficient in other ways. Nobody knows what will happen with Gus. And of course, the cause of the Alzheimer's still lurks somewhere. Maybe in ten years he'll start to deteriorate again.

"I am so grateful to you," he says to Mila when William is gone. "You have been through so much for me."

"It's okay," she says. "You'd do the same for me." Although she doesn't know what Gus would do. She doesn't know if she likes this new Gus. This big child.

"I would do the same for you," he says.

"Are you sure you wouldn't stick me in some nursing home?" she says. "Only come visit me once a month?" She tries to make her tone broad, broad enough for anyone to see this comment as a joke.

But Gus doesn't. Teasing distresses him. "No," he says now, "I promise, Mila. I would look after you the way you looked after me."

"I know, honey," she says. "I was just joking."

He frowns.

"Come on," she says. "Let's look at your homework."

He is studying for his G.E.D. It's a goal he and the therapist came up with. Mila wanted to say that Gus not only had a degree in engineering, he was certified, but of course that was the old Gus.

He's studying the Civil War, and Mila checks his homework before he goes to his G.E.D. class.

"I think I want to go to college," he says.

"What do you want to study?" she asks. She almost says, "Engineering?" but the truth is he doesn't like math. Gus was never very good at arithmetic, but he was great at conceptual math—algebra, calculus, differential equations. But now he doesn't have enough patience for the drill in fractions and square roots.

"I don't know," he says. "Maybe I want to be a therapist. I think I want to help people."

Help me, she thinks. But then she squashes the thought. He is here, he is getting better. He is not squatting in the hollyhocks. She's not afraid of him anymore. And if she doesn't love him like a husband anymore, well, she still loves him.

"What was that boy's name?" Gus says, squinting down the street. He means the home health.

For a moment she can't think and her insides twist in fear. It has started happening recently; when she forgets, she feels this sudden overwhelming fear. Is it Alzheimer's?

"William," she says. "His name is William."

"He was a nice boy," Gus says.

"Yes," Mila says, her voice and face calm, but her heart beating too fast.

Eight-Legged Story

1. Naturalistic Narrative

Cheap pens. My marriage is not going to survive this. Not the pens—I bought the pens because no pen is safe when Mark is around; his backpack is a black hole for pens—so I bought this package of cheap pens, one of which doesn't work (although rather than throw it away, I stuck it back in the pen jar, which is stupid), and two of them don't click right when you try to make the point come out and then go back. It's good to have them, though, because I'm manning the phone. Tim, my husband, is out combing the Buckeye Trail in the National Park with volunteers, looking for my nine-year-old stepson, Mark. Mark has been missing for twenty-two hours. One minute he was with them, the next minute he wasn't. I am worried about Mark. I am sure that if he is dead, I will feel terrible. I wish I liked him better. I wish I'd let him take some of these pens. Not that Tim will ever find out that I told Mark he couldn't have any of these pens.

The phone rings. It's Mark's mother, Tina. "Hello?" she says, "hello, Amelia? Hello?" Her voice is thick with medication and tears. Tina is a manic-depressive and lives in Texas.

"Hi, Tina," I say. "No word yet."

"Oh God," Tina says.

Get off the line, I think. But I can't throw Mark's mother off the phone.

"Was he wearing his jacket?" she asks. She has asked that every time she's called. As if *she* ever noticed whether or not he had his jacket on. .

"He did," I say, soothing. "He's a smart kid."

"He could have just turned his ankle," she says. "They'll find him." I offered this scenario a couple of hours ago, but she's forgotten I suggested it, and she thinks she is comforting me. I allow myself to sound comforted. She says she'll call back in an hour. I'm convinced he is drowned. I can see it; the glimmer of his white hands and face in the metallic water. I can't say it to anyone.

What will happen to my marriage? When a child dies, divorce is pretty common. Two people locked in their grief, unable to connect. But I won't grieve like Tim, and some part of me will be relieved. I'm honest with myself about this. The secret in our marriage will slowly reveal itself. He will learn that I didn't love Mark, and how can you love someone who didn't love your only son?

When I married Tim, Mark was only six. He was the child of a dysfunctional marriage. He was prone to angry outbursts. He was resentful. All they had were plastic glasses, and I bought cheap glass tumblers, but Mark didn't like them. He wanted "their" glasses. I made the dinners, and I hated the lime green plastic cups. I wanted to sit at a nice table.

It was a classic stepfamily drama. It's in the books. I compromised. I used the ghastly plates from his mother, the ones with country geese on them, but insisted on the glass tumblers. It was our family table, I explained. A mix of old and new, like our family. Mark hated everything I cooked. I used the same canned sloppy joe mix that his father had always used, and Mark sat at the table, a blond boy who was small for his age, crying silently into his sandwich. He hated sloppy joes.

His father couldn't stand to hear him cry that he was hungry. I sat on the bed in the master bedroom. Maybe I should have given in. It was hard to decide. He was six years old, and he didn't have a bedtime, didn't dress himself for school in the morning. He lay on the floor crying while I put his socks on. I made his father put him in bed at nine each night. Before we'd married, Mark had terrible headaches, so terrible that his father had taken him to the hospital and they'd done CAT scans. After we got married and we started eating at a regular time and he had a bedtime, the headaches disappeared.

I should have given in on the green glasses. But why should I have had to eat at an ugly table, when he had taken all the joy out of the dinner anyway? When it was always a screaming battle? What was I supposed to do? When was it important that he have his own things, and when was it important that he not get his own way?

The phone doesn't ring. That's good, because when it does, it will be Tina.

When they say they have found his body, I will comfort Tim. I'll just comfort him with my hands. I'll just be there. Not talking. Just there. Like something out of *Jane Eyre*. Actually, I'll get impatient, because I finally have him to myself and yet Mark will have him. You can't compete with the dead. I always thought that if we were married long enough, eventually we would get that time that people without children get when they are first married. We'll be fifty-year-old newlyweds going out to see a movie on a whim and not worrying about child care.

I can't think about any of it.

This is the last moment of my marriage. Or maybe my marriage is already gone.

I have the sudden urge to get up and go out and get in my little beat-up eight-year-old Honda that I bought with my own money, and drive. I took the freeway to my first job, working in an amusement park for the summer when I was sixteen. I hated the job, and I hated to be home. I used to get on the freeway headed north and think that I could just keep going, up to Detroit, across to Windsor, Ontario and up to Quebec, where I would get a job at a fast food place and learn to speak French.

The doorbell rings. It's Annette, the neighbor down the street. I like Annette, although I have always suspected that she disapproved of Mark and, therefore, of Tim and me as parents. Annette has two daughters, and when we all moved onto the street her daughters were five and seven while Mark was eight. Mark and the boys next door run around in hunter camouflage playing war and spying in windows.

She sits and has a cup of tea. Annette is a working mother. Here in the suburbs there are working mothers and there are housewives and there is me. I'm an architectural landscaper, and I work out of my home.

"Funny that Tim is the one out wandering the wilderness," I say to Annette.

"Yeah?" Annette says.

"Well," I say, "Tim hates the outdoors, hates yard work, hates plants." Tim is an engineer. Computers are his landscapes.

She laughs a little for me. "You're holding up really well, you know that?" she says.

Of course I'm holding up well. If her daughter was out there, Annette would be devastated. If Tim had disappeared, I would be incoherent. I wish I was incoherent about Mark.

The phone rings. I pick it up, expecting to hear Tina saying, "Amelia?"

"Amelia?" says a man's voice.

"Yes?" I say, only realizing afterward that it's Tim.

"We found him," he says. "He's okay. A little bit of hypothermia and a little dehydrated. We're going into the clinic to have him checked. Can you meet me there?"

Tim sounds normal.

I start to cry when I hang up the phone, because I'm terrified.

2. Exposition

An eight-legged essay is a Chinese form. It consists of eight parts, each of which presents an example from an earlier classic. Together, the parts are seen as the argument. The conclusion is assumed to be apparent to the reader. It is implicit rather than explicit. It's not better or worse than argument and conclusion, it's different. It is more like a story. This is not an eight-legged essay. If it were, I would use examples from the classic literature. Once upon a time there was a girl named Cinderella. Once upon a time there was a girl named Snow White.

We enter into all major relationships with no real clue of where we are going: marriage, birth, friendship. We carry maps we believe are true:

our parents' relationship, what it says in the baby books, the landscape of our own childhood. These maps are approximate at best, dangerously misleading at worst. Dysfunctional families breed dysfunctional families. Abuse is handed down from generation to generation. That this is the stuff of 12-Step programs and talk shows doesn't make it any less true or any less profound.

The map of stepparenting is one of the worst, because it is based on a lie. The lie is that you will be mom or you will be dad. If you've got custody of the child, you're going to raise it. You'll be there, or you won't. Either I mother Mark and pack his lunches, go over his homework with him, drive him to and from Boy Scouts, and tell him to eat his carrots, or I'm neglecting him. After all, Mark needs to eat his carrots. He needs someone to take his homework seriously. He needs to be told to get his shoes on, it's time for the bus. He needs to be told not to say "shit" in front of his grandmother and his teachers.

But he already has a mother, and I'm not his mother, and I never will be. He knows it, I know it. Stepmothers don't represent good things for children. Mark could not have his father and mother back together without somehow getting me out of the picture. It meant that he would have to accept a stranger whom he didn't know and maybe wouldn't really like into his home. It meant he was nearly powerless.

That is the first evil thing I did.

The second evil thing that stepparents do is take part of a parent away. Imagine this, you're married, and your spouse suddenly decides to bring someone else into the household, without asking you. You're forced to accommodate. Your spouse pays attention to the Other, and while they are paying attention to the Other, they are not paying attention to you. Imagine the Other was able to make rules. In marriages it's called bigamy, and it's illegal.

At the hospital, the parking garage is a maze. I follow arrows to the stairs and down past the walkway to the front entrance, which is nearly inaccessible from the street. The walkway is planted with geraniums paid for by the hospital auxiliary, and the center of the front drive is an abstract statue surrounded by the ubiquitous mass of daylilies, Stella d'Oro. The building front is all angles, and the entrance is a revolving door. How do they get wheelchairs out a revolving door? But angled so that people like me won't see it right away is a huge sliding door for accessibility.

The elevators are nowhere near the receptionist. I am trying to decide how to compose my face. I can't manage joyous. Relieved? I am relieved, but I'm not, too. Mark doesn't handle stress very well, even by nine-year-old standards. Things are going to be difficult after this. We'll get calls from the teacher about his behavior at school. I pass a Wendy's (in a hospital? But then it seems like a pretty good idea) and the gift shop and turn left at the elevators.

Mark isn't in a hospital room; he's asleep in some sort of examining room in a curtained-off bed. Tim is sitting on the edge of the bed wearing his baseball cap that says "Roswell Institute for UFO Studies." I bought him that as a joke.

"He's okay," Tim whispers. "We can take him home whenever."

"Are you okay?" I ask.

"I'm okay," Tim says. "Are you okay?"

I say I'm fine, and we float becalmed in a sea of "okays."

We hug. Tim is six feet tall.

"I think in some ways you were more worried than I was," Tim says. "I know you care a lot for him. I think more than you know."

I smile a lie.

Mark is sleeping like a much younger child, abandoned to exhaustion. His mouth is open slightly, and he has one fist curled next to his cheek. Tim picks him up, and he stirs to rest on Tim's shoulder but doesn't wake.

We walk through the lobby; the happy family, the family that brushed disaster and escaped.

3. Fairy Tales—Beauty and the Beast

Before Mark gets lost, we are living in another town. We are both employed by the same firm. I am studying architectural landscaping. The firm that employs us is a large company that sells many different products: detergents and diapers and potato chips.

In March they call our division together and say that the company will be restructuring, but that they don't intend to lay anyone off. As we walk out of the cafeteria where the meeting has been, Tim says, "That means layoffs for sure." I laugh, and he starts calling headhunters.

They lay one hundred and fifty people off four months later. They ask some of us to stay during the transition and offer Tim and me positions as contractors with a rather lucrative bonus for staying until December 31.

Tim finds another job in September, and moves four hours away.

After Tim has gone, on Fridays Mark and I go out for pizza. Mark is seven. We go to a pizza place where the middle part of the restaurant is shaped like the leaning tower of Pisa except that it's only three stories tall. It's called Tower Pizza, and the pizza is mediocre but they have a special children's room where they play videos of Disney movies on a large screen TV.

It is snowing, so it must be November or so. The video is of *Beauty and the Beast.*

"This sucks," Mark says. "They always show this one. I hate this one."

"Do you want to sit in the regular part of the restaurant?" I ask.

"No," Mark says. "This is okay."

He wants a Mountain Dew because it has the most caffeine. "Caffeine is cool," he says. "When's Dad coming home?"

"Late tonight," I say. "First pizza, then we'll get a video, and you can take it home and watch it, and we'll wait for your dad."

"I wish Dad were here now," Mark says.

"So do I," I say. "How was school?"

"I hate school," Mark says.

"Did you have gym today?" I try to ask specific questions that will elicit a positive response. "How was school" is a tactical mistake, and I know it as soon as I've said it.

"Yeah," he says. "I'm not hungry."

If I take him home, he'll be hungry five minutes after we get in the car, and nothing I have at home will be what he wanted. What he really wants is his dad, of course. "Just have some pizza," I say. "You'll be hungry once you taste it."

He doesn't answer. He's watching the little broken teacup dance around. "Can I go over by the TV?" he asks.

"Sure," I say.

I read my book while he watches TV, and when the pizza comes I call him. Pepperoni pizza. I don't really like pepperoni pizza, but it's the only kind that Mark eats.

"How much do I have to eat?" he asks.

"Two pieces," I say.

He sighs theatrically.

After pizza we stop and get a Christmas movie about a character named Ernest. We had seen the first Ernest movie, the Ernest Halloween movie, and the movie that involved the giant cannon and the hidden treasure. Ernest is terminally stupid, and this is supposed to be funny. At least Ernest is an adult, and there aren't the usual clueless parents in this one.

"Will you watch it with me?" Mark asks.

"Okay," I say. I sit with him and read my book and wish I could go to bed. By Friday I'm so tired I can't think. Tim will get home about eleven. It's seven thirty. I have three and a half hours, and then he'll be in charge.

"Can I have some popcorn?" Mark asks.

"You just had pizza," I say.

"I'm hungry," his voice rises.

"No," I say. "If you were hungry, you should have eaten more pizza."

"I wasn't hungry then," he says, "but now I'm hungry."

"Why is food always a battle with you?" I say because I'm tired.

Mark starts to cry.

I slap the tape in the VCR and go upstairs. I sit on the bed. I think about going downstairs and saying I'm sorry. I think about smacking him.

The phone rings, and I run for it. It's Tim.

"Amelia?" he says.

"Where are you?" I say. He should be about halfway home.

"I'm not even out of town yet. My car broke down," he says. "I'm at a BP on Route 16. You remember the Big Boy where we had breakfast? It's right there. I had to stand on the highway for half an hour. It's snowing like a son of a bitch."

"Can they fix it?"

"Amelia," he says, exasperated, "it's almost eight, and there isn't a mechanic here. I have to call a tow truck and get it towed to a garage and then see. I can't get home tonight."

You left me. You left me here with your child. "Okay," I say. "Will you tell Mark?" Otherwise he will blame me. Seven-year-olds blame the messenger.

"Sure," he says, resigned.

"Mark?" I call. No answer, although I can hear Ernest on the TV. "Mark?" After a moment I say to Tim, "Hold on," and I go downstairs. Mark is sitting on the couch, deaf to the world. "Mark!" I say loudly.

He starts. "What!"

"Your dad is on the phone."

He jumps off the couch and runs for the kitchen phone calling, "Dadddyyyy!" It is artificial. It is the behavior of a child raised on sitcoms. It sets my teeth on edge.

I go back upstairs and hang up the extension.

Mark is sobbing when I come back downstairs. He hands me the phone and runs and throws himself face down on the couch.

"Amelia?" Tim says. He sounds tired. He is standing out in the cold; he doesn't know how much the car is going to cost him. I've been a shit, of course. "I'll call you tomorrow," he says.

"Okay," I say.

I go in and I rub Mark's back. After a while he turns his tear-stained face toward the TV and watches, and I go back to my book.

Saturday morning I sit on the steps while he tells me about the car. The phone cord is stretched from the kitchen to the foyer.

In a tiny, whining little girl voice, I say, "You have to come home." Mark is watching cartoons, and I don't want him to hear me crying. "You have to come home."

"I can't," he says. "The car won't be fixed until late today, if at all today."

"Can't you rent a car?"

He hasn't thought of that. "I don't know," he says.

"You have to come home," I say. I whisper. I can't think of anything else to say. Who am I? Who is this insipid woman whose voice is coming out of my mouth, begging, sobbing?

"I'll come home," he says. "I'll call you back."

When he comes home, I can't talk to him. I'm afraid that if I open my mouth, toads and beetles and worms will pour out, and I will say something. Something irrevocable.

Mark has been lying on the couch. At one point he was screaming because he said he wanted his daddy and he wanted him right now, but his father was only about halfway home. Well, only about halfway to our home. His daddy doesn't live here anymore. The house is up for sale. We will leave at the end of December.

I wanted to tell Mark that if it wasn't for me, his daddy wouldn't have come home this weekend at all. But I don't say anything. I close my mouth so that no ugly thing will come out.

I am good. I am trying hard to be good.

4. Correspondence

Dear Mr. and Mrs. Friehoff,

Mark is a bright child, fully capable of doing the assigned work. He is often a charming child. He has quite a sense of humor. However, he has poor impulse control, does not stay in his seat, talks out inappropriately in class, and hits other children when he is frustrated. His grades reflect his inability to control himself.

He has been referred for screening through the guidance office, however, I don't think that Mark suffers from hyperactivity or ADD. He is maturing emotionally and physically more slowly than he is intellectually. Children mature at different rates, and this isn't cause for alarm.

Please call me to set up an appointment. I'm best reached between 12:15 and 12:50 or after school . . .

5. Authorial Intrusion

It is important to note that this story is a story of particulars. Most step-children live with their mother, so the situation in this story is unusual, although not unique. There are three common reasons why a court will grant full custody to the father, and these are: 1) abandonment by the biological mother; 2) significant and documented mental instability in the mother; or 3) a history of substance abuse in the mother.

The greatest threat to stepchildren is the adult partner of the bio-logical parent. Boyfriends account for a large proportion of child abuse. I would cite the source on this, but I read it in *McCall's* or *Better Homes and Gardens* while I was waiting at the HMO to have my prescription filled, and I didn't feel right taking the magazine. Stepmothers account for a significant proportion of child abuse cases, too, I'm sure.

What isn't documented is the affect on the child of living with some-one who does not physically abuse or neglect them, who is apparently a decent, caring parent, who goes through all the forms of parenthood with-out ever really feeling what a parent feels. This is not abuse, it is just fate. If anyone is at fault, it is the adult, but how do you force something you don't feel? What is the duty of the adult? What is the duty of the child?

6. Choices

Tim calls home from work at four. Mark gets off the bus at three thirty. "Hi Sweetie," Tim says. "How is everything?"

"Okay," I say. "Mark got a two." Mark gets a note every day at school rating his behavior on a five-point scale from *poor* to *excellent!*. Two is one notch above *poor*. Call it *fair*.

"What did you say?" Tim asks.

"Just the usual. You know, 'What happened? Are you sure it's all Keith's fault? Did you have anything to do with it? Is there anything you could have done to keep it from happening?' That stuff."

Tim sighs on the other end of the phone. "What's he doing now?"

"He's supposed to be doing his homework," I say. "I think he's playing with the cat."

"Oh. Let me talk to him."

"Mark!" I call down the stairs. No answer. There never is. "Mark? Your dad's on the phone." I listen for a long moment. Just about the time I decide he hasn't heard me, Mark picks up and breathes, "Hello?"

I hang the phone up gently. I sit on the bed beside the upstairs phone and wonder what they are saying. I smooth the wrinkles out of the crimson bedspread. I want to tell Tim about the school open house, and if I don't tell him now, I'll forget to tell him tonight. I'd forgotten every evening all last week.

I pick up the phone, and Tim is saying, ". . . and don't upset Amelia."

"Okay," Mark breathes, as if this is a familiar litany.

"Tim?" I say.

"Amelia," he says. "Okay Mark, hang up."

"I wanted to tell you about the open house Thursday."

"Mark," Tim says, "hang up." I hear the strain in his voice.

"Okay." Mark hangs up with a clatter.

I chatter about the open house, about how I keep forgetting to tell him. Tim promises to be home in time. "I'll pick up Mark and then we'll get some fast food and go to the open house."

"I'll go with you," I say.

"If you want," Tim says. "You don't have to go."

"It's okay," I say.

"You really don't have to," Tim says. "He's my kid." Before he finishes, I hear someone say something in the background, his manager, probably irritated that Tim is spending time on personal phone calls. Tim cups his hand over the receiver and says something. "Gotta go," he says to me.

"Okay," I say. I stay on the phone after he has hung up, listening for a moment to the empty air.

7. Pillow Talk

At open houses you don't get to talk to the teachers. You just sit with a bunch of other parents, and the teacher tells you all what school is like.

In a month there will be parent-teacher conferences. Tim grimly writes down the dates for the conference in his organizer. I suspect it will be a familiar experience. "Mark is a very bright boy, but he has trouble staying in his seat. Did you know he cries very easily?"

Mark likes the novelty of having us at school. "Do you want to see the gym?" He leads us purposefully through the low-ceilinged halls. The hallways always seemed so big when I was a child. He takes us to the art room. He likes art. He has a papier-mâché fish on the wall. It is huge and blue and green, with an open mouth and a surprised expression. A big, glorious fish.

"It's great," I say. "It's really neat."

Mark is bouncing on his toes, not appearing to have heard me.

Tim says, "Mark! Stand still!"

I touch Tim's arm. "It's okay," I say. "He's not bothering anything."

That's who Mark is, and maybe we should ease up on him a bit. Asking him to be still is asking him to do something he's wired wrongly for.

I will try, I promise myself, to give Mark spaces where he can vibrate a little.

At home that night Tim, and I crawl into bed. We haven't made love in a month, and I don't suggest it now.

"Do you mind if I watch the weather?" Tim asks.

I turn on my side with my back to him and try to sleep. The news flickers when I close my eyes, like flames. Like . . . something. I don't know what. I want to cry.

"Do you ever feel pulled?" I ask.

"Is this a talk?" Tim says. It's a joke between us. He says the worst words a wife can utter are, "Oh Tim, we have to talk."

"Do you feel pulled between making me happy and making Mark happy?"

"Sometimes," he says.

"Are you afraid of me?" I ask.

"Afraid of you?" Tim says. He laughs.

"Not that way," I say. "I mean, afraid about how I'll act with Mark. Afraid I'll be mad at him or something."

Tim is silent for a moment. Finally he says, "I'm afraid you'll get so tired of my rotten kid you'll run away."

I am thinking that I cannot live like this. I cannot be the one that everyone fears. I am thinking that if I leave, Mark will have been abandoned again. I am thinking that I am coming to understand Mark, like tonight, at the school, in ways that Tim cannot. And Mark needs that.

I am thinking I am trapped.

Think of it like a prison sentence, I tell myself. In nine years, Mark will be eighteen and he'll be gone.

I despise myself.

8. Perspectives

We are meeting with a counselor, as a family. It's Tim's idea, based on the teacher's note about Mark possibly being an ADD child. It seems to me that ADD is a description of personality. The therapist is a woman named Karen Poletta. I like her; she's middle-aged and a little overweight. Professional with kids without being a kind of mother figure. I like her gray hair: straight, smooth, and shining. I like the way she looks right at me.

By the year 2010, there will be more stepfamilies than, than, what is the right word, natural families? Nuclear families? Normal families? It's a vaguely comforting thought. I can imagine an army of us, stepmothers, marching across the country. Not marching: creeping. I can't imagine us marching.

I am saying some of my concerns. "I don't trust myself," I am saying. "I don't trust my reactions." Tim is watching me. Karen Poletta is watching me. This is a session without Mark, who is at my mother's. I look at the bookshelf with the Legos and the puppets. Family counseling. I'm glad she hasn't had Mark do anything with puppets. "I don't know if I'm being too strict, if I'm just getting mad. I don't know if, for example, I'm letting him stay out too late in the evening because I don't want him around because it's quieter when he's not around. So I try to see what the other parents do, and do what they do."

Karen Poletta looks thoughtful. "How is that different from a biological parent?" she asks. "Particularly when you have a child like Mark, who is a difficult child. You're not the only parent of a difficult child who wants some relief. I think some of the things that you think are because you are a stepmother are stepmother issues, but some of them are just parent issues."

It's not, I think, it's not the same. I don't love him. I don't like him.

Karen Poletta is talking about how much better off Mark is with us than with his mother. That sometimes things aren't perfect, but they are good enough. That Mark has a safe and stable home.

But suddenly, I'm not sure. What if it is the same, some of it? Parent issues?

There's air in the room, and I realize I am taking deep breaths. Big, gulping breaths.

"But he needs a mother," I say, interrupting.

"And he doesn't have one," the therapist says. "But he has a father and a stepmother."

It is what we have.

The Beast

I was thirteen. It was spring, the barren time in March when you cannot be sure if it is really warmer, but you are so desperate for change that you tell yourself the mud at the edge of the sidewalk is different from winter mud and you are sure that the smell of wet soil has suddenly a bit of the scent of summer rains, of grass and drowned earthworms. And it has, because it is spring and inside the ground something is stirring. I was wearing a yellow linen dress which my mother had picked out and which I therefore disliked although I knew it flattered me. My shoes were white and I was concentrating on keeping them out of the mud. My father and I were going to mass—my mother did not go; she was Protestant. My father put his hand on top of my hair, his palm on my head, and I could feel the bone of my skull and my skin and his hot palm, so dry and strong. When I was a little girl, he did that often, and called me Muscles. He had not called me Muscles or put his hand on my head for a long time. I could not help arching my back a little, I wanted to push against his hand like a cat but the instinct that comes with being thirteen, the half-understood caution that makes a girl timid, or wild, the shyness told me to just walk. I wanted to feel the rough edge of the pocket of his coat against my cheek, but I was too tall. I wanted to be seven again, and safe. But I still wanted to push against his hand and put my hand in his pocket and steal the leather palmed glove, that secret animal.

Instead I went into the church, took a Bulletin, dipped my finger in Holy Water and genuflected. The inside of the church smelled like damp wood and furniture polish, not alive at all. My father took off his coat and draped it over the edge of the pew and when I came back from communion I stole his glove. The paper taste of the wafer was still in my mouth and I took a deep breath of the leather. It smelled like March.

We walked back through the school because it was drizzling, my father tall in his navy suit and my shoes going click on the linoleum. There were two classes of each grade, starting at the sixth and going down to the first. The hall ended in a T and we went left through the gym, walked underneath the bleachers and stood next to the side door, waiting for the rain to stop.

It was dark under the bleachers. My father was a young man, thirty-five, younger because he liked to be outside, to play softball on Saturday and to take my mother and me camping on vacation. He stood rocked back on his heels with his coat thrown over his shoulders and his hands in his pockets. I thought of bacon and eggs, toast with peach jam out of the jar. I was so hungry.

The space under the bleachers was secret and dark. There were things in the shadows; a metal pail, a mop, rags. Next to the door was a tall wrought-iron candle holder—the kind that stood at either end of the altar. There was no holder and the end was jagged. On the floor was a wrapper from a French Chew. They were sold at eighth-grade basketball games on Friday nights. The light from the door made the shadows under the bleachers darker, the long space stretched far away.

I heard the rain and the faint rustle of paper and smelled damp concrete. I did not go near my father but kept my hand in my pocket, feeling the soft leather glove.

There was a rustling on the concrete and the drizzle of soft rain. I wondered if anyone ever went back under the bleachers, if there were crickets or mice there. The rustling might have been mice. I wished the rain would stop. I wanted to go home. I made noises with my heels but they were too loud so I stopped. Something else clicked and I tried to see what it was but couldn't see anything. It wasn't as loud as my heels.

My father cleared his throat, looking out the door.

I imagined a man down there in the dark, an escaped convict or a madman.

It had nearly stopped raining. In fifteen minutes we would be home and my mother would fry eggs.

I heard a noise like paper. My father heard it, too, but he pretended not to, at least he didn't turn his head. And there was a heavier sound, a rasp, like a box pulled over concrete. I looked at my father but he didn't turn his head. I wished he would turn his head. There was a click again and the rustle, and I could not think of what it could be. I had no explanation for the particular combination of sounds. No doubt there was, some two things that happened to be making noises at the same time. Once in a fever I heard thousands of birds outside my window and I was terrified that they would fling themselves through the glass and attack me, but it was only the rain on the eaves.

Since then I had learned that the world was more regular than I had supposed; birds did not amass outside windows, preying mantises did not become tall, there was nothing under my bed except dust, and escaped lunatics did not crouch under the bleachers at the Catholic school. But I heard the sound of the box being dragged again. My father did not turn his head and I could not think of what it might be except suddenly there was a smell like wet dog.

The clicks sounded like a dog's toenails on concrete, then there was the rustle again and the dragging sound. Looking at my father I said, "Is it a dog?" and he finally turned his head.

And it was there. It was tall and had an absurdly small head, a bird's head with a beak hard and short like a sparrow's except the tip curved cruelly down. The feathers on its head were yellowed and it had gnats in a cloud around its golden eyes. It had a body like some big tan furry animal, fur thinning over its sharp hips, not like a horse, maybe like a lion, and feet scaled like a bird's. Except they were thicker and stronger, the cabled tendons darkening from gold to satiny gray and the feet ending in thick graphite claws. It was as tall as my father.

It stood there, one forepaw raised, and its black bird tongue moved as it panted. Its breath smelled like wet dog. I thought it would speak. I couldn't stand it if it spoke. I wondered if this was the end of the world, but I wasn't ready.

My father took a step back, the heel of his dress shoe scraped on the floor. The beast leaned its head towards us and turned it sideways, its tongue black and wet like a snail. My father grabbed the wrought iron candlestick. The beast reared up and it screamed like a girl, a strange terrible sound to come out of the beast's throat, and my father threw the heavy iron into its chest and the point went through it as if it were paper. The beast folded around it the way a wet sheet on a line will grab you if you run into it, and my father grabbed me. The beast's scream echoed in the gym.

I was pushed against my father's coat and he held my head and murmured, "Don't scream, it's okay. Sssh."

But I hadn't screamed. I had not made any sound at all. My father's coat wrapped around me and hid me and I was afraid to look out, afraid the world would be changed. I did not know any more, even though he had stopped it, if I could count on my father to be enough any more.

"The rain has stopped," my father said as if everything was normal and I looked around. There was no beast, only the wrought-iron candlestick thrown under the bleachers. Outside it was wet and smelled of spring. My father let go of me and adjusted his coat on his shoulders and I felt embarrassed.

I stepped outside, careful of my white patten shoes; the cars were all gone from the parking lot and the sign in front of the school said, "Easter Vacation; April 4-11, Drive Carefully." A wet sparrow sat in the bushes.

I looked back at my father, still in the darkness of the doorway. His face was strange, empty. His eyes were golden and where the pupils would be they reflected red, like a cat in the dark, but when he came outside he looked like himself.

I wanted to be home eating peach jam on toast, so I forgot. At home my mother was waiting. When she asked my father what had happened to his glove he didn't know.

And I did not say.

Nekropolis

ow I came to be jessed. Well, like most people who are jessed, I was sold. I was twenty-one, and I was sold three times in one day, one right after another. First to a dealer who looked at my teeth and in my ears and had me scanned for augmentation; then to a second dealer where I sat in the back office drinking tea and talking with a gap-toothed boy who was supposed to be sold to a restaurant owner as a clerk; and finally that afternoon to the restaurant owner. The restaurant owner couldn't really have wanted the boy anyway, since the position was for his wife's side of the house.

I have been with my present owner since I was twenty-one. That was pretty long ago, I am twenty-six now. I was a good student, I got good marks, so I was purchased to oversee cleaning and supplies. This is much better than if I were a pretty girl and had to rely on looks. Then I would be used up in a few years. I'm rather plain, with a square jaw and unexceptional hair.

I liked my owner, liked my work. But now I would like to go to him and ask him to sell me.

"Diyet," he would say, taking my hand in his fatherly way, "Aren't you happy here?"

"Mardin-salah," I would answer, my eyes demurely on my toes. "You are like a father and I have been only too happy with you." Which is true even beyond being jessed. I don't think I would mind being part of Mardin's household even if I were unbound. Mostly Mardin pays no attention to me, which is how I prefer things. I like my work and my room. I like being jessed. It makes things simpler.

All would be fine if it were not for the new one.

I have no problems with AI. I don't mind the cleaning machine, poor thing, and as head of the women's household, I work with the household intelligence all the time. I may have had a simple, rather conservative upbringing, but I have come to be pretty comfortable with AI. The Holy Injunction doesn't mean that all AI is abomination. But AI should not be biologically constructed. AI should not be made in the image of humanity.

It thinks of itself. It has a name. It has gender.

It thinks it is male. And it's head of the men's side of the house, so it thinks we should work together.

It looks human male, has curly black hair and soft honey-colored skin. It flirts, looking at me sideways out of black, vulnerable gazelle eyes. Smiling at me with a smile which is not in the slightest bit vulnerable. "Come on, Diyet," it says, "we work together. We should be friends. We're both young, we can help each other in our work."

I do not bother to answer.

It smiles wickedly (although I know it is not wicked, it is just something grown and programmed. Soulless. I am not so conservative that I condemn cloning, but it is not a clone. It is a biological construct.) "Diyet," it says, "you are so solemn. Tell me, is it because you are jessed?"

I do not know how much it knows, does it understand the process of jessing? "The Second Koran says that just as a jessed hawk is tamed, not tied, so shall the servant be bound by affection and duty, not chains."

"Does the Second Koran say it should not make you sad, Diyet?"

Can something not human blaspheme?

In the morning, Mardin calls me into his office. He offers me tea, translucent green and fragrant with flowers, which I sip, regarding my sandals and my pink toenails. He pages through my morning report, nodding, making pleased noises, occasionally slurping his tea. Afternoons and evenings, Mardin is at his restaurant. I have never been in it, but I understand that it is an exceptional place.

"What will you do this afternoon?" he asks.

It is my afternoon free. "My childhood friend, Kari, and I will go shopping, Mardin-salah."

"Ah," he says, smiling. "Spend a little extra silver," he says, "buy yourself earrings or something. I'll see the credit is available."

I murmur my thanks. He makes a show of paging through the report, and the sheets of paper whisper against each other.

"And what do you think of the harni, Akhmim? Is he working out?"

"I do not spend so much time with it, Mardin-salah. Its work is with the men's household."

"You are an old-fashioned girl, Diyet, that is good." Mardin-salah holds the report a little farther away, striking a very dignified pose in his reading. "Harni have social training, but no practice. The merchant recommended to me that I send it out to talk and meet people as much as possible."

I wriggle my toes. He has stopped referring to it as a person, which is good, but now he is going to try to send it with me. "I must meet my friend Kari at her home in the Nekropolis, Mardin-salah. Perhaps it is not a good place to take a harni." The Nekropolis is a conservative place.

Mardin-salah waves his hand airily. "Everything is in order, Diyet," he says, referring to the reports in front of him. "My wife has asked that you use a little more scent with the linens."

His wife thinks I am too cheap. Mardin-salah likes to think that he runs a frugal household. He does not, money hemorrhages from this house, silver pours from the walls and runs down the street into the pockets of everyone in this city. She wanted to buy *it*, I am certain. She is like that, she enjoys toys. Surrounds herself with things, projects still more things, until it is difficult to know what is in her quarters and what comes out of the walls. She probably saw it and had to have it, the way she had to have the little long-haired dog—nasty little thing that Fadina has to feed and bathe. Fadina is her body servant.

I hope Mardin will forget about the harni but he doesn't. There is no respite. I must take it with me.

It is waiting for me after lunch. I am wearing lavender and pale yellow, with long yellow ribbons tied around my wrists.

"Jessed, Diyet," it says. "You wouldn't have me along if you weren't."

Of course I am jessed. I always wear ribbons when I go out. "The Second Koran says ribbons are a symbol of devotion to the Most Holy, as well as an earthly master."

It runs its long fingers through its curly hair, shakes its head, and its golden earring dances. Artifice, the pretense of humanity. Although I guess even a harni's hair gets in its eyes. "Why would you choose to be jessed?" it asks.

"Jessing only heightens my natural tendencies," I say.

"Then why are you so sad?" it asks.

"I am not sad!" I snap.

"I am sorry," it says immediately. Blessedly, it is silent while we go down to the tube. I point which direction we are going and it nods and follows. I get a seat on the tube and it stands in front of me. It glances down at me. Smiles. I fancy it looks as if it feels pity for me. (Artifice. Does the cleaning machine feel sorry for anyone? Even itself? Does the household intelligence? The body chemistry of a harni may be based on humanity, but it is carefully calculated.)

It wears a white shirt. I study my toenails.

The tube lets us off at the edge of the Nekropolis, at the Moussin of the White Falcon. Mourners in white stand outside the Moussin, and I can faintly smell the incense on the hot air. The sun is blinding after the cool dark tube, and the Moussin and the mourners' robes are painful to look at. They are talking and laughing. Often, mourners haven't seen each other for years, family is spread all across the country.

The harni looks around, as curious as a child or a jackdaw. The Nekropolis is all white stone, the doorways open onto blackness.

I grew up in the Nekropolis. We didn't have running water, it was delivered every day in a big lorritank and people would go out and buy it by the *karn*, and we lived in three adjoining mausoleums instead of a flat, but other than that, it was a pretty normal childhood. I have a sister and two brothers. My mother sells paper funeral decorations, so the Nekropolis is a very good place for her to live, no long tube rides every day. The part we lived in was old. Next to my bed were the dates for the person buried behind the wall, 3673 to 3744. All of the family was dead hundreds of years ago, no one ever came to this death house to lay out paper flowers and birds. In fact, when I was four, we bought the rights to this place from an old woman whose family had lived here a long time before us.

Our house always smelled of cinnamon and the perfume my mother used on her paper flowers and birds. In the middle death-house, there were funeral arrangements everywhere, and when we ate we would clear a space on the floor and sit surrounded. When I was a little girl, I learned the different uses of papers; how my mother used translucent paper for carnations, stiff satiny brittle paper for roses, and strong paper with a grain like linen for arrogant falcons. As children, we all smelled of perfume, and when I stayed the night with my friend Kari, she would wrap her arms around my waist and whisper in my neck, "You smell so good."

I am not waiting for the harni. It has to follow, it has no credit for the tube ride. If it isn't paying attention and gets lost, it will have to walk home.

When I glance back a block and a half later, it is following me, its long curly hair wild about its shoulder, its face turned artlessly toward the sun. Does it enjoy the feeling of sunlight on skin? Probably, that is a basic biological pleasure. It must enjoy things like eating.

Kari comes out, running on light feet. "Diyet!" she calls. She still lives across from my mother but now she has a husband and a pretty two-year-old daughter, a chubby toddler with black hair and clear skin the color of amber. Tariam, the little girl, stands clinging to the doorway, her thumb in her mouth. Kari grabs my wrists and her bracelets jingle. "Come out of the heat!" She glances past me and says, "Who is this?"

The harni stands there, one hand on his hip, smiling.

Kari drops my wrists and pulls a little at her rose-colored veil. She smiles, thinking of course that I have brought a handsome young man with me.

"It is a harni," I say and laugh, shrill and nervous. "Mardin-salah asked me to bring him with me."

"A harni?" she asks, her voice doubtful.

I wave my hand. "You know, the mistress, always wanting toys. He is in charge of the men's household." "He," I say. I meant "it." "It is in charge." But I don't correct myself, not wanting to call attention to my error.

"I am called Akhmim," it says smoothly. "You are a friend of Diyet's?"

Its familiarity infuriates me. Here I am, standing on the street in front of my mother's house, and it is pretending to be a man, with no respect for my reputation. If it is a man, what am I doing escorting a strange man? And if people know it is a harni, that is as bad. In the Nekropolis, people do not even like AI like the cleaning machine.

"Kari," I say, "Let's go."

She looks at the harni a moment more, then goes back to her little girl, picks her up and carries her inside. Normally I would go inside, sit and talk with her mother, Ena. I would hold Tariam on my lap and wish I had a little girl with perfect tiny fingernails and such a clean, sweet milk smell. It would be cool and dark inside, the environment controlled, and we would eat honeysweets and drink tea. I would go across the street, see my mother and youngest brother, who is the only one at home now.

The harni stands in the street, looking at the ground. It seems uncomfortable. It does not look at me; at least it has the decency to make it appear we are not together.

Kari comes out, bracelets ringing. While we shop, she does not refer to the harni, but, as it follows us, she glances back at it often. I glance back and it flashes a white smile. It seems perfectly content to trail along, looking at the market stalls with their red canopies.

"Maybe we should let him walk with us," Kari says. "It seems rude to ignore him."

I laugh, full of nervousness. "It's not human."

"Does it have feelings?" Kari asks.

I shrug. "After a fashion. It is AI."

"It doesn't look like a machine," she says.

"It's not a machine," I say, irritated with her.

"How can it be AI if it is not a machine?" she presses.

"Because it's manufactured. A technician's creation. An artificial combination of genes, grown somewhere."

"Human genes?"

"Probably," I say. "Maybe some animal genes. Maybe some that they made up themselves, how would I know?" It is ruining my afternoon. "I wish it would offer to go home."

"Maybe he can't," Kari says. "If Mardin-salah told him to come, he would have to, wouldn't he?"

I don't really know anything about harni.

"It doesn't seem fair," Kari says. "Harni," she calls, "come here."

He tilts his head, all alert. "Yes, mistress?"

"Are harni prescripted for taste?" she inquires.

"What do you mean, the taste of food?" he asks. "I can taste, just as you do, although," he smiles. "I personally am not overly fond of cherries."

"No, no," Kari says. "Colors, clothing. Are you capable of helping make choices? About earrings for example?"

He comes to look at the choices, and selects a pair of gold and rose enamel teardrops and holds them up for her. "I think my taste is no better than that of the average person," he says, "but I like these."

She frowns, looks at him through her lashes. She has got me thinking of it as "him." And she is flirting with him! Kari! A married woman!

"What do you think, Diyet?" she asks. She takes the earrings, holds one beside her face. "They are pretty."

"I think they're gaudy."

She is hurt. In truth, they suit her.

She frowns at me. "I'll take them, "she says. The stallman names a price.

"No, no, no," says the harni, "you should not buy them, this man is a thief." He reaches to touch her, as if he would pull her away, and I hold my breath in shock—as if the thing should touch her!

But the stallman interrupts with a lower price. The harni bargains. He is a good bargainer, but he should be, he has no compassion, no concern for the stallkeeper. Charity is a human virtue. The Second Koran says, "A human in need becomes every man's child."

Interminable, this bargaining, but finally, the earrings are Kari's. "We should stop and have some tea," she says.

"I have a headache," I say, "I think I should go home."

"If Diyet is ill, we should go," the harni says.

Kari looks at me, looks away, guilty. She *should* feel guilt.

I come down the hall to access the Household AI and the harni is there. Apparently busy, but waiting for me. "I'll be finished in a minute and out of your way," it says. Beautiful fingers, wrist bones, beautiful face, and dark curling hair showing just where its shirt closes; it is constructed elegantly. Lean and long-legged, like a hound. When the technician constructed it, did he know how it would look when it was grown? Are they designed aesthetically?

It takes the report and steps aside, but does not go on with its work. I ignore it, doing my work as if it were not there, standing so it is behind me.

"Why don't you like me?" it finally asks.

I consider my answers. I could say it is a thing, not something to like or dislike, but that isn't true. I like my bed, my things. "Because of your arrogance," I say to the system.

A startled hiss of indrawn breath. "My . . . arrogance?" it asks.

"Your presumption." It is hard to keep my voice steady, every time I am around the harni I find myself hating the way I speak.

"I . . . I am sorry, Diyet," it whispers. "I have so little experience. I didn't realize I had insulted you."

I am tempted to turn around and look at it, but I do not. It does not really feel pain, I remind myself. It is a thing, it has no more feelings than a fish. Less.

"Please, tell me what I have done?"

"Your behavior. This conversation, here," I say. "You are always trying to make people think that you are human."

Silence. Is it considering? Or would it be better to say processing? "You blame me for being what I am," the harni says. It sighs. "I cannot help being what I am."

I wait for it to say more, but it doesn't. I turn around, but it is gone.

After that, every time it sees me, if it can it makes some excuse to avoid me. I do not know if I am grateful or not. I am very uncomfortable.

My tasks are not complicated; I see to the cleaning machine, and set it loose in the women's household when it will not inconvenience the mistress. I am jessed to Mardin, although I serve the mistress. I am glad I am not jessed to her; Fadina is, and she has to put up with a great deal. I am careful never to blame the mistress in front of her. Let her blame the stupid little dog for crapping on the rug. She knows that the mistress is unreasonable, but of course, emotionally, she is bound to affection and duty.

On Friday mornings, the mistress is usually in her rooms, preparing for her Sunday *bismek*. On Friday afternoons, she goes out to play the Tiles with her friends and gossip about husbands and wives who aren't there. I clean on Friday afternoons. I call the cleaning machine and it follows me down the hallway like a dog, snuffling along the baseboards for dust.

I open the door and smell attar of roses. The room is different, white marble floor veined with gold and amethyst, covered with purple rugs. Braziers and huge open windows looking out on a pillared walkway, beyond that vistas down to a lavender sea. It's the mistress' *bismek* setting. A young man is reading a letter on the walkway, a girl stands behind him, her face is tearstained.

Interactive fantasies. The characters are generated from lists of traits, they're projections controlled by whoever is game-mistress of the *bismek* and fleshed out by the household AI. Everyone else comes over and becomes characters in the setting. There are poisonings and love affairs. The mistress' setting is in ancient times and seems to be quite popular. Some of her friends have two or three identities in the game.

She usually turns it off when she goes out. The little cleaning machine stops. It can read the difference between reality and the projection, but she has ordered it never to enter the projection because she says the sight of the thing snuffling through walls damages her sense of the alternate reality. I reach behind the screen and turn the projection off so that I can clean. The scene disappears, even the usual projections, and there is the mistress' rooms and their bare walls. "Go ahead," I tell the machine and start for the mistress' rooms to pick up things for the laundry.

To my horror, the mistress steps out of her bedroom. Her hair is loose and long and disheveled, and she is dressed in a day robe, obviously not intending to go out. She sees me in the hall and stops in astonishment. Then her face darkens, her beautiful, heavy eyebrows folding toward her nose, and I instinctively start to back up. "Oh, Mistress," I say, "I am sorry, I didn't know you were in, I'm sorry, let me get the cleaning machine and leave, I'll just be out of here in a moment, I thought you had gone out to play the Tiles, I should have checked with Fadina, it is my fault, mistress—"

"Did you turn them off?" she demands. "You stupid girl, *did you turn Zarin and Nisea off?*"

I nod mutely.

"Oh Holy One," she says. "Ugly, incompetent girl! Are you completely lacking in sense? Did you think they would be there and I wouldn't be here? It's difficult enough to prepare without interference!"

"I'll turn it back on," I say.

"Don't touch anything!" she shrieks. "FADINA!" The mistress has a very popular *bismek* and Fadina is always explaining to me how difficult it is for the mistress to think up new and interesting scenarios for her friends' participation.

I keep backing up, hissing at the cleaning machine, while the mistress follows me down the hall shrieking "FADINA!" and because I am watching the mistress I back into Fadina coming in the door.

"Didn't you tell Diyet that I'd be in this afternoon?" the mistress says.

"Of course," Fadina says.

I am aghast. "You did not!" I say.

"I did, too," Fadina says. "You were at the access. I distinctly told you and you said you would clean later."

I start to defend myself and the mistress slaps me in the face. "Enough of you, girl," she says. And then the mistress makes me stand there and berates me, reaching out now and then to grab my hair and yank it painfully, because of course she believes Fadina when the girl is clearly lying to avoid punishment. I cannot believe that Fadina has done this to me; she is in terror of offending the mistress, but she has always been a good girl, and I am innocent. My cheek stings, and my head aches from having my hair yanked, but, worse, I am so angry and so, so humiliated.

Finally we are allowed to leave. I know I should give Fadina a piece of my mind, but I just want to escape. Out in the hall, Fadina grabs me so hard that her nails bite into the soft part under my arm. "I told you she was in an absolute frenzy about Saturday," she whispers. "I can't believe you did that! And now she'll be in a terrible mood all evening and I'm the one who will suffer for it!"

"Fadina," I protest.

"Don't you 'Fadina' me, Diyet! If I don't get a slap out of this, it will be the intervention of the Holy One!"

I have already gotten a slap, and it wasn't even my fault. I pull my arm away from Fadina and try to walk down the hall without losing my dignity. My face is hot and I am about to cry. Everything blurs in tears, so I duck into the linens and sit down on a hamper. I want to leave this place, I don't want to work for that old woman. I realize that my only friend in the world is Kari and now we are so far apart, and I feel so hurt and lonely that I just sob.

The door to the linens opens and I turn my back thinking, "Go away, whoever you are."

"Oh, excuse me," the harni says.

At least *it* will go away. But the thought that the only thing around is the harni makes me feel even lonelier. I cannot stop myself from sobbing.

"Diyet," it says hesitantly, "are you all right?"

I can't answer. I want it to go away, and I don't.

After a moment, it says from right behind me, "Diyet, are you ill?" I shake my head.

I can feel it standing there, perplexed, but I don't know what to do and I can't stop crying and I feel so foolish. I want my mother. Not that she would do anything other than remind me that the world is not fair. My mother believes in facing reality. Be strong, she always says. And that makes me cry harder.

After a minute, I hear the harni leave, and awash in self-pity, I even cry over that. My feelings of foolishness are beginning to outweigh my feelings of unhappiness, but perversely enough I realize that I am enjoying my cry. That it has been inside me, building stronger and stronger, and I didn't even know it.

Then someone comes in again, and I straighten my back again, and pretend to be checking towels. The only person it could be is Fadina.

It is the harni, with a box of tissues. He crouches beside me, his face full of concern. "Here," he says.

Embarrassed, I take one. If you didn't know, you would think he was a regular human. He even smells of clean man-scent. Like my brothers.

I blow my nose, wondering if harni ever cry. "Thank you," I say.

"I was afraid you were ill," he says.

I shake my head. "No, I am just angry."

"You cry when you are angry?" he asks.

"The mistress is upset at me and it's Fadina's fault, but I had to take the blame." That makes me start to cry again, but the harni is patient and he just crouches next to me in among the linens, holding the box of tissues. By the time I collect myself, there is a little crumpled pile of tissues and some have tumbled to the floor. I take two tissues and start folding them into a flower, like my mother makes.

"Why are you so nice to me when I am so mean to you?" I ask.

He shrugs. "Because you do not want to be mean to me," he says. "It makes you suffer. I am sorry that I make you so uncomfortable."

"But you can't help being what you are," I say. My eyes are probably red. Harni never cry, I am certain. They are too perfect. I keep my eyes on the flower.

"Neither can you," he says. "When Mardin-salah made you take me with you on your day off, you were not even free to be angry with him. I knew that was why you were angry with me." He has eyes like Fhassin, my brother (who had long eyelashes like a girl, just like the harni).

Thinking about Mardin-salah makes my head ache a little and I think of something else. I remember and cover my mouth in horror. "Oh no."

"What is it?" he asks.

"I think . . .I think Fadina *did* tell me that the mistress would be in, but I was, was thinking of something else, and I didn't pay attention." I was standing at the access, wondering if the harni was around, since that was where I was most likely to run into him.

"It is natural enough," he says, unnatural thing that he is. "If Fadina weren't jessed, she would probably be more understanding."

He is prescripted to be kind, I remind myself. I should not ascribe human motives to an AI. But I haven't been fair to him, and he is the only one in the whole household sitting here among the linens with a box of tissues. I fluff out the folds of the flower and put it among the linens. A white tissue flower, a funeral flower.

"Thank you . . . Akhmim." It is hard to say his name.

He smiles. "Do not be sad, Diyet."

I am careful and avoid the eye of the mistress as much as I can. Fadina is civil to me, but not friendly. She says hello to me, politely, and goes on with whatever she is doing.

It is Akhmim the harni, who stops me one evening and says, "The mistress wants us for *bismek* tomorrow." It's not the first time I've been asked to stand in, but usually it's Fadina who lets me know and tells me what I'm supposed to do. Lately, however, I have tried to be kind to Akhmim. He is easy to talk to, and like me he is alone in the household.

"What are we supposed to be?" I ask.

The harni flicks his long fingers dismissively. "Servants, of course. What's it like?"

"*Bismek?*" I shrug. "Play-acting."

"Like children's games?" he asks, looking doubtful.

"Well, yes and no. It's been going on couple of years now and there are hundreds of characters," I say. "The ladies all have roles, and you have to remember to call them by their character names and not their real names, and you have to pretend it's all real. All sorts of things happen; people get in trouble and they all figure out elaborate plots to get out of trouble and people get strange illnesses and everybody professes their undying affection. The mistress threw her best friend in prison for awhile, Fadina said that was very popular."

He looks at me for a moment, blinking his long eyelashes. "You are making fun of me, Diyet," he says, doubtful.

"No," I say laughing, "it is true." It is, too. "Akhmim, no one is ever really hurt or uncomfortable."

I think he cannot decide whether to believe me or not.

Saturday afternoon, I am dressed in a pagan-looking robe that leaves one shoulder bare. And makes me look ridiculous, I might add. I am probably a server. Projections are prettier than real people, but they aren't very good at handing out real food.

I am in the mistress' quarters early. The scent of some heavy, almost bitter incense is overwhelming. The cook is laying out real food, using our own service, but the table is too tall to sit at on the floor, and there are candles and brass bowls of dates to make it look antique. Without the projection, the elaborate table looks odd in the room, which is otherwise empty of furniture. Akhmim is helping, bringing in lounging chairs so that the guests can recline at the table. He is dressed in a white robe that comes to his knees and brown sandals that have elaborate crisscross ties, and, like me, his shoulder is bare. But the harni looks graceful. Maybe people really did wear clothes like this. I am embarrassed to be seen by a man with my shoulder and neck bare. Remember, I think, Akhmim is what he is, he is not really a man or he wouldn't be here. The mistress wouldn't have a man at *bismek*, not in her quarters. Everyone would be too uncomfortable, and Mardin-salah would never allow it.

Akhmim looks up, smiles at me, comes over. "Diyet," he says, "Fadina says that the mistress is in a terrible mood."

"She is always in a terrible mood when she is nervous," I say.

"*I'm* nervous."

"Akhmim!" I say, laughing, "don't worry."

"I don't understand any of this playing pretend," he wails softly, "I never had a childhood!"

I take his hand and squeeze it. If he were a man, I would not touch him. "You'll do fine. We don't have to do much anyway, just serve dinner. Surely you can manage that, probably better than I can."

He bites his lower lip, and I am suddenly so reminded of my brother Fhassin I could cry. But I just squeeze his hand again. I'm nervous, too, but not about serving dinner. I have avoided the mistress since the incident with the cleaning machine.

Fadina comes in and turns on the projection, and suddenly the white marble room glows around us, full of servants and musicians tuning up. I feel better, able to hide in the crowd. Akhmim glances around. "It's exciting," he says thoughtfully.

There are five guests. Fadina greets them at the door and takes them back to the wardrobe to change. Five middle-aged woman, come to pretend. I tell Akhmim their character names as they come in so that he knows what to call them.

The musicians start playing; projections, male and female, recline on projected couches. I know some of their names. Of course, they have projected servers and projected food. I wish I knew what the scenario was, usually Fadina tells me ahead of time, but she doesn't talk much to me these days. Pretty soon the mistress comes in with the real guests, and they all find the real couches, where they can talk to each other. First is bread and cheese, already on the table, and Akhmim has to pour wine, but I just stand there, next to a projected servant. Even this close, she seems real, exotic with her pale hair. I ask her what her name is and she whispers, "Miri." Fadina is standing next to the mistress' couch, she glares at me. I'm not supposed to make the household AI do extra work.

The first part of the meal is boring. The mistress' friends get up once in a while to whisper to each other or a projection, and projections do the same thing. There's some sort of intrigue going on, people look very tense and excited. Akhmim and I glance at each other and he smiles. While I am serving, I whisper to him, "Not so bad, is it?"

The two lovers I turned off are at this dinner, I guess they are important characters right now. The mistress' friends are always there, but the projections change so fast. The girl is apparently supposed to be the daughter of one of the mistress' friends. It will be something to do with the girl, I imagine.

Almost two hours into the dinner, the girl is arguing with her lover and stands up to leave—her eyes roll back in her head and she falls to the marble floor, thrashing. There is hysterical activity, projected characters rushing to the girl, the woman whose character is supposed to be the mother of the girl behaving with theatrical dignity in the circle of real women. The male lover is hysterical, kneeling and sobbing. It makes me uncomfortable, both the seizures and the reactions. I look for Akhmim, he is standing against the wall, holding a pitcher of wine, observing. He looks thoughtful. The girl's lover reaches onto the table and picks up her wine glass while everybody else watches him. The action is so highlighted that only an idiot would fail to realize that it's supposed to be important. The "mother" shrieks suddenly, "Stop him! It's poison!" And there is more hysterical activity, but they are too late. The lover drinks down the wine. The "mother" is "held back" by her friends, expeditious since the other characters are projections and she would look foolish trying to touch them.

I am embarrassed by the melodrama, by the way these women play with violence. I look back at Akhmim, but he's still observing. What does he think, I wonder.

There is a call for a physician, projections rush to and fro. There is a long, drawn-out death scene for the girl, followed by an equally long death for the lover. The women are openly sobbing, including Fadina. I clasp my hands together, squeeze them, look at the floor. Finally, everything is played out. They sit around the "dining room" and discuss the scenario and how masterful it was. The mistress looks drained but pleased. One by one the women pad back and change, then let themselves out until only the mistress and the "mother" are left.

"It was wonderful," she keeps telling the mistress.

"As good as when Hekmet was ill?" the mistress asks.

"Oh, yes. It was wonderful!" Finally they go back to change, Fadina following to help, and Akhmim and I can start clearing the dishes off the table.

"So what did you think," I ask, "was it what you expected?"

Akhmim makes a noncommittal gesture.

I stack plates and dump them on a tray. Akhmim boosts the tray, balancing it at his shoulder like a waiter. He is really much stronger than he looks. "You don't like it," he says finally.

I shake my head.

"Why not, because it's not real?"

"All this violence," I say. "Nobody would want to live this way. Nobody would want these things to happen to them." I am collecting wine glasses, colored transparent blue and rose like soap bubbles.

He stands looking at me, observing me the way he did the women, I think. What do we look like to harni? He is beautiful, the tray balanced effortlessly, the muscles of his bare arm and shoulder visible. He looks pagan enough in his white robe, with his perfect, timeless face. Even his long curly hair seems right.

I try to explain. "They entertain themselves with suffering."

"They're only projections," he says.

"But they seem real, the whole point is to forget they're projections, isn't it?" The glasses ring against each other as I collect them.

Softly he says, "They are bored women, what do they have in their lives?"

I want him to understand how I am different. "You can't tell me it doesn't affect the way they see people, look at the way the mistress treats Fadina!" Akhmim tries to interrupt me, but I want to finish what I am saying. "She wants excitement, even if it means watching death. Watching a seizure, that's not entertaining, not unless there's something wrong. It's decadent, what they do, it's . . . it's sinful! Death isn't entertainment."

"Diyet!" he says.

Then the mistress grabs my hair and yanks me around and all the glasses in my arms fall to the floor and shatter.

Sweet childhood. Adulthood is salty. Not that it's not rewarding, mind you, just different. The rewards of childhood are joy and pleasure, but the rewards of adulthood are strength. I am punished, but it is light punishment, not something that demands so much strength. The mistress beats me. She doesn't really hurt me much, it's noisy and frightening, and I cut my knee where I kneel in broken glass, but no serious damage. I am locked in my room and only allowed punishment food: bread, tea, and a little cheese, but I can have all the paper I want, and I fill my rooms with flowers. White paper roses, white iris with petals curling down to reveal their centers, snowy calla lilies like trumpets and poppies and tulips of luscious paper with nap like velvet. My walls are white, and the world is white, filled with white flowers.

"How about daisies," Akhmim asks. He comes to bring me my food and my paper.

"Too innocent," I say. "Daisies are only for children."

Fadina recommended to the mistress that Akhmim be my jailer. She thinks that I hate to have him near me, but I couldn't have asked for better company than the harni. He's never impatient, never comes to me asking for attention to his own problems. He wants to learn how to make flowers. I try to teach him but he can never learn to do anything but awkwardly copy my model. "You make them out of your own head," he says. His clever fingers stumble and crease the paper or turn it.

"My mother makes birds, too," I say.

"Can you make birds?" he asks.

I don't want to make birds, just flowers.

I think about the Nekropolis. Akhmim is doing his duties and mine, too, so he is busy during the day and mostly, I am alone. When I am not making flowers I sit and look out my window, watching the street, or I sleep. It is probably because I am not getting so much to eat, but I can sleep for hours. A week passes, then two. Sometimes I feel as if I have to get out of this room, but then I ask myself where I would want to go and I realize that it doesn't make any difference. This room, the outside, they are all the same place, except that this room is safe.

The place I want to go is the Nekropolis, the one in my mind, but it's gone. I was the eldest, then my sister, Larit, then my brother, Fhassin, and then the baby boy, Michim. In families of four, underneath the fighting, there is always pairing, two and two. Fhassin and I were a pair. My brother. I think a lot about Fhassin and about the Nekropolis, locked in my room.

I sleep, eat my little breakfast that Akhmim brings me, sleep again. Then I sit at the window or make flowers, sleep again. The only time that is bad is late afternoon, early evening, when I have slept so much that I can't sleep any more and my stomach is growling and growling. I feel fretful and teary. When Akhmim comes in the evening with dinner he bruises my senses until I get accustomed to his being there; his voice has so many shades, his skin is so much more supple, so much more oiled and textured than paper, that he overwhelms me.

Sometimes he sits with his arms around my shoulders and I lean against him. I pretend intimacy doesn't matter because he is only a harni, but I know that I am lying to myself. How could I ever have thought him safe because he was made rather than born? I understood from the first that he wasn't to be trusted, but actually it was I that couldn't be trusted.

He is curious about my childhood, he says he never was a child. To keep him close to me I tell him everything I can remember about growing up, all the children's games, teach him the songs we skipped rope to, the rhymes we used to pick who was it, everybody with their fists in the center, tapping a fist on every stress as we chanted:

ONCE my SIS-ter HAD a HOUSE,
THEN she LEFT it TO a MOUSE,
SING a SONG,
TELL a LIE,
KISS my SIS-ter,
SAY good-BYE.

"What does it mean?" he asks, laughing.

"It doesn't mean anything," I explain, "it's a way of picking who is it. Who is the fox, or who holds the broom while everybody hides." I tell him about fox and hounds, about how my brother Fhassin was a daredevil and one time to get away he climbed to the roof of Kari's grandmother's house and ran along the roofs and how our mother punished him. And of how we got in a fight and I pushed him and he fell and broke his collarbone.

"What does Kari do?" he asks.

"Kari is married," I say. "Her husband works, he directs lorritanks, like the one that delivers water."

"Did you ever have a boyfriend?" he asks.

"I did, his name was Zard."

"Why didn't you marry?" He is so innocent.

"It didn't work," I say.

"Is that why you became jessed?"

"No," I say.

He is patient, he waits.

"No," I say again. "It was because of Shusilina."

And then I have to explain.

Shusilina moved into the death house across the street, where Kari's grandfather had lived until he died. Kari's grandfather had been a soldier when he was young, and to be brave for the Holy he had a Serinitin implant, so that when he was old he didn't remember who he was anymore. And when he died, Shusilina and her husband moved in. Shusilina had white hair and had had her ears pointed and she wanted a baby. I was only twenty, and trying to decide whether I should marry Zard. He had not asked me, but I thought he might, and I wasn't sure what I should answer. Shusilina was younger than me, nineteen, but she wanted a baby, and that seemed terribly adult. And she had come from outside the Nekropolis, and had pointed ears, and everybody thought she was just a little too good for herself.

We talked about Zard, and she told me that after marriage everything was not milk and honey. She was very vague on just what she meant by that, but I should know that it was not like it seemed now, when I was in love with Zard, I should give myself over to him, but I should hold some part of myself private, for myself, and not let marriage swallow me.

Now I realize that she was a young bride trying to learn the difference between romance and life, and the conversations are so obvious and adolescent, but then it seemed so adult to talk about marriage this way.

It was like something sacred, and I was being initiated into mysteries. I dyed my hair white.

My sister hated her. Michim made eyes at her all the time but he was only thirteen. Fhassin was seventeen and he laughed at Michim. Fhassin laughed at all sorts of things. He looked at the world from under his long eyelashes, so in contrast with his sharp-chinned face and monkey grin. That was the year Fhassin, who had always been shorter than everybody, almost shorter than Michim, suddenly grew so tall. He was visited by giggling girls, but he never took any of them seriously.

It was all outside, not inside the family. In the evenings we sat on the floor in the middle of our three death houses and made paper flowers. We lived in a house filled with perfume. I was twenty, Larit was nineteen, but nobody had left my mother's house, and we never thought that was strange. But it was, the way we were held there.

So when did Fhassin stop seeing her as silly and begin to see Shusilina as a person? I didn't suspect it. The giggling girls still came by the house, and Fhassin still grinned and didn't really pay much attention. They were careful, meeting in the afternoon when her husband was building new death-houses at the other end of the Nekropolis and the rest of us were sleeping. I think Fhassin did it because he was always a daredevil, like walking on the roofs of the death-houses, or the time he took money out of our mother's money pot so he could sneak out and ride the Tube. He was lost in the city for hours, finally sneaking back onto the Tube and risking getting caught as a free-farer.

No, that isn't true. The truth must be that he fell in love with her. I had never been in love with Zard, maybe I have never been in love with anyone. How could I understand? I couldn't stand the thought of leaving the family to marry Zard, how could *he* turn his back on the family for Shusilina? But some alchemy must have transformed him, made him see her as something other than a vain and silly girl—yes, it's a cliché to call her a vain and silly girl, but that's what she was. She was married, and it wasn't very exciting anymore, not nearly as interesting as when her husband was courting her. Fhassin made her feel important, look at the risk he was taking, for her. For her!

But what was going on in Fhassin? Fhassin despised romantic love, sentimentality.

Her husband suspected, laid in wait and caught them, the neighborhood poured out into the street to see my brother, shirtless, protecting Shusilina whose hair was all unbound around her shoulders. Fhassin had a razor, and was holding off her screaming husband. The heat poured all over his brown, adolescent shoulders and chest. We stood in the streets, sweating. And Fhassin was laughing, deadly serious, but laughing. He was so alive. Was it the intensity? Was that the lure for Fhassin? This was my brother, who I had known all my life, and he was a stranger.

I realized that the Nekropolis was a foreign place, and I didn't know anyone behind the skinmask of their face.

They took my brother and Shusilina, divorced her from her husband for the adultery trial, and flogged them both, then dumped them in prison for seven years. I did not wait for Zard to ask me to marry him—not that he would have, now. I let my hair go black. I became a dutiful daughter. When I was twenty-one, I was jessed, impressed to feel duty and affection for whoever would pay the fee of my impression.

Akhmim doesn't understand. He has to go. I cry when he's gone.

Finally, after twenty-eight days, I emerge from my room, white and trembling like Iqurth from the tomb, to face the world and my duties. I don't know what the mistress has told Mardin, but I am subjected to a vague lecture I'm sure Mardin thinks of as fatherly. Fadina avoids meeting my eyes when she sees me. The girl who works with the cook watches the floor. I move like a ghost through the women's quarters. Only the mistress sees me, fastens her eyes on me when I happen to pass her, and her look is cruel. If I hear her, I take to stepping out of the hall if I can.

Friday afternoon, she is playing the Tiles, and I take the cleaning machine to her room. I have checked with Fadina to confirm that she is not in, but I cannot convince myself that she has left. Perhaps Fadina has forgotten, perhaps the mistress has not told her. I creep in and stand listening. The usual projection is on—not *bismek* but the everyday clutter of silks and fragile tables with silver lace frames, antique lamps, paisley scarves and cobalt pottery. The cleaning machine will not go in. I stop and listen, no sound but the breeze through the window hangings. I creep through the quarters, shaking. The bed is unmade, a tumble of blue and silver brocade. That's unusual, Fadina always makes it. I think about making it, but I decide I had better not, do what I always do or the mistress will be on me. Best do only what is safe. I pick up the clothes off the floor and creep back and turn off the projection. The machine starts.

If she comes back early what will I do? I stand by the projection switch, unwilling to leave even to put the clothing in the laundry. If she comes back, when I hear her, I will snap on the projection machine. The cleaning machine will stop and I will take it and leave. It is the best I can do.

The cleaning machine snuffles around, getting dust from the windowsills and table tops, cleaning the floor. It is so slow. I keep thinking I hear her and snapping on the projection. The machine stops and I listen, but I don't hear anything so I snap the projection off and the cleaning machine starts again. Finally the rooms are done, and the cleaning machine and I make our escape. I have used extra scent on the sheets in the linen closet, the way she likes them, and I have put extra oil in the rings on the lights, and extra scent in the air freshener. It is all a waste, all that money, but that's what she likes.

I have a terrible headache. I go to my room and wait and try to sleep until the headache is gone. I am asleep when Fadina bangs on my door and I feel groggy and disheveled.

"The mistress wants you," she snaps, glaring at me.

I can't go.

I can't *not* go. I follow her without doing up my hair or putting on my sandals.

The mistress is sitting in her bedroom, still dressed up in saffron and veils. I imagine she has just gotten back. "Diyet," she says, "did you clean my room?"

What did I disturb? I didn't do anything to this room except pick up the laundry and run the cleaning machine; is something missing? "Yes, mistress," I say. Oh, my heart.

"Look at this room," she hisses.

I look, not knowing what I am looking for.

"Look at the bed!"

The bed looks just the same as it did when I came in, blankets and sheets tumbled, shining blue and silver, the scent of her perfume in the cool air.

"Come here," the mistress commands, "kneel down." I kneel down so that I am not taller than she is. She looks at me for a moment, so angry that she does not seem able to speak. Then I see it coming but I can't do anything, up comes her hand and she slaps me. I topple sideways, mostly from surprise. "Are you too stupid to even know to make a bed?"

"Fadina always makes your bed," I say. I should have made it, I should have. Holy One, I am such an idiot.

"So the one time Fadina doesn't do your work you are too lazy to do it yourself?"

"Mistress," I say, "I was afraid to—"

"You *should* be afraid!" she shouts. She slaps me, both sides of my face, and shouts at me, her face close to mine. On and on. I don't listen, it's just sound. Fadina walks me to the door. I am holding my head up, trying to maintain some dignity. "Diyet," Fadina whispers.

"What?" I say, thinking maybe she has realized that it's the mistress, that it's not my fault.

But she just shakes her head. "Try not to upset her, that's all. Just don't upset her." Her face is pleading, she wants me to understand.

Understand what? That she is jessed? As Akhmim says, we are only what we are.

But I understand what it is going to be like now. The mistress hates me, and there's nothing I can do. The only way to escape is to ask Mardin to sell me off, but then I would have to leave Akhmim. And since he's a harni he can't even ride the tube without someone providing credit. If I leave, I'll never see him again.

The room is full of whispers. The window is open and the breeze rustles among the paper flowers. There are flowers everywhere, on the dresser, the chairs. Akhmim and I sit in the dark room, lit only by the light from the street. He is sitting with one leg underneath him. Like some animal, a panther, indolent.

"You'll still be young when I am old," I say.

"No," he says. That is all, just the one word.

"Do you get old?"

"If we live out our natural span. About sixty, sixty-five years."

"Do you get wrinkles? White hair?"

"Some. Our joints get bad, swell, like arthritis. Things go wrong." He is so quiet tonight. Usually he is cheerful.

"You are so patient," I say.

He makes a gesture with his hands. "It does not matter."

"Is it hard for you to be patient?"

"Sometimes," he says. "I feel frustration, anger, fear. But we are bred to be patient."

"What's wrong?" I ask. I sound like a little girl, my voice all breathy.

"I am thinking. You should leave here."

The mistress is always finding something. Nothing I do is right. She pulls my hair, confines me to my room. "I can't," I say. "I am jessed."

He is so still in the twilight.

"Akhmim," I say, suddenly cruel. "Do you want me to go?"

"Harni are not supposed to have 'wants,'" he says, his voice flat. I have never heard him say the word "harni." It sounds obscene. It makes me get up, his voice. It fills me with nervousness, with aimless energy. If he is despairing, what is there for me? I touch all the furniture, and take an armload of flowers, crisp and cool, and I drop them in his lap. "What?" he says. I take more flowers and throw them over his shoulders. His face is turned up at me, lit by the light from the street, full of won-der. I gather flowers off the chair, drop them on him. There are flowers all over the bed, funeral flowers. He reaches up, flowers spilling off his sleeves, and takes my arms to make me stop, saying, "Diyet, what?" I lean forward and close my eyes.

I wait, hearing the breeze rustle the lilies, the poppies, the roses on the bed. I wait forever. Until he finally kisses me.

He won't do any more than kiss me. Lying among all the crushed flowers he will stroke my face, my hair, he will kiss me, but that is all. "You have to leave," he says, desperately. "You have to tell Mardin, tell him to sell you."

I won't leave. I have nothing to go to.

"Do you love me because you have to? Is it because you are a harni and I am a human and you have to serve me?" I ask.

He shakes his head.

"Do you love me because of us?" I press. There are no words for the questions I am asking him.

"Diyet," he says.

"Do you love the mistress?"

"No," he says.

"You should love the mistress, shouldn't you, but you love me."

"Go home, go to the Nekropolis. Run away," he urges, kissing my throat, tiny little kisses, as if he was been thinking of my throat for a long time.

"Run away? From Mardin? What would I do for the rest of my life? Make paper flowers?"

"What would be wrong with that?"

"Would you come with me?" I ask.

He sighs and raises up on his elbow. "You should not fall in love with me."

This is funny. "This is a fine time to tell me."

"No," he says, "it is true." He counts on his fine fingers. "One, I am a harni, not a human being, and I belong to someone else. Two, I have caused all of your problems, if I had not been here, you would not have had all your troubles. Three, the reason it is wrong for a human to love a harni is because harni-human relationships are bad paradigms for human behavior, they lead to difficulty in dealing with human-to-human relationships—"

"I don't *have* any human-to-human relationships," I interrupt.

"You will, you are just young."

I laugh at him. "Akhmim, you're younger than *I* am! Prescripted wisdom."

"But wisdom nevertheless," he says, solemnly.

"Then why did you kiss me?" I ask.

He sighs. It is such a human thing, that sigh, full of frustration. "Because you are so sad."

"I'm not sad right now," I say. "I'm happy because you are here." I am also nervous. Afraid. Because this is all so strange, and even though I keep telling myself that he's so human, I am afraid that underneath he really is alien, more unknowable than my brother. But I want him to stay with me. And I am happy. Afraid but happy.

My lover. "I want you to become my lover," I say.

"No." He sits up. He is beautiful, even disheveled. I can imagine what I look like. Maybe he does not even like me, maybe he has to act this way because I want it. He runs his fingers through his hair, his earring gleams in the light from the street.

"Do harni fall in love?" I ask.

"I have to go," he says. "We've crushed your flowers." He picks up a lily whose long petals have become twisted and crumpled and tries to straighten it out.

"I can make more. Do you have to do this because I want you to?"

"No," he says very quietly. Then more clearly, like a recitation, "Harni don't have feelings, not in the sense that humans do. We are loyal, flexible, and affectionate."

"That makes you sound like a smart dog," I say, irritated.

"Yes," he says, "that is what I am, a smart dog, a very smart dog. Good night, Diyet."

When he opens the door, the breeze draws and the flowers rustle, and some tumble off the bed, trying to follow him.

"Daughter," Mardin says, "I am not sure that this is the best situation for you." He looks at me kindly. I wish Mardin did not think that he had to be my father.

"Mardin-salah?" I say, "I don't understand, has my work been unsatisfactory?" Of course my work has been unsatisfactory, the mistress hates me. But I am afraid they have somehow realized what is between Akhmim and me—although I don't know how they could. Akhmim is avoiding me again.

"No, no," he waves his hand airily, "your accounts are in order, you have been a good and frugal girl. It is not your fault."

"I . . . I am aware that I have been clumsy, that perhaps I have not always understood what the mistress wished, but, Mardin-salah, I am improving!" I am getting better at ignoring her, I mean. I don't want him to feel inadequate. Sitting here, I realize the trouble I've caused him. He hates having to deal with the household in any but the most perfunctory way. I am jessed to this man, his feelings matter to me. Rejection of my services is painful. This has been a good job, I have been able to save some of my side money so that when I am old I won't be like my mother, forced to struggle and hope that the children will be able to support her when she can't work anymore. Mardin is uncomfortable. The part of me that is not jessed can see that this is not the kind of duty that Mardin likes. This is not how he sees himself; he prefers to be the benevolent patriarch. "Daughter," he says, "you have been exemplary, but wives. . . ." he sighs. "Sometimes, child, they get whims, and it is better for me, and for you, if we find you some good position with another household."

At least he hasn't said anything about Akhmim. I bow my head because I am afraid I will cry. I study my toes. I try not to think of Akhmim. Alone again. Oh Holy One, I am so tired of being alone. I will be alone my whole life; jessed women do not marry. I cannot help it, I start to cry. Mardin takes it as a sign of my loyalty and pats me gently on the shoulder. "There, there, child, it will be all right."

I don't want Mardin to comfort me. The part of me that watches, that isn't jessed, doesn't even really *like* Mardin—but at the same time, I want to make him happy, so I gamely sniff and try to smile. "I . . . I know you know what is best," I manage. But my distress makes him uncomfortable. He says when arrangements are made he will tell me.

I look for Akhmim, to tell him, but he stays in the men's side of the house, away from the middle where we eat, and far away from the women's side.

I begin to understand. He didn't love me, it was just that he was a harni, and it was *me* . . . I led him to myself. Maybe I am no better than Shusilina, with her white hair and pointed ears. So I work, what else is there to do? And I avoid the mistress. Evidently Mardin has told her he is getting rid of me, because the attacks cease. Fadina even smiles at me, if distantly. I would like to make friends with Fadina again, but she doesn't give me a chance. So I will never see him again. He isn't even that far from me, and I will never see him again.

There is nothing to do about it. Akhmim avoids me. I look across the courtyard or across the dining room at the men's side, but I almost never see him. Once in a while he's there, with his long curly hair and his black gazelle eyes, but he doesn't look at me.

I pack my things. My new mistress comes. She is a tall, gray-haired woman, slightly pop-eyed. She has a breathy voice and a way of hunching her shoulders as if she wished she were actually a very small woman. I am supposed to give her my life? It is monstrous.

We are in Mardin's office. I am upset. I want desperately to leave, I am so afraid of coming into a room and finding the mistress. I am trying not to think of Akhmim. But what is most upsetting is the thought of leaving Mardin. Will the next girl understand that he wants to pretend that he is frugal, but that he really is not? I am nearly overwhelmed by shame because I have caused this. I am only leaving because of my own foolishness, and I have failed Mardin, who only wanted peace.

I will not cry. These are impressed emotions. Soon I will feel them for this strange woman. Oh Holy, what rotten luck to have gotten this woman for a mistress. She wears bronze and white—bronze was all the fashion when I first came and the mistress wore it often—but this is years after and these are second-rate clothes, a young girl's clothes and not suited to my mistress at all. She is nervous, wanting me to like her, and all I want to do is throw myself at Mardin's feet and embarrass him into saying that I can stay.

Mardin says, "Diyet, she has paid the fee." He shows me the credit transaction and I see that the fee is lower than it was when I came to Mardin's household. "I order you to accept this woman as your new mistress."

That's it. That's the trigger. I feel a little disoriented. I never really noticed how the skin under Mardin's jaw was soft and lax. He is actually rather nondescript. I wonder what it must be like for the mistress to have married him. She is tall and vivid, if a bit heavy, and was a beauty in her day. She must find him disappointing. No wonder she is bitter.

My new mistress smiles tentatively. Well, she may not be fashionable, the way my old mistress was, but she looks kind. I hope so, I would like to live in a kind household. I smile back at her.

That is it. I am impressed.

My new household is much smaller than the old one. The mistress' last housekeeper was clearly inefficient. I am busy for days, just trying to put things in order. I must be frugal; there's a lot less money in this house. It is surprising how much I have gotten accustomed to money at Mardin's house; this is much more like I grew up.

I do inventories of the linens and clean all the rooms from top to bottom. At first I am nervous, but my new mistress is not like the old one at all. She watches me work, as if astounded, and she is never offended if she walks in her room and I have the cleaning machine going. I learn not to work too much around her, she is oddly sensitive about it. She won't say anything, but she will start to make funny little embarrassed/ helpful gestures, or suggest that I get myself some tea. Her husband is an old man. He smiles at me and tells me very bad jokes, puns, and I have to laugh to be polite. I would like to avoid him because he bores me nearly to tears. They have a daughter who is a terror. She is in trouble all the time. She spends money, takes her mother's credit chip without asking—they have been forced to put a governor on daily purchases and they are in the process of locking the girl out of the parents' credit.

The daughter is nice enough to me, but her politeness is false. She argues with her mother about spending money on getting a jessed servant, instead of sending her to school. But the daughter's marks at academy are dreadful and the mistress says she will not waste money on more.

Akhmim. I think of him all the time.

Emboldened by my mistress' approval, I rearrange the furniture. I take some things she has—they are not very nice—and put them up. I reprogram the household AI. It is very limited, insufficient for anything as complicated as *bismek*, but it can handle projections, of course. I remember the things my old mistress used to like and I put around cobalt vases and silver framed pictures. Marble floors would overwhelm these rooms, but the tile I pick is nice.

My days are free on Tuesday and half-a-day Sunday. Tuesday my mistress apologizes to me. They are a little tight on credit and she can't advance my leisure allowance until Sunday, do I mind?

Well, a little, but I say I don't. I spend the afternoon making flowers.

When I make flowers I think of Akhmim and myself on the bed surrounded by crushed carnations and iris. It isn't good to think about Akhmim, he doesn't miss me, I'm sure. He is a harni, always an owned thing, subject to the whims of his owners. If they had constructed him with lasting loyalties, his life would be horrible. Surely when the technician constructed his genes, he made certain that Akhmim would forget quickly. He told me that harni do not love. But he also told me that they did. And he told me he didn't love the old mistress, but maybe he only said that because he had to, because I did not love the old mistress and his duty is to make humans happy.

I put the flowers in a vase. My mistress is delighted, she thinks they are lovely.

Long lilies, spiked stamens and long petals like lolling tongues. Sometimes feelings are in me that have no words, and I look at the paper flowers and want to rip them to pieces.

On Sunday, my mistress has my leisure allowance. Mardin used to add a little something extra, but I realize that in my new circumstances I can't expect that. I go to the Moussin of the White Falcon, on the edge of the Nekropolis, to listen to the service.

Then I take the tube to the street of Mardin's house. I don't even intend to walk down the street, but of course I do. And I stand outside the house, looking for a sign of Akhmim. I'm afraid to stand long. I don't want anyone to see me. What would I tell them, that I'm homesick? I'm jessed.

I like to take something to do on the tube, so the ride is not so boring. I have brought a bag of paper to make flowers. I think I'll earn a little money on the side by making wreaths. I am not allowed to give it to my mistress, that's against the law. It's to protect the jessed that this is true.

In the Nekropolis, we lived in death houses, surrounded by death. Perhaps it isn't odd that I'm a bit morbid, and perhaps this is why I pull a flower out of my bag and leave it on a windowsill on the men's side of the house. After all, something did die, although I can't put in words exactly what it was. I don't really know which window is Akhmim's, but it doesn't matter, it's just a gesture. It only makes me feel foolish.

Monday I wake early and drink hot mint tea. I take buckets of water and scrub down the stone courtyard. I make a list of all the repairs that need to be done. I take the mistress' printouts and bundle them. She saves them, she subscribes to several services and she feels that they might be useful. My old mistress would have quite a lot to say about someone who would save printouts. The mistress goes out to shop, and I clean everything in her storage. She has clothes she should throw out, things fifteen years old and hopelessly out of date. (I remember when I wore my hair white. And later when we used to wrap our hair in veils, the points trailing to the backs of our knees. We looked so foolish, so affected. What are young girls wearing now? How did I get to be so old? I'm not even thirty.)

I put aside all the things I should mend, but I don't want to sit yet. I run the cleaning machine, an old clumsy thing even stupider than the one at Mardin's. I push myself all day, a whirlwind. There is not enough in this house to do, even if I clean the cleaning machine, so I clean some rooms twice.

Still, when it is time to sleep, I can't. I sit in my room making a funeral wreath of carnations and tiny, half-open roses. The white roses gleam like satin.

I wake up on my free day, tired and stiff. In the mirror, I look ghastly, my hair tangled and my eyes puffy. Just as well the harni never saw me like this, I think. But I won't think of Akhmim any more. That part of my life is over, and I have laid a flower at its death house. Today I will take my funeral wreaths around and see if I can find a shop that will buy them. They are good work, surely someone will be interested. It would just be pocket money, take a little of the strain off my mistress, she would not feel then as if she wasn't providing extras for me if I can provide them for myself.

I take the tube all the way to the Nekropolis, carefully protecting my wreaths from the other commuters. All day I walk through the Nekropolis, talking to stall keepers, stopping sometimes for tea, and when I have sold the wreaths, sitting for awhile to watch the people, letting my tired mind empty.

I am at peace, now I can go back to my mistress.

The Second Koran tells us that the darkness in ourselves is a sinister thing. It waits until we relax, it waits until we reach the most vulnerable moments, and then it snares us. I want to be dutiful. I want to do what I should. But when I go back to the tube, I think of where I am going; to that small house and my empty room. What will I do tonight? Make more paper flowers, more wreaths? I am sick of them. Sick of the Nekropolis.

I can take the tube to my mistress' house, or I can go by the street where Mardin's house is. I'm tired. I'm ready to go to my little room and relax. Oh, Holy One, I dread the empty evening. Maybe I should go by the street just to fill up time. I have all this empty time in front of me. Tonight and tomorrow and the week after and the next month and all down through the years as I never marry and become a dried-up woman. Evenings spent folding paper. Days cleaning someone else's house. Free afternoons spent shopping a bit, stopping in tea shops because my feet hurt. That is what lives *are*, aren't they? Attempts to fill our time with activity designed to prevent us from realizing that there *is* no meaning? I sit at a tiny table the size of a serving platter and watch the boys hum by on their scooters, girls sitting behind them, clutching their waists with one hand, holding their veils with the other, while the ends stream and snap behind them, glittering with the shimmer of gold (this year's fashion).

So I get off the tube and walk to the street where Mardin lives. And I walk up the street past the house. I stop and look at it. The walls are pale yellow stone. I am wearing rose and sky blue, but I have gone out without ribbons on my wrists.

"Diyet," Akhmim says, leaning on the windowsill, "you're still sad."

He looks so familiar and it is so easy, as if we do this every evening. "I live a sad life," I say, my voice even. But my heart is pounding. To see him! To talk to him!

"I found your token," he says.

"My token," I say, not understanding.

"The flower. I thought today would be your free day so I tried to watch all day. I thought you had come and I missed you." Then he disappears for a moment, and then he is sitting on the windowsill, legs and feet outside, and he jumps lightly to the ground.

I take him to a tea shop. People look at us, wondering what a young woman is doing unescorted with a young man. Let them look. "Order what you want," I say, "I have some money."

"Are you happier?" he asks. "You don't look happier, you look tired."

And he looks perfect, as he always does. Have I fallen in love with him precisely because he *isn't* human? I don't care, I feel love, no matter what the reason. Does a reason for a feeling matter? The feeling I have for my mistress may be there only because I am impressed, but the *feeling* is real enough.

"My mistress is kind," I say, looking at the table. His perfect hand, beautiful nails and long fingers, lies there.

"Are you happy?" he asks again.

"Are you?" I ask.

He shrugs. "A harni does not have the right to be happy or unhappy."

"Neither do I," I say.

"That's *your* fault. Why did you do it?" he asks. "Why did you choose to be jessed? You were free." His voice is bitter.

"It's hard to find work in the Nekropolis, and I didn't think I would ever get married."

He shakes his head. 'Someone would marry you. And if they didn't, is it so awful not to get married?"

"Is it so awful to be jessed?" I ask.

"Yes."

That is all he says. I suppose to him it looks as if I threw everything away, but how can he understand how our choices are taken from us? He doesn't even understand freedom and what an illusion it really is.

"Run away," he says.

Leave the mistress? I am horrified. "She needs me, she cannot run that house by herself and I have cost her a great deal of money. She has made sacrifices to buy me."

"You could live in the Nekropolis and make funeral wreaths," he urges. "You could talk to whomever you wished and no one would order you around."

"I don't want to live in the Nekropolis," I say.

"Why not?"

"There is nothing there for me!"

"You have friends there."

"I wouldn't if I ran away."

"Make new ones," he says.

"Would you go?" I ask.

He shakes his head. "I'm not a person, I can't live."

"What if you could make a living, would you run away?"

"Yes," he says, "yes." He squares his shoulders defiantly and looks at me. "If I could be human, I would be." He is shaming me.

Our tea comes. My face is aflame with color. I don't know what to say. I don't know what to think. He feels morally superior. He thinks he knows the true worth of something I threw away. He doesn't understand, not at all.

"Oh, Diyet," he says softly. "I am sorry. I shouldn't say these things to you."

"I didn't think you could have these feelings," I whisper.

He shrugs again. "I can have any feelings," he says. "Harni aren't jessed."

"You told me to think of you as a dog," I remind him. "Loyal."

"I am loyal," he says. "You didn't ask who I was loyal to."

"You're supposed to be loyal to the mistress."

He drums the table with his fingers, *taptaptaptap, taptaptaptap.* "Harni aren't like geese," he says, not looking at me. His earring is golden, he is rich and fine-looking. I had not realized at my new place how starved I had become for fine things. "We don't impress on the first person we see." Then he shakes his head. "I shouldn't talk about all this nonsense. You must go, I must go back before they miss me."

"We have to talk more," I say.

"We have to go," he insists. Then he smiles at me and all the unhappiness disappears from his face. He doesn't seem human anymore, he seems pleasant; *harni*. I get a chill. He is so alien. I understand him less than I understand people like my old mistress. We get up and he looks away as I pay.

Outside Mardin's house I tell him, "I'll come back next Tuesday."

It's good I did so much before, because I sleepwalk through the days. I leave the cleaning machine in the doorway where the mistress almost trips over it. I forget to set the clothes in order. I don't know what to think.

I hear the mistress say to the neighbor, "She is a godsend, but so moody. One day she's doing everything, the next day she can't be counted on to remember to set the table."

What right does she have to talk about me that way? Her house was a pigsty when I came.

What am I thinking? What is wrong with me that I blame my mistress? Where is my head? I feel ill, my eyes water and head fills. I can't breathe, I feel heavy. I must be dutiful. I used to have this feeling once in a while when I was first jessed, it's part of the adjustment. It must be the change. I have to adjust all over again.

I find the mistress, tell her I'm not feeling well, and go lie down.

The next afternoon, just before dinner, it happens again. The day after that is fine, but then it happens at midmorning of the third day. It is Sunday and I have the afternoon off. I force myself to work through the morning. My voice is hoarse, my head aches. I want to get everything ready since I won't be there to see to dinner in the afternoon. White cheese and olives and tomatoes on a platter. My stomach rebels and I have to run to the bathroom.

What is wrong with me?

I go to the Moussin in the afternoon, lugging my bag, which is heavy with paper, and sit in the cool dusty darkness, nursing my poor head. I feel as if I should pray. I should ask for help, for guidance. The Moussin is so old that the stone is irregularly worn, and through my slippers I can feel the little ridges and valleys in the marble. Up around the main worship hall there are galleries hidden by arabesques of scroll-work. Kari and I used to sit up there when we were children. Above that, sunlight flashes through clerestory widows. Where the light hits the marble floor it shines hard, hurting my eyes and my head. I rest my forehead on my arm, turned sideways on the bench so I can lean on the back. With my eyes closed I smell incense and my own scent of perfume and perspiration.

There are people there for service, but no one bothers me. Isn't that amazing?

Or maybe it is only because anyone can see that I am impure.

I get tired of my own melodrama. I keep thinking that people are looking at me, that someone is going to say something to me. I don't know where to go.

I don't even pretend to think of going back to my room. I get on the tube and go to Mardin's house. I climb the stairs from the tube—these are newer, but, like the floor of the moussin, they are unevenly worn, sagging in the centers from the weight of this crowded city. What would it be like to cross the sea and go north? To the peninsula, Ida, or north from there, into the continent? I used to want to travel, to go to a place where people had yellow hair, to see whole forests of trees. Cross the oceans, learn other languages. I told Kari that I would even like to taste dog, or swine, but she thought I was showing off. But it's true, once I would have liked to try things.

I am excited, full of energy and purpose. I can do anything. I can understand Fhassin, standing in the street with his razor, laughing. It is worth it, anything is worth it for this feeling of being alive. I have been jessed, I have been asleep for so long.

There are people on Mardin's street. It's Sunday and people are visiting. I stand in front of the house across the street. What am I going to say if someone opens the door? I am waiting to meet a friend. What if they don't leave, what if Akhmim sees them and doesn't come out.

The sun bakes my hair, my head. Akhmim, where are you? Look out the window. He is probably waiting on the mistress. Maybe there is a *bismek* party and those women are poisoning Akhmim. They could do anything, they *own* him. I want to crouch in the street and cover my head in my hands, rock and cry like a widow woman from the Nekropolis. Like my mother must have done when my father died. I grew up without a father, maybe that's why I'm so wild. Maybe that's why Fhassin is in prison and I'm headed there. I pull my veil up so my face is shadowed. So no one can see my tears.

Oh my head. Am I drunk? Am I insane? Has the Holy One, seeing my thoughts, driven me mad?

I look at my brown hands. I cover my face.

"Diyet?" He takes my shoulders.

I look up at him, his beautiful familiar face, and I am stricken with terror. What is he? What am I trusting my life, my future to?

"What's wrong," he says, "are you ill?"

"I'm going insane," I say. "I can't stand it, Akhmim, I can't go back to my room——"

"Hush," he says, looking up the street and down. "You have to. I'm only a harni. I can't do anything, I can't help you."

"We have to go. We have to go away somewhere, you and I."

He shakes his head. "Diyet, please. You must hush."

"You said you wanted to be free," I say. My head hurts so bad. The tears keep coming even though I am not really crying.

"I can't be free," he says. "That was just talk."

"I have to go now," I say. "I'm jessed, Akhmim, it is hard, if I don't go now I'll never go."

"Your mistress——"

"DON'T TALK ABOUT HER!" I shout. If he talks about her I may not be able to leave.

He looks around again. We are a spectacle, a man and a woman on the street.

"Come with me, we'll go somewhere, talk," I say, all honey. He cannot deny me, I see it in him. He has to get off the street. He would go anywhere. Any place is safer than this.

He lets me take him into the tube, down the stairs to the platform. I clutch my indigo veil around my face We wait in silence, he has his hands in his pockets. He looks like a boy from the Nekropolis, standing there in just his shirt, no outer robe. He looks away, shifts his weight from one foot to the other, ill at ease. So human. Events are making him more human. Taking away all the uncertainties.

"What kinds of genes are in you?" I ask.

"What?" he asks.

"What kinds of genes?"

"Are you asking for my chart?" he says.

I shake my head. "Human?"

He shrugs. "Mostly. Some artificial sequences."

"No animal genes," I say. I sound irrational because I can't get clear what I mean. The headache makes my thoughts skip, my tongue thick.

He smiles a little. "No dogs, no monkeys."

I smile back, he is teasing me. I am learning to understand when he teases. "I have some difficult news for you, Akhmim. I think you are a mere human being."

His smile vanishes. He shakes his head. "Diyet," he says. He is about to talk like a father.

I stop him with a gesture. My head still hurts.

The train whispers in, sounding like wind. Oh the lights. I sit down, shading my eyes, and he stands in front of me. I can feel him looking down at me. I look up and smile, or maybe grimace. He smiles back, looking worried. At the Moussin of the White Falcon, we get off. Funny that we are going into a cemetery to live. But only for a while, I think. Somehow I will find a way we can leave. We'll go north, across the sea, up to the continent, where we'll be strangers. I take him through the streets and stop in front of a row of death houses, like the Lachims', but an inn. I give Akhmim money and tell him to rent us a place for the night. "Tell them your wife is sick," I whisper.

"I don't have any credit. If they take my identification, they'll know," he says.

"This is the Nekropolis," I say. "They don't use credit. Go on. Here you are a man."

He frowns at me but takes the money. I watch him out of the corner of my eye, bargaining, pointing at me. Just pay, I think, even though we have so little money. I just want to lie down, to sleep. And finally he comes out and takes me by the hand and leads me to our place. A tiny place of rough whitewashed walls, a bed, a chair, a pitcher of water and two glasses. "I have something for your head," he says. "The man gave it to me." He smiles ruefully. "He thinks you are pregnant."

My hand shakes when I hold it out. He puts the white pills in my hand and pours a glass of water for me. "I'll leave you here," he says. "I'll go back. I won't tell anyone that I know where you are."

"Then you were lying to me," I say. I don't want to argue, Akhmim, just stay until tomorrow. Then it will be too late. "You said if you could be free, you would. You *are* free."

"What can I do? I can't live," he says in anguish. "I can't get work!"

"You can sell funeral wreaths. I'll make them."

He looks torn. It is one thing to think how you will act, another to be in the situation and do it. And I know, seeing his face, that he really is human, because his problem is a very human problem. Safety or freedom.

"We will talk about it tomorrow," I say. "My head is aching."

"Because you are jessed," he says. "It is so dangerous. What if we don't make enough money? What if they catch us?"

"That is life," I say. I will go to prison. He will be sent back to the mistress. Punished. Maybe made to be conscript labor.

"Is it worth the pain?" he asks in a small voice.

I don't know, but I can't say that. "Not when you have the pain," I say, "but afterward it is."

"Your poor head." He strokes my forehead. His hand is cool and soothing.

"It's all right," I say. "It hurts to be born."

Frankenstein's Daughter

I'm at the mall with my sister Cara, doing my robot imitation. Zzzt-choo. Zzzt. Zzzt. Pivot on my heel stiffly, 45 degrees, readjust forward, headed towards Sears, my arms stiff and moving with mechanical precision.

"Robert!" Cara says. It's easy to get her to laugh. She likes the robot stuff a lot. I first did it about a year ago, and it feels a little weird to do it in public, in the mall. But I want to keep Cara happy. Cara is six, but she's retarded so she's more like three or four and she'll probably never be more than about four or five. Except she's big. She was born big. Big bones like a cow. Big jaw, big knuckles. Big blue eyes. Only her blond hair is wispy. You have to look really hard to see how she resembles Kelsey. Kelsey was my big sister. I'm fourteen. Kelsey was hit by a car when she was thirteen. She'd be twenty now. Cara is Kelsey's clone, except, of course, Kelsey wasn't retarded or as big as a cow. In our living room there's a picture of Kelsey in her gymnast's leotard, standing next to the balance beam. You can kind of see how Cara looks like her.

"Let's go in Spencer's," I say.

Cara follows me. Spencer's is like heaven for a retarded girl—all the fake spilled drinks and the black lights and the lava lamps and optical projections and Cara's favorite, the Japanese string lights. They're back with the strings of chili pepper lights and the Coca-Cola lights. They sort of look like weird Christmas lights. If you look right at them, all they do is flicker, but if you look kind of sideways at them, you see all these Japanese letters and shit. Cara just stares at them. I think it's the flicker. While she's staring, I wander towards the front of the store.

Spencer's is shoplifter paradise, so they've got really good security. There's this chubby guy in the back, putting up merchandise and sweating up a storm. There are the cameras. There's a girl at the front cash register who is bored out of her mind and fiddling with some weird Spencer's Gifts pen but who can pretty much see anything in the store if she bothers to look. But I've got Cara. That, and I understand the secret of shoplifting, which is to have absolutely no emotions. Be cold about the whole thing. I can switch off everything and I'm just a thinking machine, doing everything according to plan. If you're nervous, then people notice you. Iceman. That's my name, my tag. That's the nickname I use in chatrooms. That's me.

I look at the bedroom board games. I stand at the shelf so that I pretty much block anything anyone could see in a camera. I don't know exactly where the cameras are, but if I don't leave much space between me and the shelf, how much can they really see? I wait. After a minute or two, Cara is grabbing the light strings and after another couple of minutes, the girl who's watching from the cash register has called someone to go intercept Cara and I palm a deck of *Wedding Night Playing Cards.* They're too small to have an anti-theft thing. I don't even break a sweat, increase my heart rate, nothing. The ice man. I head back to Cara.

Everyone's just watching the weird retarded girl except this one chubby guy who's trying to get her to put down the lights but who's afraid to touch her.

"Not supposed to touch those," he says. "Where's your mom? Is your mom here?"

"Sorry!" I say.

The chubby guy frowns at me.

"Cara," I say. "No hands."

Cara looks at me, looks at the lights. I gently try to take them.

"No!" she wails. "Pretty!"

"I'm sorry," I say, "I'm her brother. She's developmentally delayed.

Cara! Cara, no. No hands."

She wails, but lets me disentangle her hands.

"I'm sorry," I say again, the concerned big brother. "I was just looking around and thought she was right with me, you know? Our mom's down at Dillard's."

Chubby guy kind of hovers until I get the lights away from Cara and as soon as I put them on the shelf he grabs them and starts straightening them out and draping them back over the display.

I herd Cara towards the front of the store, mouthing *sorry* at the front cashier. She's kind of pretty. She smiles at me. Nice big brother with retarded sister.

Back out in the mall, Cara is wailing, which could start an asthma attack, so to distract her I say, "You want a cookie?"

Mom has Cara on a diet, so of course she wants a cookie. She perks up the way Shelby, our Shetland Sheepdog does, when you say 'treat.' I take her to the food court and buy her an M&M cookie and buy myself a Mountain Dew and then while she's eating her cookie, I pull the deck of cards out of my pocket and unwrap it. We've got another fifteen minutes before we have to meet my mom.

The idea is to play fish except every time you get a match you're supposed to do what it says. *Tie partner's hands with a silk scarf. Kiss anywhere you like and see how long your partner can keep from moving or making any noise. The one who lasts the longest gets to draw an extra card.*

Tame, but pretty cool. I can't wait to show Toph and Len.

Cara has chocolate smeared on her mouth, but she lets me wipe her face off.

"You ready to go back to see Mom?" I say.

When we pass Spencer's again, she stops. "Uhhh," she says, pointing to the store. Mom always tries to get her to say what she wants, but I know what she wants and I don't want to fight with her.

"No," I say. "Let's go see Mom."

Cara's face crumples up and she hunches her thick shoulders. "Uhhh," she says, mad.

"It's okay," I say. "Come on."

She swings at me. I grab her hand and pull her behind me. She tries to sit down, but I just keep on tugging and she follows me, gulping and wailing.

"What did you do?" my mom says when she sees us. My mom had to buy stuff, like gym shorts for me and underwear for herself, so I told her that I'd take Cara with me while she bought her stuff. She's holding a Dillard's bag.

"She wanted to go in Spencer's," I say. "We went in but she kept grabbing stuff and I had to take her out and now she's upset."

"Robert," my mom says, irritated. She crouches down. "Ah, Cara mia, don't cry."

We trail out of the store, Cara holding Mom's hand and sniffling.

By the time we get to the car, though, Cara's wheezing. Mom digs out Cara's inhaler and Cara dutifully takes a hit. I tried it once and it was pretty dreadful. It felt really weird, trying to get that stuff in my lungs, and it made me feel a little buzzy but it didn't even feel good, so it's pretty amazing that Cara will do it.

Cara sits in her booster seat in the back of the car, wheezing all the way home, getting worse and worse, and by the time we pull in the driveway, she's got that white look around her mouth.

"Robert," Mom says, "I'm going to have to take her to the Emergency Room."

"Okay," I say and get out of the car.

"You want to call your dad?" Mom asks. "I don't know how long we'll be." Mom checks her watch. It's three something now. "We may not be home in time for dinner."

I don't want to call my dad who is probably with Joyce, his girlfriend, anyway. Joyce is always trying to be likable and it gets on my nerves after awhile—she tries way too hard. "I can just make a sandwich," I say.

"I want you to stay at home, then," she says. "I've got my cell phone if you need to call."

"Can Toph and Len come over?" I ask.

She sighs. "Okay. But no roughhousing. Remember you have school tomorrow." She opens the garage door so I can get in.

I stand there and watch her back down the driveway. She turns back, watching where she's going, and she needs to get her hair done again because I can really see the gray roots. Cara is watching me through the watery glass, her mouth a little open. I wave good-bye.

I'm glad they're gone.

I watch my daughter try to breathe. When Cara is having an asthma attack she becomes still; conserving, I think. Her face becomes empty. People think Cara looks empty all the time, but her face is usually alive—maybe with nothing more than some faint, reflected flicker of the world around her, like those shimmers of light on the bottom of a pool, experience washing over her.

"Cara mia," I say. She doesn't understand why we won't pick her up anymore, but she weighs over sixty-five pounds and I just can't.

She doesn't like the Emergency Room but it doesn't scare her. She's familiar with it. I steer her through the doors, my hand on her back, to the reception desk. I don't know today's receptionist. I hand her my medical card. When Cara was born, we officially adopted her, just as if we had done a conventional in-vitro fertilization in a surrogate and adopted the child, so Cara is on our medical plan. Now, of course, medical plans don't cover cloned children, but Cara was one of the early ones.

The receptionist takes all the information. The waiting room isn't very full. "Is Dr. Ramanathan on today?" I ask. Dr. Ramanathan, a softspoken Indian with small hands, is familiar with Cara. He's good with her, knows the strange idiosyncrasies of her condition—that her lungs are oddly vascularized, that she sometimes reacts atypically to medication. But Dr. Ramanathan isn't here.

We go sit in the waiting room.

The waiting room chairs don't have arms, so I lay Cara across a chair with her head on my lap and stroke her forehead. Calming her helps keep the attack from getting too bad. She needs her diaper changed. I didn't think to bring any. We were making some headway on toilet training until about two months ago, but then she just decided she hated the toilet.

I learned not to force things when she decided to be difficult about dinner. She's big and although she's not terribly strong, when she gets mad she packs a wallop. The last time I tried to teach her about using a fork, I tried to fold her hand round it and she started screaming. It's a shrill, furious scream, not animal at all, but full of something terribly human and too old for such a little girl. I grabbed her hand and she hit me in the face with her fist and broke my reading glasses. So I don't force things anymore.

The nurse calls us at a little after five.

I settle Cara on the examining table. It's cold so I wrap her in a blanket. She watches me, terribly patient, her mouth open. She has such blue eyes. The same eyes as Kelsey and the same eyes as my ex-husband, Allan. I can hear the tightness in her chest. I sit down next to her and hum and she rubs my arm with the flat of her hand, as if she were smoothing out a wrinkle in a blanket.

I don't know the doctor who comes in. He is young and his face seems good-humored and kind. He has a pierced ear. He isn't wearing an earring, but I can see the crease where his ear is pierced and it cheers me a little. A little unorthodox, and kind. It seems like a good combination. His name is Dr. Guidall. I do my little speech—that she has asthma, that she had an attack and didn't respond to the inhaler, that she is developmentally delayed.

"Have you been to the Emergency Room before?" he asks.

"Many times," I say. "Right, Cara?"

She doesn't answer, she just watches me.

He examines her and he is careful. He tells her the stethoscope is going to be cold and treats her like a person, which is a good sign.

"She has odd pulmonary vascularization," I say.

"Are you a doctor?" he asks.

When Cara's sister Kelsey had her accident, I was in charge of the international division of Kleinhoffer Foods. Now I sell real estate. "No," I say. "I've just learned a lot with Cara. Sometimes we see Dr. Ramanathan. He's familiar with Cara's problems."

The doctor frowns. Maybe he doesn't care for Dr. Ramanathan. He's young. Emergency Room doctors are usually young, at least at the hospital where I take Cara.

"She's not Down's Syndrome, is she?" he says.

"No," I say. I don't want to say more.

He looks at me, and I realize he's pieced something together. "Is your daughter the clone?"

The clone. "Yes," I say. Dr. Ramanathan asked me if he could write up his observations of Cara to publish and I said yes, because he seems to really care about her. I get requests from doctors to examine her. When she was first born I got hate mail, too. People saying that she should never have been born. That she was an abomination in the sight of God. I'm upset that Dr. Ramanathan would talk about her with someone else.

Dr. Guidall is silent, examining her. I imagine his censure. Maybe I'm wrong. Maybe he's just surprised.

"Is she allergic to anything?"

"She isn't allergic, but she has atypical reactions to some drugs like leukotriene receptor antagonists." I keep a list of drugs in my wallet. I pull it out and hand it to him. The list is worn, the creases so sharp that the paper is starting to tear.

"Do you use a nebulizer?" he asks. "And what drug are you using?"

"Budesonide," I say. I'm not imagining it. He's curt with me.

The doctor puts a nebulizer—a mask rather than an inhaler so she won't have to do anything but breathe—on her face. He leaves to pull her chart from records.

I know we'll be here a long time. I've spent a lot of time in hospitals.

The doctor wants to punish me, I think. He does a thorough exam of Cara, who has fallen asleep as the asthma attack waned. He listens to her lungs and checks her reflexes and looks in her ears. He doesn't need to look in her ears. But how many cloned children will he get to examine? Cloning humans is illegal in the United States, although there's no law against having your child cloned in, say, Israel and then bringing the adopted child into the U.S.

"I don't like what I'm hearing in her breathing," he says. "I would like to run some tests."

He has gotten more formal, which means that something is wrong. I want to go home so bad, I don't want things to start tonight. *Things.*

The crisis doesn't always come when you're tired and thinking about the house you're going to show tomorrow, but often it does.

The doctor is very young, and very severe. It's easy to be severe when you're young. I can imagine what he would like to ask. *Why the hell did you do it? How do you justify it?* Cara's respiratory defects will kill her, probably before she is twelve, almost certainly before she is eighteen.

He is perhaps furious at me. But Cara is right here. What would the angry people have me do, take her home and put a pillow over her face? How do I tell him, tell them, that when Cara was conceived, I wasn't sane? Nothing prepares you for the death of a child. Nothing teaches you how to live with it.

If he says anything I will ask him, *Do you have any children? I hope you never lose one*, I will say.

He doesn't ask.

Nobody is impressed with the wedding-night playing cards because Toph has scored really big. His dad took him along to Computer Warehouse so his dad could buy some sort of accounting software and while Toph was hanging out playing video games, some salesperson got out *Hacker Vigilante* to show to some customer, and then got paged and forgot to lock it back up. "So I just picked it up and slid it under my shirt," Toph says, "and then when my dad and me got to the car, I slid it under the seat before he got in."

We are in awe, Len and me. It's the biggest thing anyone has ever gotten away with. Toph is studying the box, like it's no big deal but we can tell he's really buggin' on the whole thing.

I'm not allowed to have *Hacker Vigilante*. In it, you have to do missions to track down terrorists and you do all these things to raise money, like steal stuff. My mom won't let me have it because one of the things that you can do to get money is pick up two teenaged girls at the bus station and get them to make a porn movie for you and then post it on the Internet. You don't really get to see anything, the girls just start taking off their shirts and the hotel room door closes but it's hysterical.

I am dying. I can't believe it. "Man, that was lucky," I say, because it was. No salesperson ever left anything that cool out in front of me.

"Hey," Toph says, "You just gotta know how to be casual."

"I'm casual," I say. "I'm way casual. But that just fuckin' fell in your lap."

"You loser," Toph says, laughing at me. "Fuck you." Len is laughing at me, too. I can feel my face turning red and my ears feel hot and I'm so mad I want to smash their faces in. Toph is just picking up stuff left lying around by dumbass salesdroids and I'm setting up scams in fucking Spencer's Gifts which everybody knows is really hard to score at because security is like bugfuck tight.

"You wait, asshole," I say. "You wait. I've got an idea for a score. You watch on the bus going to school tomorrow and you'll see."

"What?" Len says. "What are you going to do?"

"You'll see," I say.

By the time they check Cara into a room it's almost seven. I manage to get to a phone and call Allan. Joyce, his girlfriend, answers the phone. "Hi, Joyce," I say, "this is Jenna. Is Allan around?"

"Sure," she says. "Hold on, Jenna."

Joyce. Jenna. Allan likes 'J' women. Actually, Allan likes thin women with dark hair and a kind of relentlessly Irish look. Joyce and I could be cousins. Joyce is prettier than I am. And younger. Every time I talk to her I use her name too much and she uses mine too much. We are working hard to be friendly.

"Jenna?" says Allan, "what's up?"

"I'm at the hospital with Cara," I say.

"Do you need me to come down?" he says, too fast. Allan is conscientious. He is bracing himself. *Is it a crisis?* is what he wants to know.

"No, it's just an asthma attack but the doctor in the emergency room didn't like her oxygen levels or something and they want to keep her. But Robert is home by himself and they want to do some more tests tonight . . . "

"Ah. Okay," he says. "Let me think a moment."

It's Sunday night? What can he be doing on a Sunday night? "Are you busy? I mean, am I calling at a bad time—"

"No, no," he says. "Joyce and I were supposed to meet some friends, but I can call them and let them know. It wasn't anything important."

I try to think of what they could be doing on a Sunday night.

"It's just Joyce's church," Allan says into the pause. "They have a social thing, actually a kind of study thing on Sunday nights."

I didn't know Joyce was religious. "Well," I say, "maybe you could just check in on him? I mean, will it take you too far out of your way?"

"No," Allan says, "I'll go over there."

"See how things are. If you think he's all right, maybe you can just call and make sure he's in bed by ten or something?"

"No," Allan says, "I can stay with him. You're going to be there for hours, I know."

"He's fourteen," I say. "Use your judgment. I mean, I hate to impose on you and Joyce."

"It's okay," Allan says. "They're my kids."

I feel rather guilty so I hang up without saying, 'Church?' One Christmas my dippy older sister was talking about God protecting her from some minor calamity, some domestic crisis involving getting a dent in her husband's Ford pickup, and later, as we drove home, Allan said, grinning, "I'm so glad that God is looking after Matt's pickup. Makes up for whatever he was doing during, you know, Cambodia, or the Black Plague."

He's going to church for Joyce.

Well, he went through the whole cloning thing for me. I don't exactly have the moral high ground.

I go to bed early because my dad and his girlfriend have shown up to baby-sit for me. Toph and Len bug out as soon as Dad shows up. Joyce is being so nice it feels fake but she's acting weird towards my dad, really nice to him. They've brought a movie they rented and when my dad asks her if she wants popcorn with it she says things like, "That would be really nice, thank you." Like they barely know each other.

So I play computer games in my room for awhile and then I go to bed. Shelby, our dog, leaps onto the bed with me. She usually sleeps at the foot of my bed. I get under the covers with my jeans on, and I don't mean to fall asleep, but I do. Shelby wakes me up when my mom gets home because she hears Mom and starts slapping the bed with her tail. My mom talks with my dad and Joyce for a few minutes——I can't hear what they're saying, but I can hear the murmur. I pretend to still be asleep when my mom checks in on me. Shelby is all curled up, but happy to see Mom and my mom comes in and says 'shhh' and pets her a minute.

The hard part is staying awake after that. My clock says 11:18 when my mom leaves my room and I want to give her at least half an hour to be good and sound asleep. But I nod off and when I wake up with a jerk, it's 1:56 A.M.

I almost don't get up. I'm really tired. But I make myself get up. Shelby wakes up and leaps off my bed. Shelby is my big worry about sneaking out. If I lock her in my room she'll scratch and then she'll bark. So she follows me downstairs and I let her out back. Maybe Mom will just think that Shelby had to go out, although usually if Shelby has to go out I sleep right through it and she goes downstairs and pees in the dining room and then my mom gets really twisted at me the next morning.

I almost fall asleep on the couch waiting for Shelby to come back in. I could tell Toph and Len that my dad came over and I couldn't sneak out, and do it tomorrow night. But while Shelby is out I make myself go into the basement and get a can of black spray paint. My mom used black spray paint to repaint the patio furniture and most of this can is still left.

I have a navy hooded sweatshirt and I slide open the back door, let Shelby in and go out the back. That way the door only opened twice, once to let Shelby out, and then to let Shelby in.

The backyard is dark and the cold is kind of startling. Mom keeps saying that she can't believe that in four weeks it will be Memorial Day and the pools will be open, but I like the cold. I look up at the stars. The only constellation I know is Orion, but if it is up, it's behind the trees or on the other side of the house. I bet Shelby is watching me through the window when I come around the front of the house. I can't see her, but I know what she looks like 'cause she does it every time people go out in the car; she's standing on the couch so she can look out the window, but all we'd be able to see is just this little, miniature Lassie face with her ears up all cute.

I walk down the street and I feel like people are watching me out the windows, watching me like Shelby. But all the windows are dark. Still, anyone looking out would see me, and it's after curfew. I should cut through the yards, but they're too dark and people's dogs would bark and people would think I was stealing stuff and call the police—and mostly I just don't want to.

It's a couple of miles to the police station—which is past the middle school. After a while I stop feeling like people are looking at me. They're all in their beds and I'm out here. I'm the only one moving. I can picture them, all cocooned in their beds. Unaware.

I'm aware. All you sleeping people. I'm out here. And you don't know anything about me. I could do stuff while you sleep.

It's so cool. It's great. I'm like some sort of assassin or something. The Iceman. That's me. Moving out here in the dark. I'm a wolf and you're all just rabbits or something.

I'm feeling so good. I'm not cold because I'm walking and I'm feeling so good. By the time I get to the police station, I feel better than anything. Better than after I steal something, which up until now has been the best. But this is the best. The Iceman out moving in the dark. The dark is my friend. I watch the police station for a while but nothing's moving. I shake the paint can and the ball bearing in it sounds loud and for a moment my heart hammers, but then I'm okay again.

I'm casual. I'm better than casual. I'm Special Forces. I'm fucking terror in the streets.

I take a minute and look at the wall. I spray the words on the side, really big, big enough to be seen from the bus:

TO REPORT A CRIME CALL 425-1234

I sketch them fast, and then carefully fill them in. Then I sketch my tag—'Iceman.' I make the letters all sharp and spiky. It's a bitch that I've only got black paint—it should be blue and white with black outline. I carefully start darkening the 'I'. Toph and Len will just die. It's so funny to me that I've got this grin on my face. They're going to come by on the bus and there it will be. Tagging the fucking police station. 425-1234 really is the police phone number. First I was going to put PROTECTED BY NEIGHBORHOOD BLOCK WATCH, but I thought this was funnier.

Then the squad car coasts up behind me and turns the floodlights on and the whole world is white.

I had no idea that police stations had waiting rooms, but when I go to pick up Robert, that's where I end up. It's a room, with seats along the walls and fluorescent lights and a bullet-proof window. The window has one of those metal circles in it, like movie theaters. I tell the young woman that I'm Robert's mother and I got a call to come down and get my son and she picks up a phone to tell someone I'm here.

A cop comes out with Robert. Robert looks properly scared. The cop, who has sandy hair and a handlebar mustache and looks rather boyish, introduces himself as Bruce Yoder. Yoder is an Amish name, although Bruce Yoder obviously isn't Amish. I bet his parents are Mennonite, which is less strict than Amish. It's what you do if you're Amish and you don't have any high-school education but you want a car. You become Mennonite. And now their son is a cop, the route to assimilation of my Irish ancestors. Why am I thinking this while my son, who is almost as tall as the cop, stands sullen and afraid with his hands jammed in the front pocket of his sweatshirt?

We walk outside and around the building so I can survey Robert's handiwork.

The police station is pale sandstone—colored brick and the black letters, as tall as me, stand out even in the dim light. I don't know what to say. Finally I say, "What's 'Iceman'?"

When he doesn't answer I say, "Robert?"

"A nickname," he says.

The cop says to me, "You're the family with the little girl, the clone."

"Yes," I say. "Cara." When people call her "the clone," I always feel compelled to tell them her name. The cop looks a little embarrassed.

We go back inside and I talk to the cop. Robert has been booked and he'll have a hearing in front of a family court referee. I say "I'm sorry" a number of times. A family court referee. That's what we need. That's what everyone needs, someone to tell us the rules. When the phone rang, I thought it was the hospital, that something had happened to Cara, and then I was washed with clear, cold rage. *How can you do this to me?* But it isn't about me, of course.

Allan walks in. I called him before I left the house and he said, as soon as he understood that it wasn't Cara, as soon as he understood what was going on, "He'll have to come live with me. You can't do this, not with Cara."

I am so glad to see him. There have been times I loved him, times I hated him, but now he is kin. For all his flaws and for all my flaws, seeing Allan walk in wearing an old University of Michigan sweatshirt, with his hair tousled so I can see how thin it is getting, and his poor vulnerable temples, I feel only relief and my eyes fill with tears. It's unexpected, this crying.

Allan talks to the cop, the ex-Amish cop, while I sniffle into a wadded-up and ancient Kleenex I found in the pocket of my jacket.

We walk back outside. "I think I should take him home with me tonight," Allan says. "We'll follow you to the house, get him some things. I'll call in tomorrow and start arranging for him to go to school in Marshall."

Robert says, "What?"

Allan says, "You're going to come live with me."

Robert says, his voice cracking across the syllables, "For how long?"

"For good, I suppose," Allan says.

"Is Joyce—" I almost say 'Is Joyce at your place,' but I can't ask that.

"Joyce left early, she's got to go to work tomorrow," Allan says, and he looks off across the parking lot, his mouth pursed. This is a problem for him, a monkey wrench.

I start to reach out and say "I'm sorry" again, and tears well up, again.

"What about school?" Robert asks. "I've got to go to school tomorrow. I've got an algebra test on Tuesday!"

"That," Allan says quietly, "is the least of your problems."

"What about my friends!" Robert says. "You can't do this to me!" I can see his eyes glistening, too. The family that cries together.

"I can," Allan says, "and I will. Now you've put your mother and me through enough, get in the car."

"No!" Robert says, "You can't make me!"

Allan reaches for his arm, to grab him, and Robert slips away, dancing, tall and gangly, and then blindly turns and runs.

I open my mouth, drawing in the breath to shout his name, and he is running, long legs like his father's, full of health and desperation, running pointlessly. It's inescapable, what he is running from, but in the instant before I shout his name I am glad, glad to see him running, this boy of mine who will, I think, survive. "Robert!" I shout, exactly the same time as his father, but Robert is heading down the street, head up, arms pumping. He won't go far.

"Robert!" his father shouts again.

I am glad, oh so glad. *Run,* I think joyfully. *Run, you sweet bastard. Run!*

Reading Group Guide

The Evil Stepmother: An Essay
Author Interview
Talking Points

The Evil Stepmother

My nine-year-old stepson Adam and I were coming home from kung fu. "Maureen," Adam said—he calls me 'Maureen' because he was seven when Bob and I got married and that was what he had called me before. "Maureen," Adam said, "are we going to have a Christmas tree?"

"Yeah," I said, "of course." After thinking a moment. "Adam, why didn't you think we were going to have a Christmas tree?"

"Because of the new house," he said, rather matter-of-fact. "I thought you might not let us."

It is strange to find that you have become the kind of person who might ban Christmas trees.

We joke about me being the evil stepmother. In fact, the joke is that I am the Nazi Evil Stepmother From Hell. It dispels tension to say it out loud. Actually, Adam and I do pretty good together. But the truth is that all stepmothers are evil. It is the nature of the relationship. It is, as far as I can tell, an unavoidable fact of step relationships.

We enter into all major relationships with no real clue of where we are going; marriage, birth, friendship. We carry maps we believe are true; our parents' relationship, what it says in the baby book, the landscape of our own childhood. These maps are approximate at best, dangerously misleading at worst.

Dysfunctional families breed dysfunctional families. Abuse is handed down from generation to generation. That it's all the stuff of 12-Step programs and talk shows doesn't make it any less true or any less profound.

The map of stepparenting is one of the worst, because it is based on a lie. The lie is that you will be mom or you will be dad. If you've got custody of the child, you're going to raise it. You'll be there, or you won't. Either I mother Adam and pack his lunches, go over his homework with him, drive him to and from Boy Scouts, and tell him to eat his carrots, or I'm neglecting him. After all, Adam needs to eat his carrots. He needs someone to take his homework seriously. He needs to be told to get his shoes on, it's time for the bus. He needs to be told not to say 'shit' in front of his grandmother and his teachers.

But he already has a mother, and I'm not his mother, and no matter how deserving or undeserving she is or I am, I never will be. He knows it, I know it. Stepmothers don't represent good things for children. When I married Adam's father it meant that Adam could not have his father and mother back together without somehow getting me out of the picture. It meant that he would have to accept a stranger whom he didn't know and maybe wouldn't really like into his home. It meant he was nearly powerless. It doesn't really matter that Adam's father and mother weren't going to get back together, because Adam wanted to see his mom, and he wanted to be with his dad, and the way that it was easiest for him to get both those things was for his parents to be together.

It's something most stepparents aren't prepared for because children often court the future stepparent. You're dating, and it's exciting. Adam was excited that his father was going to marry me. He wanted us to do things together. But a week before the wedding, he also wanted to know if his mother and father could get back together. It wasn't that he didn't understand that the two things were mutually exclusive, it was more that they were unrelated for him. When I came over I was company, it was fun. But real life was mom and dad.

Marriage stopped that. That is the first evil thing I did.

The second evil thing that stepparents do is take part of a parent away. Imagine this, you're married, and your spouse suddenly decides to bring someone else into the household, without asking you. You're forced to accommodate. Your spouse pays attention to the Other, and while they are paying attention to the Other, they are not paying attention to you. Imagine the Other was able to make rules. In marriages it's called bigamy, and it's illegal.

What's worse for the child is that they have already lost most of one parent. Now someone else is laying claim on the remaining parent. The weapons of the stepchild are the weapons of the apparently powerless, the weapons of the guerilla. Subterfuge. Sabotage. The artless report of the hurtful things his real mother has said about you. Disliking the way you set the table, not wanting you to move the furniture. And stepchildren—even more than children in non-step relationships—are hyperalert to division between parent and stepparent.

I was thirty-three when I married; I had no children of my own and never wanted any. I'm a book person, so before I got married I went out and bought books about being a stepmother. I asked that we all do some family counseling before and during the time we were getting married. The books painted a dismal picture. Women got depressed. Women felt like maids. Women got sick. There were lots of rules—the child needs to spend some time alone with their natural parent and some time alone with their stepparent in a sort of round robin of quality time; a stepmother should have something of her own that gives her a feeling of her own identity; don't move into their house, start a new house together if you possibly can.

I liked that there were rules so I followed them and they helped a lot (even though I suspect that, like theories of child-raising, our theories of step relationships are a fad and the advice in the books will all be different fifty years from now). But I was still evil, and that was the most disheartening thing of all. I felt trapped in a role not my own choosing. Becoming a stepmother redefined who I am, and nothing I did could resist that inexorable redefining. I suppose motherhood redefines who you are, too. Part of the redefinition of me has been just that—sitting on the bench with the row of anxious mothers at the Little League game or at martial arts. Going to school and being Adam's mother. Being Adam's mom. It has made me suddenly feel middle-aged in funny ways. I used to go through the grocery line and buy funky things like endive, a dozen doughnuts, a bottle of champagne and two tuna steaks. Now I buy carts full of cereal and hamburger and juice boxes. I used to buy overpriced jackets and expensive suits. Now I go to Sears and buy four sweatshirts and two packages of socks in the boys department.

When I bought endive and champagne, the check-out clerk used to ask me what I was making. But no one asks you what you are making when you buy cereal and hamburger.

Beyond all this loomed the specter of Adam at sixteen. The rebellious teenage boy from the broken home, hulking about the house, always in trouble, always resentful. Like many stepchildren, Adam came with an enormous amount of behavioral baggage. He acted out the tensions of his extended family. He was sullen, tearful, resentful of me and equally resentful of his mother. I knew that Adam was the victim in all this, but when you're up to your ass in alligators, it is hard to remember that your original intention is to drain the swamp. I had read that I would be resentful, but nothing prepared me for a marriage that was about this alien child. I didn't marry Adam, he didn't marry me, and yet that is what my marriage came down to. By the time Adam was dealt with, my husband and I were too exhausted to be married.

My relationship with Adam was good, better than the relationships described in all those books. He was a happier, healthier, more behaved child than he had been when I married Bob—after all, it is easier to parent when there are two of you. People complimented me on what a fine job I had done. I was the only one who suspected that there was a coldness in the center of our relationship that Adam and I felt. I could console myself that he had been better off than he was before I married Bob, and he was. But I knew that something was a lie.

One day Adam said angrily that I treated the dog better than I treated him. Of course, I liked the dog, the dog adored me, and Adam, well Adam and I had something of a truce. The kind of relationship a child would have with an adult who might ban Christmas trees from the house. So the accusation struck home.

I started to deal with my stepson the way I deal with my dog. Quite literally. A boy and a stepmother have a strange tension in a physical relationship. I hug Adam and I kiss him on the forehead, on the nose, anywhere but on the mouth. I am careful about how I touch him. I suspect that the call from Child Protective Services is the nightmare of every stepparent. But after that comment I began to ruffle his hair the way I ruffle the dog's ears. I rubbed Adam's back. I petted him. I occasionally gave Adam a treat, the way I occasionally give the dog one. At first it was all calculated, but within a very short time, it was natural to reassure Adam.

It has made all the difference.

Adam is almost twelve, and the specter of the delinquent teenager in the dysfunctional family still haunts me, but it doesn't seem so likely at the moment. As Adam grows older, my husband and I have more time to be married.

Speaking from the land of the stepparent, I tell you, this business of being evil is hard. It is very hard. Being a stepparent is the hardest thing I have ever done. And what rewards there are, are small. No one pats me on the head for having given up the pleasures of endive and champagne and tuna steaks for spaghetti sauce and hamburger. That's what mothers do. Except, of course, they get to be the mom.

Author Interview

Q. The title of the collection identifies the recurring motif of mothers, and their interactions with other family members, a motif central to many of these stories. Was this a conscious choice or a pattern that you recognized after writing and publishing the stories?

A. I started writing stories about mothers because of something the writer Karen Joy Fowler said at a workshop. In a story by another writer, the main character's mom called, and Karen made the offhand comment that she was glad to see a mother in a story. At the time I was struggling mightily with the whole exercise of being a stepmother and one of the things I had trouble sorting out was the difference between issues that were 'step' issues and just the same stuff that comes up for every parent. In my eyes, everything was because I wasn't my kid's 'real mom'. (We had full custody of my stepson.) Some of those things were just parent things. When something is important to me and I don't understand it, I often write about it.

Mothers were just expected to be so perfect, you know?

Some of the pieces in the collection had already been written by this point, but I found that mothers had already started coming up in my fiction, and came up more and more. I had been thinking about a collection on and off for years and kicking around names, most of which were pretty stupid. Then Small Beer Press asked me to do a collection and I realized the name of the collection was *Mothers & Other Monsters*, and everything just sort of jelled around that.

Q. What is it that makes mothers such rich territory in fiction?

A. Nobody much writes about them. There are some great stories about mothers, but for the most part, motherhood is a very rigid role. A Hollywood actor observed recently that she had reached the point where she had two choices in roles, Good Mommy and Psycho Mommy. (Shirley MacLaine specializes in the grandmother version of these roles—but Psycho Grandmothers also Dispense Wisdom and Allow Children To Be Themselves.) I'm a different mother than any of my kid's friend's mothers. And they're all different from each other in ways a good deal more complicated than Good Mother and Bad Mother.

There are some really good things written about motherhood. Tillie Olsen's story, "I Stand Here Ironing" is one. Lorrie Moore's harrowing "People Like That Are the Only People Here" is another wonderful short story. But for the most part, we can explore the relationships between lovers and between fathers and sons, but we're nervous about talking about mothers and children.

Q. You are also able to focus closely on the experiences of children and teenagers in such stories as "Interview: On Any Given Day" and "Laika Comes Back Safe." What are the difficulties involved in capturing the voices of these younger characters?

A. Language. My language for teenagers is inevitably a bit lame. My son helped me a bit. I told myself that even if their language was dead on, in five years it would sound preposterous, and just wrote it anyway. I'm also oddly protective of my teenagers. I work really hard not to embarrass them. My memories of being an adolescent usually involve one humiliating moral or social failure after another. I tend to shy away from doing that to them.

But I'm really comfortable with coming-of-age stories. I think my generation has never believed we were adults.

Q. It seems as if literary fiction is finally returning to a broader, more inclusive spectrum than the realism that has been predominant for so long. Your stories often work with speculative elements. How do you view the role of realism in fiction?

A. You know, I always get this question asked from the other direction—how do I view speculative elements. This is a *great* question. I was drawn to science fiction for the ways in which it allowed me to skip parts of real life I hated. I liked SF that made life more romantic. I liked Andre Norton's protagonists finding out they weren't ordinary. I wanted to be a mutant, an escapee from a different reality where I was special.

I studied writing for years. Some of that was formal—I have a masters degree from New York University that would be an MFA in creative writing if I got it today. Some of it was the more traditional way to become of writer. Write a lot, most of it bad, find people who can tell you it's bad. Learn to get better. I found power in realism. I liked psychological realism when I read it. Those details—the moments we have all experienced but maybe never seen written down—work like a kind of electric jolt in a good story. In the Lorrie Moore story I mentioned, her two-year-old son has cancer. She describes being in the office of the pediatric oncologist and her son is doing that thing toddlers do so joyously, flicking on and off the light switch, while the pediatric oncologist explains what the cancer means and what they'll do. How many times have I seen a toddler entranced with a switch—a flashlight, a vacuum cleaner, anything. And juxtaposed against the patient doctor explaining the moment is almost unbearable.

Q. How do you think working with fantastic or science fictional elements enriches your work?

A. It's like a lens. It takes the story and throws the elements of relationship in high relief. In "Frankenstein's Daughter," the situation is not so uncommon. The daughter has chronic health problems that will potentially be fatal. The mother pays very little attention to her son because her daughter is so often in a life-or-death situation. The fact that the daughter is a clone of her dead daughter just heightens the situation. It justifies the very common feeling 'this is my fault' because she chose her daughter's existence. And it startles the story in some way. I like that the daughter's physiological problems come right out of the scientific literature on cloning. But I also like that, as I wrote the story, I found that the family was very much like a lot of other families.

Q. Your stories have been recognized both inside and outside the SF genre. Do you feel more at home as a writer in either field?

A. Both and neither, I guess. Science fiction has been really good to me, but I am conscious of having disappointed a lot of readers. People complain that I write boring stories. Depressing stories. That my stories could be about today if you took the speculative element out. Some of my stories, like "Laika Comes Back Safe," may not even have a speculative element. (Although just because I think that doesn't mean it's true.)

But outside the field, I think I'm seen as a little precious. I write science fictional stories about moms. Kind of a niche. The way feminist writing is seen as a niche. I feel that for years my stories weren't read outside the field. So inside the field I was seen as not science fictional enough and outside the field I was too science fictional.

This is a little like stepparenting/parenting issues. The non-genre writers I know also have difficulties with the ways in which their work is visibly shaped for the market. Any time a book or story is in the world, it's in some place in a book store, in some specific magazine that means some people see it and others don't. Often there are people who don't see it who might very much like it, and people who do see it who feel misled by the packaging.

Q. Your stories often deal with the domestic, although usually in bold, original settings. Do you feel fiction that focuses on older women or domestic life is treated differently?

A. Sometimes. For one thing, I get asked about the fathers a lot. Where are the fathers? But mostly no. I've been really well received, and I've gotten extraordinary attention from my peers. I'd say that my fiction has been treated very well by people from workshops like Sycamore Hill and Rio Hondo, and by the East Side Writers and the local SF writer's group. They grappled directly with it, called me to account on it, and in large part let me become the writer I am today. Editors have always published my work, they haven't marginalized it.

Q. Several of the stories in the collection—most notably "Oversite" and "Presence"—feature characters dealing with the fallout of Alzheimer's or dementia in their lives. What are you exploring in these stories?

A. Alzheimer's, like other brain disorders, calls into question the very nature of self. What is self? Who are we? I think we are our physical selves, particularly our brains. I have a particular fear of dementia and of loss of self. More so, I would say, than a fear of death. The irony of that is that now my mother has dementia, so for the past few years I have been privy to a close-up look of the way in which her 'self' is dissolving. The 'self,' I must say, is very persistent. Even as my mother loses aspects of language and some of her personality changes, there is a stubborn core of something that, at this point at least, is still recognizably connected to the historic 'her.'

Q. Consciousness and identity emerge as two strong themes within the collection. What did you want to say in dealing with these?

A. I don't know that I wanted to say anything. I think I don't understand consciousness or identity. There's a saying in fiction, 'Write what you know.' I think better fiction comes out of writing about the things that are important to me, but that I'm fundamentally uncertain about. That doesn't mean I sit down and say, 'I'm going to write a story about identity.' I always think I'm writing a story about a girl who thinks her best friend is a werewolf. It just happens that I circle back to those issues of identity.

As a writer, I have a couple of itches that I scratch, things I return to again and again. I tend to be drawn to motherhood because I'm trying to find a way to convince myself that I wasn't a monster. I'll get an idea for a story and think, I know, I'll make the mother have Alzheimer's. Not thinking about the connection between a teenager finding her way and an old woman losing her way and a mother helpless in the middle to ease either passage. I find out about all those things years later. I put them there, because those things are by default interesting to me. But it's not conscious.

Q. Did you learn anything new about these stories in the process of choosing and ordering them for the book?

A. I find it difficult to reread my own fiction. It was nice to see that a lot of it had held up. And I was surprised at how much the same things kept coming up, again and again. The mother in "The Lincoln Train," for example, has some form of dementia.

Q. How are these stories different from your novels, if at all? How does your writing process differ between the two?

A. I often write short stories to a deadline. Often, anymore, a workshop. They are more likely to be ideas that I'm not at all sure will work out. I can take more risks because most of the time I know that in a couple of months I'll at least have a draft.

Two of my novels have come out of short stories, so at some level, there is some overlap. But when I intentionally start a novel, I'm thinking it will have more ingredients than a short story. More loose ends. More questions and more stuff.

Q. You've talked in the past about workshopping with other writers being an important part of your writing life. What do you take from those experiences?

A. As I get older, I think I get better at reading and understanding stories, and some of that is from workshopping.

Mostly it's been very rare for someone not to tell me something that didn't show me a way to read the story I'd written. A lot of times it wasn't the way I wanted the story read. And a lot of times it said stuff about the story and about my writing that I wasn't very good at hearing.

But it's the only way I know to get better.

Q. Who are some writers you admire or who have influenced your work?

A. At any given time, anyone I'm reading who strikes me is going to have a pretty strong affect on me.

When I was in my twenties I was really taken by the work of Samuel R. Delany and the novels of Joan Didion. I think I was drawn to the romanticism of Delany. I was also really taken with the way so much of Didion's stories happened off the page. I was also strongly drawn to a little book by Marguerite Yourcenar called *Coup de Grâce.* I reread it a couple of years ago and saw all sorts of aspects of it that distress me now that I'm in my forties but it affected me powerfully when I was younger.

A few years ago I found myself utterly charmed by the sheer artificialness of Raymond Carver's stories. I had always thought of them as very psychologically realistic. Minimal. All that. But what I like about them now is how artificial they are. Perfect little setups that spring shut at conclusion. Lately I've been reading the short fiction of Joy Williams. It's really astonishing.

I like the work of Kelly Link a lot.

I like the Harry Potter novels. Great escapism.

When I was younger, I expected what I thought of as a rigorous kind of lack of sentimentality in novels. Anything else struck me as cheating. Lately I have been drawn more and more to certain kinds of sentiment. Books like *I Capture the Castle* by Dodie Smith.

Q. What can we expect to see from you next?

I'm working on a novel. I've been working on it for six or seven years. But this time, I swear I'm going to finish it.

Interview by Gwenda Bond.

Talking Points

Some things to talk about. There are no right answers.

1. What is your take on the title of this collection—*Mothers & Other Monsters*? Is it that mothers are monstrous? How about the mothers in this collection? Who are the *Other Monsters*?

2. Science-fiction stories may be set in places real or imaginary, in real or imaginary times. Even so, they are usually about the here and now. Do you feel McHugh is able to address contemporary issues in a more—or a less—effective way through the use of her imaginary settings? What contemporary issues seem to interest her most?

3. Advances in technology allow parents to monitor their children in ways that were impossible a generation ago. What along these lines has already changed since you were a teenager? Would you prefer to be a teenager now? Would you prefer to have been a parent then?

4. How much oversight is too much?

5. Does McHugh's treatment of stepmothers seem accurate? What are some of the difficulties stepmothers face here? Why are stepmothers traditionally seen as wicked? With more families being headed by single parents, will the stereotype of the wicked stepmother lose popularity?

6. McHugh works within a number of literary traditions including realism ("Eight-Legged Story"), ghost stories ("In the Air"), science fiction ("The Cost to Be Wise"), fantasy ("Ancestor Money"), fairy tales ("The Beast"), and narrative nonfiction ("Interview: On Any Given Day"). Science fiction has been characterized as a literature of exploration and therefore seen as especially appropriate for teenagers. Are these stories you would give to a teenager to read? What aspects of these stories would you have enjoyed as a teenager?

7. One of the effects of Alzheimer's Disease is that life decisions for an individual have to be made by someone else. Do the reactions of the Alzheimer's sufferer's families in these stories seem realistic to you? How about the treatment of and the treatments for the disease?

8. What would you do if your partner were cured of Alzheimer's but was not quite the person they had once been? (As in "Presence")

9. In "Laika Comes Back Safe," is Tye a werewolf or a kid who thinks he's a werewolf? Which is scarier?

10. In "Ancestor Money," a woman burns an offering for her grandmother. In China, these offerings include paper money called 'Hell Money' and elaborate paper models of houses, cars and even things like paper model fax machines and paper model cell phones. The idea is that when they are burned, the ancestors receive them as goods and money. What would you send your ancestors?

11. McHugh's protagonists are frequently trapped in some way—by love, by law, by history, by illness. How do you feel about reading stories in which the narrator has little power and few choices? How well do you think McHugh's narrators do in the circumstances in which they find themselves?

12. When it's possible to rejuvenate your body, will you?

13. Would you describe these as love stories?

14. Did this collection remind you of any other books? What did these stories gain by being collected together? What differences do you experience between reading stories separately in magazines as compared to reading them in a collection or anthology?

About the Author

Maureen F. McHugh has spent most of her life in Ohio, but has lived in New York City and, for a year, in Shijiazhuang, China. She is the author of four novels. Her first novel, *China Mountain Zhang*, won the Tiptree Award and her latest novel, *Nekropolis*, was a Book Sense 76 pick and a *New York Times* Editor's Choice. McHugh has also written for the I Love Bees and Last Call Poker alternate reality games. McHugh has taught at John Carroll University and the Imagination and Clarion workshops. She lives with her husband and two dogs next to a dairy farm. Sometimes, in the summer, black and white Holsteins look over the fence at them.

Publication History

These stories were previously published as follows:

Ancestor Money, *SciFiction*, October 2003
In the Air, *Killing Me Softly* (HarperPrism)
The Cost to Be Wise, *Starlight* 1 (Tor)
The Lincoln Train, *The Magazine of Fantasy & Science Fiction*, April 1995
Interview: *On Any Given Day, Starlight* 3 (Tor)
Oversite, *Asimov's*, September 2004
Wicked appears here for the first time.
Laika Comes Back Safe, *Polyphony* (Wheatland Press)
Presence, *The Magazine of Fantasy & Science Fiction*, March 2002
Eight-Legged Story, *Trampoline* (Small Beer Press)
The Beast, *Asimov's*, March 1992
Nekropolis, *Asimov's*, April 1994
Frankenstein's Daughter, *SciFiction*, April 2003

Small Beer Press

Alan DeNiro · *Skinny Dipping in the Lake of the Dead* · 1931520178 · $16
"Here's Alan DeNiro, whose *Skinny Dipping in the Lake of the Dead* was always my favorite.
I'm thrilled to see him in bookstores at last."—Jonathan Lethem (*The Fortress of Solitude*)

Carol Emshwiller · *The Mount* · 1931520038 · $16
"Best of the Year"—*Book Magazine, Locus, San Francisco Chronicle*
★ "Brilliantly conceived and painfully acute."—*Publishers Weekly* (starred review)
—— · *Report to the Men's Club* · 193152002X · $16
"Elliptical, funny and stylish."—*Time Out New York*

Angélica Gorodischer · *Kalpa Imperial* · 1931520054 · $16
Translated by Ursula K. Le Guin
★ "Should appeal to [Le Guin's] fans as well as to those of literary fantasy and Latin
American fiction."—*Library Journal* (starred review)

Ellen Kushner · *The Privilege of the Sword* · 1931520208 · $35
"Unholy fun, and wholly fun…an elegant riposte, dazzlingly executed."
—Gregory Maguire (*Wicked*)

Kelly Link · *Magic for Beginners* · 1931520151 · $24
"Play in a place few writers go, a netherworld between literature and fantasy, Alice
Munro and J.K. Rowling."—*Time Magazine: Best Books of 2005*
—— · *Stranger Things Happen* · 1931520003 · $16
"Best of the Year"—*Salon, Village Voice, San Francisco Chronicle*
—— editor · *Trampoline: an anthology* · 1931520046 · $17
20 astounding stories by Emshwiller, Jeffrey Ford, Karen Joy Fowler, & others.
"No unblinkered, gloveless reader can resist the stream of associations unleashed by
Ford's story and the rest of *Trampoline*: influences as disparate as science fiction, magic
realism, pulp, and *Twilight Zone* morality plays."—*The Village Voice*

Jennifer Stevenson · *Trash Sex Magic* · 1931520127 · $16
"This just absolutely rocks. It's lyrical, it's weird and it's sexy in a very funky way."
—Audrey Niffenegger, *The Time Traveler's Wife*

Sean Stewart · *Perfect Circle* · 1931520119 · $15
★ "All-around terrific."—*Booklist* (starred review)
"Stephen King meets Ibsen. Trust me."—Neal Stephenson, *The Confusion*
—— · *Mockingbird* · 1931520097 · $14
"Hands down the best novel I have read in 2005, and one of the best I've ever had the
privilege to read."—Park Road Books, Charlotte, NC

Ray Vukcevich · *Meet Me in the Moon Room* · 1931520011 · $16
"Vukcevich is a master of the last line. . . . ingenious with the short-story form."
—*Review of Contemporary Fiction*

Kate Wilhelm · *Storyteller: Writing Lessons & More from 27 years of the Clarion Writers' Workshop* · 193152016X · $16
"Oh, but this is a lovely book. . . . Wilhelm fills *Storyteller* with lessons about how to write,
and just as important, how not to write."—*Strange Horizons*

Peapod Classics

Howard Waldrop · *Howard Who?* · 1931520186 · $14
> Revised introduction by George R.R. Martin (*A Song of Ice and Fire*): "If this is your first taste of Howard, I envy you. Bet you can't read just one."

> "Clever, humorous, idiosyncratic, oddball, personal, wild, and crazy."
> —*Library Journal*

> "The resident Weird Mind of his generation, he writes like a honkytonk angel."
> —*Washington Book World*

Naomi Mitchison · *Travel Light* · 1931520143 · $14
> Halla's travels take her from the darkest medieval forests to the intrigues of early modern Constantinople. Every page glitters with imagination. This is a book to treasure. A fabulous novel which will appeal to fans of Diana Wynne Jones, Harry Potter, and T. H. White's *The Sword in the Stone*.

> "A 78-year-old friend staying at my house picked up *Travel Light*, and a few hours later she said, 'Oh, I wish I'd known there were books like this when I was younger!' So, read it now—think of all those wasted years!"—Ursula K. Le Guin (*Gifts*)

Carol Emshwiller · *Carmen Dog* · 1931520143 · $14
> "An inspired feminist fable. . . . A wise and funny book."—*The New York Times*

> "A first novel that combines the cruel humor of *Candide* with the allegorical panache of *Animal Farm*."—*Entertainment Weekly*

Chapbook Series

Richard Butner, *Horses Blow Up Dog City*
Christopher Rowe, *Bittersweet Creek*
Benjamin Rosenbaum, *Other Cities*
Mark Rich, *Foreigners, and Other Familiar Faces*
Judith Berman, *Lord Stink and Other Stories*
Alex Irvine, *Rossetti Song: Four Stories*

Lady Churchill's Rosebud Wristlet

A twice-yearly fiction &c zine ("Tiny, but celebrated."—*The Washington Post*) edited by Kelly Link and Gavin J. Grant publishing writers including Carol Emshwiller, Karen Joy Fowler, Jeffrey Ford, Eliot Fintushel, James Sallis, Molly Gloss, and many others. Fiction and nonfiction from *LCRW* has been reprinted in *The Year's Best Fantasy & Horror*, *The Best of the Rest*, and *The Zine Yearbook*. Many subscription options (including chocolate) available on our website.

www.smallbeerpress.com